"DICK FRANCIS IS A WONDER. . . .
A TIGHT, TAUT THRILLER . . .
GRIPPING."
The Cleveland Plain Dealer

"The ex-jockey proves, once again, that he hasn't lost his sense of balance—or his desire for a strong finish."
Chicago Tribune

"Once again on home turf in British horse country, Francis takes us along on a gallop to the finish line. His track record surpasses all contenders. . . . LONGSHOT delivers with all the speed and form we've come to expect from him."
The Philadelphia Inquirer

"Writing in typically fine form, Francis' LONGSHOT is a sure shot with fans."
New York Daily News

"Francis creates a cast of vivid characters, hides the killer's identity nicely and works his descriptions of survival skills into the story smoothly."
The Seattle Times

Please turn the page for more glowing reviews from all across America. . . .

Also by Dick Francis:

NERVE*
FOR KICKS*
ODDS AGAINST*
FLYING FINISH*
BLOOD SPORT*
DEAD CERT*
ENQUIRY*
FORFEIT*
SLAYRIDE*
THE SPORT OF QUEENS
TRIAL RUN*
WHIP HAND*
HIGH STAKES*
REFLEX*
TWICE SHY*
BANKER*
BONECRACK
KNOCKDOWN
IN THE FRAME
THE DANGER*
RISK
SMOKESCREEN
RAT RACE
PROOF*
A JOCKEY'S LIFE: The Biography of Lester Piggott*
BREAK IN*
BOLT*
HOT MONEY*
THE EDGE*
STRAIGHT*

*Published by Fawcett Books

LONGSHOT

Dick Francis

FAWCETT CREST • NEW YORK

With love to

JOCELYN
MATTHEW
BIANCA
TIMOTHY
WILLIAM

Our grandchildren

and acknowledgments to

The SAS Survival Handbook
by John Wiseman

and

No Need to Die
by Eddie McGee

A Fawcett Crest Book
Published by Ballantine Books
Copyright © 1990 by Dick Francis

All rights reserved under International and Pan-American Copyright Conventions. Published in the United States by Ballantine Books, a division of Random House, Inc., New York

This book, or parts thereof, may not be produced in any form without permission.

Library of Congress Catalog Card Number: 90-41145

ISBN 0-449-21955-0

This edition published by arrangement with G.P. Putnam's Sons

Manufactured in the United States of America

First International Ballantine Books Edition: August 1991
First U.S. Ballantine Books Edition: April 1992

1

I accepted a commission that had been turned down by four other writers, but I was hungry at the time.

Although starving in a garret had seemed a feasible enough plan a year earlier, the present realities of existence under the frozen eaves of a friend's aunt's house in a snowy January were such that without enough income to keep well fed and warm I was a knockover for a risky decision.

My state of course was my own fault. I could easily have gone out looking for paid muscular employment. I didn't have to sit shivering in a ski suit, biting the end of a pencil, hunched over a notebook, unsure of myself, of my ability and of the illuminations crashing about in my head.

The spartan discomfort was not, either, a self-pitying morass of abject failure, but more the arctic doldrums between the high elation of the recent acceptance of my first novel for publication and the distant date of its launch into literary orbit. This was the downside after the heady receipt of the first advance payment and its division into past debts, present expenses and six months' future rent.

Give it two years, I'd thought, kissing farewell to the security of a salary: if I can't get published in two years I'll admit that the compulsion to write fiction is fool's gold and settle for common sense. Tossing away the paychecks had been a fairly desperate step, but I'd tried writing before work and after, in trains and at weekends, and had produced only dust. A stretch of no-excuse solitude, I'd thought, would settle things one way or another. Incipient hypothermia wasn't in any way diminishing the intense happiness of having put my toe into the first crack of the rockface.

I did as it happened know quite a lot about survival in adverse circumstances, and the prospect of lean times hadn't worried me. I'd rather looked forward to them as a test of ingenuity. I just hadn't realized that sitting and thinking in itself made one cold. I hadn't known that a busy brain sneakily stole warmth from inactive hands and feet. In every freezing configuration I'd lived through before, I'd been moving.

The letter from Ronnie Curzon came on a particularly cold morning when there was ice like a half-descended curtain over the inside of my friend's aunt's attic window. The window, with its high view over the Thames at Chiswick, over the ebb-tide mud and the wind-sailing sea gulls, that window, my delight, had done most, I reckoned, to release invention into words. I'd rigged a chair onto a platform so that I could sit there to write with a long view to the tree-chopped horizon over Kew Gardens. I'd never yet managed an even passable sentence when faced with a blank wall.

The letter said:

"Dear John,

"Care to drop into the office? There's been a suggestion about American rights in your book. You might be interested. I think we might discuss it, anyway.

Yours ever, Ronnie.

Why can't you have a telephone like everyone else?"

American rights! Incredible words.

The day warmed up miraculously. American rights were things that happened to successful authors, not to people struggling in an unfamiliar landscape, afflicted by self-doubts and insecurities, with a need to be told over and over that the book is OK, it's OK, don't worry so much.

"Don't worry," Ronnie had said heartily, summoning me to his presence after reading the manuscript I'd dumped unheralded on his desk a couple of weeks earlier. "Don't worry, I'm sure we can find you a publisher. Leave it to me. Let me see what I can do."

Ronnie Curzon, authors' agent, with his salesman's subtle tongue, had indeed found me a publisher, a house more prestigious than I would have aimed for.

"They have a large list," Ronnie explained kindly. "They can afford to take a risk on a few first-timers, though it's all much harder than it used to be." He sighed. "The tyrannical bottom line and so on. Still," he beamed, "they've asked you to lunch to get acquainted. Look on the bright side."

I'd grown used to Ronnie's fast swings to pessimism and back. He'd told me in the same breath that I'd sell two thousand copies if I was very lucky indeed, and that a certain lady novelist counted her paperbacks in millions.

"Everything's possible," he said encouragingly.

"Including falling flat on one's face?" I asked.

"Don't worry so much."

On the day of the American rights letter I walked as usual

from the friend's aunt's house to Ronnie's office four miles away in Kensington High Street and, as I'd learned a thing or two by that time, I went not precipitously as soon as possible but later in the morning, so as to arrive at noon. Shortly after that hour, I'd discovered, Ronnie tended to offer wine to his visitors and to send out for sandwiches. I hadn't told him much about my reduced domestic arrangements; he was naturally and spontaneously generous.

I misjudged things to the extent that the door of his own room was firmly shut, where normally it stood open.

"He's with another client," Daisy said.

Daisy smiled easily, an unusual virtue in a receptionist. Big white teeth in a black face. Wild hair. A neat Oxford accent. Going to night school for Italian classes.

"I'll let him know you're here," she said, lifting her telephone, pressing a button and consulting with her boss.

"He wants you to wait," she reported, and I nodded and passed some time with patience on one of the two semicomfortable chairs arranged for the purpose.

Ronnie's suite of offices consisted of a large outer room, partly furnished by the desks of Daisy and of her sister Alice, who kept the firm's complicated accounts, and partly by a wall of box-files on shelves and a large central table scattered with published books. Down a passage from the big room lay on one side the doors to three private offices (two housing Ronnie's associates) and on the other the entrance into a windowless store like a library, where from floor to ceiling were ranked copies of all the books that Ronnie and his father before him had nursed to birth.

I spent the time in the outer room looking at a framed corkboard on which were pinned the dust jackets of the crop still in the shops, wondering yet again what my own baby would look like. First-time authors, it seemed, were allowed little input in the design department.

"Trust the professionals," Ronnie had said comfortingly. "After all, they know what will sell books."

I'd thought cynically that sometimes you'd never guess. All I could do, though, was hope.

Ronnie's door opened and out came his head, his neck and a section of shoulder.

"John? Come along in."

I went down to his room which contained his desk, his swiveling armchair, two guest chairs, a cupboard and roughly a thousand books.

"Sorry to keep you," he said.

He was as expansively apologetic as if I'd had a definite appointment and waved me into his office with every appearance of being delighted by my presence. He showed the same manner to everyone. A very successful agent, Ronnie.

He was rounded and enthusiastic. Cuddly was almost the word. Short, with smooth dark hair and soft dry hands, wearing always a business suit over a white shirt and a striped tie. Authors, his presentation seemed to say, could turn up if they pleased in pale-blue and red ski-suits and snow-defeating moon boots, but serious business took place in sober worsted.

"A cold day," he said, eyeing my clothes forgivingly.

"The slush in the gutters has frozen solid."

He nodded, only half listening, his eyes on his other client, who had remained settled in his chair as if there for the day. It seemed to me that Ronnie was stifling exasperation under a façade of aplomb, a surprising configuration when what he usually showed was unflagging effortless bonhomie.

"Tremayne," he was saying jovially to his guest, "this is John Kendall, a brilliant young author."

As Ronnie regularly described all his authors as brilliant, even with plentiful evidence to the contrary, I remained unembarrassed.

Tremayne was equally unimpressed. Tremayne, sixtyish, gray-haired, big and self-assured, was clearly not pleased at the interruption.

"We haven't finished our business," he said ungraciously.

"Time for a glass of wine," Ronnie suggested, ignoring the complaint. "For you, Tremayne?"

"Gin and tonic."

"Ah . . . I meant, white wine or red?"

After a pause Tremayne said with a show of annoyed resignation, "Red, then."

"Tremayne Vickers," Ronnie said to me noncommittally, completing the introduction. "Red do you, John?"

"Great."

Ronnie bustled about, moving heaps of books and papers, clearing spaces, producing glasses, bottle and corkscrew and presently pouring with concentration.

"To trade," he said with a smile, handing me a glass. "To success," he said to Vickers.

"Success! What success? All these writers are too big for their boots."

Ronnie glanced involuntarily at my own boots, which were big enough for anyone.

"It's no use you telling me I'm not offering a decent fee," Tremayne told him. "They ought to be glad of the work." He eyed me briefly and asked me without tact, "What do you earn in a year?"

I smiled as blandly as Ronnie and didn't answer.

"How much do you know about racing?" he demanded.

"Horse racing?" I asked.

"Of course horse racing."

"Well," I said. "Not a lot."

"Tremayne," Ronnie protested, "John isn't your sort of writer."

"A writer's a writer. Anyone can do it. You tell me I've been wrong looking for a big name. Very well then, find me a smaller name. You said your friend here is brilliant. So how about *him*?"

"Ah," Ronnie said cautiously. "Brilliant is just . . . ah . . . a figure of speech. He's inquisitive, capable and impulsive."

I smiled at my agent with amusement.

"So he's *not* brilliant?" Tremayne asked ironically, and to me he said, "What have you written, then?"

I answered obligingly, "Six travel guides and a novel."

"Travel guides? What sort of travel guides?"

"How to live in the jungle. Or in the Arctic. Or in deserts. That sort of thing."

"For people who like difficult holidays," Ronnie said, with all the indulgent irony of those devoted to comfort. "John used to work for a travel agency which specializes in sending the intrepid out to be stretched."

"Oh." Tremayne looked at his wine without enthusiasm and after a while said testily, "There must be someone who'd leap at the job."

I said, more to make conversation than out of urgent curiosity, "What is it that you want written?"

Ronnie made a gesture that seemed to say "Don't ask," but Tremayne answered straightforwardly.

"An account of my life."

I blinked. Ronnie's eyebrows rose and fell.

Tremayne said, "You'd think those race-writing johnnies would be falling over themselves for the honor, but they've all turned me down." He sounded aggrieved. "Four of them."

He recited their names, and such was their eminence that even I, who seldom paid much attention to racing, had heard of them all. I glanced at Ronnie, who showed resignation.

"There must be others," I said mildly.

"There's some I wouldn't let set foot through my door." The truculence in Tremayne's voice was one of the reasons, I reflected, why he was having trouble. I lost interest in him, and Ronnie, seeing it, cheered up several notches and suggested sandwiches for lunch.

"I hoped you'd be lunching me at your club," Tremayne said grouchily, and Ronnie said vaguely "Work" with a flap of the hand to indicate the papers on his desk. "I mostly have lunch on the run these days."

He went over to the door and put the same section of himself through it as before.

"Daisy?" He called to her along the passage. "Phone down to the shop for sandwiches, would you? Usual selection. Everyone welcome. Count heads, would you? Three of us here."

He brought himself in again without more discussion. Tremayne went on looking disgruntled and I drank my wine with gratitude.

It was warm in Ronnie's office. That, too, was a bonus. I took off the jacket of the ski suit, hung it over a chair back and sat down contentedly in the scarlet sweater I wore underneath. Ronnie winced as usual over the brightness of my clothes but in fact I felt warmer in red, and I never discounted the psychology of colors. Those of my travel-agency friends who dressed in army olive-browns were colonels at heart.

Tremayne went on niggling away at his frustration, not seeming to mind if I learned his business.

"I offered to have them to stay," he complained. "Can't do fairer than that. They all said the sales wouldn't be worth the work, not at the rate I was offering. Arrogant lot of bastards." He gloomily drank and made a face over the taste. "My name alone would sell the book, I told them, and they had the gall to disagree. Ronnie says it's a small market." He glowered at my agent. "Ronnie says that he can't get the book commissioned by a publisher without a top-rank writer, and maybe not even then, and that no top-rank writer will touch it without a commission. See where that gets me?"

He seemed to expect an answer, so I shook my head.

"It gets me into what they call vanity publishing. Vanity! Bloody insult. Ronnie says there are companies that will print and bind any book you give them, but *you* have to pay *them.* Then I'd also have to pay someone to write the book. Then I'd also have to sell the book myself, as I would be my own publisher, and Ronnie says there's no way I'd sell enough to cover the costs, let alone make a profit. He says that's why no regular publisher will take the book. Not enough sales. And I ask you, why not? Why not, eh?"

I shook my head again. He seemed to think I should know who he was, that everyone should. I hardly liked to say I'd never heard of him.

He partially enlightened me. "After all," he said, "I've trained getting on for a thousand winners. The Grand National, two Champion Hurdles, a Gold Cup, the Whitbread, you name it. I've seen half a century of racing. There's stories in all of it. Childhood . . . growing up . . . success . . . My life has been *interesting,* dammit."

Words temporarily failed him, and I thought that everyone's life was interesting to themselves, tragedies and all. Everyone had a story to tell: the trouble lay in the few who wanted to read it, the fewer still who were ready to pay for the privilege.

Ronnie soothingly refilled the glasses and gave us a regretful summary of the state of the book trade, which was in one of its periodical downswings on account of current high interest rates and their adverse effects on mortgage payments.

"It's the people with mortgages who usually buy books," he said. "Don't ask me why. For every mortgage there are five people saving into the building societies, and when interest rates are high *their* incomes go up. They've more money to spend, but they just don't seem to buy books with it."

Tremayne and I looked blank over this piece of sociology, and Ronnie further told us, without noticeably cheering us up, that for a publisher in the modern world turnover was all very well but losses weren't, and that it was getting more and more difficult to get a marginal book accepted.

I felt more grateful than ever that he'd got one particular

marginal book accepted, and remembered what the lady from the publisher's had said when she'd taken me for the getting-acquainted lunch.

"Ronnie could sweet-talk the devil. He says we need to catch new authors like you in their early thirties, otherwise we won't have any big names ten years from now. No one knows yet how you'll turn out in ten years. Ronnie says that all salmon are small fry to begin with. So we're not promising you the world, but an opportunity, yes."

An opportunity was all one could ask, I thought.

Daisy at length appeared in the doorway to say the food had arrived, and we all went along to the big room where the central table had been cleared of books and relaid with plates, knives, napkins and two large platters of healthy-looking sandwiches decorated with a drizzle of cress.

Ronnie's associates emerged from their rooms to join us, which made seven altogether, including Daisy and her sister, and I managed to eat a lot without, I hoped, it being noticeable. Fillings of beef, ham, cheese, bacon: once-ordinary things that had become luxuries lately. Free lunch, breakfast and dinner. I wished Ronnie would write summoning notes oftener.

Tremayne harangued me again over the generic short-comings of racing writers, holding his glass in one hand and waving a sandwich in the other as he made his indignant points, while I nodded in sympathetic silence and munched away as if listening carefully.

Tremayne made a great outward show of forceful self-confidence, but there was something in his insistence which curiously belied it. It was almost as if he needed the book to be written to prove he had lived; as if photographs and records weren't enough.

"How old are you?" he said abruptly, breaking off in midflow.

I said with my mouth full, "Thirty-two."

"You look younger."

I didn't know whether "good" or "sorry" was appropriate, so I merely smiled and went on eating.

"Could you write a biography?" Again the abruptness.

"I don't know. Never tried."

"I'd do it myself," he said belligerently, "but I haven't got time."

I nodded understandingly. If there was one biography I didn't want to cut my teeth on, I thought, it was his. Much too difficult.

Ronnie fetched up beside him and wheeled him away, and in between finishing the beef-and-chutney and listening to Daisy's problems with scrambled software I watched Ronnie across the room, nodding his head placatingly under Tremayne's barrage of complaints. Eventually, when all that was left on the plates were a few pallidly wilting threads of cress, Ronnie said a firm farewell to Tremayne, who still didn't want to go.

"There's nothing I can usefully offer at the moment," Ronnie was saying, shaking an unresponsive hand and practically pushing Tremayne doorward with a friendly clasp on his shoulder. "But leave it to me. I'll see what I can do. Keep in touch."

With ill grace Tremayne finally left, and without any hint of relief Ronnie said to me, "Come along then, John. Sorry to have kept you all this time," and led the way back to his room.

"Tremayne asked if I'd ever written a biography," I said, taking my former place on the visitors' side of his desk.

Ronnie gave me a swift glance, settling himself into his own padded dark-green leather chair and swiveling gently from side to side as if in indecision. Finally he came to a stop and asked, "Did he offer you the job?"

"Not exactly."

"My advice to you would be not to think of it." He gave me no time to assure him that I wouldn't, and went straight on, "It's fair to say he's a good racehorse trainer, well

11

known in his own field. It's fair to say he's a better man than you would have guessed today. It's even fair to agree he's had an interesting life. But that isn't enough. It all depends on the writing." He paused and sighed. "Tremayne doesn't really believe that. He wants a big name because of the prestige, but you heard him, he thinks anyone can write. He doesn't really know the difference."

"Will you find him someone?" I asked.

"Not on the terms he's looking for." Ronnie considered things. "I suppose I can tell you," he said, "as he made an approach to you. He's asking for a writer to stay in his house for at least a month, to go through all his cuttings and records and interview him in depth. None of the top names will do that, they've all got other lives to lead. Then he wants seventy percent of royalty income, which isn't going to amount to much in any case. No top writer is going to work for thirty percent."

"Thirty percent . . . including the advance?"

"Right. An advance no bigger than yours, if I could get one at all."

"That's starvation."

Ronnie smiled. "Comparatively few people live by writing alone. I thought you knew that. Anyway"—he leaned forward, dismissing Tremayne and saying more briskly—"about these American rights . . ."

It seemed that a New York literary agent, an occasional associate of Ronnie's, had asked my publishers routinely whether they had anything of interest in the pipeline. They had steered him back to Ronnie. Would I, Ronnie asked, care to have him send a copy of my manuscript to the American agent, who would then, if he thought the book salable in the American market, try to find it an American publisher.

I managed to keep my mouth shut but was gaping and gasping inside.

"Well?" Ronnie said.

"I . . . er . . . I'd be delighted," I said.

"Thought you would. Not promising anything, you realize. He's just taking a look."

"Yes."

"If you remember, we gave your publisher here only British and Commonwealth rights. That leaves us elbow room to maneuver." He went on for a while discussing technicalities and possibilities that I only half understood, raising hopes and damping them in his pendulum way. I was left with a feeling that things might be going to happen but on the other hand probably not. The market was down, everything was difficult, but the publishing machine needed constant fodder and my book might be regarded as a bundle of hay. . . . He would let me know, he said, as soon as he got an opinion back from the New York agent.

"How's the new book coming along?" he asked.

"Slowly."

He nodded. "The second one's always difficult. But just keep going."

"Yes."

He rose to his feet, looking apologetically at his waiting paperwork, shaking my hand warmly in farewell. I thanked him for the lunch. Any time, he said automatically, his mind already on his next task, and I left him and walked along the passage, stopping at Daisy's desk on the way out.

"You're sending my manuscript to America," I said, zipping up my jacket and bursting to tell someone, anyone, the good news.

"Yes." She beamed. "I posted it last Friday."

"Did you indeed!"

I went on out to the elevator not sure whether to laugh or be vaguely annoyed at Ronnie's asking permission for something he had already done. I wouldn't have minded at all if he'd simply told me he'd sent the book off. It was his job to do the best for me that he could; I would have thought it well within his rights.

I rode down two floors and went out into the bitter afternoon air thinking of the steps that had led to his door.

Finishing the book had been one thing, finding a publisher another. The six small books I'd previously written, though published and on sale to the public, had all been part of my work for the travel firm, who had paid me pretty well for writing them besides sending me to far-flung places to gather the knowledge. The travel firm owned the guides and published them themselves, and they weren't in the market for novels.

I'd taken my precious typescript personally to a small but well-known publisher (looking up the address in the phone book) and had handed it to a pretty girl there who said she would put it in the slush pile and get around to it in due course.

The slush pile, she explained, showing dimples, was what they called the heap of unsolicited manuscripts that dropped through their letterbox day by day. She would read my book while she commuted. I could return for her opinion in three weeks.

Three weeks later, the dimples still in place, she told me my book wasn't really "their sort of thing," which was mainly "serious literature," it seemed. She suggested I should take it to an agent, who would know where to place it. She gave me a list of names and addresses.

"Try one of those," she said. "I enjoyed the book very much. Good luck with it."

I tried Ronnie Curzon for no better reason than I'd known where to find his office, as Kensington High Street lay on my direct walk home. Impulse had led to good and bad all my life, but when I felt it strongly, I usually followed it. Ronnie had been good. Opting for poverty had been so-so. Accepting Tremayne's offer was the pits.

2

As I walked back to Chiswick from Ronnie's office, I hadn't the slightest intention of ever meeting Tremayne Vickers again. I forgot him. I thought of the present book I was writing: especially of how to get one character down from a runaway experimental helium-filled balloon with its air pumps out of order. I had doubts about the balloon. Maybe I'd rethink the whole thing. Maybe I'd scrap what I'd done and start again. The character in the balloon was shitting himself with fear. I thought I knew how he felt. The chief unexpected thing I'd learned from writing fiction was fear of getting it wrong.

The book that had been accepted, which was called *Long Way Home,* was about survival in general and in particular about the survival, physical and mental, of a bunch of people isolated by a disaster. Hardly an original theme, but I'd followed the basic advice to write about something I knew, and survival was what I knew best.

15

In the interest of continuing to survive for another week or ten days, I stopped at the supermarket nearest to the friend's aunt's house and spent my food allotment on enough provisions for the purpose: bunch of packet soups, loaf of bread, box of spaghetti, box of porridge oats, pint of milk, a cauliflower and some carrots. I would eat the vegetables raw whenever I felt like it, and otherwise enjoy soup with bread in it, soup on spaghetti and porridge with milk. Items like tea, Marmite and salt cropped up occasionally. Crumpets and butter came at scarce intervals when I could no longer resist them. Apart from all that I bought once a month a bottle of vitamin pills to stuff me full of any oddments I might be missing and, dull though it might seem and in spite of frequent hunger, I had stayed in resounding good health all along.

I opened the front door with my latchkey and met the friend's aunt in the hall.

"Hello, dear," she said. "Everything all right?"

I told her about Ronnie sending my book to America, and her thin face filled with genuine pleasure. She was roughly fifty, divorced, a grandmother, sweet, fair-haired, undemanding and boring. I understood that she regarded the rent I paid her (a fifth of what I had had to fork out for my former flat) as more a bribe to get her to let a stranger into her house than as an essential part of her income. In addition, though, she had agreed I could put milk in her fridge, wash my dishes in her sink, shower in her bathroom and use her washer-drier once a week. I wasn't to make a noise or ask anyone in. We had settled these details amicably. She had installed a coin-in-the-slot electric meter for me, and approved a toaster, a kettle, a tiny tabletop cooker and new plugs for a television and a razor.

She'd been introduced to me as "Aunty" and that's what I called her, and she seemed to regard me as a sort of extension nephew. We had lived for ten months in harmony, our lives adjacent but uninvolved.

"It's very cold . . . are you warm enough up there?" she asked kindly.

"Yes, thank you," I said. The electric heater ate money. I almost never switched it on.

"These old houses . . . very cold under the roofs."

"I'm fine," I said.

She said, "Good, dear," amiably, and we nodded to each other, and I went upstairs thinking that I'd lived in the Arctic Circle and if I hadn't been able to deal with a cold London attic I would have been ashamed of myself. I wore silk jersey, long-sleeved undershirts and long johns under sweaters and jeans under the ski suit, and I slept warmly in a sleeping bag designed for the North Pole. It was writing that made me cold.

Up in my eyrie I struggled for a couple of hours to resolve the plight of the helium balloon but ended with only a speculation on nerve pathways. Why didn't terror make one *deaf*, for instance? How did it always beeline to the bowel? My man in the balloon didn't know and was too miserable to care. I thought I'd have to invent a range of mountains dead ahead for him to come to grief on. Then he would merely have the problem of descending from an Everest-approximation with only fingers, toes and resolution. Much easier. I knew a tip or two about that, the first being to look for the longest way down because it would be the least steep. Sharp-faced mountains often had sloping backs.

My attic, once the retreat of the youngest of Aunty's daughters, had a worn pink carpet and cream wallpaper sprigged with pink roses. The resident furniture of bed, chest of drawers, tiny wardrobe, two chairs and a table was overwhelmed by a veritable army of crates, boxes and suitcases containing my collected worldly possessions: clothes, books, household goods and sports equipment, all top quality and in good shape, acquired in carefree bygone affluence. Two pairs of expensive skis stood in their covers in a corner. Wildly extravagant cameras and lenses rested in dark foam beds. I kept in working order a windproof, sandproof, bug-proof tent which self-erected in seconds and weighed only three pounds. I checked also climbing gear and a camcorder from time to time. A word processor with a laser printer, which I still used, was wrapped most of the time in sheeting. My helicopter pilot's license lay in a drawer, automatically expired now since I hadn't flown for a year. A life on hold, I thought. A life suspended.

I thought occasionally that I could eat better if I sold something, but I'd never get back what I'd paid for the skis, for instance, and it seemed stupid to cannibalize things that had given me pleasure. They were mostly, anyway, the tools of my past trade and I might need them again. They were my safety net. The travel firm had said they would take me back once I'd got this foolishness out of my system.

If I'd known I was going to do what I was doing, I would have planned and saved a lot more in advance, perhaps: but between the final irresistible impulse and its execution there had been only about six weeks. The vague intention had been around a lot longer; for most of my life.

Helium balloon . . .

The second half of the advance on *Long Way Home* wasn't due until publication day, a whole long year ahead. My small weekly allotted parcels of money wouldn't last that long, and I didn't see how I could live on much less. My rent-in-advance would run out at the end of June. If, I thought, if I could finish this balloon lark by then and if it were accepted and if they paid the same advance as before, then maybe I'd just manage the full two years. Then if the books fell with a dull thud, I'd give up and go back to the easier rigors of the wild.

That night the air temperature over London plummeted still further, and in the morning Aunty's house was frozen solid.

"There's no water," she said in distress when I went

downstairs. "The central heating stopped and all the pipes have frozen. I've called the plumber. He says everyone's in the same boat and just to switch everything off. He can't do anything until it thaws, then he'll come to fix any leaks." She looked at me helplessly. "I'm very sorry, dear, but I'm going to stay in a hotel until this is over. I'm going to close the house. Can you find somewhere else for a week or two? Of course I'll add the time on to your six months, you won't lose by it, dear."

Dismay was a small word for what I felt. I helped her close all the stopcocks I could find and made sure she had switched off her water heaters, and in return she let me use her telephone to look for another roof.

I got through to her nephew, who still worked for the travel firm.

"Do you have any more aunts?" I inquired.

"Good God, what have you done with that one?"

I explained. "Could you lend me six feet of floor to unroll my bedding on?"

"Why don't you gladden the life of your parents on that Caribbean island?"

"Small matter of the fare."

"You can come for a night or two if you're desperate," he said. "But Wanda's moved in with me, and you know how tiny the flat is."

I also didn't much like Wanda. I thanked him and said I would let him know, and racked my brains for somewhere else.

It was inevitable I should think of Tremayne Vickers.

I phoned Ronnie Curzon and put it to him straight. "Can you sell me to that racehorse trainer?"

"What?"

"He was offering free board and lodging."

"Take me through it one step at a time."

I took him through it and he was all against it.

"Much better to get on with your new book."

19

"Mm," I said. "The higher a helium balloon rises the thinner the air is and the lower the pressure, so the helium balloon expands, and goes on rising and expanding until it bursts."

"*What?*"

"It's too cold to invent stories. Do you think I could do what Tremayne wants?"

"You could probably do a workmanlike job."

"How long would it take?"

"Don't do it," he said.

"Tell him I'm brilliant after all and can start at once."

"You're mad."

"I might as well learn about racing. Why not? I might use it in a book. And I can ride. Tell him that."

"Impulse will kill you one of these days."

I should have listened to him, but I didn't.

I was never sure exactly what Ronnie said to Tremayne, but when I phoned again at noon he was mournfully triumphant.

"Tremayne agreed you can write his book. He quite took to you yesterday, it seems." Pessimism vibrated down the wire. "He's agreed to guarantee you a writing fee." Ronnie mentioned a sum which would keep me eating through the summer. "It's payable in three installments—a quarter after a month's work, a quarter when he approves the full manuscript, and half on publication. If I can get a regular publisher to take it on, the publisher will pay you, otherwise Tremayne will. He's agreed you should have forty percent of any royalties after that, not thirty. He's agreed to pay your expenses while you research his life. That means if you want to go to interview people who know him, he'll pay for your transport. That's quite a good concession, actually. He thinks it's odd that you haven't a car, but I reminded him that people who live in London often don't. He says you can drive one of his. He was pleased you can ride. He says you should take riding clothes with you and also a dinner jacket, as he's to be guest of honor at some dinner or other and he wants you to witness it. I told him you were an expert photographer so he wants you to take your camera."

Ronnie's absolute and audible lack of enthusiasm for the project might have made me withdraw even then had Aunty not earlier given me a three o'clock deadline for leaving the house.

"When does Tremayne expect me?" I asked Ronnie.

"He seems pathetically pleased that anyone wants to take him on, after the top men turned him down. He says he'd be happy for you to go as soon as you can. Today, even, he said. Will you go today?"

"Yes," I said.

"He lives in a village called Shellerton, in Berkshire. He says if you can phone to say what train you're catching, someone will meet you at Reading station. Here's the number." He read it out to me.

"Fine," I said. "And Ronnie, thanks very much."

"Don't thank me. Just . . . well, just write a brilliant chapter or two and I'll try to get the book commissioned on the strength of them. But go on writing fiction. That's where your future is."

"Do you mean it?"

"Of course I mean it." He sounded surprised I should ask. "For someone who's not afraid of jungles you exhibit the strangest self-confidence deficiency."

"I know where I am in jungles."

"Go and catch your train," he said, and wished me luck.

I caught, instead, a bus, as it was much cheaper, and was met outside the Reading bus station by a shivering young woman in a padded coat and woolen hat who visually checked me over from boots six feet up via ski suit to dark hair and came to the conclusion that I was, as she put it, the writer.

"You're the writer?" She was positive, used to authority, not unfriendly.

"John Kendall," I said, nodding.

"I'm Mackie Vickers. That's m,a,c,k,i,e," she spelled. "Not Maggie. Your bus is late."

"The roads are bad," I said apologetically.

"They're worse in the country." It was dark and extremely cold. She led the way to a chunky jeeplike vehicle parked not far away and opened the rear door. "Put your bags in here. You can meet everyone as we go along."

There were already four people in the vehicle, it seemed, all cold and relieved I had finally turned up. I stowed my belongings and climbed in, sharing the backseat with two dimly seen figures who moved up to give me room. Mackie Vickers positioned herself behind the wheel, started the engine, released the brake and drove out into a stream of cars. A welcome trickle of hot air came out of the heater.

"The writer says his name is John Kendall," Mackie said to the world in general.

There wasn't much reaction to the introduction.

"You're sitting next to Tremayne's head lad," she went on, "and his wife is beside him."

The shadowy man next to me said, "Bob Watson." His wife said nothing.

"In front," Mackie said, "next to me, are Fiona and Harry Goodhaven."

Neither Fiona nor Harry said anything. There was an intense quality in the collective atmosphere that dried up any conversational remark I might have thought of making, and it had little to do with temperature. It was as if the very air were scowling.

Mackie drove for several minutes in continuing silence, concentrating on the slush-lined surface under the yellowish lights of the main road west out of Reading. The traffic was heavy and slow moving, the ill-named rush hour crawling along with flashing scarlet brake lights, a procession of curses.

Eventually Mackie said to me, turning her head over her shoulder as I was sitting directly behind her, "We're not good company. We've spent all day in court. Tempers are frayed. You'll just have to put up with it."

"No trouble," I said.

Trouble was the wrong word to use, it seemed.

As if releasing tension Fiona said loudly, "I can't *believe* you were so stupid."

"Give it a rest," Harry said. He'd already heard it before.

"But you know damned well that Lewis was drunk."

"That doesn't excuse anything."

"It *explains* things. You know damned well he was drunk."

"Everyone *says* he was drunk," Harry said, sounding heavily reasonable, "but I don't *know* it, do I? I didn't *see* him drinking too much."

Bob Watson beside me said "Liar" on a whispered breath, and Harry didn't hear.

"Nolan is going to *prison*," Fiona said bitterly. "Do you realize? *Prison.* All because of you."

"You don't *know* he is," Harry complained. "The jury haven't found him guilty yet."

"But they *will,* won't they? And it will be *your fault.* Dammit, you were under *oath.* All you had to do was say Lewis was drunk. Now the jury thinks he wasn't drunk, so he must be able to remember everything. They think he's lying when he says he can't remember. Christ Almighty, Nolan's whole *defense* was that Lewis can't remember. How could you be so *stupid?*"

Harry didn't answer. The atmosphere if possible worsened, and I felt as if I'd gone into a movie halfway through and couldn't grasp the plot.

Mackie without contributing any opinions turned from the Great West Road onto the M4 motorway and made better time westward along an unlit uninhabited stretch between snow-covered wooded hills, ice crystals glittering in the headlights.

"*Bob* says Lewis was drunk," Fiona persisted, "and he should know, he was serving the drinks."

"Then maybe the jury will believe Bob."

"They believed him until you stood there and blew it."

"They should have had *you* in the witness box," Harry said defensively. "Then you could have sworn he was paralytic and had to be scraped off the carpet, even if you weren't there."

Bob Watson said, "He wasn't paralytic."

"You keep out of it, Bob," Harry snapped.

"Sorr-ee," Bob Watson said, again under his breath.

"All you had to do was swear that Lewis was drunk." Fiona's voice rose with fury. "That's *all* the defense called you for. Then you didn't say it. Nolan's lawyer could have killed you."

Harry said wearily, "*You* didn't have to stand there answering that prosecutor's questions. You heard what he said, how did I know Lewis was drunk? Had I given him a breath test, a blood test, a urine test? On what did I base my judgment? Did I have any clinical experience? You heard him. On and on. How many drinks did I see Lewis take? How did I know what was in the drinks? Had I ever heard of Lewis having blackouts any other time after drinking?"

"That was disallowed," Mackie said.

"You let that prosecutor tie you in *knots*. You looked absolutely *stupid* . . ." Fiona ran on and on, the rage in her mind unabating.

I began to feel mildly sorry for Harry.

We reached the Chievely interchange and left the motorway to turn north on the big A34 to Oxford. Mackie had sensibly taken the cleared major roads rather than go over the hills, even though it was further that way, according to the map. I'd looked up the whereabouts of Tremayne's village on the theory that it was a wise man who knew his destination, especially when it was on the Berkshire Downs a mile from nowhere.

Silence had mercifully struck Fiona's tongue by the time Shellerton showed up on a signpost. Mackie slowed, signaled, and cautiously turned off the main road into a very narrow secondary road that was little more than a lane, where snow had been roughly pushed to the sides but still lay in shallow frozen brown ruts over much of the surface. The tires scrunched on them, cracking the ice. Mist formed quickly on the inside of the windscreen and Mackie rubbed it away impatiently with her glove.

There were no houses beside the lane: it was well over a mile across bare downland, I found later, from the main road to the village. There were also no cars: no one was out driving if they could help it. For all Mackie's care one could sometimes feel the wheels sliding, losing traction for perilous seconds. The engine, engaged in low gear, whined laboriously up a shallow incline.

"It's worse than this morning," Mackie said, sounding worried. "This road's a skating rink."

No one answered her. I was hoping, as I expect they all were, that we would reach the top of the slope without sliding backwards, and we did, only to see that the downside looked just as hazardous, if not more so. Mackie wiped the windscreen again and with extra care took a curve to the right.

Caught by the headlights, stock-still in the middle of the lane, stood a horse. A dark horse buckled into a dark rug, its head raised in alarm. There was the glimmer of sheen on its skin and luminescence in its wide eyes. The moment froze like the landscape.

"*Hell!*" Mackie exclaimed, and slammed her foot on the brake.

The vehicle slid inexorably on the ice and although

Mackie released the brakes a moment later it did as much harm as good.

The horse, terrified, tried to plunge out of the lane into the field alongside. Intent on missing him, and at the same time fighting the skid, Mackie miscalculated the curve, the camber and the speed, though to be fair to her it would have taken a stunt driver to come out of there safely.

The jeep slid to the side of the lane, spun its wheels on the snow-covered grass shoulder, mounted it, ran along and across as if making for the open fields under its own volition and tipped over sideways into an unseen drainage ditch, cracking with noises like pistol shots through a covering sheet of ice.

We'd been going slowly enough for it not to be an instantly lethal crunch, though it was a bang hard enough to rattle one's teeth. The curbside wheels, both front and back, finished four feet lower than road level, the far side of the ditch supporting the length of the roof of the vehicle so that it lay not absolutely flat on its side. I was opening my door, which was half sloping skyward, and hauling myself out more or less before the engine had had time to stall.

The downland wind, always on the move, stung my face sharply with a freezing warning. Wind-chill was an unforgiving enemy, deadly to the unwary.

Bob Watson had fallen on top of his wife. I reached down into the car and grasped him, and began to pull him out.

He tried to free himself from my hands, crying "Ingrid" urgently, and then in horror, "It's wet . . . she's in water."

"Come out," I said peremptorily. "Then we can both pull her. Come out, you're heavy on her. You'll never get her out like that."

Some vestige of sense got through to him and he let me yank him out far enough so that he could stretch back in for his wife. I held him and he held her, and between the two of us we brought her out onto the roadway.

The ditch was almost full of muddy freezing water under

its coating of ice. Even as we lifted Ingrid out, the water deepened fast in the vehicle, and in the front seat Fiona was yelling to Harry to get her out, and Harry, I saw in horror, was underneath her and in danger of drowning.

The one headlight which had still been shining suddenly went out.

Mackie hadn't moved to save herself. I pulled open her door and found her dazed and semiconscious, held in her place by her seat belt.

"Get us out," Fiona yelled.

Harry, below her, was struggling in water and heaving, whether to save her or himself was impossible to tell. I felt around Mackie until I found the seat-belt clasp, released it, hauled her out bodily and shoved her into Bob Watson's arms.

"Sit her on the shoulder," I said. "Clear the snow off the grass. Hold her. Shield her from the wind."

"Bob," Ingrid said piteously, standing helplessly on the road and seeming to think her husband should attend to her alone, "Bob, I need you. I feel awful."

Bob glanced at his wife but took Mackie's weight and helped her to sit down. She began moving and moaning and asking what had happened, showing welcome signs of life.

No blood, I thought. Not a drop. Bloody lucky. My eyes became accustomed to the dark.

Fiona, halfway panic-stricken, put her arms up to mine and came out easily into the air, lithe and athletic. I let go of her and leaned in for Harry, who now had his seat belt unfastened and his head above water and had got past the stage of abject fright. He helped himself to climb out and went dripping over to Mackie, showing most concern for her, taking her support from Bob Watson.

Ingrid stood in the road, soaked, thin, frightened, helpless and crying. The wind was piercing, relentless . . . infinitely dangerous. It was easy to underestimate how fast cold could kill.

I said to Bob Watson, "Take all your wife's clothes off."

"What?"

"Take her wet clothes off or she'll freeze into a block of ice."

He opened his mouth.

"Start at the top," I said. "Take everything off and put my jacket on her, quickly. It's warm." I unzipped it and took it off, folding it together so as to keep the warmth of my body in it as much as possible. The cold bit through my sweater and undershirt as if they were invisible. I was infinitely grateful to be dry.

"I'll help Ingrid," Fiona said, as Bob still hesitated. "You don't mean her bra as well?"

"Yes, everything."

While the two women unbuttoned and tugged I went to the rear of the overturned vehicle and found to my relief that the luggage door would still open. I pushed up my sleeves and literally fished out my two bags, and Harry, close beside me, watched the water drip off them with gloom.

"Everything will be wet," he said defeatedly.

"No." Waterproof, sandproof, bugproof were the rules I traveled by, even in rural England. I found the aluminum camera case under the water and set it on the road beside the bags.

"Which would you prefer," I asked Harry, "bathrobe or dinner jacket?"

He actually laughed.

"Strip off," I said, "in case the iceman cometh. Top half first."

They had all been dressed for a day in court, not for trudging about in the open. Even Mackie and Bob Watson, who were dry, hadn't enough on for the circumstances.

Bob Watson took over again with Mackie, and Harry began to struggle out of his sodden overcoat, business suit, shirt and tie, wincing with pain as the cold hit his wet flesh. His undershirt was sticking to him. I gave him a hand.

"What did you say your name was?" he said, teeth clenched, shuddering.

"John."

I handed him a navy-blue silk undershirt and long johns, two sweaters, gray trousers and the bathrobe. No one ever dived into clothes faster. My shoes were a size too big, he ironically complained, hopping around and pulling them on over dry socks.

Fiona had changed Ingrid to the waist and was waiting to do the second half. I took off my boots and then my ski pants, which Fiona put on Ingrid after trying to shield her brief lower nakedness from my eyes, which amazed me. It was hardly the time for fussing. The boots looked enormous, once they were on, and Ingrid was nine inches shorter than my ski suit.

For myself I brought out a navy blazer and jodhpur boots, feeling the ice strike up through wool to my toes.

"My feet are squelching," Fiona said, eyeing the boots with strong shivers, "and I'm wet to the neck. Is there anything left?"

"You'd better have these."

"Well . . . I . . ." She looked at my bare socks, hesitating.

I thrust the boots and blazer into her hands. My black evening shoes, which were all that remained in the way of footwear, would have fallen off her at every step.

I dug into the bag again for jodhpurs, black socks and a sweatshirt. "These any good to you?" I asked.

She took all the clothes gratefully and hid behind Ingrid to change. I put on my black shoes and the dinner jacket: a lot better than nothing.

When Fiona reappeared her shivers had grown to shakes. She still had too few layers, even if now dry. The only useful thing still unused in my belongings was the plastic bag which had contained my dinner jacket. I put it over Fiona's head, widening the hole where the hanger usually went, and if she didn't care to be labeled "Ace Cleaners" at intervals front and back, at least it stopped the wind a bit and kept some body heat in.

"Well," Harry said with remarkable cheerfulness, eyeing the dimly seen final results of the motley redistribution, "thanks to John we should live to see Shellerton. All you lot had better start walking. I'll stay with Mackie and we'll follow when we can."

"No," I said. "How far is it to the village?"

"A mile or so."

"Then we all start now. We'll carry Mackie. It's too cold, believe me, for hanging about. How about a chair lift?"

So Harry and I sat the semiconscious Mackie on our linked wrists and draped her arms around our necks, and we set off towards the village with Bob Watson carrying all the wet clothes in one of my bags, Fiona carrying dry things in the other and Ingrid shuffling along in front in the moon boots with my camera case, lighting the way with the dynamo flashlight from my basic travel kit.

"Squeeze it." I showed her how. "It doesn't have batteries. Shine it on the road, so we can all see."

"Thank God it isn't snowing," Harry said: but there were ominous clouds hiding the stars. What little natural light there was, was amplified by the whiteness of the snow, the only good thing about it. I was glad it wasn't too far to the village. Mackie wasn't draggingly heavy, but we were walking on ice.

"Doesn't any traffic ever come along this road?" I asked in frustration when we'd gone half a mile and still seen no one.

"There are two other ways into Shellerton," Harry said. "God, this wind's the devil. My ears are dropping off."

My own head also was achingly cold. Mackie and Fiona had woolen hats, Ingrid was warmest in the hood of my ski suit, Bob Watson wore a cap. Ingrid had my gloves. Harry's hands and mine were going numb under Mackie's bottom.

If I'd brought any more socks we could have used them as mitts.

"It's not far now," Bob said. "Once we're round the bend you'll see the village."

He was right. Electricity twinkled not far below us, offering shelter and warmth. Let's not have a power cut, I prayed.

Mackie suddenly awoke to full consciousness on the last stretch and began demanding to know what was happening.

"We skidded into a ditch," Harry said succinctly.

"The horse! Is the horse all right? Why are you carrying me. Put me down."

We stopped and set her on her feet, where she swayed and put a hand to the side of her head.

"Did we hit the horse?" she said.

"No," Harry answered. "Better let us carry you."

"What happened to the horse?"

"It buggered off across the Downs. Come on, Mackie, we're literally freezing to death standing here." Harry swung his arms in my bathrobe, then hugged his body and tried to warm his hands in his armpits. "Let's get on, for God's sake."

Mackie refused to let us lift her up again, so we began to struggle on towards the village, a shadowy band slipping and sliding downhill, holding on to each other and trying not to fall, cold to the bone. I should have brought the skis, I thought, and it seemed an extraordinarily long time since that morning.

One reason for the dearth of traffic became clear as we reached the first houses: two cars lay impacted across the width of the lane, and certainly nothing was leaving the village that way.

"You'd better all come to our house," Fiona said in a shaking voice as we edged around the wreck. "It's nearest."

No one argued.

We turned into a long village street with no lighting, and passed a garage, darkly shut, and a pub, open.

"How about a quick one?" Harry suggested, half serious.

Fiona said with some of her former asperity, "I should think you've heard enough about drink for one day. And you're not going anywhere dressed like that except straight home."

It was too dark to see Harry's expression. No one cared to comment, and presently Ingrid with the flashlight turned into a driveway which wound around behind some cottages and opened into a snowy expanse in front of a big Georgian-looking house.

Ingrid stopped. Fiona said, "This way," and led a still-silent procession around to a side door, which she unlocked with a key retrieved from under a stone.

The relief of being out of the wind was like a rebirth. The warmth of the extensive kitchen we filed into was a positive life-giving luxury; and there in the lights I saw my companions clearly for the first time.

3

Everyone except Ingrid was visibly trembling, myself included. All the faces were bluish-white, suffering.

"God," Fiona said, "that was hell."

She was older than I'd thought. Forties, not thirties. The Ace Cleaners bag reached nearly to her knees, covering her arms, bordering on farcical.

"Take this damned thing off me," she said. "And don't bloody laugh."

Harry obligingly pulled the cleaner's plastic bag up and over her head, taking her knitted hat with it, freeing heavy silver-blond hair and transforming her like a *coup de théâtre* from a refugee to an assured charismatic woman in jodhpurs and blue blazer with the turtleneck sweatshirt showing white at throat and cuffs.

Although she was tall, the sleeves were all too long for her, which had been a blessing, it seemed, as she had been able

33

to tuck her hands inside them, using them as gloves. She stared at me across her kitchen, looking with curiosity at the man whose clothes she wore, seeing I supposed a tallish, thinnish, youngish brown-eyed person in jeans, scarlet sweater and incongruous dinner jacket.

I smiled at her and she, aware of the admiration in my expression, swept a reviving glance around her other unexpected guests and went over to the huge red Aga which warmed the whole place, lifting the lid, letting volumes of heat flow out. The bad temper of the journey had disappeared, revealing a sensible, competent woman.

"Hot drinks," she said decisively. "Harry, fill the kettle and get some mugs."

Harry, my height but fair and blue-eyed, complied with the instructions as though thoroughly accustomed to being bidden and began rooting around also for spoons, instant coffee and sugar. Swaddled in my blue bathrobe, he looked ready for bed; and he too was older than I'd thought. He and Fiona were revealed as well-off and perhaps rich. The kitchen was large, individual, a combination of technology and sitting room, and the manner and voices of its owners had the unself-conscious assurance of comfortable social status.

Mackie sat down uncertainly at the big central table, her fingers gingerly feeling her temple.

"I was looking at the horse," she said. "Must have hit my head on the window. Is the jeep all right?"

"Shouldn't think so," Harry said without emotion. "It's lying in water which will be frozen over again by morning. The door on my side buckled when we hit. Filthy ditchwater just rushed in."

"Damn," Mackie said wearily. "That on top of everything else."

She huddled into her fawn-colored padded coat, still deeply shivering, and it was hard to tell what she would look like warm and laughing. All I could see were reddish curls over her forehead followed by closed eyes, pale lips and the rigid muscles of distress.

"Is Perkin home?" Fiona asked her.

"He should be. God, I hope so."

Fiona, recovering faster than anyone else, perhaps because she was in her own house, went across to a wall telephone and pressed buttons. Perkin, whoever he was, apparently answered and was given a variety of bad news.

"Yes," Fiona said repeating things, "I did say the jeep's in a ditch . . . it's in that hollow just over the top of the hill after you leave the A34 . . . I don't know whose horse, dammit . . . No, we had an *abysmal* day in court. Look, can you get down here and collect everyone? Mackie's all right but she hit her head . . . Bob Watson and his wife are with us . . . Yes, we did pick up the writer, he's here too. Just *come,* Perkin, for God's sake. Stop dithering." She hung up the receiver with a crash.

Harry poured steaming water onto instant coffee in a row of mugs and then picked up a milk carton in one hand and a bottle of brandy in the other, offering a choice of additives. Everyone except Ingrid chose brandy, and Harry's idea of a decent slug cooled the liquid to drinking point.

Although if we had still been outside, the alcohol wouldn't have been such a good idea, the deep trembles in all our bodies abated and faded away. Bob Watson took off his cap and looked suddenly younger, a short stocky man with wiry brown hair and a returning glint of independence. One could still see what he must have looked like as a schoolboy, with rounded cheeks and a natural insolence not far from the surface but controlled enough to keep him out of trouble. He had called Harry a liar, but too quietly for him to hear. That rather summed up Bob Watson, I thought.

Ingrid, swamped in the ski suit, looked out at the world from a thinly pretty face and sniffed at regular intervals. She sat beside her husband at the table, unspeaking and forever in his shadow.

Standing with his backside propped against the Aga, Harry warmed both hands around his mug and looked at me with the glimmering amusement that, when not under stress from giving evidence, seemed to be his habitual cast of mind.

"Welcome to Berkshire," he said.

"Thanks a lot."

"I would have stayed by the jeep and waited for someone to come," he said.

"I thought someone would," I agreed.

Mackie said, "I hope the horse is all right," as if her mind were stuck in that groove. No one else, it seemed to me, cared an icicle for the survival of the cause of our woes, and I suspected, perhaps unfairly, that Mackie kept on about the horse so as to reinforce in our consciousness that the crash hadn't been her fault.

Warmth gradually returned internally also and everyone looked as if they had come up to room temperature, like wine. Ingrid pushed back the hood of my ski suit revealing soft mouse-brown hair in need of a brush.

No one had a great wish to talk, and there was something of a return to the pre-crash gloom, so it was a relief when wheels, slammed doors and approaching footsteps announced the arrival of Perkin.

He hadn't come alone. It was Tremayne Vickers who advanced first into the kitchen, his loud voice and large personality galvanizing the subdued group drinking coffee.

"Got yourselves into a load of shit, have you?" he boomed with a touch of not wholly unfriendly scorn. "Roads too much for you, eh?"

Mackie went defensively into the horse routine as if she'd merely been rehearsing earlier.

The man who followed Tremayne through the door looked like a smudged carbon copy: same height, same build, same basic features, but none of Tremayne's bullishness. If that was Perkin, I thought, he must be Tremayne's son.

The carbon copy said to Mackie crossly, "Why didn't you go round the long way? You ought to have more sense than to take that shortcut."

"It was all right this morning," Mackie said, "and I always go that way. It was the horse . . ."

Tremayne's gaze fastened on me. "So you got here. Good. You've met everyone? My son, Perkin. His wife, Mackie."

I'd assumed, I realized, that Mackie had been either Tremayne's own wife or perhaps his daughter; hadn't thought of daughter-in-law.

"Why on earth are you wearing a dinner jacket?" Tremayne asked, staring.

"We got wet in the ditch," Harry said briefly. "Your friend the writer lent us dry clothes. He issued his dinner jacket to himself. Didn't trust me with it, smart fellow. What I've got on is his bathrobe. Ingrid has his ski suit. Fiona is his from head to foot."

Tremayne looked briefly bewildered but decided not to sort things out. Instead he asked Fiona if she'd been hurt in the crash. "Fiona, my dear . . ."

Fiona, his dear, assured him otherwise. He behaved to her with a hint of roguishness, she to him with easy response. She aroused in all men, I supposed, the desire to flirt.

Perkin belatedly asked Mackie about her head, awkwardly producing anxiety after his ungracious criticism. Mackie gave him a tired understanding smile, and I had a swift impression that she was the one in that marriage who made allowances, who did the looking after, who was the adult to her good-looking husband-child.

"But," he said, "I do think you were silly to go down that road." His reaction to her injury was still to blame her for it, but I wondered if it weren't really a reaction to fright, like a parent clouting a much-loved lost-but-found infant. "And there was supposed to be a police notice at the turnoff saying it was closed. It's been closed since those cars slid into each other at lunchtime."

"There wasn't any police notice," Mackie said.

"Well, there must have been. You just didn't see it."

"There was no police notice in sight," Harry said, and we all agreed, we hadn't seen one.

"All the same . . ." Perkin wouldn't leave it.

"Look," Mackie said, "if I could go back and do it again then I wouldn't go along there, but it looked all right and I'd come up in the morning, so I just *did,* and that's that."

"We all saw the *horse,*" Harry said, drawling, and from the dry humor lurking in his voice one could read his private opinion of Perkin's behavior.

Perkin gave him a confused glance and stopped picking on Mackie.

Tremayne said, "What's done's done," as if announcing his life's philosophy, and added that he would "give the police a ring" when he got home, which would be very soon now.

"About your clothes," Fiona said to me, "shall I send them to the cleaners with all our wet things?"

"No, don't bother," I said. "I'll come and collect them tomorrow."

"All right." She smiled slightly. "I do realize we have to thank you. Don't think we don't know."

"Don't know what?" Perkin demanded.

Harry said in his way, "Fellow saved us from ice-cubery."

"From *what?*"

Ingrid giggled. Everyone looked at her. "Sorry," she whispered, subsiding.

"Quite likely from death," Mackie said plainly. "Let's go home." She stood up, clearly much better for the warmth and the stiffly laced coffee and also, it seemed to me, relieved that her father-in-law hadn't added his weight to her husband's bawling-out. "Tomorrow," she added slowly, "which of us is going back to Reading?"

"Oh, God," Fiona said. "For a minute I'd forgotten."

"Some of us will have to go," Mackie said, and it was clear that no one wanted to.

After a pause Harry stirred. "I'll go. I'll take Bob. Fiona doesn't have to go, nor does Ingrid. Mackie . . ." He stopped.

"I'll come with you," she said. "I owe him that."

Fiona said, "So will I. He's my cousin, after all. He deserves us to support him. Though after what Harry did today I don't know if I can look him in the face."

"What did Harry do?" Perkin asked.

Fiona shrugged and retreated. "Mackie can tell you." Fiona, it seemed, could attack Harry all she liked herself, but she wasn't throwing him to other wolves. Harry was no doubt due for further tongue-lashing after we'd gone, and in fact was glancing at his wife in a mixture of apprehension and resignation.

"Let's be off," Tremayne said. "Come along, Bob."

"Yes, sir."

Bob Watson, I remembered, was Tremayne's head lad. He and his Ingrid went over to the door, followed by Mackie and Perkin. I put down my mug, thanking Harry for the reviver.

"Come this time tomorrow to fetch your clothes," he said. "Come for a drink. An ordinary drink, not an emergency."

"Thank you. I'd like that."

He nodded amiably, and Fiona also, and I picked up my dry-clothes bag and the camera case and followed Tremayne and the others out again into the snow. The six of us squeezed into a large Volvo, Tremayne driving, Perkin sitting beside him, Ingrid sitting on Bob's lap in the back with Mackie and me. At the end of the village Tremayne stopped to let Bob and Ingrid get out, Ingrid giving me a sketchy smile and saying Bob would bring my suit and boots along in the morning, if that would be all right. Of course, I said.

They turned away to walk through a garden gate towards

a small shadowy house, and Tremayne started off again towards open country, grousing that the trial would take his head lad away for yet another day. Neither Mackie nor Perkin said anything, and I still had no idea what the trial was all about. I didn't know them well enough to ask, I felt.

"Not much of a welcome for you, John, eh?" Tremayne said over his shoulder. "Did you bring a typewriter?"

"No. A pencil, actually. And a tape recorder."

"I expect you know what you're doing." He sounded cheerfully more sure of that than I was. "We can start in the morning."

After about a mile of cautious crawling along a surface much like the one we'd come to grief on, he turned in through a pair of imposing gateposts and stopped outside a very large house where many lights showed dimly through curtains. As inhabitants of large houses seldom used their front doors, we went into this one also at the side, not directly into the kitchen this time but into a warm carpeted hall leading to doorways in all directions.

Tremayne, saying, "Bloody cold night," walked through a doorway to the left, looking back for me to follow. "Come on in. Make yourself at home. This is the family room, where you'll find newspapers, telephone, drinks, things like that. Help yourself to whatever you want while you're here."

The big room looked comfortable in a sprawling way, not tidy, not planned. There was a mixture of patterns and colors, a great many photographs, a few poinsettias left over from Christmas and a glowing log fire in a wide stone fireplace.

Tremayne picked up a telephone and briefly told the local police that his jeep was in the ditch in the lane, not to worry, no one had been hurt, he would get it picked up in the morning. Duty done, he went across to the fire and held out his hands to warm them.

"Perkin and Mackie have their own part of the house, but this room is where we all meet," he said. "If you want to leave a message for anybody, pin it to that board over there." He pointed to a chair on which was propped a cork-board much like the one in Ronnie's office. Red drawing pins were stuck into it at random, one of them anchoring a note which in large letters announced briefly, BACK FOR GRUB.

"That's my other son," Tremayne said, reading the message from a distance. "He's fifteen. Unmanageable." He spoke however with indulgence. "I expect you'll soon get the hang of the household."

"Er . . . *Mrs.* Vickers?" I said tentatively.

"Mackie?" He sounded puzzled.

"No . . . Your wife?"

"Oh. Oh, I see. No, my wife took a hike. Can't say I minded. There's just me and Gareth, the boy. I've a daughter, married a frog, lives outside Paris, has three children, they come here sometimes, turn the place upside down. She's the eldest, then Perkin. Gareth came later."

He was feeding me facts without feelings, I thought. I'd have to change that, if I were to do any good: but maybe it was too soon for feelings. He was glad I was there, but jerky, almost nervous, almost—now we were alone—shy. Now that he had got what he wanted, now that he had secured his writer, a lot of the agitation and anxiety he'd displayed in Ronnie's office seemed to have abated. The Tremayne of today was running on only half-stress.

Mackie, coming into the room, restored him to his confident self. Carrying an ice bucket, she glanced quickly at her father-in-law as if to assess his mood, to find out if his tolerance in Fiona and Harry's kitchen was still in operation. Reassured in some way, she took the ice over to a table bearing a tray of bottles and glasses and began mixing a drink.

She had taken off her padded coat and woolly hat, and was wearing a blue jersey dress over knee-high narrow black boots. Her red-brown hair, cut short, curled neatly on a well-shaped head and she was still pale, without lipstick or vivacity.

The drink she mixed was gin and tonic, which she gave to Tremayne. He nodded his thanks, as for something done often.

"For you?" Mackie said to me. "John?"

"The coffee was fine," I said.

She smiled faintly. "Yes."

Truth to tell I was hungry, not thirsty. Thanks to no water in the friend's aunt's house, all I had had that day apart from the coffee was some bread and Marmite and two glasses of milk, and even that had been half frozen in its carton. I began to hope that Gareth's return, "back for grub," was imminent.

Perkin appeared carrying an already full glass of brown liquid that looked like Coca-Cola. He sank into one of the armchairs and began complaining again about the loss of the jeep, not seeing that he was lucky not to have lost his wife.

"The damned thing's insured," Tremayne said robustly. "The garage can tow it out of the ditch in the morning and tell us if it can be salvaged. Either way, it's not the end of the world."

"How will we manage without it?" Perkin grumbled.

"Buy another," Tremayne said.

This simple solution silenced Perkin, and Mackie looked grateful. She sat on a sofa and took her boots off, saying they were damp from snow and her feet were freezing. She massaged her toes and looked across at my black shoes.

"Those shoes of yours are meant for dancing," she said, "and not for carrying females across ice. I'm sorry, I really am."

"Carrying?" Tremayne said, eyebrows rising.

"Yes, didn't I tell you? John and Harry carried me for about a mile, I think. I can remember the crash, then I sort of passed out and I woke up just outside the village. I do

vaguely remember them carrying me . . . it's a bit of a blur
. . . I was sitting on their wrists . . . I knew I mustn't fall off
. . . it was like dreaming."

Perkin stared, first at her, then at me. Not pleased, I
thought.

"I'll be damned," Tremayne said.

I smiled at Mackie and she smiled back, and Perkin very
obviously didn't like that. I'd have to be careful, I thought.
I was not there to stir family waters but simply to do a job,
to stay uninvolved and leave everything as I'd found it.

Thankful for the heat of the fire, I shed the dinner
jacket, laying it on a chair and feeling less like the decadent
remains of an orgy. I wondered how soon I could decently
mention food. If it hadn't been for the bus fare I might
have bought something sustaining like chocolate. I wondered if I could ask Tremayne to reimburse the bus fare.
Frivolous thoughts, mental rubbish.

"Sit down, John," Tremayne said, waving to an armchair.
I sat as instructed. "What happened in court?" he asked
Mackie. "How did it go?"

"It was awful." She shuddered. "Nolan looked so . . . so
vulnerable. The jury think he's guilty, I'm sure they do. And
Harry wouldn't swear after all that Lewis was drunk . . ."
She closed her eyes and sighed deeply. "I wish to God we'd
never had that damned party."

"What's done is done," Tremayne said heavily, and I
wondered how many times they'd each repeated those regrets.

Tremayne glanced at me and asked Mackie, "Have you
told John what's going on?" She shook her head and he
enlightened me a little. "We gave a party here last year in
April to celebrate winning the Grand National with Top
Spin Lob. Celebrate! There were a lot of people here, well
over a hundred, including of course Fiona and Harry, who
you met. I train horses for them. And Fiona's cousins were
here, Nolan and Lewis. They're brothers. No one knows for

sure what happened, but at the end of the party, when most people had gone home, a girl died. Nolan swears it was an accident. Lewis was there . . . he should have been able to settle it one way or the other, but he says he was drunk and can't remember."

"He *was* drunk," Mackie protested. "Bob testified he was drunk. Bob said he served him getting on for a dozen drinks during the evening."

"Bob Watson acted as barman," Tremayne told me. "He always does, at our parties."

"We'll never have another," Mackie said.

"Is Nolan being tried for murder?" I asked, into a pause.

"For assault resulting in death," Tremayne said. "The prosecution are trying to prove intent, which would make it murder. Nolan's lawyers say the charge means manslaughter but they are pressing hard for involuntary manslaughter, which could be called negligence or plain accident. The case has been dragging on for months. At least tomorrow it will end."

"He'll appeal," Perkin said.

"They haven't found him guilty yet," Mackie protested.

Tremayne told me, "Mackie and Harry walked together into Mackie and Perkin's sitting room and found Nolan standing over the girl, who was lying on the floor. Lewis was sitting in an armchair. Nolan said he'd put his hands round the girl's neck to give her a shaking, and she just went limp and fell down, and when Mackie and Harry tried to revive her, they found she was dead."

"The pathologist said in court today that she died from strangulation," Mackie said, "but that sometimes it takes very little pressure to kill someone. He said she died of vagal inhibition, which means the vagus nerve stops working, which it apparently can do fairly easily. The vagus nerve keeps the heart beating. The pathologist said it's always dangerous to clasp people suddenly round the neck, even in fun. But there's no doubt Nolan was furious with

Olympia—that's the girl—and he had been furious all the evening, and the prosecution produced someone who'd heard him say, 'I'll strangle the bitch,' so that he had it in his mind to put his hands round her neck . . ." She broke off and sighed again. "There wouldn't have been a trial at all except for Olympia's father. The pathologist's original report said it could so easily have been an accident that there wasn't going to be a prosecution, but Olympia's father insisted on bringing a private case against Nolan. He won't let up. He's obsessed. He was sitting there in court glaring at us."

"If he'd had his way," Tremayne confirmed, "Nolan would have been behind bars all this time, not out on bail."

Mackie nodded. "The prosecution—and that's Olympia's father talking through his lawyers—wanted Nolan to be remanded in jail tonight, but the judge said no. So Nolan and Lewis have gone back to Lewis's house, and God knows what state they're in after the mauling they got in court. It's Olympia's father who deserves to be strangled for all the trouble he's caused."

It seemed to me that on the whole it was Nolan who had caused the trouble, but I didn't say so.

"Well," Tremayne said, shrugging, "it happened in this house but it doesn't directly concern my family, thank God."

Mackie looked as if she weren't so sure. "They are our friends," she said.

"Hardly even that," Perkin said, looking my way. "Fiona and Mackie are friends. That's where it starts. Mackie came to stay with Fiona, and I met her in Fiona's house"—he smiled briefly—"and so, as they say, we were married."

"And lived happily ever after," Mackie finished loyally, though I reckoned if she were happy she worked at it. "We've been married two years now. Two and a half, almost."

"You won't put all this Nolan business in my book, will you?" Tremayne asked.

"I shouldn't think so," I said, "not if you don't want me to."

"No, I don't. I was saying good-bye to some guests when that girl died. Perkin came to tell me, and I had to deal with it, but I didn't know her, she'd come with Nolan and I'd never met her before. She isn't part of my life."

"All right," I said.

Tremayne showed no particular relief, but just nodded. Seen in his own home, standing by his own fire, he was a big-bodied man of substantial presence, long accustomed to taking charge and ruling his kingdom. This was the persona, no doubt, that the book was to be about: the face of control, of worldly wisdom and success.

So be it, I thought. If I were to sing for my supper I'd sing the songs he chose. But meanwhile, *where* was the supper?

"In the morning," Tremayne said to me, changing the subject and apparently tired of the trial and its tribulations, "I thought you might come out with me to see my string at morning exercise."

"I'd like to," I said.

"Good. I'll wake you at seven. The first lot pulls out at seven-thirty, just before dawn. Of course, at present, with this freeze we can't do any schooling but we've got an all-weather gallop. You'll see it in the morning. If it should be snowing hard, we won't go."

"Right."

He turned his head to Mackie. "I suppose you won't be out for first lot?"

"No, sorry. We'll have to leave early again to get to Reading."

He nodded, and to me he said, "Mackie's my assistant."

I glanced at Mackie and then at Perkin.

"That's right," Tremayne said, reading my thought. "Perkin doesn't work for me. Mackie does. Perkin never wanted to be a trainer and he has his own life. Gareth . . . well . . . Gareth might take over from me one day, but he's too young to know what he'll want. But when Perkin married Mackie he brought me a damned smart assistant, and it's worked out very well."

Mackie looked pleased at his audible sincerity and it seemed the arrangement was to Perkin's liking also.

"This house is huge," Tremayne said, "and as Perkin and Mackie couldn't afford much of a place of their own yet, we divided it, and they have their private half. You'll soon get the hang of it." He finished his drink and went to pour himself another. "You can have the dining room to work in," he said to me over his shoulder. "Tomorrow I'll show you where to find the cuttings, videotapes and form books, and you can take what you like into the dining room. We'll fix up the video player there."

"Fine," I said. Food in the dining room would be better, I thought.

Tremayne said, "As soon as it thaws I'll take you racing. You'll soon pick it up."

"Pick it up?" Perkin repeated, surprised. "Doesn't he *know* about racing?"

"Not a lot," I said.

Perkin raised ironic eyebrows. "It's going to be some book."

"He's a writer," Tremayne said, a touch defensively. "He can learn."

I nodded to back him up. It was true that I had learned the habits and ways of life of dwellers in far places, and didn't doubt I could do the same to the racing fraternity at home in England. To listen, to see, to ask, to understand, to check; I would use the same method that I'd used six times before, and this time without needing an interpreter. Whether I could present Tremayne's life and times in a shape others would enjoy, that was the real, nagging, doubtful question.

Gareth at long last blew in with a gust of cold air and,

stripping off an eye-dazzling psychedelic padded jacket, asked his father, "What's for supper?"

"Anything you like," Tremayne said, not minding.

"Pizza, then." His gaze stopped on me. "Hello, I'm Gareth."

Tremayne told him my name and that I would be writing the biography and staying in the house.

"Straight up?" the boy said, his eyes widening. "Do you want some pizza?"

"Yes, please."

"Ten minutes," he said. He turned to Mackie. "Do you two want some?"

Mackie and Perkin simultaneously shook their heads and murmured that they'd be off to their own quarters, which appeared to be what Gareth and Tremayne expected.

Gareth was perhaps five foot six with a strong echo of his father's self-confidence and a voice still half broken, coming out hoarse and uneven. He gave me an all-over glance as if assessing what he'd got to put up with for the length of my visit and seemed neither depressed nor elated.

"I heard the weather news at Coconut's," he told his father. "Today's been the coldest for twenty-five years. Coconut's father's horses have their duvet rugs on under the jute."

"So have ours," Tremayne said. "Did they forecast more snow?"

"No, just cold for a few more days. East winds from Siberia. Have you remembered to send my school fees?"

Tremayne clearly hadn't.

"If you'll just sign the check," his son said, "I'll give it to them myself. They're getting a bit fussed."

"The checkbook's in the office," Tremayne said.

"Right." Gareth took his Joseph's coat with him out of the door and almost immediately returned. "I suppose there isn't the faintest chance," he said to me, "that you can cook?"

4

In the morning I went downstairs to find the family room dark but lights on in the kitchen.

It wasn't a palatial kitchen like Fiona's but did contain a big table with chairs all around it as well as a solid-fuel cooker whose warmth easily defeated the pre-dawn refrigeration. I had been hoping to borrow a coat from Tremayne to go out to watch the horses, but on a chair I found my boots, gloves and ski suit with a note attached by a safety pin, "Thanks ever so much."

Smiling, I unpinned the note and put on the suit and boots, and Tremayne, in a padded jacket, cloth cap and yellow scarf came in blowing on his bare hands and generally bringing the arctic indoors.

"Ah, there you are," he said, puffing. "Good. Bob Watson brought up your clothes when he came to feed. Ready?"

I nodded.

"I'll just get my gloves." He checked also that I had gloves. "It's as cold as I've ever known it. We won't stay out long, the wind's terrible. Come along."

As we went through the hall I asked him about the feeding.

"Bob Watson comes at six," he said briefly. "All horses in training get an early-morning feed. High protein. Keeps them warm. Gives them energy. A thoroughbred on a high-protein diet generates a lot of heat. Just as well in weather like this. You rarely find a bucket of water frozen over in a horse's box, however cold it is outside. Mind you," he said, "we do our best to stop draughts round the doors, but you have to give them fresh air. If you don't, if you mollycoddle them too much, you get viruses flourishing."

As we stepped out into the open, the wind pulled his last words away and sucked the breath out of our lungs and I reckoned we were still dealing with perhaps ten degrees of frost, plus chill factor, the same as the evening before. It wouldn't go on freezing for as long as in nineteen sixty-three, I thought: that had been the coldest winter since seventeen forty.

A short walk took us straight into the stable yard, dark the night before and dimly seen, now lit comprehensively and bustling with activity.

"Bob Watson," Tremayne said, "is no ordinary head lad. He has all sorts of skills, and takes pride in them. Any odd job, carpentering, plumbing, laying concrete, anything to improve the yard and working conditions, he suggests it and mostly does it himself."

The object of this eulogy came to meet us, noticing I wore the ski suit, acknowledging my thanks.

"All ready, guv'nor," he said to Tremayne.

"Good. Bring them out, Bob. Then you'd better be off, if you're going to Reading."

Bob nodded and gave some sort of signal and from many open doors came figures leading horses, riders in hard helmets, horses in rugs. In the lights and the dark, with plumes of steam swirling as they breathed, with the circling movements and the scrunching of icy gravel underfoot, the great elemental creatures raised in me such a sense of enjoyment and excitement that I felt for the first time truly enthusiastic about what I'd set my hand to. I wished I could paint, but no canvas, and not even film, could catch the feeling of primitive life or the tingle and smell of the frosty yard.

Bob moved through the scene giving a leg-up to each lad and they resolved themselves into a line, perhaps twenty of them, and processed away through a far exit, horses stalking on long strong legs, riders hunched on top, heads bobbing.

"Splendid," I said to Tremayne, almost sighing.

He glanced at me. "Horses get to you, don't they?"

"To you too? Still?"

He nodded and said "I love them," as if such a statement were no more than normal, and in the same tone of voice went on, "As the jeep's in the ditch we'll have to go up to the gallops on the tractor. All right with you?"

"Sure," I said, and got my introduction to the training of steeplechasers perched high in a cab over chain-wrapped wheels which Tremayne told me had been up to the Downs with his groundsman once already that morning to harrow the tracks and make them safe for the horses to walk on. He drove the tractor himself with the facility of long custom, spending most of his time not looking where he was going but at anything else visible around him.

His house and stables, I discovered, were right on the edge of the grassy uplands, so that the horses had merely to cross one public road to be already on a downland track, and the road surface itself had been thinly covered with unidentified muck to make the icy crossing easier.

Tremayne waited until his whole string was safely over before following them at enough distance not to alarm them, then they peeled off to the right while we lumbered onwards and upwards over frozen rutted mud, making for a horizon that slowly defined itself out of shadows as the firmament grew lighter.

Through the wind Tremayne remarked that perfectly still mornings on the long east-west sweep of downland across Berkshire and Wiltshire were as rare as honest beggars. Apart from that, the day broke clear and high with a pale-gray washed sky that slowly turned blue over the rolling snow-dusted hills. When Tremayne stopped the tractor and the silence and isolation crept into the senses, it was easy to see that this was what it had looked like up here for thousands of years, that this primordial scene before our present eyes had also been there before man.

Tremayne prosaically told me that if we had continued up over the next brow we would have been close to the fences and hurdles of his schooling ground where his horses learned to jump. Today, he said, they would be doing only half-speed gallops on the all-weather track, and he led the way on foot from the tractor across a stretch of powdery snow to a low mound from where we could see a long dark ribbon of ground winding away down the hill and curving out of sight at the bottom.

"They'll come up here towards us," he said. "The all-weather surface is wood chips. Am I telling you what you already know?"

"No," I said. "Tell me everything."

He grunted noncommittally and raised a pair of binoculars powerful enough to see into the riders' minds. I looked where he was looking, but it took me much longer to spot the three dark shapes moving over the dark track. They seemed to be taking a long time to come up head-on towards us but the slowness was an illusion merely. Once they drew near and passed us their speed was vivid, stirring, a matter of muscles stretching and hooves thudding urgently on the quiet surface.

Two or three at a time they all came up in their turn. "Both of those are Fiona's," Tremayne said from behind the binoculars, giving me a commentary as a pair of chestnuts scurried past, and, "The one on the left of this next three is my Grand National winner, Top Spin Lob."

With interest I watched the pride of the stable go past us and begin to pull up as he reached the brow of the rise, but beside me Tremayne was stiffening in dismay and saying, "What the hell—"

I looked back down the hill in the direction of his binoculars but could see only three more horses coming up the track, two in front, one behind. It wasn't until they were almost upon us that I realized that the one at the rear had no rider.

The three horses passed us and began to slow down and Tremayne said "Shit" with fervor.

"Did the lad fall off?" I asked inanely.

"No doubt he did," Tremayne said forcefully, watching through his glasses, "but he's not one of mine."

"How do you mean?"

"I mean," Tremayne said, "that's not my horse. Just look at him. That's not my rug. That horse isn't saddled and has no bridle. Can't you see?"

When I looked, when he'd told me what to look for, then I could see. Tremayne's horses had fawn rugs with horizontal red and blue stripes, rugs which covered the ribs and hindquarters but left the legs free for full movement. The rug of the riderless horse was brownish-gray, much thicker, and fastened by straps running under the belly and around in front of the shoulders.

"I suppose you'll think me crazy," I said to Tremayne, "but maybe that's the horse that was loose in the lane last night when we crashed. I mean, I saw it for only a split second, really, but it looked like that. Dark, with that sort of rug."

"Almost every racehorse wears that sort of rug at night in the winter," Tremayne said. "I'm not saying you're wrong, though. In a minute, I'll find out."

He swung his binoculars back to where another couple of his string were putting on their show and calmly watched them before referring again to the stranger.

"They're the last," he said as they sped past us. "Now let's see what's what."

He began to walk up beside the gallop in the direction of the horses and I followed, and we soon came over the brow to where his whole string was circling on snowy grass, steam swelling in clouds from their breath after their exertions. They were silhouetted against the eastern sun, their shapes now black, now gleaming. Brilliant, freezing, moving; unforgettable morning.

Away to the left, apart from the string, the riderless horse made his own white sun-splashed plume, his nervousness apparent, his herding instincts propelling him towards his kin, his wild nature urging flight.

Tremayne reached his horses and spoke to his lads.

"Anyone know whose horse that is?"

They shook their heads.

"Walk on back to the yard then. Go back down the all-weather track. No one else is using it this morning. Take care crossing the road."

They nodded and began to form into a line as they had in the stables, walking off in self-generated mist towards the end of the gallop.

Tremayne said to me, "Go back to the tractor, will you? Don't make any sudden moves. Don't alarm this fellow." His eyes slid in the direction of the loose horse. "In the tractor's cab you'll find a rope. Bring it back here. Move slowly when you're coming into sight."

"Right," I said.

He nodded briefly and as I turned to go on the errand he reached into a pocket and produced a few horse-feed cubes which he held out to the runaway, speaking to him directly.

"Come on, now, fella. Nice and easy. Come along now,

you must be hungry . . ." His voice was calm and cajoling, absolutely without threat.

I walked away without haste and retrieved the rope from the cab, and by the time I cautiously returned over the brow into Tremayne's sight he was standing close to the horse, feeding him cubes with his left hand and holding a bunch of mane with his right.

I stopped, then went forward again slowly. The horse quivered, his head turning my way, his alarm transmitting like electricity. With small movements I made a big loop in one end of the supple old rope and tied a running bowline, then went slowly forward holding the rope open, not in a small circle that might frighten the horse more but in a big loop drooping almost to my knees.

Tremayne watched and continued to talk soothingly, feeding horse cubes one by one. I walked cautiously forwards, suppressing anything that could seem like doubt or anxiety, and paused again a step or two away from the horse.

"There's a good fella," Tremayne said to him, and to me in the same tone, "If you can put the rope over his head, do it."

I took the last two paces and without stopping walked alongside the horse on the far side from Tremayne so that the horse's head came as if naturally into and through the dangling loop. Tremayne moved his hand with the horse cubes away from the black muzzle just long enough for the rope to pass, and then still without abruptness I pulled the slack through the bowline until the noose was snug but not tight around the horse's neck.

"Good," Tremayne said. "Give me the rope. I'll walk him down to my yard. Can you drive the tractor?"

"Yes."

"Wait until I'm out of sight at the bottom. We don't want him bolting from fright. I couldn't hold him if he did."

"Right."

Tremayne fished a few more cubes out of his pocket and offered them as before but tugged gently on the rope at the same time. Almost as if making up his mind, as if settling for food and captivity, the great creature moved off with him peacefully, and the two of them trailed down to the dark strip of wood chips and plodded towards home.

Food and warmth, I thought. Maybe I had a lot in common with that horse. What had I settled for, but a form of captivity?

I shrugged. What was done was done, as Tremayne would say. I went down to the tractor and in due course drove it back and parked it where it had been before we started out.

In the now sunlit kitchen Tremayne was standing by the table, talking crossly into a telephone.

"You'd have thought someone would have noticed by now that they're missing a horse!" He listened a bit, then said, "Well, I've one here that's surplus to requirements, so let me know." He put the receiver down with destructive force. "No one's told the police, would you believe it?"

He took off his coat, scarf and cap and hung them on a single peg, revealing a big diamond-patterned golfing sweater over a boldly checked open-necked shirt. The same eye-clutter as in the family room; same taste.

"Coffee?" he said, going towards the Aga. "You won't mind getting your own breakfast, will you? Look around, take anything you want." He slid the heavy kettle onto the hot plate and went along to a refrigerator which disgorged sliced bread, a tub of yellowish spread and a pot of marmalade. "Toast?" he said, putting two slices in a wire mesh holder which he slid under the second hot plate lid of the cooker. "There's cornflakes, if you'd rather. Or cook an egg."

Toast would be fine, I said, and found myself delegated to making sure it didn't burn while he put through two more phone calls, both fairly incomprehensible to my ears.

"Plates," he said, pointing to a cupboard, and I found

those and mugs also and, in a drawer, knives, forks and spoons. "Hang your jacket in the cloakroom, next door."

He went on talking; positive, decisive. I hung my jacket, made the coffee and more toast. He put the receiver down with another crash and went out into the hall.

"Dee-Dee," he shouted. "Coffee."

He came back and sat down to eat, waving to me to join him, which I did, and presently in the doorway appeared a slight brown-haired woman who wore jeans and a huge gray sweater reaching to her knees.

"Dee-Dee," Tremayne said around a mouthful of toast, "this is John Kendall, my writer." To me he added, "Dee-Dee's my secretary."

I stood up politely and she told me unsmilingly to sit down. My first impression of her as she went across to the Aga to make her own coffee was that she was like a cat, ultra soft-footed, fluid in movement and totally self-contained.

Tremayne watched me watching her and smiled with amusement. "You'll get used to Dee-Dee," he said. "I couldn't manage without her."

She took the compliment without acknowledgment and sat half on a chair as if temporarily, as if about to retreat.

"Phone up a few people to see if they've lost a horse," Tremayne told her. "If anyone's panicking, he's here. Unhurt. We've given him water and feed. He was out all night on the Downs, it seems. Someone's in for a bollocking."

Dee-Dee nodded.

"The jeep's in a ditch on the south road to the A34. Skidded last evening with Mackie. No one hurt. Get the garage to fish it out."

Dee-Dee nodded.

"John, here, will be working in the dining room. Anything he wants, give it to him. Anything he wants to know, tell him."

Dee-Dee nodded.

"Get the blacksmith over for two of the string who lost

57

shoes on the gallop this morning. The lads found the shoes, we don't need new ones."

Dee-Dee nodded.

"If I'm not here when the vet comes, ask him to take a look at Waterbourne after he's cut the colt. She's got some heat in her near-fore fetlock."

Dee-Dee nodded.

"Check that the haulage people will be on time delivering the hay. We're running low. Don't take snow for an answer."

Dee-Dee smiled, which in a triangular way looked feline also, although far from kittenish. I wondered fleetingly about claws.

Tremayne ate his toast and went on giving sporadic instructions which Dee-Dee seemed to have no trouble remembering. When the spate slowed she stood, picked up her mug and said she would finish her coffee in the office while she got on with things.

"Utterly reliable," Tremayne remarked to her departing back. "There's always ten damned trainers trying to poach her." He lowered his voice. "A shit of an amateur jockey treated her like muck. She's not over it yet. I make allowances. If you find her crying, that's it."

I was amazed by his compassion and felt I should have recognized earlier how many unexpected layers there were to Tremayne below the loud executive exterior: not just his love of horses, not just his need to be recorded, not even just his disguised delight in Gareth, but other, secret, unrevealed privacies which maybe I would come to in time, and maybe not.

He spent the next half hour on the telephone both making and receiving calls: it was the time of day, I later discovered, when trainers could most reliably be found at home. Toast eaten, coffee drunk, he reached for a cigarette from a packet on the table and brought a throwaway lighter out of his pocket.

"Do you smoke?" he asked, pushing the pack my way.

"Never started," I said.

"Good for the nerves," he commented, inhaling deeply. "I hope you're not an anti fanatic."

"I quite like the smell."

"Good." He seemed pleased enough. "We'll get on well."

He told me that at ten o'clock, by which time the first lot would have been given hay and water and the lads would have had their own breakfasts, he would drive the tractor back to the gallops to watch his second lot work. He said I needn't bother with that: I could set things up in the dining room, arrange things however I liked working. As all racing was off from frost, he could, if I agreed, spend the afternoon telling me about his childhood. When racing began again, he wouldn't have so much time.

"Good idea," I said.

He nodded. "Come along, then, and I'll show you where things are."

We went out into the carpeted hall and he pointed to the doorway opposite.

"That's the family room, as you know. Next to the kitchen . . ." he walked along and opened a closed door, ". . . is my dining room. We don't use it much. You'll have to turn the heating up, I dare say."

I looked into the room I was to get to know well: a spacious room with mahogany furniture, swagged crimson curtains, formal cream-and-gold-striped walls and a plain dark-green carpet. Not Tremayne's own choice, I thought. Much too coordinated.

"That'll be great," I said obligingly.

"Good." He closed the door again and looked up the stairs we had climbed to bed the night before. "We put those stairs in when we divided the house. This passage beside them, this leads to Perkin and Mackie's half. Come along, I'll show you." He walked along a wide, pale-green-carpeted corridor with pictures of horses on both walls and opened double white-painted doors at the end.

"Through here," he said, "is the main entrance hall of the house. The oldest part."

We passed onto a big wood-blocked expanse of polished floor from which two graceful wings of staircase rose to an upper gallery. Under the gallery, between the staircases, was another pair of doors, which Tremayne, crossing, opened without flourish, revealing a vista of gold and pale-blue furnishings in the same formal style as the dining room.

"This is the main drawing room," he said. "We share it. We hardly use it. We used it last for that damned party . . ." He paused. "Well, as Mackie said, I don't know when we'll have another."

A pity, I thought. It looked a house made for parties. Tremayne closed the drawing-room door and pointed straight across the hall.

"That's the front entrance, and those double doors on the right open into Perkin and Mackie's half. We built a new kitchen for them and another new staircase. We planned it as two separate houses, you see, with this big common section between us."

"It's great," I said to please him, but also meaning it.

He nodded. "It divided quite well. No one needs houses this size these days. Take too much heating." Indeed, it was cold in the hall. "Most of this was built about nineteen six. Edwardian. Country house of the Windberry family, don't suppose you've ever heard of them."

"No," I agreed.

"My father bought the place for peanuts during the Depression. I've lived here all my life."

"Was your father a trainer also?" I asked.

Tremayne laughed. "God, no. He inherited a fortune. Never did a day's work. He liked going racing, so he bought a few jumpers, put them in the stables that hadn't been used since cars replaced the carriages and engaged a trainer for them. When I grew up, I just took over the horses. Built another yard, eventually. I've fifty boxes at present, all full."

He led the way back through the doors to his own domain and closed them behind us.

"That's more or less all," he said, "except for the office."

Once back in his own hall he veered through the last of the doorways there and I followed him into yet another big room in which Dee-Dee looked lost behind a vast desk.

"This used to be the Windberrys' billiards room," Tremayne said. "When I was a child, it was our playroom."

"You had brothers and sisters?"

"One sister," he said briefly, looking at his watch. "I'll leave you to Dee-Dee. See you later."

He went away purposefully, and after the time it would have taken him to replace coat, cap and scarf, the door out to the yard slammed behind him. He was a natural slammer, I thought; there seemed to be no ingredient of ire.

Dee-Dee said, "How can I help you?" without any great enthusiasm.

"Don't you approve of the biography project?" I asked.

She blinked. "I didn't say that."

"You looked it."

She fiddled lengthily with some papers, eyes down.

"He's been on about it for months," she said finally. "It's important to him. I think . . . if you must know . . . that he should have held out for someone better . . ." She hesitated. "Better *known,* anyway. He met you one day and the next day you're here, and I think it's too *fast.* I suggested that we should at least run a check on you but he said Ronnie Curzon's word was good enough. So you're here." She looked up, suddenly fierce. "He deserves the best," she said.

"Ah."

"What do you mean by 'Ah?'"

I didn't answer at once but looked around the jumbo office, seeing the remains of the classical decorative style overlaid by a host of modern bookshelves, filing cabinets, cupboards, copier, fax, computer, telephones, floor safe, television, tapes by the dozen, cardboard boxes, knee-high stack of newspapers and another corkboard with red drawing-pinned memos. There was an antique kneehole desk with an outsize leather chair, clearly Tremayne's own territory, and on the floor a splatter of overlapping Persian rugs in haphazard patterns and colors covering most of an old gray carpet. Pictures of horses passing winning posts inhabited the walls alongside a bright row of racing silks hanging on pegs.

I ended the visual tour where I'd begun, on Dee-Dee's face.

"The more you help," I said, "the more chance he has."

She compressed her mouth obstinately. "That doesn't follow."

"Then the more you obstruct, the less chance he has."

She stared at me, her antagonism still clear, while logic made hardly a dent in emotion.

She was about forty, I supposed. Thin but not emaciated, from what one could see via the sweater. Good skin, bobbed straight hair, unremarkable features, pink lipstick, no jewelry, small, strong-looking hands. General air of reserve, of holding back. Perhaps that was habitual; perhaps the work of the shit of an amateur jockey who had treated her like muck.

"How long have you worked here?" I asked, voice neutral, merely inquiring.

"Eight years, about." Straightforward answer.

"What I chiefly need," I said, "are cuttings books."

She almost smiled. "There aren't any."

With dismay I protested, "There must be. He mentioned cuttings."

"They're not in books, they're in boxes." She turned her head, nodding directions. "In that cupboard over there. Help yourself."

I went across and opened a white-painted door and inside

found stacked on shelves from floor to head height a whole array of uniform white-cardboard boxes, all like shirt boxes but about eight inches deep, all with dates written on their ends in black marker ink.

"I reboxed all the cuttings three or four years ago," Dee-Dee said. "Some of the old boxes were falling to bits. The newspaper is yellow and brittle. You'll see."

"Can I take them all into the dining room?"

"Be my guest."

I loaded up four of the boxes and set off with them, and in a minute found her following me.

"Wait," she said inside the dining room door. "Mahogany gets scratched easily."

She went over to a large sideboard and from a drawer drew out a vast green baize cloth which she draped over the whole expanse of the large oval table.

"You can work on that," she said.

"Thank you."

I put down the boxes and went to fetch another load, ferrying them until the whole lot was transferred. Dee-Dee meanwhile went back to her desk and her work, which largely consisted of the telephone. I could hear her still talking on and off while I arranged the boxes of cuttings chronologically and took the lid off the first, realizing from the date on its end that it had to go back beyond Tremayne; that he hadn't started training when he was a baby. Tattered yellow pieces of newsprint informed me that Mr. Loxley Vickers, of Shellerton House, Berkshire, had bought Triple Subject, a six-year-old gelding, for the record sum for a steeplechaser of twelve hundred guineas. A house, an astonished reporter wrote, could be bought for less.

I looked up, smiling, and found Dee-Dee standing in the doorway, hesitantly hovering.

"I've been talking to Fiona Goodhaven," she said abruptly.

"How is she?"

"All right. Thanks to you, it seems. Why didn't you tell me about your rescue job?"

"It didn't seem important."

"Are you mad?"

"Well, it didn't seem important in the context of whether I could or couldn't do justice to Tremayne's biography."

"God Almighty." She went away but shortly came back. "If you turn that thermostat," she said, pointing, "it will get warmer in here."

She whisked away again before I could thank her, but I understood that peace had been declared, or, at the very least, hostilities temporarily suspended.

Tremayne returned in time. I heard him talking forcefully into an office telephone and presently he strode into the dining room to tell me that someone had finally found they had a horse missing.

"It came over the hill from the next village. They're sending a box to pick it up. How are you doing?"

"Reading about your father."

"A lunatic. Had an obsession about how things would look in his stomach after he'd eaten them. He used to make his butler put an extra serving of everything he was going to eat in a bucket and stir it round. If my father didn't like the look of it, he wouldn't eat his dinner. Drove the cook mad."

I laughed. "What about your mother?"

"She'd fallen off the perch by then. He wasn't so bad when she was alive. He went screwy after."

"How old were you when she . . . er . . . fell off the perch?"

"Ten. Same age as Gareth when *his* mother finally hopped it. You might say I know what it's like to be Gareth. Except *his* mother's still alive and he sees her sometimes. I can't remember mine very clearly, to be honest."

After a moment I said, "How much can I ask you?"

"Ask anything. If I don't want to answer, I'll say so."

"Well . . . you said your father inherited a fortune. Did he . . . er . . . leave it to you?"

Tremayne laughed in his throat. "A fortune seventy or eighty years ago is not a fortune now. But yes, in a way he did. Left me this house. Taught me the principles of land-owning which he'd learnt from *his* father but hardly practiced. My father spent, my grandfather accumulated. I'm more like my grandfather, though I never knew him. I tell Gareth sometimes that we can't afford things even if we can. I don't want him to turn out a spender."

"What about Perkin?"

"Perkin?" For a second Tremayne looked blank. "Perkin has no money sense at all. Lives in a world of his own. It's no use talking to Perkin about money."

"What does he do," I asked, "in his world?"

Tremayne looked as if his elder son's motivations were a mystery, but somewhere also I sensed a sort of exasperated pride.

"He makes furniture," he said. "Designs it. Makes it himself, piece by piece. Chests, tables, screens, anything. Two hundred years from now they will be valuable antiques. That's Perkin's money sense for you." He sighed. "Best thing he ever did was marry a smart girl like Mackie. She sells his pieces, makes sure he makes a profit. He used to sell things sometimes for less than they cost to make. Absolutely hopeless."

"As long as he's happy."

Tremayne made no comment on his son's state of happiness but asked about my tape recorder.

"Didn't it get wet last night? Won't it be ruined?"

"No. I keep everything in waterproof bags. Sort of habit."

"Jungles and deserts?" he asked, remembering.

"Mm."

"Then you go and fetch it, and we'll start. And I'll move the office television in here with the video player so you can watch the races I've won. And if you want any lunch," he added as an afterthought, "I nearly always have beef sandwiches; buy them by the fifty, ready made from the super-market, and put them in the freezer."

We both ate mostly thawed uninteresting beef sandwiches in due course and I thought that even if Tremayne's house-keeping were slightly eccentric, at least he hadn't stirred his food up first in a bucket.

5

At about six-thirty that day I walked down to Shellerton to collect my clothes from the Goodhavens, Fiona and Harry. Darkness had fallen but it seemed to me that the air temperature hadn't, and there was less energy in the wind than in the morning.

I had by that time taped three hours' worth of Tremayne's extraordinary childhood and walked around with him to inspect his horses at evening stables. At every one of the fifty doors he had stopped to check on the inmate's welfare, discussing it briefly with the lad and dispensing carrots to inquiring muzzles with little pats and murmurs of affection.

In between times as we moved along the rows he explained that the horses would now be rugged up against the frost in wool blankets and duvets, then covered with jute rugs (like sacking) securely buckled on. They would be given their main feed of the day and be shut up for the night to remain undisturbed until morning.

"One of us walks round last thing at night," he said, "Bob or Mackie or I, to make sure they're all right. Not kicking their boxes and so on. If they're quiet they're all right, and I don't disturb them."

Like fifty children, I thought, tucked up in bed.

I'd asked him how many lads he had. Twenty-one, he said, plus Bob Watson, who was worth six, and the traveling head lad and a box driver and a groundsman. With Mackie and Dee-Dee, twenty-seven full-time employees. The economics of training racehorses, he remarked, put the book trade's problems in the shade.

When I reminded him that I was going down to Fiona and Harry's to fetch my belongings he offered me his car.

"I quite like walking," I said.

"Good God."

"I'll cook when I get back."

"You don't have to," he protested. "Don't let Gareth talk you into it."

"I said I would, though."

"I don't care much what I eat."

I grinned. "Maybe that will be just as well. I'll be back soon after Gareth, I expect."

I'd discovered that the younger son rode his bicycle each morning to the house of his friend Coconut, from where both of them were driven to and from a town ten miles away, as day boys in a mainly boarding school. The hours were long, as always with that type of school: Gareth was never home much before seven, often later. His notice BACK FOR GRUB seemed to be a fixture. He removed it, Tremayne said, only when he knew in the morning that he would be out until bedtime. Then he would leave another message instead, to say where he was going.

"Organized," I commented.

"Always has been."

I reached the main street of Shellerton and tramped along to the Goodhavens' house, passing three or four cars in their driveway and walking around to the kitchen door to ring the bell.

After an interval the door was opened by Harry, whose expression changed from inhospitable to welcoming by visible degrees.

"Oh, hello, come in. Forgot about you. Fact is, we've had another lousy day in Reading. But home without crashing, best you can say."

I stepped into the house and he closed the door behind us, at the same time putting a restraining hand on my arm.

"Let me tell you first," he said. "Nolan and Lewis are both here. Nolan got convicted of manslaughter. Six months' jail suspended for two years. He won't go behind bars but no one's happy."

"I don't need to stay," I said. "Don't want to intrude."

"Do me a favor, dilute the atmosphere."

"If it's like that . . ."

He nodded, removed his hand and walked me through the kitchen into a warm red hallway and on into a pink and green chintzy sitting room beyond.

Fiona, turning her silver-blond head said, "Who was it?" and saw me following Harry. "Oh, good heavens, I'd forgotten." She came over, holding out a hand, which I shook, an odd formality after our previous meeting.

"These are my cousins," she said. "Nolan and Lewis Everard." She gave me a wide don't-say-anything stare, so I didn't. "A friend of Tremayne's," she said to them briefly. "John Kendall."

Mackie, sitting exhaustedly in an armchair, waggled acknowledging fingers. Everyone else was standing and holding a glass. Harry pressed a pale-gold drink into my hand and left me to discover for myself what lay under the floating ice. Whisky, I found, tasting it.

I had had no mental picture of either Nolan or Lewis, but their appearance all the same was a surprise. They were both short, Nolan handsome and hard, Lewis swollen and soft.

Late thirties, both of them. Dark hair, dark eyes, dark jaws. I supposed I had perhaps expected them to be like Harry in character if not in appearance, but it was immediately clear that they weren't. In place of Harry's amused urbanity, Nolan's aristocratic-sounding speech was essentially violent and consisted of fifty percent obscenity. The gist of his first sentence was that he wasn't in the mood for guests.

Neither Fiona nor Harry showed embarrassment, only weary tolerance. If Nolan had spoken like that in court, I thought, it was no wonder he'd been found guilty. One could quite easily imagine him throttling a nymph.

Harry said calmly, "John is writing Tremayne's biography. He knows about the trial and the Top Spin Lob party. He's a friend of ours, and he stays."

Nolan gave Harry a combative stare which Harry returned with blandness.

"Anyone can know about the trial," Mackie said. "It was in all the papers this morning, after all."

Harry nodded. "To be continued in reel two."

"It's not an expletive joke," Lewis said. "They took photos of us when we were leaving." His peevish voice was like his brother's though a shade higher in pitch and, as I progressively discovered, instead of truly offensive obscene words he had a habit of using euphemisms like "expletive," "bleep" and "deleted." In Harry's mouth it might have been funny; in Lewis's it seemed a form of cowardice.

"Gird up such loins as you have," Harry told him peaceably. "The public won't remember by next week."

Nolan said between four-letter words that everyone that mattered would remember, including the Jockey Club.

"I doubt if they'll actually warn you off," Harry said. "It wasn't as if you hadn't paid your bookmaker."

"Harry!" Fiona said sharply.

"Sorry, m'dear," murmured her husband, though his lids half veiled his eyes like blinds drawn over his true feelings.

Tremayne and I had each read two accounts of the previous day's proceedings while dealing with the sandwiches, one in a racing paper, another in a tabloid. Tremayne's comments had been grunts of disapproval, while I had learned a few facts left out by the Vickers family the evening before.

Fiona's cousin Nolan, for starters, was an amateur jockey ("well-known," in both papers) who often raced on Fiona's horses, trained by Tremayne Vickers. Nolan Everard had once briefly been engaged to Magdalene Mackenzie (Mackie), who had subsequently married Perkin Vickers, Tremayne's son. "Sources" had insisted that the three families, Vickerses, Goodhavens and Everards, were on friendly terms. The prosecution, not disputing this, had suggested that indeed they had all closed ranks to shield Nolan from his just deserts.

A demure photograph of Olympia (provided by her father) showed a fair-haired schoolgirl, immature, an innocent victim. No one seemed to have explained why Nolan had said he would strangle the bitch, and now that I'd heard him talk I was certain those had not been his only words.

"The question really is," Fiona said, "not whether the Jockey Club will warn him off racecourses altogether, because I'm sure they won't, they let real villains go racing, but whether they'll stop him riding as an amateur."

Harry said, as if sympathetically, to Nolan, "It's rather put paid to your ambitions to be made a *member* of the Jockey Club, though, hasn't it, old lad?"

Nolan looked blackly furious and remarked with venom that Harry hadn't helped the case by not swearing to hell and back that Lewis had been comprehensively pissed.

Harry didn't reply except to shrug gently and refill Lewis's glass, which was unquestionably comprehensively empty.

If one made every possible allowance for Nolan, I thought, if one counted the long, character-withering ordeal of waiting to know if he were going to prison, if one threw in the stress of having undoubtedly killed a young woman, even by accident, if one added the humiliations he would forever face because of his conviction, if one granted all that, he was still unattractively, viciously ungrateful.

His family and friends had done their best for him. I thought it highly likely that Lewis had in fact perjured himself, and that Harry had also, very nearly, in the matter of the alcoholic blackout. Harry had at the last minute shrunk from either a positive opinion or from an outright lie, and I'd have put my money on the second. They had all gone again to court to support Nolan when they would much rather have stayed away.

"I still think you ought to appeal," Lewis said.

Nolan's pornographic reply was to the effect that his lawyer had advised him not to push his luck, as Lewis very well knew.

"Bleep the lawyer," Lewis said.

"Appeal courts can *increase* sentences, I believe," Fiona said warningly. "They might cancel the suspension. Doesn't bear thinking about."

"Olympia's father was incandescent afterwards," Mackie said gloomily, nodding. "He wanted Nolan put away for life. Life for a life, that's what he was shouting."

"You can't just appeal against a sentence because you don't happen to like it," Harry pointed out. "There has to be some point of law that was conducted wrongly at the trial."

Lewis said obstinately, "If Nolan doesn't appeal it's as good as admitting he's expletive guilty as charged."

There was a sharp silence all around. They all did think him guilty, though maybe to different degrees. Don't push your luck seemed good pragmatic advice.

I looked speculatively at Mackie, wondering about her sometime engagement to Nolan. She showed nothing for him now but concerned friendship: no lingering love and no hard feelings. Nolan showed nothing but concern for himself.

Fiona said to me, "Stay to dinner?" and Harry said, "Do," but I shook my head.

"I promised to cook for Gareth and Tremayne."

"Good God," Harry said.

Fiona said, "That'll make a change from pizza! They have pizza nine nights out of ten. Gareth just puts one in the microwave, regular as clockwork."

Mackie put down her glass and stood up tiredly. "I think I'll go too. Perkin will be waiting to hear the news."

Nolan, between words beginning with *f*, remarked tartly that if Perkin had bothered to put in an appearance at Reading he would know the news already.

"He wasn't needed," Harry said mildly.

"Olympia died in his half of the house," Lewis said. "You'd have thought he'd have taken an interest."

Nolan remembered with below-the-waist indelicacies that Tremayne hadn't supported him either.

"They were both busy," Mackie said gamely. "They both work, you know."

"Meaning we don't?" Lewis asked waspishly.

Mackie sighed. "Meaning whatever you like." To me she said, "Did you come in Tremayne's car?"

"No, walked."

"Oh! Then . . . do you want a lift home?"

I thanked her and accepted and Harry came with us to see us off.

"Here are your clothes in your bag," he said, handing it to me. "Can't thank you enough, you know."

"Any time."

"God forbid."

Harry and I looked at each other briefly in the sort of appreciation that's the beginning of friendship, and I wondered whether he, of all of them, would have been least sorry to see Nolan in the cells.

"He's not always like that," Mackie said as she steered

out of the drive. "Nolan, I mean. He can be enormously good fun. Or rather, he used to be, before all this."

"I read in today's paper that you were once engaged to him."

She half laughed. "Yes, I was. For about three months, five years ago."

"What happened?"

"We met in February at a Hunt Ball. I knew who he was. Fiona's cousin, the amateur jockey. I'd been brought up in eventing. Had ponies before I could walk. I told him I sometimes went to stay with Fiona. Small world, he said. We spent the whole evening together and . . . well . . . the whole night. It was sudden, like lightning. Don't tell Perkin. Why does one tell total strangers things one never tells anyone else? Sorry, forget it."

"Mm," I said. "What happened when you woke up?"

"It was like a roller-coaster. We spent all our time together. After two weeks he asked me to marry him and I said yes. Blissful. My feet never touched the ground. I went to the races to watch him . . . he was spellbinding. Kept winning, saying I'd brought him luck." She stopped, but she was smiling.

"Then what?"

"Then the jumping season finished. We began planning the wedding . . . I don't know. Maybe we just got to know each other. I can't say which day I realized it was a mistake. He was getting irritable. Flashes of rage, really. I just said one day, 'It won't work, will it?' and he said, 'No' so we fell into each other's arms and had a few tears and I gave him his ring back."

"You were lucky," I commented.

"Yes. How do you mean?"

"To come out of it without a fighting marriage and a spiteful divorce."

"You're so right." She turned into Tremayne's drive and came to a halt. "We've been friends ever since, but Perkin has always been uncomfortable with him. See, Nolan is brilliant and brave on horses and Perkin doesn't ride all that well. We don't talk about horses much, when we're alone. It's restful, actually. I tell Perkin he ought to be grateful to Nolan that I was free for *him,* but I suppose he can't help how he feels."

She sighed, unbuckled her seat belt and stood up out of the car.

"Look," she said, "I like you, but Perkin does tend to be jealous."

"I'll ignore you," I promised.

She smiled vividly. "A touch of old-fashioned formality should do the trick." She began to turn away, and then stopped. "I'm going in through our own entrance, Perkin's and mine. I'll see how he's doing. See if he's stopped work. We'll probably be along for a drink. We often do, at this time of day."

"OK."

She nodded and walked off, and I went around and into Tremayne's side of the house as if I'd lived there forever. Yesterday morning, I thought incredulously, I awoke to Aunty's freeze.

Tremayne had lit the log fire in the family room and poured his gin and tonic and, standing within heating range of the flames, he listened with disillusion to the outcome of Nolan's trial.

"Guilty but unpunished," he observed. "Newfangled escape clause."

"Should the guilty always be punished?"

He looked at me broodingly. "Is that a character-assessment question?"

"I guess so."

"It's unanswerable, anyway. The answer is, I don't know." He turned and with a foot pushed a log further into the fire. "Help yourself to a drink."

"Thanks. Mackie said they might be along."

Tremayne nodded, taking it for granted, and in fact she and Perkin came through from the central hall while I was dithering between the available choices of whisky or gin, neither of which I much liked. Perkin solved the liquid question for himself by detouring into the kitchen and reappearing with a glass of Coke.

"What do you actually *like*?" Mackie asked, seeing my hesitation as she poured tonic into gin for herself.

"Wine, I suppose. Red for preference."

"There will be some in the office. Tremayne keeps it for owners when they come to see their horses. I'll get it."

She went without haste and returned with a Bordeaux-shaped bottle and a sensible corkscrew, both of which she handed over.

Tremayne said, as I liberated the Château Kirwan, "Is that stuff any good?"

"Very," I said, smelling the healthy cork.

"It's all grape juice as far as I'm concerned. If you like the stuff, put it on the shopping list."

"The shopping list," Mackie explained, "is a running affair pinned to the kitchen corkboard. Whoever does the shopping takes the list with him. Or her."

Perkin, slouching in an armchair, said I might as well get used to the idea of doing the shopping myself, particularly if I like eating.

"Tremayne takes Gareth to the supermarket sometimes," he said, "and that's about it. Or Dee-Dee goes, if there's no milk for the coffee three days running." He looked from me to Mackie. "I used to think it quite normal until I married a sensible housekeeper."

Perkin, I thought, as he reaped a smile from his wife, was a great deal more relaxed than on the evening before, though the faint hostility he'd shown towards me was still there. Tremayne asked him his opinion of the verdict on Nolan, and Perkin consulted his glass lengthily as if seeking illumination.

"I suppose," he said finally, "that I'm glad he isn't in jail."

It was a pretty ambiguous statement after so much thought, but Mackie looked pleasantly relieved. Only she of the three, it was clear, cared much for Nolan the man. To father and son, having Nolan in jail would have been an inconvenience and an embarrassment which they were happy to avoid.

Looking at the two of them, the differences were as powerful as the likenesses. If one discounted Tremayne's hair, which was gray where Perkin's was brown, and the thickness in Tremayne's neck and body that had come with age, then physically they were of one cloth; but where Tremayne radiated strength, Perkin was soggy, where Tremayne was a leader, Perkin retreated. Tremayne's love was for living horses, Perkin's was for passive wood.

It came as a shock to me to wonder if Tremayne wanted his own achievements written in an inheritable book because Perkin's work would be valuable in two hundred years. Wondered if the strong father felt he had to equal his weaker son. I dismissed the idea as altogether too subtle and as anyway tactless in an employed biographer.

Gareth came home with his usual air of a life lived on the run and eyed me with disapproval as I sat in an armchair drinking wine.

"I thought you said—" he began, and stopped, shrugging, an onset of good manners vying with disappointment.

"I will," I said.

"Oh, really? Now?"

I nodded.

"Good. Come on, then, I'll show you the freezers."

"Let him alone," Mackie said mildly. "Let him finish his drink."

Perkin reacted to this harmless remark with irritation. "As he said he'd cook, let him do it."

"Of course," I said cheerfully, getting up. I glanced at Tremayne. "All right with you?"

"You're all right with me until further notice," he said, and Perkin didn't like that testimony of approval either, but Gareth did.

"You're home and dried with Dad," he told me happily, steering me through the kitchen. "What did you do to him?"

"Nothing."

"What did you do to me?" he asked himself comically, and answered himself. "Nothing. I guess that's it. You don't have to do anything, it's just the way you are. The freezers are through here, in the utility room. If you go straight on through the utility room you get to the garage. Through that door there." He pointed ahead to a heavy-looking door furnished with businesslike bolts. "I keep my bike through there."

There were two freezers, both upright, both with incredible contents.

"This one," Gareth said, opening the door, "is what Dad calls the peezer freezer."

"Or the pizza frizza?" I suggested.

"Yes, that too."

It was stacked with pizzas and nothing else, though only half full.

"We eat our way down to the bottom," Gareth said reasonably, "then fill up again every two or three months."

"Sensible," I commented.

"Most people think we're mad."

He shut that freezer and opened the other, which proved to contain four packs of beef sandwiches, fifty to a pack. There were also about ten sliced loaves (for toast, Gareth explained), one large turkey (someone gave it to Tremayne for Christmas), pints galore of chocolate ripple ice cream (Gareth liked it) and a whole lot of bags of ice cubes for gins and tonic.

Was it for this, I surmised wildly, that I'd sold my soul?

"Well," I said in amusement, "what do we have in the larder?"

"What larder?"

"Cupboards, then."

"You'd better look," Gareth said, closing the second freezer's door. "What are you going to make?"

I hadn't the faintest idea, but what Tremayne, Gareth and I ate not very much later was a hot pie made of beef extracted from twenty defrosted sandwiches and chopped small, then mixed with undiluted condensed mushroom soup (a find) and topped with an inch-thick layer of sandwich breadcrumbs fried crisp.

Gareth watched the simple cooking with fascination, and I found myself telling him about the techniques I'd been taught of how to live off the countryside without benefit of shops.

"Fried worms aren't bad," I said.

"You're kidding me."

"They're packed with protein. Birds thrive on them. And what's so different from eating snails?"

"Could you really live off the land? You yourself?"

"Yes, sure," I said. "But you can die of malnutrition eating just rabbits."

"How do you *know* these things?"

"It's my business, really. My trade." I told him about the six travel guides. "The company used to send me to all those places to set up holiday expeditions for real rugged types. I had to learn how to get them out of all sorts of local trouble, especially if they struck disasters like losing all their equipment in raging torrents. I wrote the books and the customers weren't allowed to set off without them. Mind you, I always thought the book on how to survive would have been lost in the raging torrent with everything else, but maybe they would remember some of it, you never know."

Gareth, helping make breadcrumbs in a blender, said a shade wistfully, "How did you ever start on something like that?"

"My father was a camping nut. A naturalist. He worked

in a bank, really, and still does, but every spare second he would head for the wilds, dragging me and my mother along. Actually I took it for granted, as just a fact of life. Then after college I found it was all pretty useful in the travel trade. So bingo."

"Does he still go camping? Your father, I mean?"

"No. My mother got arthritis and refused to go anymore, and he didn't have much fun without her. He's worked in a bank in the Cayman Islands for three or four years now. It's good for my mother's health."

Gareth asked simply, "Where are the Cayman Islands?"

"In the Caribbean, south of Cuba, west of Jamaica."

"What do you want me to do with these breadcrumbs?"

"Put them in the frying pan."

"Have *you* ever been to the Cayman Islands?"

"Yes," I said, "I went for Christmas. They sent me the fare as a present."

"You are *lucky*," Gareth said.

I paused from cutting up the beef. "Yes." I agreed, thinking about it. "Yes, I am. And grateful. And you've got a good father, too."

He seemed extraordinarily pleased that I should say so, but it seemed to me, unconventional housekeeping or not, that Tremayne was making a good job of his younger son.

Notwithstanding Tremayne's professed lack of interest in food, he clearly enjoyed the pie, which three healthy appetites polished off to the last fried crumb. I got promoted instantly to resident chef, which suited me fine. Tomorrow I could do the shopping, Tremayne said, and without ado pulled out his wallet and gave me enough to feed the three of us for a month, though he said it was for a week. I protested it was too much and he kindly told me I had no idea how much things cost. I thought wryly that I knew how much things cost to the last anxious penny, but there was no point in arguing. I stowed the money away and asked them what they didn't like.

"Broccoli," Gareth said instantly. "Yuk."

"Lettuce," said Tremayne.

Gareth told his father about fried worms and asked me if I had any of the travel guides with me.

"No, sorry, didn't think of bringing them."

"Couldn't we possibly get some? I mean, I'd buy them with my pocket money. I'd like to keep them. Are they in the shops?"

"Sometimes, but I could ask the travel company to send a set," I suggested.

"Yes, do that," Tremayne said, "and I'll pay for them. We'd all like to look at them, I expect."

"But Dad . . ." Gareth protested.

"All right," Tremayne said, "get two sets."

I began to appreciate Tremayne's simple way of solving problems and in the morning, after I'd driven him on the tractor up to the Downs to see the horses exercise and after orange juice, coffee and toast, I phoned my friend in the travel agency and asked him to organize the books.

"Today?" he said, and I said, "Yes, please," and he said he would Red Star–parcel them by train, if I liked. I consulted Tremayne, who thought it a good idea and told me to get them sent to Didcot station where I could go to pick them up when I went in to do the shopping.

"Fair enough," the friend said. "You'll get them this afternoon."

"My love to your aunt," I said, "and thanks."

"She'll swoon." He laughed. "See you."

Tremayne began reading the day's papers, both of which carried the results of the trial. Neither paper took any particular stance either for or against Nolan, though both quoted Olympia's father at length. He came over as a sad obsessed man whose natural grief had turned to self-destructive anger and one could feel sorry for him on many counts. Tremayne read and grunted and passed no opinion.

The day slowly drifted into a repetition of the one before.

Dee-Dee came into the kitchen for coffee and instructions and when Tremayne had gone out again with his second lot of horses I returned to the boxes of clippings in the dining room.

I decided to reverse yesterday's order and start at the most recent clippings, and work backwards.

It was Dee-Dee, I had discovered, who cut the sections out of the newspapers and magazines, and certainly she had been more zealous than whoever had done it before her, as the boxes for the last eight years were much fuller.

I laid aside the current box as it was still almost empty and worked through from January to December of the previous year, which had been a good one for Tremayne, embracing not only his Grand National with Top Spin Lob but many other successes important enough to get the racing hacks excited. Tremayne's face smiled steadily from clipping after clipping including, inappropriately, those dealing with the death of the girl, Olympia.

Drawn irresistibly, I read a whole batch of accounts of that death from a good many different papers, the number of them suggesting that someone had gone out and bought an armful of everything available. In total, they told me not much more than I already knew, except that Olympia was twice described as a "jockette," a word I somehow found repulsive. It appeared that she had ridden in several ladies' races at point-to-point meetings, which one paper, to help the ignorant, described as "the days the hunting classes stop chasing the fox and chase each other instead." Olympia the jockette had been twenty-three, had come from a "secure suburban background" and had worked as an instructor in a riding school in Surrey. Her parents, not surprisingly, were said to be "distraught."

Dee-Dee came into the dining room, offering more coffee, and saw what I was reading.

"That Olympia was a sexpot bimbo," she remarked flatly.

"I was there at the party and you could practically smell it. Secure little suburban riding instructor, my foot."

"Really?"

"Her father made her out to be a sweet innocent little saint. Perhaps he even believes it. Nolan never said any different because it wouldn't have helped him, so no one told the truth."

"What was the truth?"

"She had no underclothes on," Dee-Dee said calmly. "She wore only a long scarlet strapless dress slit halfway up her thigh. You ask Mackie. She knows, she tried to revive her."

"Er . . . quite a lot of women don't wear underclothes," I said.

"Is that a fact?" She gave me an ironic look.

"My blushing days are over."

"Well, do you or don't you want any coffee?"

"Yes, please."

She went out to the kitchen and I continued reading clippings, progressing from "no action on the death at Shellerton House" to "Olympia's father brings private prosecution" and "Magistrates refer Nolan Everard case to Crown Court." A *sub judice* silence then descended and the clippings stopped.

It was after a bunch of end-of-jumping-season statistics that I came across an oddity from a Reading paper published on a Friday in June.

"Girl groom missing," read the headline, and there was an accompanying photo of Tremayne, still looking cheerful.

Angela Brickell, 17, employed as a 'lad' by prominent racehorse trainer Tremayne Vickers, failed to turn up for work on Tuesday afternoon and hasn't been seen in the stables since. Vickers says lads leave without notice all too often, but he is puzzled that she didn't ask for pay due to her. Anyone knowing Angela Brickell's whereabouts is asked to get in touch with the police.

Angela Brickell's parents, like Olympia's, were reported to be "distraught."

6

By the following week Angela Brickell's disappearance had been taken up by the national dailies, who all mentioned the death of Olympia at Shellerton two months earlier but drew no significant conclusions.

Angela, I learned, lived in a stable hostel with five other girls, who described her as "moody." An indistinct photograph of her showed the face of a child, not a young woman, and pleas to "Find This Girl" could realistically never have been successful if they depended on recognizing her from her likeness in newsprint.

There was no account in fact of her having been found, and after a week or so the clippings about her stopped.

There were no cuttings at all for July, when it seemed the jump-racing fraternity took a holiday, but they began again with various accounts of the opening of the new season in Devon in August: "Vickers Victories Continue!"

Nolan had ridden a winner on one of Fiona's horses: "the well-known amateur now out on bail facing charges of assault resulting in death . . ."

In early September Nolan had hit the news again, this time in giving evidence at a Jockey Club inquiry in defense of Tremayne, who stood accused of doping one of his horses.

With popping eyes, since Tremayne to me even on such short acquaintance seemed the last person to put his whole way of life in jeopardy for so trivial a reason, I read that one of his horses had tested positive to traces of the stimulants theobromine and caffeine, prohibited substances.

The horse in question had won an amateurs' race back in May. Belonging to Fiona, it had been ridden by Nolan, who said he had no idea how the drugs had been administered. He had himself been in charge of the horse that day, since Tremayne hadn't attended the meeting. Tremayne had sent the animal in the care of his head traveling lad and a groom, and neither the head lad nor Tremayne knew how the drugs had been administered. Mrs. Fiona Goodhaven could offer no explanation either, though she and her husband had attended and watched the race.

The Jockey Club's verdict at the end of the day had been that there was no way of determining who had given the drugs or how, since they couldn't any longer question the groom who had been in charge of the horse as she, Angela Brickell, could not be found.

Angela Brickell. Good grief, I thought.

Tremayne had nevertheless been adjudged guilty as charged and had been fined fifteen hundred pounds. A slapped wrist, it seemed.

Upon leaving the inquiry Tremayne had shrugged and said, "These things happen."

The drug theobromine, along with caffeine, commented the reporter, could commonly be found in chocolate. Well, well, I thought. Never a dull moment in the racing industry.

The rest of the year seemed an anticlimax after that, though there had been a whole procession of notable wins. "The Stable in Form" and "More Vim to Vickers" and "Loadsa Vicktories," according to which paper or magazine one read.

I finished the year and was simply sitting and thinking when Tremayne breezed in with downland air still cool on his coat.

"How are you doing?" he said.

I pointed to the pile of clippings out of their box. "I was reading about last year. All those winners."

He beamed. "Couldn't put a foot wrong. Amazing. Sometimes things just go right. Other years, you get the virus, horses break down, owners die, you have a ghastly time. All the luck of the game."

"Did Angela Brickell ever turn up?" I asked.

"Who? Oh, her. No, silly little bitch, God knows where she made off to. Every last person in the racing world knows you mustn't give chocolate to horses in training. Pity really, most of them love it. Everybody also knows a Mars bar here or there isn't going to make a horse win a race, but there you are, by the rules chocolate's a stimulant, so bad luck."

"Would the girl have got into trouble if she'd stayed?"

He laughed. "From me, yes. I'd have sacked her, but she'd gone before I heard the horse had tested positive. It was a routine test; they test most winners." He paused and sat down on a chair across the table from me, staring thoughtfully at a heap of clippings. "It could have been anyone, you know. Anyone here in the yard. Or Nolan himself, though God knows why he should. Anyway"—he shrugged—"it often happens because the testing techniques are now so highly developed. They don't automatically warn off trainers anymore, thank God, when odd things turn up in the analysis. It has to be gross, has to be beyond interpretation as an accident. But it's still a risk every trainer runs. Risk of crooks. Risk of plain malice. You take what precautions you can and pray."

"I'll put that in the book, if you like."

He looked at me assessingly. "I got me a good writer after all, didn't I?"

I shook my head. "You got one who'll do his best."

He smiled with what looked like satisfaction and after lunch (beef sandwiches) we got down to work again on taping his early life with his eccentric father. Tremayne seemed to have soared unharmed over such psychological trifles as being rented out in Leicestershire as a harness and tack cleaner to a fox-hunting family and a year later as stableboy to a polo player in Argentina.

"But that was child abuse," I protested.

Tremayne chuckled unconcernedly. "I didn't get buggered, if that's what you mean. My father hired me out, picked up all I earned and gave me a crack or two with his cane when I said it wasn't fair. Well, it wasn't fair. He told me that that was a valuable lesson, to learn that things weren't fair. Never expect fairness. I'm telling you what he told me, but you're lucky, I won't beat it into you."

"Will you pay me?"

He laughed deeply. "You've got Ronnie Curzon looking after that." His amusement continued. "Did your father ever beat you?"

"No, he didn't believe in it."

"Nor do I, by God. I've never beaten Perkin, nor Gareth. Couldn't. I remember what it felt like. But then, see, he did take me with him to Argentina and all round the world. I saw a lot of things most English boys don't. I missed a lot of school. He was mad, no doubt, but he gave me a priceless education, and I wouldn't change anything."

"You had a pretty tough mind," I said.

"Sure." He nodded. "You need it in this life."

You might need it, I reflected, but tough minds weren't regulation issue. Many children would have disintegrated where Tremayne learned and thrived. I tended to feel at home with stoicism and, increasingly, with Tremayne.

About midafternoon, when we stopped taping, he lent me his Volvo to go to Didcot to fetch the parcel of books from the station and to do the household shopping, advising me not to slide into any ditches if I could help it. The roads however were marginally better and the air not so brutally cold, though the forecasters still spoke of more days' frost. I shopped with luxurious abandon for food and picked up the books, getting back to Shellerton while Tremayne was still out in his yard at evening stables.

He came into the house with Mackie, both of them stamping their feet and blowing onto their fingers as they discussed the state of the horses.

"You'd better ride Selkirk in the morning," Tremayne said to her. "He's a bit too fresh these days for his lad."

"Right."

"And I forgot to tell Bob to get the lads to put two rugs on their mounts if they're doing only trotting exercise."

"I'll remind him."

"Good."

He saw me in the kitchen as I was finishing stowing the stores and asked if the books had arrived. They had, I said.

"Great. Bring them into the family room. Come on, Mackie, gin and tonic."

The big logs in the family-room fireplace never entirely went cold: Tremayne kicked the embers smartly together, adding a few small sticks and a fresh chunk of beech to renew the blaze. The evening developed as twice before, Perkin arriving as if on cue and collecting his Coke.

With flattering eagerness Tremayne opened the package of books and handed some of them to Mackie and Perkin. So familiar to me, they seemed to surprise the others, though I wasn't sure why.

Slightly larger than paperbacks, they were more the size of videotapes and had white shiny hard covers with the title in various bright black-edged colors: *Return Safe from the Jungle* in green, *Return Safe from the Desert* in orange, *Return Safe from the Sea* in blue, *Return Safe from the Ice* in purple, *Return Safe from Safari* in red, *Return Safe from the Wilderness* in a hot rusty brown.

"I'll be damned," Tremayne said. "Real books."

"What did you expect?" I asked.

"Well . . . pamphlets, I suppose. Thin paperbacks, perhaps."

"The travel agency wanted them glossy," I explained, "and also useful."

"They must have taken a lot of work," Mackie observed, turning the pages of *Ice* and looking at illustrations.

"There's a good deal of repetition in them, to be honest," I said. "I mean, quite a lot of survival techniques are the same wherever you find yourself."

"Such as what?" Perkin asked, faintly belligerent as usual.

"Lighting fires, finding water, making a shelter. Things like that."

"The books are fascinating," Mackie said, looking at *Sea,* "but how often do people get marooned on desert islands these days?"

I smiled. "Not often. It's just the *idea* of survival that people like. There are schools where people on holiday go for survival courses. Actually the most lethal place to be is up a British mountainside in the wrong clothes in a cold mist. A fair number of people each year don't survive *that.*"

"Could you?" Perkin asked.

"Yes, but I wouldn't be up there in the wrong clothes in the first place."

"Survival begins before you set out," Tremayne said, reading the first page of *Jungle:* he looked up, amused, quoting, " 'Survival is a frame of mind.' "

"Yes."

"I have it," he said.

"Indeed you do."

All three of them went on reading the books with obvious interest, dipping into the various sections at random, flicking over pages and stopping to read more: vindicating, I thought, the travel agency's contention that the back-to-nature essentials of staying alive held irresistible attractions for ultra-cosseted sophisticates, just as long as they never had to put them into practice in bitter earnest.

Gareth erupted into the peaceful scene like a rehearsing poltergeist.

"What are you all so busy with?" he demanded, and then spotted the books. "Boy, oh *boy*. They've come!"

He grabbed up *Return from the Wilderness* and plunged in, and I sat drinking wine and wondering if I would ever see four people reading *Long Way Home*.

"This is pretty earthy stuff," Mackie said after a while, laying her book down. "Skinning and degutting animals . . . ugh."

"You'd do it if you were starving," Tremayne told her.

"I'd do it *for* you," Gareth said.

"So would I," said Perkin.

"Then I'll arrange not to get stranded anywhere without you both." She was teasing, affectionate. "And I'll stay in camp and grind the corn." She put a hand to her mouth in mock dismay. "Dear heaven, may feminists forgive me."

"It's pretty boring about all these jabs," Gareth complained, not being interested in gender typing.

" 'Better the jabs than the diseases,' it says here," Tremayne said.

"Oh well, then."

"And you've had tetanus jabs already."

"I guess so," Gareth agreed. He looked at me. "Have you had all these jabs?"

"Afraid so."

"Tetanus?"

"Especially."

"There's an awful lot about first aid," he said, turning

pages. "How to stop wounds bleeding . . . pressure points. A whole map of arteries. How to deal with poisons . . . swallow *charcoal*!" He looked up. "Do you mean it?"

"Sure," I said. "Scrape it into water and drink it. The carbon helps take some sorts of poison harmlessly through the gut, if you're lucky."

"Good God," Tremayne said.

His younger son went on reading. "It says here you can drink urine if you distill it."

"Gareth!" Mackie said, disgusted.

"Well, that's what it says. 'Urine is sterile and cannot cause diseases. Boil it and condense the steam, which will then be pure distilled water, perfectly safe to drink.' "

"John, really!" Mackie protested.

"It's true," I said, smiling. "Lack of water is a terrible killer. If you've a fire but no water, you now know what to do."

"I couldn't."

"Survival is a frame of mind," Tremayne repeated. "You never know what you could do until you had to."

Perkin asked me, "Have you ever drunk it?"

"Distilled water?"

"You know what I mean."

I nodded. "Yes, I have. To test it for the books. And I've distilled all sorts of other things too. Filthy jungle water. Wet mud. Seawater, particularly. If the starter liquid is watery and not fermenting, the steam is pure H_2O. And when seawater boils dry you have salt left, which is useful."

"What if the starter liquid *is* fermenting?" Gareth asked.

"The steam is alcohol."

"Oh, yes, I'm supposed to have learned that in school."

"Gin and tonic in the wilderness?" Tremayne suggested.

I said with enjoyment, "I could certainly get you *drunk* in the wilderness, but actual gin would depend on juniper bushes, and tonic on chinchona trees for quinine, and I don't think they'd both grow in the same place, but you never know." I paused. "Ice cubes might be a problem in the rain forest."

Tremayne laughed deep in his chest. "Did you ever rely on all this stuff to save your life?"

"Not entirely," I said. "I lived by these techniques for weeks at a time, but someone always knew roughly where I was. I had escape routes. I was basically testing what was practicable and possible and sensible in each area where the agency wanted to set up adventure holidays. I've never had to survive after a plane crash in the mountains, for instance."

There had been a plane crash in the Andes in 1972 when people had eaten other people in order to stay alive. I didn't think I would tell Mackie, though.

"But," she said, "did things ever go wrong?"

"Sometimes."

"Like what? Do say."

"Well . . . like insect bites and eating things that disagreed with me."

They all looked as if these were everyday affairs, but I'd been too ill a couple of times to care to remember.

I said with equal truth but more drama, "A bear smashed up my camp in Canada once and hung around it for days. I couldn't reach anything I needed. It was a shade fraught there for a bit."

"Do you mean it?" Gareth was openmouthed.

"Nothing happened," I said. "The bear went away."

"Weren't you afraid he would come back?"

"I packed up and moved somewhere else."

"Wow," Gareth said.

"Bears eat people," his brother told him repressively. "Don't get any ideas about copying John."

Tremayne looked at his sons mildly. "Have either of you ever heard of vicarious enjoyment?"

"No," Gareth said. "What is it?"

"Dreaming," Mackie suggested.

Perkin said, "Someone else does the suffering for you."

"Let Gareth dream," Tremayne said, nodding. "It's natural. I don't suppose for one moment he'll go chasing bears."

"Boys do stupid things, Gareth included."

"Hey," his brother protested. "Who's talking? Who climbed onto the roof and couldn't get down?"

"Shut your face," Perkin said.

"Do give it a rest, you two," Mackie said wearily. "Why do you always quarrel?"

"We're nothing compared with Lewis and Nolan," Perkin said. "They can get really vicious."

Mackie said reflectively, "They haven't quarreled since Olympia died."

"Not in front of us," her husband agreed, "but you don't know what they've said in private."

Diffidently, because it wasn't really my business, I asked, "Why do they quarrel?"

"Why does anyone?" Tremayne said. "But those two envy each other. You met them last night, didn't you? Nolan has the looks and the dash, Lewis is a drunk with brains. Nolan has courage and is thick, Lewis is a physical disaster but when he's sober he's a whiz at making money. Nolan is a crack shot, Lewis misses every pheasant he aims at. Lewis would like to be the glamorous amateur jockey and Nolan would like to be upwardly disgustingly rich. Neither will ever manage it, but that doesn't stop the envy."

"You're too hard on them," Mackie murmured.

"But you know I'm right."

She didn't deny it, but said, "Perhaps the Olympia business has drawn them together."

"You're a sweet young woman," Tremayne told her. "You see good in everyone."

Perkin said, "Hands off my wife" in what might or might not have been a joke. Tremayne chose to take it lightly, and I thought he must be well used to his son's acute possessiveness.

He turned from Perkin to me and with a swift change of subject said, "How well do you ride?"

"Er . . ." I said. "I haven't ridden a racehorse."

"What then?"

"Hacks, dude-ranch horses, pony trekking, Arab horses in the desert."

"Hm." He pondered. "Care to ride my hack with the string in the morning? Let's see what you can do."

"OK." I must have sounded halfhearted, because he pounced on it.

"Don't you want to?" he demanded.

"Yes, please."

"Right, then," he nodded. "Mackie, tell Bob to have Touchy saddled up for John, if you're out in the yard before me."

"Right."

"Touchy won the Cheltenham Gold Cup," Gareth told me.

"Oh, did he?" Some hack.

"Don't worry," Mackie said, smiling, "he's fifteen now and almost a gentleman."

"Dumps people regularly on Fridays," Gareth said.

With apprehension I went out into the yard on the following morning, Friday, in jodhpurs, boots, ski jacket and gloves. I hadn't sat on a horse of any sort for almost two years and, whatever Mackie might say, my idea of a nice quiet return to the saddle wasn't a star steeplechaser, pensioned or not.

Touchy was big, with bulging muscles; he would have to be, I supposed, to carry Tremayne's weight. Bob Watson gave me a grin, a helmet and a leg-up, and it seemed a fair way down to the ground.

Oh, well, I thought. Enjoy it. I'd said I could ride: time to try and prove it. Tremayne, watching me appraisingly with his head on one side, told me to take my place behind Mackie, who would be leading the string. He himself would be driving the tractor. I could take Touchy up the all-weather gallop at a fast canter when everyone else had worked.

"All right," I said.

He smiled faintly and walked away and I collected the reins and a few thoughts and tried not to make a fool of myself.

Bob Watson appeared again at my elbow.

"Get him anchored when you set off up the gallop," he said, "or he'll pull your arms out."

"Thanks," I said, but he had already moved on.

"All out," he was saying, and out they all came from the boxes, circling in the lights, breathing plumes, moving in circles as Bob threw the lads up, all as before, only now I was part of it, now on the canvas in the picture, as if alive in a Munnings painting, extraordinary.

I followed Mackie out of the yard and across the road and onto the downland track, and found that Touchy knew what to do from long experience but would respond better to pressure with the calf rather than to strong pulls on his tough old mouth.

Mackie looked back a few times as if to make sure I hadn't evaporated and watched while I circled with the others as it grew light and we waited for Tremayne to reach the top of the hill.

Drifting alongside, she asked, "Where did you learn to ride?"

"Mexico," I said.

"You were taught by a Spaniard!"

"Yes, I was."

"And he had you riding with your arms folded?"

"Yes, how do you know?"

"I thought so. Well, tuck your elbows in on old Touchy."

"Thanks."

She smiled and went off to oversee the dividing of the string into twos or threes for the gallops.

Snow still lay thinly over everything and it was another clear morning, stingingly, beautifully cold. January dawn on the Downs; once felt, never forgotten.

Section by section the string set off up the wood-chippings track until only Mackie and I were left.

"I'll ride on the right of you," she said, coming up behind me. "Then Tremayne can see how you ride."

"Thanks very much," I said ironically.

"You'll do all right."

She swayed suddenly in the saddle and I put out a hand to steady her.

"Are you OK?" I asked anxiously. "You should have rested more after that bang on the head." She was pale. Huge-eyed. Alarming.

"No . . . I . . ." She took an unsteady breath. "I just felt . . . oh . . . oh . . ."

She swayed again and looked near to fainting. I leaned across and put my right arm around her waist, holding her tight to prevent her falling. Her weight sagged against me limply until I was supporting her entirely, and since she had an arm through her reins her horse was held close to mine, their heads almost touching.

I took hold of her reins in my left hand and simply held her tight with my right, and her horse moved his rump sideways away from me until she slid off out of her saddle altogether and finished half lying across my knee and Touchy's withers, held only by my grasp.

I couldn't let her fall and I couldn't dismount without dropping her, so with both hands I pulled and heaved her up onto Touchy until she was half sitting and half lying across the front of my saddle, held in my arms. Touchy didn't much like it and Mackie's horse had backed away sharply to the length of his reins and was on the edge of bolting, and I began to wonder if I should just let him go free in spite of the icy dangers everywhere lurking. I might then manage to walk Touchy back to the stable with his double cargo and we might yet not have a worse disaster than Mackie's unconsciousness. The urgency of getting help for her made more things possible than I could have thought.

Touchy got an unmistakable signal from my leg and obediently turned towards home. I decided I would hold on to Mackie's horse as long as it would come too, and as if by magic he got the going-home message and decided not to object any further.

We had gone perhaps three paces in this fashion when Mackie woke up and came to full consciousness as if a light had been switched on.

"What happened . . . ?"

"You fainted. Fell this way."

"I can't have done." But she could see that she must have. "Let me down," she said. "I feel awfully sick."

"Can you stand?" I asked worriedly. "Let me take you home like this."

"No." She rolled against me onto her stomach and slid down slowly until her feet were on the ground. "What a stupid thing to do," she said. "I'm all right now, I am really. Give me my reins."

"Mackie . . ."

She turned away from me suddenly and vomited convulsively onto the snow.

I hopped down off Touchy with the reins of both horses held fast and tried to help her.

"God," she said weakly, searching for a tissue, "must have eaten something."

"Not my cooking."

"No." She found the tissue and smiled a fraction. She and Perkin hadn't stayed for the previous evening's grilled chicken. "I haven't felt well for days."

"Concussion," I said.

"No, even before that. Tension over the trial, I suppose." She took a few deep breaths and blew her nose. "I feel perfectly all right now. I don't understand it."

She was looking at me in puzzlement, and I quite clearly saw the thought float into her head and transfigure her face into wonderment and hope . . . and joy.

"Oh!" she said ecstatically. "Do you think . . . I mean, I've been feeling sick every morning this week . . . and after two years of trying I'd stopped expecting anything to happen, and anyway, I didn't know it could make you feel so ill right at the beginning . . . I mean, I didn't even *suspect* . . . I'm always wildly irregular." She stopped and laughed. "Don't tell Tremayne. Don't tell Perkin. I'll wait a bit first, to make sure. But I *am* sure. It explains all sorts of odd things that have happened this last week. Like my nipples itching. My hormones must be rioting. I can't believe it. I think I'll burst."

I thought that I had never before seen such pure uncomplicated happiness in anyone, and was tremendously glad for her.

"What a revelation!" she said. "Like an angel announcing it . . . if that's not blasphemous."

"Don't hope too much," I said cautiously.

"Don't be silly. I *know*." She seemed to wake suddenly to our whereabouts. "Tremayne will be going mad because we haven't appeared."

"I'll ride up and tell him you're not well and have gone home."

"No, definitely not. I *am* well. I've never felt better in my whole life. I am gloriously and immensely well. Give me a leg-up."

I told her she needed to rest but she obstinately refused, and in the end I bowed to her judgment and lifted her lightly into the saddle, scrambling up myself onto Touchy's broad back. She shook up her reins as if nothing had happened and set off up the wood chippings at a medium canter, glancing back for me to follow. I joined her expecting to go the whole way at that conservative pace but she quickened immediately when I reached her and I could hardly hang back and say hold on a minute, I haven't done this in a while and could easily fall off. Instead, I tucked in my elbows as instructed and relied on luck.

Towards the end Mackie kicked her horse into a frank gallop and it was at that speed that we both passed Tremayne. I was peripherally aware of him standing four-square on the small observation mound, though all my direct attention was acutely focused on balance, grip and what lay ahead between Touchy's ears.

Touchy, I thanked heaven, slowed when Mackie slowed and brought himself to a good-natured halt without dumping his rider, Friday or not. I was breathless and also exhilarated and thought I could easily get hooked on Touchy after a fix or two more like that.

"Where the hell did you get to?" Tremayne inquired of me, joining us and the rest of the string. "I thought you'd chickened out."

"We were just talking," Mackie said.

Tremayne looked at her now glowing face and probably drew the wrong conclusion but made no further comment. He told everyone to walk back down the gallop and dismount and lead them the last part of the way, as usual.

Mackie, taking her place at the head, asked me to ride at the back, to make sure everyone returned safely, which I did. Tremayne's tractor followed slowly, at a distance.

He came stamping into the kitchen, where I was fishing out orange juice and without preamble demanded, "What were you and Mackie talking about?"

"She'll tell you," I said, smiling.

He said belligerently, "Mackie's off limits."

I put down the orange juice and straightened, not knowing quite what to say.

"If you mean do I fancy Mackie," I said, "then yes, she's a great girl. But off limits is right. We were not flirting, chatting up, or whatever else you care to call it. *Not.*"

After a grudging minute he said, "All right then," and I

thought that in his way he was as possessive of Mackie as Perkin was.

A short while later, munching the toast I'd made for him, he seemed to have forgotten it.

"You can ride out every morning," he said, "if you'd like."

He could see I was pleased. I said, "I'd like it very much."

"Settled, then."

The day passed in the way that had become routine: clippings, beef sandwiches, taping, evening drinks, Gareth home, cook the dinner. Dee-Dee's distrust of me had vanished; Perkin's hadn't. Tremayne seemed to have accepted my assurance of the morning, and Mackie smiled into her plain tonic and carefully avoided my eyes for fear of revealing that a secret lay between us.

On Saturday morning I rode Touchy again but Mackie didn't materialize, having phoned Tremayne to say she wasn't well: but she and Perkin appeared in the kitchen during breakfast, he with an arm around her shoulders in a supremely proprietary way.

"We've something to tell you," Perkin said to Tremayne.

"Oh, yes?" Tremayne was busy with some papers.

"Yes. Do pay attention. We're having a baby."

"We think so," Mackie said.

Tremayne paid attention abruptly and was clearly profoundly delighted. Not an overdemonstrative man, he didn't leap up to embrace them but literally purred in his throat like a cat and beat the table with his fist. Son and daughter-in-law had no difficulty in reading the signals and looked smugly pleased with themselves, sitting down, drinking coffee and working out that the birth would occur in September, but they weren't quite sure of the date.

Mackie gave me a shy smile which Perkin forgave. Each of them looked more in love with the other, more relaxed, as if the earlier failure to conceive had caused tension between them, now relieved.

After that excitement I labored all morning again on the clippings, unsustained by cups from Dee-Dee, who didn't work on Saturdays. Gareth went to Saturday morning school and pinned a second message on the corkboard—FOOTBALL MATCH PM—leaving BACK FOR GRUB in place.

Tremayne, cursing the persistent absence of racing even on television, taped the saga of his younger life up to the time he accompanied his father to a brothel.

"My father wouldn't have anybody but the madam and she said she'd retired long ago but she accommodated him in the end. Couldn't resist him, the mad old charmer."

In the evening I fed the three of us on lamb chops, peas and potatoes in their skins and on Sunday morning Fiona and Harry came to the stables to see her horses and drink with Tremayne afterwards in the family room. Nolan came with them, but not Lewis. An aunt of Harry's, another Mrs. Goodhaven, tagged quietly along. Mackie, Perkin and Gareth congregated as if to a normal ritual.

Mackie couldn't keep her good news to herself, and Fiona and Harry hugged her while Perkin looked important and Nolan gave halfhearted congratulations. Tremayne opened champagne.

At about that time, ten miles away in lonely woodland, a gamekeeper came across what was left of Angela Brickell.

7

The discovery made no impact on Shellerton on that Sunday because at first no one knew whose bones lay among the dead brambles and the dormant oaks.

The gamekeeper went home to his Sunday lunch and telephoned the local police after he'd eaten, feeling that as the bones were old it wouldn't matter if they waited one hour longer.

In Tremayne's house, when the toasts to the future Vickers had been drunk, Gareth showed Fiona a couple of the travel guides and Fiona in astonishment showed Harry. Nolan picked up *Safari* as if absentmindedly and said that no one but a bloody fool would go hunting tigers in Africa.

"There aren't any tigers in Africa," Gareth said.

"That's right. He'd be a bloody fool."

"Oh . . . it's a joke," Gareth said, obviously feeling that it was he who'd been made a fool of. "Very funny."

Nolan, though the shortest man there, physically dominated the room, eclipsing even Tremayne. His strong animal
vigor and powerful saturnine features seemed to charge the
very air with static, as if his presence alone could generate
sparks. One could see how Mackie had been struck by lightning. One could see how Olympia might have died by violent
accident. One's reactions to Nolan had little to do with
reason, all with instinct.

Harry's aunt was looking into *Ice* in a faintly superior
way as if confronted with a manifestation of the lower orders.

"How frightfully *rugged*," she said, her voice as languid as
Harry's but without the God-given amusement.

"Er," Harry said to me. "I didn't introduce you properly.
I must present you to my aunt, Erica Goodhaven. She's a
writer."

There was a subterranean flood of mischief in his eyes.
Fiona glanced at me with a hint of a smile and I thought
both of them looked as though I were about to be thrown to
the lions for their entertainment. Anticipation of enjoyment,
loud and clear.

"Erica," Harry said, "John wrote these books."

"And a novel," Tremayne said defensively, coming to an
aid I didn't realize I needed. "It's going to be published. And
he's writing my biography."

"A *novel*," Harry's aunt said, in the same way as before.
"Going to be published. How *interesting*. I, also, write novels. Under my unmarried name, Erica Upton."

Thrown to a literary lion, I perceived. A real one, a lion-
ess. Erica Upton's five-star prize-winning reputation was for
erudition, elegant syntax, esoteric backgrounds, elegiac
characters and a profound understanding of incest.

"Your aunt?" I said to Harry.

"By marriage."

Tremayne refilled my glass with champagne as if I would
need it and muttered under his breath, "She'll eat you."

From across the room she did look faintly predatory at that moment, though was otherwise a slender, intense-looking gray-haired woman in a gray wool dress with flat shoes and no jewelry. A quintessential aunt, I thought; except that most people's aunts weren't Erica Upton.

"What is your novel *about*?" she inquired of me. Her voice was patronizing but I didn't mind that: she was entitled to it.

The others all waited with her to hear my answer. Incredible, I thought, that nine people in one room weren't carrying on several noisy separate conversations, as usually happened.

"It's about survival," I said politely.

Everyone listened. Everyone always listened to Erica Upton.

"What sort of survival?" she asked. "Medical? Economic? Creative?"

"It's about some travelers cut off by an earthquake. About how they coped. It's called *Long Way Home*."

"How *quaint*," she said.

She wasn't intending to be outright offensive, I thought. She seemed merely to know that her own work was on a summit I would never reach, and in that she was right. All the same I felt again the mild recklessness that I had on Touchy: even if I lacked confidence, relax and have a go.

"My agent says," I said neutrally, "that *Long Way Home* is really about the spiritual consequences of deprivation and fear."

She knew a gauntlet when she heard one. I saw the stiffening in her body and suspected it in her mind.

She said, "You are too young to write with authority of spiritual consequences. Too young for your soul to have been tempered. Too young to have learned the intensity of understanding that comes only through deep adversity."

Was that true? I wondered. How old was old enough?

I said, "Shouldn't contentment be allowed its insights?"

"It has none. Insight grows best on stony ground. Unless you have suffered or are poor or can tap into melancholy, you have defective perception."

I rolled with that one. Sought for a response.

"I *am* poor," I said. "Well, fairly. Poor enough to perceive that poverty is the enemy of moral strength."

She peered at me as if measuring a prey for the pounce.

"You are a lightweight person," she said, "if you have no conception of the moral strength of redemption and atonement in penury."

I swallowed. "I don't seek sainthood. I seek insight through a combination of imagination and common sense."

"You are not a serious writer." A dire accusation; her worst.

"I write to entertain," I said.

"I," she said simply, "write to enlighten."

I could find no possible answer. I said wryly, with a bow, "I am defeated."

She laughed with pleasure, her muscles loosening. The lion had devoured the sacrifice and all was well. She turned away to begin talking to Fiona, and Harry made his way to my side, watching me dispatch my champagne with a gulp.

"You didn't do too badly," he said. "Nice brisk duel."

"She ran me through."

"Oh, yes. Never mind. Good sport, though."

"You set it up."

He grinned. "She phoned this morning. She comes occasionally for lunch, so I told her to beetle over. Couldn't resist it."

"What a pal."

"Be honest. You enjoyed it."

I sighed. "She outguns me by far."

"She's more than twice your age."

"That makes it worse."

"Seriously," he said, as if he thought my ego needed

patching, "these survival guides are pretty good. Do you mind if we take a few of them home?"

"They're Tremayne's and Gareth's, really."

"I'll ask them, then." He looked at me shrewdly. "Nothing wrong with your courage, is there?"

"How do you mean?"

"You took her on. You didn't have to."

I half laughed. "My agent calls it impulsive behavior. He says it will kill me, one day."

"You're older than you look," he said cryptically, and went off to talk to Tremayne.

Mackie, her drink all but untouched, took his place as kind blotter of bleeding feelings.

"It's not fair of her to call you lightweight," she said. "Harry shouldn't have brought her. I know she's highly revered but she can make people cry. I've seen her do it."

"My eyes are dry," I said. "Are you drinking that champagne?"

"I'd better not, I suppose."

"Care to give it to the walking wounded?"

She smiled her brilliant smile and we exchanged glasses.

"Actually," she said, "I didn't understand all Erica was saying."

"She was saying she's cleverer than me."

"I."

"I," I agreed.

"I'll bet she can't catch people who're fainting off horses."

Mackie was, as Tremayne had said, a sweet young woman.

Angela Brickell's remains lay on the Quillersedge Estate at the western edge of the Chilterns.

The Quillersedge gamekeeper arranged on the telephone for the local police to collect him from his cottage on the estate and drive as near to the bones as possible on the estate's private roads. From there, everyone would have to go through the woods on foot.

The few policemen on duty on Sunday afternoon thought of cold wet undergrowth and shivered.

In Tremayne's house, the informal party lingered cheerfully. Fiona and Mackie sat on a sofa, silver-blond head beside dark red–brown, talking about Mackie's baby. Nolan discussed with Tremayne the horses Nolan hoped still to be riding when racing resumed. Gareth handed around potato chips while eating most of them himself, and Perkin read aloud how to return safely from getting lost. " 'Go downhill, not up,' " he read. " 'People live in valleys. Follow streams in their flow direction. People live beside rivers. 'I can't imagine I'll ever need this advice. I steer clear of jungles.' "

"You could need it in the Lake District," I said mildly.

"I don't like walking, period."

Harry said, "John, Erica wants to know why you've ignored mountain climbing in your guides."

"Never got round to it," I said, "and there are dozens of mountain climbing books already."

Erica, the sparkle of victory still in her eyes, asked who was publishing my novel. When I told her she raised her eyebrows thoughtfully and made no disparaging remark.

"Good publishers, are they?" Harry asked, his lips twitching.

"Reputable," she allowed.

Fiona, getting to her feet, began to say good-byes, chiefly with kisses. Gareth ducked his but she stopped beside me and put her cheek on mine.

"How long are you staying?" she asked.

Tremayne answered for me forthrightly. "Three more weeks. Then we'll see."

"We'll fix a dinner," Fiona said. "Come along, Nolan. Ready, Erica? Love you, Mackie, take care of yourself."

When they'd gone Mackie and Perkin floated off home on

cloud nine and Tremayne and I went around collecting glasses and stacking them in the dishwasher.

Gareth said, "If we can have beef sandwich pie again, I'll make it for lunch."

At about the time we finally ate the pie, two policemen and the gamekeeper reached the pathetic collection of bones and set nemesis in motion. They tied ropes to trees to ring and isolate the area and radioed for more instructions. Slowly the information percolated upwards until it reached Detective Chief Inspector Doone, Thames Valley Police, who was sleeping off his Yorkshire pudding.

He decided, as daylight would die within the hour, that first thing in the morning he would assemble and take a pathologist for an on-site examination and a photographer for the record. He believed the bones would prove to belong to one of the hundreds of teenagers who had infested his patch with all-night parties the summer before. Three others had died on him from drugs.

In Tremayne's house Gareth and I went up to my bedroom because he wanted to see the survival kit that he knew I'd brought with me.

"Is it just like the ones in the books?" he asked as I brought out a black waterproof pouch that one could wear around one's waist.

"No, not entirely." I paused. "I have three survival kits at present. One small one for taking with me all the time. This one here for longer walks and difficult areas. And one that I didn't bring, which is full camping survival gear for going out into the wilds. That's a backpack on a frame."

"I wish I could see it," Gareth said wistfully.

"Well, one day, you never know."

"I'll hold you to it."

"I'll show you the smallest kit first," I said, "but you'll

have to run down and get it. It's in my ski-suit jacket pocket in the cloakroom."

He went willingly but presently returned doubtfully with a flat tin, smaller than a paperback book, held shut with black insulating tape.

"Is this it?" he said.

I nodded. "Open it carefully."

He did as I said, laying out the contents on the white counterpane on the bed and reciting them aloud.

"Two matchbooks, a bit of candle, a little coil of thin wire, a piece of jagged wire, some fishhooks, a small pencil and piece of paper, needles and thread, two bandages and a plastic bag folded up small and held by a paper clip." He looked disappointed. "You couldn't do much with those."

"Just light a fire, cut wood, catch food, collect water, make a map and sew up wounds. That jagged wire is a flexible saw."

His mouth opened.

"Then I always carry two things on my belt." I unstrapped it and showed it to him. "The belt itself has a zipped pocket all along the inside where you can keep money. What's in there at the moment is your father's. I don't often carry a wallet. Those other things on the belt, one is a knife, one is a multi-purpose survival tool."

"Can I look?"

"Yes, sure."

The knife, in a black canvas sheath with a flap fastened by Velcro, was a strong folding knife with a cunningly serrated blade, very sharp indeed, nine inches overall when open, only five when closed. Gareth opened it until it locked with a snap and stood looking at it in surprise.

"That's some knife," he said. "Were you wearing it while we were having drinks?"

"All the time. It weighs only four and a half ounces, about one-eighth of a kilo. Weight's important too, don't forget.

Always travel as light as you can if you have to carry everything."

He opened the other object slotted onto the belt, a small leather case about three inches by two and a half, which contained a flat metal rectangular object a shade smaller in dimension: total weight altogether, three and a half ounces.

"What's this?" he asked, taking it out onto his hand. "I've never seen anything like this."

"I carry that instead of an ordinary penknife. It has a blade slotted in one side and scissors in the other. That little round thing is a magnifying glass for starting fires if there's any sun. With those other odd-shaped edges you can make holes in a tin of food, open crown-cork bottles, screw in screws, file your nails and sharpen knives. The sides have inches and centimeters marked like a ruler, and the back of it all is polished like a mirror for signaling."

"Wow." He turned it over and looked at his own face. "It's really cool."

He began to pack all the small things back into the flat tin and remarked that fishhooks wouldn't be much good away from rivers.

"You can catch birds on fishhooks. They take bait like fish."

He stared at me. "Have you eaten birds?"

"Chicken are birds."

"Well . . . ordinary birds?"

"Pigeons? Four and twenty blackbirds? You eat anything if you're hungry enough. All our ancestors lived on whatever they could get hold of. It was normal, once."

Normal for him was a freezer full of pizzas. He had no idea what it was like to be primevally alone with nature, and it was unlikely he would ever find out, for all his present interest.

I'd spent a month once on an island without any kit or anything modern at all, knowing only that there was water and that I would be collected at the end, and even with those certainties and all the craft I'd ever learned, I'd had a hard job lasting out; and it was then that I'd discovered for myself that survival was a matter of mind rather than body.

The travel agency, on my urgent advice, had decided against offering holidays of that sort.

"What about a group?" they said. "Not one alone."

"A group eats more," I pointed out. "The tensions are terrible. You'd have a murder."

"All right. Full camping kit then, with essential stores and radios."

"And choose the leader before they set out."

Even so, few of the "marooned" holidays had passed off without trouble, and in the end the agency had abandoned them.

Gareth replaced the coil of fine wire in the tin and said, "I suppose this wire is for all the traps in the books?"

"Only the simplest ones."

"Some of those traps are really sneaky."

"I'm afraid so."

"There you are, a harmless rabbit hopping along about your business and you don't see the wire hidden in dead leaves and you trip over it and suddenly pow! You're all tied up in a net or squashed under logs. Have you done all that?"

"Yes, lots of times."

"I like the idea of the bow and arrows better," he said.

"Yes, well, I put in the instructions of how to make them effectively because our ancestors had them, but it's not easy to hit anything if it's moving. Impossible if it's small. It's not the same as using a custom-made bow shooting metal arrows at a nice round stationary target, like in archery competitions. I've always preferred traps."

"Didn't you ever hit *anything* with a bow and arrow?"

I smiled. "I shot an apple off a tree in our garden once when I was small because I was only allowed to eat windfalls, and there weren't any. Bad luck that my mother was looking out of the window."

"Mothers!"

"Tremayne says you see yours sometimes."

"Yes, I do." He glanced up at me quickly and down again. "Did Dad tell you my mother isn't Perkin's mother?"

"No," I said slowly. "I guess we haven't come to that bit yet."

"Perkin and Jane's mother died years ago. Jane's my sister—well, half sister really. She's married to a French trainer and they live in Chantilly, which is a sort of French Newmarket. It's good fun, staying with Jane. I go summers. Couple of weeks."

"Do you speak French?"

He grinned. "Some. I always seem to come home just when I'm getting the hang of it. What about you?"

"French a bit, but Spanish more, only I'm rusty in both now too."

He nodded and fiddled for a bit putting the insulating tape back on the tin.

I watched him, and in the end he said, "My mother's on television quite a lot. That's where Dad means I see her."

"Television! Is she an actress?"

"No. She cooks. She does one of those afternoon programs sometimes."

"A *cook*?" I could hardly believe it. "But your father doesn't care about food."

"Yeah, that's what he says, but he's been eating what you've made, hasn't he? But I think she used to drive him barmy always inventing weird fancy things he didn't like. I didn't care that much except that I never got what I liked either, so when she left us we sort of relapsed into what we *did* like, and we stayed like that. Only recently I've been wishing I could make custard and I tried but I burned the milk and it tasted awful. Did you know you could burn milk? So, anyway, she's married to someone else now. I don't like him though. I don't bother with them much."

He sounded as if he'd said all he wanted to on the subject

and seemed relieved to go back to simple things like staying alive, asking to see inside kit number two, the black pouch.

"You're not bored?" I said.

"Can't wait."

I handed it to him and let him open its three zipped and Velcroed pockets, to lay the contents again on the bed. Although the pouch itself was waterproof, almost every item inside it was further wrapped separately in a small plastic bag, fastened with a twist tie; safe from sand and insects. Gareth undid and emptied some of the bags and frowned over the contents.

"Explain what they are," he said. "I mean, twenty matchbooks are for lighting fires, right, so what are the cotton-wool balls doing with them?"

"They burn well. They set fire to dry leaves."

"Oh. The candle is for light, right?"

"And to help light fires. And wax is useful for a lot of things."

"What's this?" He pointed to a short fat spool of thin yellow thread.

"That's Kevlar fiber. It's a sort of plastic, strong as steel. Six hundred yards of it. You can make nets of it, tie anything, fish with it, twist it into fine unbreakable rope. I didn't come across it in time to put it in the books."

"And this? This little jar of whitish liquid packed with the sawn-off paintbrush."

I smiled. "That's in the *Wilderness* book. It's luminous paint."

He stared.

"Well," I said reasonably, "if you have a camp and you want to leave it to go and look for food or firewood, you want to be able to find your way back again, don't you? Essential. So as you go, you paint a slash of this on a tree trunk or a rock, always making sure you can see one slash from another, and then you can find your way back even in the dark."

"Cool," he said.

"That little oblong metal thing with the handle," I said, "that's a powerful magnet. Useful but not essential. Good for retrieving fishhooks if you lose them in the water. You tie the magnet on a string and dangle it. Fishhooks are precious."

He held up a transparent film case, one of about six in the pouch. "More fishhooks in here," he said. "Isn't this what film comes in? I thought they were black."

"Fuji films come in these clear cases. As you can see what's inside, I use them all the time. They weigh nothing. They're everything-proof. Perfect. These other cases contain more needles and thread, safety pins, aspirins, water-purifying tablets, things like that."

"What's this knobbly-looking object? Oh, it's a telescope!" He laughed and weighed it in his hand.

"Two ounces," I said, "but eight by twenty magnification."

He passed over as mundane a flashlight that was also a ball-point pen, the light in the tip for writing, and wasn't enthralled by a whistle, a Post-it pad or a thick folded wad of aluminum foil. ("For wrapping food to cook in the embers," I said.) What really fascinated him was a tiny blowtorch which shot out a fierce blue flame hot enough to melt solder.

"Cool," he said again. "That's really *ace*."

"Infallible for lighting fires," I said, "as long as the butane lasts."

"You said in the books that fire comes first."

I nodded. "A fire makes you feel better. Less alone. And you need fire for boiling river water to make it OK to drink, and for cooking, of course. And signaling where you are, if people are looking for you."

"And to keep warm."

"That too."

Gareth had come to the last thing, a pair of leather gloves, which he thought were sissy.

"They give your hands almost double grip," I said. "They save you from cuts and scratches. And apart from that they're invaluable for collecting stinging nettles."

"I'd hate to collect stinging nettles."

"No, you wouldn't. If you boil the leaves they're not bad to eat, but the best things are the stalks. Incredibly stringy. You can thrash them until they're supple enough for lashing branches together, for making shelters and also racks to keep things off the ground away from damp and animals."

"You know so much," he said.

"I went camping in my cradle. Literally."

He methodically packed everything back as he'd found it and asked what it weighed altogether.

"About two pounds. Less than a kilo."

A thought struck him. "You haven't got a compass!"

"It's not in there," I agreed. I opened a drawer in the chest of drawers and found it for him: a slim liquid-filled compass set in a clear oblong of plastic which had inch and centimeter measures along the sides. I showed him how it aligned with maps and made setting a course relatively easy, and told him I always carried it in my shirt pocket to have it handy.

"But it was in the drawer," he objected.

"I'm not likely to get lost in Shellerton."

"You could up on the Downs," he said seriously.

I doubted it, but said I would carry it to please him, which earned the sideways look it deserved.

Putting everything on top of the chest of drawers, I reflected how little time I'd spent in that room amid the mismatched furniture and faded fabrics. I hadn't once felt like retreating to be alone there, though for one pretty accustomed to solitude it was odd to find myself living in the lives of all these people, as if I'd stepped into a play that was already in progress and been given a walk-on part in the action. I would spend another three weeks there and exit, and the play would go on without me as if I hadn't been on stage at all. Meanwhile, I felt drawn in and interested and unwilling to miss any scene.

"This room used to be Perkin's," Gareth observed, as if catching a swirl of my thought. "He took all his own stuff with him when they divided the house. It used to be terrif in here." He shrugged. "You want to see my room?"

"I'd love to."

He nodded and led the way. He and I shared the bathroom which lay between us, and along the hallway lay Tremayne's suite, into which he was liable to vanish with a brisk slam of the door.

Gareth's room was all pre-adolescent. He slept on a platform with a pull-out desk below and there were a good many white space-age fitments liberally plastered with posters of pop stars and sportsmen. Prized objects filled shelves. Clothes adorned the floor.

I murmured something encouraging but he swept his lair with a disparaging scrutiny and said he was going to do the whole thing over, Dad willing, in the summer.

"Dad got this room done for me after Mum left, and it was top ace at the time. Guess I'm getting too old for it now."

"Life's like that," I said.

"Always?"

"It looks like it."

He nodded as if he'd already discovered that changes were inevitable and not always bad, and in undemanding accord we shut the door on his passing phase and went down to the family room, where we found Tremayne asleep.

Gareth retreated without disturbing him and beckoned me to follow him through to the central hall. There he walked across and knocked briefly on Mackie and Perkin's door, which after an interval was opened slowly by Perkin.

"Can we come in for five mins?" Gareth said. "Dad's asleep in his chair. You know what he's like if I wake him."

Perkin yawned and opened his door wider though without excessive willingness, particularly on my account. He led the way into his sitting room, where it was clear he and Mackie had been spending a lazy afternoon reading the Sunday newspapers.

Mackie started to get up when she saw me and then relaxed again as if to say I was now family, not a visitor, and could fend for myself. Perkin told Gareth there was Coke in the fridge if he wanted some. Gareth didn't.

I remembered with a small jerk that it was in this room, Perkin and Mackie's sitting room, that Olympia had died. I couldn't help but glance around, wondering just where it had happened, where Mackie and Harry had found Nolan standing over the girl without underclothes in a scarlet dress, with Lewis—drunk or not—in a chair.

There was nothing left of that violent scene now in the pleasant big room, no residual shudder in the comfortable atmosphere, no regrets or grief. The trial was over, Nolan was free, Olympia was ashes.

Gareth, unconcerned, asked Perkin, "Can I show John your workroom?"

"Don't touch anything. I mean *anything*."

"Cross my heart."

With me still obediently in tow he crossed Perkin and Mackie's inner hall and opened a door which led into a completely different world, one incredibly fragrant with the scent of untreated wood.

The room where Perkin created his future antiques was of generous size, like all the rooms in the entire big house, but also no larger than the others. It was extremely tidy, which in a way I wouldn't have expected, with a polished wood-block floor swept spotless, not a shaving or speck of sawdust in sight.

When I commented on it Gareth said it was always like that. Perkin would use one tool at a time and put it away before he used another. Chisels, spokeshaves, things like that.

"Dead methodical," Gareth said. "Very fussy."

There was surprisingly a gas cooker standing against one wall. "He heats glue on that," Gareth said, seeing me looking, "and other sorts of muck like linseed oil." He pointed across the room. "That's his lathe, that's his saw-bench, that's his sanding machine. I haven't seen him working much. He doesn't like people watching him, says it interferes with the feeling for what he's doing."

Gareth's voice held disbelief, but I thought if I had to write with people watching I'd get nothing worthwhile done either.

"What's he making at the moment?" I asked.

"Don't know."

He wandered around the room looking at sheets of veneer stacked against a wall and at little orderly piles of square-cut lengths from exotic black to golden walnut. "He makes legs with those," Gareth said, pointing.

He stopped by a long solid worktop like a butcher's block and said to me over his shoulder, "I should think he's just started on this."

I went across to look and saw a pencil drawing of a display cabinet of sharply spare and unusual lines, a piece designed to draw the eye to its contents, not itself.

The drawing was held down by two blocks of wood, one, I thought, cherry, the other bleached oak, though I was better at living trees than dead.

"He often slats one sort of wood into the other," Gareth said. "Makes a sort of stripe. His things don't actually look bad. People buy them all the time."

"I'm not surprised," I said.

"Aren't you?" He seemed pleased, as if he'd been afraid I wouldn't be impressed, but I was, considerably.

As we turned to leave I said, "Was it in their sitting room that that poor girl died?"

"Gruesome," Gareth said, nodding. "I didn't see her. Perkin did, though. He went in just after Mackie and Harry and found it all happening. And, I mean, disgusting . . . there was a mess on the carpet where she'd been lying and by the time they were allowed to clean it up, they couldn't. So they got a new carpet from insurance but Perkin acts as if the mess is still there and he's moved a sofa to cover the place. Bonkers, I think."

I thought I might easily have done the same. Whoever would want to walk every day over a deathbed? We went back to the sitting room and one could see, if one knew, just which of the three chintz-covered sofas wasn't in a logical place.

We stayed only a short while before returning to the family room, where Tremayne was safely awake and yawning, getting ready to walk around his yard at evening stables. He invited me to go with him, which I did with pleasure, and afterwards I made cauliflower cheese for supper which Tremayne ate without a tremor.

When he went out at bedtime for a last look around, he came back blowing on his hands cheerfully and smiling broadly.

"It's thawing," he said. "Everything's dripping. Thank God."

The world indeed turned from white to green during the night, bringing renewed life to Shellerton and racing.

Out in the melting woodlands, Angela Brickell spent her last night in the quiet undergrowth among the small scavenging creatures that had blessedly cleaned her bones. She was without odor and without horror, weather-scrubbed, long gone into everlasting peace.

8

Tremayne promoted me from Touchy to a still actively racing steeplechaser that Monday morning, a nine-year-old gelding called Drifter. I was also permitted to do a regular working gallop and by great good fortune didn't fall off. Neither Tremayne nor Mackie made any comment on my competence or lack of it, only on the state of fitness of the horse. They were taking me for granted, I realized, and was flattered and glad of it.

When we returned from the newly greenish-brownish Downs there was a strange car in the yard and a strange man drinking coffee in the kitchen; but strange to me only. Familiar to everyone else.

He was young, short, thin, angular and bold, wearing self-assurance as an outer garment. He was also, I soon found, almost as foul-mouthed as Nolan but, unlike him, funny.

"Hello, Sam," Tremayne said. "Ready for work?"

"Too sodding right. I'm as stiff as a frigging virgin."

I wondered idly how many virgins he had personally introduced to frigging: there was something about him that suggested it.

Tremayne said to me, "This is Sam Yaeger, our jockey." To Sam Yaeger he explained my presence and said I'd been riding out.

Sam Yaeger nodded to me, visibly assessing what threat or benefit I might represent to him, running a glance over my jodhpurs and measuring my height. I imagined that because of my six feet alone he might put away fears that I could annex any of his racing territory.

He himself wore jodhpurs also, along with a brilliant yellow sweatshirt. A multicolored anorak, twin of Gareth's, hung over the back of his chair, and he had brought his own helmet, bright turquoise, with YAEGER painted large in red on the front. Nothing shy or retiring about Sam.

Dee-Dee, appearing for her coffee, brightened by fifty watts at the sight of him.

"Morning, lover-boy," she said.

Lover-boy made a stab at pinching her bottom as she passed behind him, which she seemed not to mind. Well, well, well, I thought, there was a veritable pussycat lurking somewhere inside that self-contained touch-me-not secretarial exterior. She made her coffee and sat at the table beside the jockey, not overtly flirting but very aware of him.

I made the toast, which had become my accepted job, and put out the juice, butter, marmalade and so on. Sam Yaeger watched with comically raised eyebrows.

"Didn't Tremayne say you were a writer?" he asked.

"Most of the time. Want some toast?"

"One piece, light brown. You don't look like a bloody writer."

"So many people aren't."

"Aren't what?"

"What they look like," I said. "Bloody or not."

"What do I look like?" he demanded, but with, I thought, genuine curiosity.

"Like someone who won the Grand National among eighty-nine other races last year and finished third on the jockeys' list."

"You've been peeking," he said, surprised.

"I'll be interviewing you soon for your views of your boss as a trainer."

Tremayne said with mock severity, "And they'd better be respectful."

"They bloody well would be, wouldn't they?"

"If you have any sense," Tremayne agreed, nodding.

I dealt out the toast and made some more. Sam's extremely physical presence dominated breakfast throughout and I wondered briefly how he got on with Nolan, the dark side of the same coin.

I asked Dee-Dee that question after Sam and Tremayne had gone out with the second lot; asked her in the office while I checked some facts in old form books.

"Get on?" she repeated ironically. "No, they do not." She paused, considered whether to tell me more, shrugged and continued. "Sam doesn't like Nolan riding so many of the stable's horses. Nolan rides most of Fiona's runners, he accepts that, but Tremayne runs more horses in amateur races than most trainers do. Wins more, too, of course. The owners who bet, they like it, because whatever else you can say about Nolan, no one denies he's a brilliant jockey. He's been top of the amateurs' list for years."

"Why doesn't he turn professional?" I asked.

"The very idea of that scares Sam rigid," Dee-Dee said calmly, "but I don't think it will happen. Especially not now, since the conviction. Nolan prefers his amateur status, anyway. He thinks of Sam as blue collar to his white. That's why . . ." She stopped abruptly as if blocking a revelation that was already on its way from brain to mouth, stopped so sharply that I was immediately interested, but without showing it asked, "Why what?"

She shook her head. "It's not fair to them."

"Do go on," I said, not pressing too much. "I won't repeat it to anyone."

"It wouldn't help you with the book," she said.

"It might help me to understand the way the stable works and where its success comes from, besides Tremayne's skill. It might come partly, for instance, from rivalry between two jockeys who each wants to prove himself better than the other."

She gazed at me. "You have a twisty mind. I'd never have thought of that." She paused for decision and I simply waited. "It isn't just riding," she said finally. "It's women."

"Women?"

"They're rivals there, too. The night Nolan—I mean, the night Olympia died . . ."

They all said, I'd noticed, "when Olympia died," and never "when Nolan killed Olympia," though Dee-Dee had just come close.

"Sam set out to seduce Olympia," Dee-Dee said, as if it were only to be expected. "Nolan brought her to the party and of course Sam made a beeline for her." Somewhere in her calm voice was indulgence for Sam Yaeger, censure for Nolan, never mind that Nolan seemed to be the loser.

"Did he . . . er . . . know Olympia?"

"Never set eyes on her before. None of us knew her. Nolan had been keeping her to himself. Anyway he brought her that night and she took one look at Sam and *giggled.* I know, I was there. Sam has that effect on females." She raised her eyebrows. "Don't say it. I respond to him too. Can't help it. He's fun."

"I can see that," I said.

"Can you? Olympia did. Putty in his hands, which of course were all over her the minute Nolan went to fetch her a drink. When he came back, she'd gone off with Sam. Like

I told you, she had on a low-cut long scarlet dress slit up the thigh . . . next-best thing to a written invitation. Nolan seemed to think that Sam and Olympia would have headed for the stables and he went looking for them there, but without results."

She stopped again as if doubting the wisdom of telling me these things, but it seemed harder for her to stop than to start.

"Nolan came back into the house cursing and swearing and telling me he would strangle the . . . er . . . bitch because, you see, I think he blamed *her,* not Sam, for making him feel a fool. Him, Nolan, the white-collar amateur. He wasn't going to make it public and he shut up pretty soon, though he went on being angry. So, anyway, there you are, that's really what happened."

"Which no one," I said slowly, "brought up at the trial."

"Of course not. I mean, not many people knew, and it gave Nolan a *motive.*"

"Yes, it did."

"But he didn't mean to kill her. Everyone knows that. If he'd attacked and killed *Sam,* it would have been a different matter."

I said, frowning, "It wasn't you, though, who said at the trial they'd heard him say he would strangle the bitch."

"No, of course not. Some other people heard him before he reached me, and they didn't know *why* he was saying it. It didn't seem important at that time. Of course no one ever asked me if *I* knew why he'd said it, so no one found out."

"But the prosecution must have asked *Nolan* why he said it?"

"Yes, sure, but he said it was because he couldn't find her, nothing else. Extravagant language but not a threat."

I sighed. "And *Sam* wasn't for saying why, as it would further torpedo his shaky reputation?"

"Yes. And anyway he didn't believe Nolan meant to kill her. He told me that. He said it wasn't the first time he and

Nolan had bedded the same girl, and sometimes Nolan had pinched one of his, and it was a bit of a lark on the whole, not a killing matter."

"More a lark to Sam than to Nolan," I suggested.

"Probably." She shook herself. "I'm getting no work done."

"You've done some of mine."

"Don't put it in the book," she insisted, alarmed.

"I promise I won't," I said.

I retired to the dining room and, since the shape of Tremayne's passage through life was more and more becoming clear, I began to map out the book into sections, giving each a tentative title with subheadings. I still hadn't put an actual sentence on paper and was feeling tyrannized by all the blank pages lying ahead. I'd heard of writers who leaped to their typewriters as to a lover. There were days when I'd do any chore I could think of rather than pick up a pencil, and it was never easy, never, to dig words and ideas from my brain. Half the time I couldn't believe I'd chosen this occupation; half the time I longed for the easier solitude under the stars.

I scribbled "Find something you like doing and spend your life doing it" at the end of the outline plan and decided it was enough for one day. If tomorrow it looked all right, maybe I'd let it stand, and go on.

Out in the woodland Detective Chief Inspector Doone looked morosely at Angela Brickell's jumbled bones while the pathologist told him they were those of a young female, dead probably less than a year.

The photographer took photographs. The gamekeeper marked the spot on a large-scale map. The pathologist said it was impossible to determine cause of death without a detailed autopsy, and very likely not even then.

With sketchy reverence for whoever they had been, the

skull and other bones were packed into a coffin-shaped box, carried to a van and driven to the mortuary.

Detective Chief Inspector Doone, seeing there was no point in looking for tire tracks, footprints or cigarette ends, set two constables to searching the undergrowth for clothes, shoes or anything not rotted by time; and it was in this way that under a blanket of dead leaves they came across some wet filthy jeans, a small-sized bra, a pair of panties and a T-shirt with the remains of a pattern on the front.

Detective Chief Inspector Doone watched his men pack these sad remnants into a plastic bag and reflected that none of the clothes had been on or even near the bones.

The girl, he reckoned, had been naked when she died.

He sighed deeply. He didn't like these sorts of cases. He had daughters of his own.

Tremayne came back from second lot in a good mood, whistling between his teeth. He wheeled straight into the office, fired off a fresh barrage of instructions to Dee-Dee and made several rapid phone calls himself. Then he came into the dining room to let me know the state of play and to ask a favor or two, taking it (correctly) for granted that I would oblige.

The ditched jeep had gone to the big scrap heap in the sky: a replacement had been found in Newbury, a not new but serviceable Land-Rover. If I would go to Newbury in the Volvo with Tremayne, I could drive the substitute home to Shellerton.

"Of course," I said.

The racing industry was scrambling back into action, with Windsor racecourse promising to be operational on Wednesday. Tremayne had horses entered, four of which he proposed to run. He would like me to come with him, he said, to see what his job entailed.

"Love to," I said.

He wished to go out for the evening to play poker with

friends, and he'd be back late: would I stay in for Gareth?

"Sure," I said.

"He's old enough to be safe on his own, but . . . well . . ."

"Company," I said. "Someone around."

He nodded.

"You're welcome," I said.

"Dee-Dee thinks we take advantage of you," he said bluntly. "Do we?"

"No." I was surprised. "I like what I'm doing."

"Cooking, baby-sitting, spare chauffeur, spare lad?"

"Sure."

"You have the right to say no," he said uncertainly.

"I'll tell you soon enough if I'm affronted. As of now, I'd rather be a part of things, and useful. OK?"

He nodded.

"And," I said, "this way I get to know you better for the book."

For the first time he looked faintly apprehensive, as if perhaps after all he didn't want his whole self publicly laid bare; but I would respect any secrecies I learned, I thought again, if he didn't want them told. This was not an investigative blast-the-lid-off exercise, this was to be the equivalent of a commissioned portrait, an affirmation of life. It might be fair to include a wart or two, but not to put every last blemish under magnification.

The day went ahead as planned and, in addition, in the Volvo on the way to Newbury, Tremayne galloped through his late adolescence and his introduction (by his father, naturally) to high-stakes gambling. His father's advice, he said, was always to wager more than one could afford, otherwise one would get no thrill and feel no despair.

"He was right, of course," Tremayne said, "but I'm more prudent. I play poker, I back horses, I bet a little, win a little, lose a little, it doesn't flutter my pulse. I've owners who go white and shake at the races. They look on the point of dying, they stand to lose or win so much. My father would have understood it. I don't."

"All your life's a gamble," I said.

He looked blank for a moment. "You mean training race-horses? True enough, I get thrills like Top Spin Lob, and true enough, great slabs of despair. You might say I wager my heartstrings, but not much cash."

I wrote it down. Tremayne, driving conservatively, slanted a glance at my notebook and seemed pleased to be quoted. The man himself, I thought with a stirring of satis-faction, was going to speak clearly from the pages, coming alive with little help from me.

In the evening, after Tremayne had departed to his card game, Gareth asked me to teach him to cook.

I was nonplussed. "It's easy," I said.

"How did you learn?"

"I don't know. Maybe from watching my mother." I looked at his face. "Sorry, I forgot."

"My mother makes it all difficult, not easy. And she would never let me watch her at home. She said I got under her feet."

My own mother, I reflected, had always let me clean out raw cake mixture with my finger: had always liked to talk to me while things bubbled.

"Well," I said, "what do you want to eat?"

We went into the kitchen where Gareth tentatively asked for "real" shepherd's pie, "not that stuff in supermarket boxes that tastes of cardboard and wouldn't feed a pygmy."

"Real easy shepherd's pie," I assented. "First of all, catch your shepherd."

He grinned and watched me assemble some minced beef, an onion, gravy powder and a jar of dried herbs.

"The gravy powder's sort of cheating," I said. "Your mother would be horrified, but it thickens the meat and tastes good."

I dissolved some powder into a little water, added it to the beef, chopped the onion finely, added that, sprinkled some herbs, stirred it all around in a saucepan, put the lid on and set it to cook on a low heat.

"Next thing to decide," I said, "is real potatoes or dried potato granules. How are you with peeling potatoes? No? Granules, then?"

He nodded.

"Follow the directions," I said, giving him the packet.

"Heat eight fluid ounces of water and four fluid ounces of milk," he said, reading. He looked up. "Hey, I was going to ask you . . . You know you said to boil river water before you drink it? Well, what *in?*"

I smiled. "Best thing is a Coca-Cola can. You can usually find an empty one lying about, the litter habits of this nation being what they are. You want to just shake it up with water to wash it out a few times in case there are any spiders or anything inside, but Coke cans are pretty clean."

"Ace," he said emphatically. "Well, for the potatoes we need some butter and salt . . . Will you write down all you bought last week, so I can get them again and cook when you're gone?"

"Sure thing."

"I wouldn't mind if you stayed."

Loneliness was an ache in his voice. I said, "I'll be here another three weeks." I paused. "Would you like, say perhaps next Sunday if it's a decent day, to come out with me into some fields and perhaps some woods? I could show you a few of the things in the books . . . how to do them in real life."

His face shone: my own reward.

"Could I bring Coconut?"

"Absolutely."

"Mega cool."

He whipped the potato granules happily into the hot liquid and we piled the fluffy result onto the cooked meat mixture in a round pie dish. Put it under the grill to brown the top. Ate the result with mutual fulfillment and cleared everything away afterwards.

"Can we take the survival kit?" he asked.

"Of course."

"And light a fire?"

"Perhaps on your own land, if your father will let us. You can't just light fires anywhere in England. Or anyway, you shouldn't, unless it's an emergency. People do, actually, but you're supposed to get the landowner's permission first."

"He's sure to let us."

"Yes. I'd think so."

"I really can't wait," he said.

On Tuesday morning the pathologist made his report to Detective Chief Inspector Doone.

"The bones are those of a young adult female, probably five foot four or five, possible age, twenty. Could be a year or two younger or older, but not much. There was a small remaining patch of scalp, with a few hairs still adhering: the hairs are medium brown, four inches long, can't tell what length her hair was overall."

"How long since she died?" Doone asked.

"I'd say last summer."

"And cause of death? Drugs? Exposure?"

"As to drugs, we'll have to analyze the hairs, see what we can find. But no, you've got a problem here."

Doone sighed. "What problem?"

"Her hyoid bone is fractured."

Depression settled on Doone. "You're sure?"

"Positive. She was strangled."

At Shellerton Tuesday passed uneventfully with riding out, breakfast, clippings, lunch, taping, evening drinks and dinner.

In the morning I came across Dee-Dee weeping quietly into her typewriter and offered a tissue.

"It's nothing," she said, sniffing.

"Care to unbutton?"

"I don't know why I tell you things."

"I listen."

She blew her nose and gave me a brief apologetic look. "I'm old enough to know better. I'm thirty-six." She gave her age almost in desperation, as if the figure itself were a disaster.

"Tremayne told me you'd had a disappointment in the love department," I said hesitatingly. "He didn't exactly say who."

"Disappointment! Huh!" She sniffed hard. "I loved the beast. I mean, I even ironed his shirts for him. We were lovers for ages and he dumped me from one minute to the next. And now Mackie's having a *baby*." Her eyes filled with tears again, and I saw it was the raw ache for motherhood, that fierce instinct which could cause such unassuageable pain, that grieved her at least as much as the loss of the man.

"Do you know what?" Dee-Dee said with misery. "That louse didn't want a child until after we were married. *After*. He never meant to marry me, I know it now, but I waited for his sake . . . and I wasted . . . *three years* . . ." She gulped, a sob escaping. "I'll tell you, I'll take *anyone* now. I don't need a wedding ring. I want a *child*."

Her voice died in a forlorn pining wail, a keen of mourning. With a hunger that strong she could make dreadful decisions, but who could tell which would be better for her to be in the end, reckless or barren. Either way, there would be regrets.

She dried her eyes, blew her nose again and shook herself as if straightening her emotions by force, and when I next looked in on her she was typing away collectedly in her usual self-contained manner as if our conversation had never taken place.

* * *

On Tuesday afternoon Detective Chief Inspector Doone sent his men to search the whole area where the bones had been discovered. He told them to look for shoes, also for anything else man-made. They could use metal detectors. They should look under dead leaves. They were to mark on the map where each artifact was found, and also tag the artifact, being careful not to destroy evidence.

This was now a murder investigation, he reminded them.

On Wednesday morning when we came in from first lot Sam Yaeger was again in the kitchen.

This time he came not in his car but with a borrowed pickup truck in which he proposed to collect some Burma teak that Perkin had acquired for him at trade discount.

"Sam has a boat," Tremayne told me dryly. "An old wreck that he's slowly turning into a palace fit for a harem."

Sam Yaeger grinned cheerfully and made no denials. "It's already sold, or as good as," he told me. "Every jockey's got to have an eye to the bloody future. I buy clapped-out antique boats and make them better than new. I sold the last one to one of those sodding newspaper moguls. They'll pay the earth for good stuff. No fiberglass crap."

Life was full of surprises, I thought.

"Where do you keep the boat?" I asked, making toast.

"Maidenhead. On the Thames. I bought a bankrupt boat-yard there a while back. It looks a right shambles but a bit of dilapidation's a good thing. Bloody thieves think there's nothing bloody worth stealing. Better than a Rottweiler, is a bit of squalor."

"So I suppose," Tremayne said, "that you're taking the wood to the boatyard on your way to the races."

Sam looked at me in mock amazement. "Don't know how he works these things out, do you?"

"That'll do, Sam," Tremayne said, and one could see just where he drew the line between what he would take from Sam Yaeger, and what not. He began to discuss the horses he would be running at Windsor races that afternoon, telling Sam that "Bluecheesecake is better, not worse, for the lay-off," and "Give Just the Thing an easy if you feel her wavering. I don't want her ruined while she's still green."

"Right," Sam said, concentrating. "What about Cashless? Do I ride him in front again?"

"What do you think?"

"He likes it better. He just got beat by faster horses, last time."

"Go off in front, then."

"Right."

"Nolan rides Telebiddy in the amateur race," Tremayne said. "Unless the Jockey Club puts a stop to it."

Sam scowled but spoke no evil. Tremayne told him what he would be riding on the morrow at Towcester and said he'd have no runners at all on Friday.

"Saturday I'm sending five or six to Chepstow. You'll go there. So will I. With luck, Nolan rides Fiona's horse in the Wilfred Johnstone Hunter 'Chase at Sandown. Maybe Mackie will go to Sandown; we'll have to see."

Dee-Dee came in composedly for her coffee and as before sat next to Sam. Sam might be a constant seducer, I thought, looking at them, but he wouldn't want to leave a trail of paternity problems. Dee-Dee might get him into bed but not into fatherhood. Bad luck, try again.

Tremayne gave Dee-Dee instructions about engaging transport for Saturday, which she memorized as usual.

"Remember to phone through the entries for Ludlow and Wincanton. I'll decide on the Newbury entries this morning before I go to Windsor."

Dee-Dee nodded.

"Pack the colors for Windsor."

Dee-Dee nodded.

"Phone the saddler about collecting those exercise sheets for repair."

Dee-Dee nodded.

"Right, then. That's about it." He turned to me. "We'll leave for Windsor at twelve-thirty."

"Fine," I said.

He went up to the Downs to watch the second lot, driving the newly acquired Land-Rover. Sam Yaeger took the pickup around to Perkin's half of the house and loaded up his teak. Dee-Dee took her coffee into the office and I made a determined attempt to sort each year's clippings into order of significance, the most newsworthy on top.

At about that time, Detective Chief Inspector Doone went into the formerly unused office that had been dubbed "Incident Room" for the bones investigation and laid out on a trestle table the bits and pieces that his men had gleaned from the woodland.

There were the clothes found originally, now drying out in the centrally heated air. There was also a pair of well-worn and misshapen sneakers, still sodden, which might once have been white.

Apart from those, there were four old empty and dirty soft drink cans, a heavily rusted toy fire-engine, a pair of broken sunglasses, a puckered leather belt with split stitches, a gin bottle, a blue plastic comb uncorrupted by time, a well-chewed rubber ball, a gold-plated ball-point pen, a pink lipstick, chocolate bar wrappers, a pitted garden spade and a broken dog collar.

Detective Chief Inspector Doone walked broodingly around the table, staring at the haul from all angles.

"Speak to me, girl," he said. "Tell me who you are."

The clothes and the shoes made no answer.

He called in his men and told them to go back to the woods and widen the search, and he himself, as he had the day before, went through his lists of missing persons, trying to make a match.

He knew it was possible the young woman had been a far stranger to the area but thought it more likely that she was within fifty miles of her home. They usually were, these victims. He decided automatically to beam in on the locally lost.

He had a list of twelve persistent adolescent runaways: all possibles. A list of four defaulters from youth custody. A short list of two missing prostitutes. A list of six missing for "various reasons."

One of those was Angela Brickell. The reason given was: "Probably doped a racehorse in her charge. Skipped out."

Doone's attention passed over her and fastened thoughtfully on the wayward daughter of a politician. Reason for being missing: "Mixed with bad crowd. Unmanageable."

It might do his stalled career a bit of good, Doone reckoned, if it turned out to be *her*.

9

Tremayne told me that the only place that he couldn't take me on Windsor racecourse was into the Holy of Holies, the weighing room. Everywhere else, he said, I should stay by his side. He wouldn't forever be looking back to make sure I was with him: I was to provide my own glue.

Accordingly I followed him doggedly, at times at a run. Where he paused briefly to talk to other people he introduced me as a friend, John Kendall, not as Boswell. He left me to sort out for myself the information bombarding me from all sides, rarely offering explanations, and I could see that explanations would have been a burden for him when he was so busy. His four runners, as it happened, were in four consecutive races. He took me for a quick sandwich and a drink soon after our arrival on the racecourse and from then on began a darting progress: into the weighing room to fetch his jockey's saddle and weight cloth containing the correct amount of lead, off at a trot to the saddling boxes to do up the girths himself and straighten the tack to send the horse out looking good, into the parade ring to join the owners and give last-minute orders to the jockey, off up to the stands to watch the horse run, down again to the unsaddling areas, hoping to greet a winner, otherwise to listen to the why-not story from the jockey, and then off to the weighing room to pick up another saddle and weight cloth to start all over again.

Nolan was there, anxiously asking if Tremayne had received any thumbs-down from the Jockey Club.

"No," Tremayne said. "Have you?"

"Not an effing peep."

"You ride, then," Tremayne said. "And don't ask questions. Don't invite a no. They'll tell you quick enough if they want you off. Apply your mind to winning. Telebiddy's owners are here with their betting money burning holes in their pockets, so deliver the goods, eh?"

"Tell them I want a better effing present than last time."

"Win the race first," Tremayne said.

He made one of his dives into the weighing room, leaving me outside with Nolan, who had come dressed to stifle criticism. All the same he complained to me bitterly that the effing media had snapped him coming through the main gate and he could do without their sodding attentions, the obscene so and sos.

The filth of Nolan's language tended to wash over one, I found: the brain tended finally to filter it out.

Much the same could be said about Sam Yaeger, who slouched up beside us and annoyed Nolan by patting him on the back. Sam, too, was transformed by tidiness and I gradually observed that several of the jockeys arrived and departed from the racecourse dressed for the boardroom. Their working clothes might be pink, purple and the stuff of fantasy but they were saying they were businessmen first.

The physical impact of each of them, Nolan and Sam, was

diluted and dissipated by the open air that incidentally was still as cold as their relationship.

"Go easy on Bluecheesecake," Nolan said. "I don't want him effing loused up before the Kim Muir at Cheltenham."

Sam answered, "I'm not nannying any sodding amateur."

"The Kim Muir is his main effing target."

"Eff his bloody target."

Did anyone ever grow up? I wondered. The school playground had a lot to answer for.

Away from each other, as I discovered during the afternoon, they were assured, sensible and supremely expert.

Sam made no concessions on Bluecheesecake. Through a spare pair of Tremayne's binoculars I watched his gold cap from start to finish, seeing the smooth pattern of his progress along the rails, staying in third or fourth place while others surged forward and fell back on his outside.

The steeplechase course at Windsor proved to be a winding figure-of-eight, which meant that tactics were important. At times one saw the runners from head-on; difficult to tell who was actually in front. Coming around the last of several bends, Bluecheesecake made a mess of one head-on-view fence, his nose going down to the ground, Sam's back wholly visible from shoulders down to bottom up. Tremayne beside me let go of a Nolan-strength curse, but both horse and jockey righted themselves miraculously without falling and lost, Sam said afterwards, no more than three or four lengths.

Perhaps because of having to make up for those lengths in limited time before the winning post, Sam, having given his mount precious extra seconds for recovery of balance, rode over the last two fences with what even I could see was total disregard for his own safety and pressed Bluecheesecake unceremoniously for every ounce of effort.

Tremayne put down his glasses and watched the rocketing finish almost impassively, giving no more than a satisfied grunt when in the last few strides Bluecheesecake's nose showed decisively in front.

Before the cheers had died Tremayne had set off at a run to the winner's enclosure with me in pursuit, and after he'd received his due congratulations, inspected his excited sweating breathless charge for cuts and damage (none) and talked briefly to the press, he followed Sam into the weighing room to fetch the saddle again for Just the Thing.

When he came out he was escorted by Nolan, who fell into step beside him complaining ferociously that Sam had given Bluecheesecake a viciously hard race and spoiled his, Nolan's, chances at Cheltenham.

"Cheltenham is six weeks off," Tremayne said calmly. "Plenty of time."

Nolan repeated his gripe.

Tremayne said with amazing patience, "Sam did exactly right. Go and do the same on Telebiddy."

Nolan stalked away still looking more furious than was sensible in his position and Tremayne allowed himself a sigh but no comment. He took a lot more from Nolan, I reflected, than he would allow from Sam, even though it seemed to me that he liked Sam better. A lot of things were involved there: status, accent, connections; all the signal flags of class.

Sam rode Just the Thing in the next event, a hurdle race, with inconspicuous gallantry, providing the green mare with a clear view of the jumps and urging her on at the end to give her a good idea of what was expected. She finished a respectable third to Tremayne's almost tangible pleasure: and it was fascinating to me to have heard the plans beforehand and see them put into exact effect.

While Tremayne was on his way from weighing room to saddling boxes for Telebiddy in the next race he handed me an envelope and asked me to put the contents for him on the Tote; Telebiddy, all to win.

"I don't like people to see me bet," he said, "because for

one thing it shows them I'm pretty confident, so they put their money on too, and it shortens the odds. I usually bet by phone with a bookmaker, but today I wanted to judge the state of the ground first. It can be treacherous, after snow. You don't mind, do you?"

"Not at all."

He nodded and hurried off, and I made my way to the Tote windows and disposed of enough to keep me in food for a year. Small, as in Tremayne's "small bet," was a relative term, I saw.

I joined him in the parade ring and asked if he wanted the tickets.

"No. If he wins, collect for me, will you?"

"OK."

Nolan was talking to the owners, exercising his best charm and moderating his language. In jockey's clothes he still looked chunky, strong and powerfully arrogant, but the swagger seemed to stop the moment he sat on the horse. Then professionalism took over and he was concentrated, quiet and neat in the saddle.

I tagged along behind Tremayne and the owners and from the stands watched Nolan give a display of razor-sharp competence that made most of the other amateurs look like Sunday drivers.

He saved countable seconds over the fences, his mount gaining lengths by always seeming to take off at the right spot. Judgment, not luck. The courage that Mackie loved was still there, unmistakable.

The owners, mother and daughter, were tremblers. They weren't entirely white and near to dying, but from what they said the betting money was out of their pockets and on the horse in a big way and there was a good deal of lip- and knuckle-biting from off to finish.

Nolan, as if determined to outride Sam Yaeger, hurled himself over the last three fences and won by ten lengths pulling up. Tremayne let out a deep breath and the owners hugged each other, hugged Tremayne and stopped shaking.

"You could give Nolan a good cash present for that," Tremayne said bluntly.

The owners thought Nolan would be embarrassed if they gave him such a present.

"Give it to me, to give to him. No embarrassment."

The owners said they'd better run down and lead in their winner, which they did.

"Stingy cats," Tremayne said in my ear as we watched them fuss over the horse and have their picture taken.

"Won't they really give Nolan anything?" I asked.

"It's against the rules, and they know it. Amateurs aren't supposed to be given money for winning. Nolan will have backed the horse anyway, he always does with a hot chance like this. And I get one-hundred-percent commitment from my jockey." His voice was dry with humor. "I often think the Jockey Club has it wrong, not letting professional jockeys bet on their own mounts."

He returned to the weighing room to fetch Sam's saddle and weight cloth for Cashless, and I went off to the Tote and collected his Telebiddy winnings, which approximately equaled his stake. Nolan, it appeared, had been riding the hot favorite.

When I commented on it to Tremayne in the parade ring as we watched Cashless being led around, he told me that Nolan's presence on any horse shortened its odds, and Telebiddy had won twice for him already this season. It was a wonder, Tremayne said, that the Tote had paid evens: he'd expected less of a return. I would do him a favor, he added, if I would give him his winnings on the way home, not in public, so I walked around with a small fortune I had no hope of repaying if I lost it, keeping it clutched in my left-hand trousers pocket.

We went up to the stands for the race and watched Cashless set off in front as expected, a position he easily held until right where it mattered, the last fifty yards. Then three jockeys who had been waiting behind him stepped on the accelerator, and although Cashless didn't in any way give up, the three others passed him.

Tremayne shrugged. "Too bad."

"Will you run him in front again next time?" I asked, as we went down off the stands.

"I expect so. We've tried keeping him back and he runs worse. He's one-paced in a finish, that's his trouble. He's game enough, but it's hard to find races he can win."

We reached the parade ring, where the unsuccessful runners were being unsaddled. Sam, looping girths over his arm, gave Tremayne a rueful smile and said Cashless had done his best.

"I saw," Tremayne agreed. "Can't be helped." We watched Sam walk off towards the weighing room, and Tremayne remarked thoughtfully that he might try Cashless in an amateur race, and see what Nolan could do.

"Do you play them off against each other on purpose?" I asked.

Tremayne gave me a flickering glance. "I do the best for my owners," he said. "Like a drink?"

It appeared he had arranged to meet the owners of Telebiddy in the Club bar and when we arrived they were already celebrating with a bottle of champagne. Nolan, too, was there, being incredibly nice to them but without financial results.

When the two women had left in a state of euphoria, Nolan asked belligerently whether Tremayne had told them to give him a present.

"I suggested it," Tremayne said calmly, "but you'll be lucky. Better settle for what you took from the bookmakers yourself."

"Damn little," Nolan said, or words to that effect, "and the bloodsucking lawyers will get the lot." He shouldered his way out of the bar in self-righteous outrage, which seemed to be his uppermost state of mind oftener than not.

With noncommittal half-lowered eyelids Tremayne watched him go, then transferred his gaze to me.

"Well," he asked, "what have you learned?"

"What you intended me to, I expect."

He smiled. "And a bit more than I intended. I've noticed you do that all the time." With a contented sigh he put down his empty glass. "Two winners," he said. "A better-than-average day at the races. Let's go home."

At about the time we were driving home with Tremayne's winnings safely stowed in his own pockets, not mine, Detective Chief Inspector Doone was poring over the increased pickings from the woodland.

The detective chief inspector could be said to be purring. Among some insignificant long-rusted detritus lay the star of the whole collection, a woman's handbag. Total satisfaction had been denied him, as the prize had been torn open on one side, probably by a dog, whose toothmarks still showed, so that most of the contents had been lost. All the same, he was left with a shoulder strap, a corroded buckle and at least half of a brown plastic school-style bag which still held, in an intact inner zipped pocket, a small mirror and a folded photograph frame.

With careful movements Doone opened the frame and found inside, waterstained along one edge but otherwise sharply clear, a colored snapshot of a man standing beside a horse.

Disappointed that there was still no easy identification of the handbag's past owner, Doone took a telephone call from the pathologist.

"You were asking about teeth," the pathologist said. "The dental records you gave me are definitely not those of our bones. Our girl had good teeth. One or two missing, but no fillings. Sorry."

Doone's disappointment deepened. The politician's daughter had just been ruled out. He mentally reviewed his lists again, skipped the prostitutes and provisionally paused on Angela Brickell, stable lad. Angela Brickell . . . horse.

The bombshell burst on Shellerton on Thursday.

Tremayne was upstairs showering and dressing before going to Towcester races when the doorbell rang. Dee-Dee went to answer it and presently came into the dining room looking mystified.

"It's two men," she said. "They say they're policemen. They flashed some sort of identity cards, but they won't say what they want. I've put them in the family room until Tremayne comes down. Go and keep an eye on them, would you mind?"

"Sure," I said, already on the move.

"Thanks," she said, returning to the office. "Whatever they want, it looks boring."

I could see why she thought so. The two men might have invented the word gray, so characterless did they appear at first sight. Ultimate plainclothes, I thought.

"Can I help you?" I said.

"Are you Tremayne Vickers?" one of them asked.

"No. He'll be down soon. Can I help?"

"No, thank you, sir. Can you fetch him?"

"He's in the shower."

The policeman raised his eyebrows. Trainers, however, didn't shower before morning exercise, they showered after, before going racing. That was Tremayne's habit, anyway. Dee-Dee had told me.

"He's been up since six," I said.

The policeman's eyes widened, as if I'd read his mind.

"I am Detective Chief Inspector Doone, Thames Valley Police," he said. "This is Detective Constable Rich."

"How do you do," I said politely. "I'm John Kendall. Would you care to sit down?"

They perched gingerly on chairs and said no to an offer of coffee.

"Will he be long, sir?" Doone asked. "We must see him soon."

"No, not long."

Doone, on further inspection, appeared to be about fifty, with gray-dusted light-brown hair and a heavy medium-brown mustache. He had light-brown eyes, big bony hands and, as we all slowly discovered, a habit of talking a lot in a light Berkshire accent.

This chattiness wasn't at all apparent in the first ten minutes before Tremayne came downstairs buttoning the blue-and-white-striped cuffs of his shirt and carrying his jacket gripped between forearm and chest.

"Hello," he said, "who's this?"

Dee-Dee appeared behind him, apparently to tell him, but Doone introduced himself before either she or I could do so.

"Police?" Tremayne said, unworried. "What about?"

"We'd like to speak to you alone, sir."

"What? Oh, very well."

He asked me with his eyes to leave with Dee-Dee, shutting the door behind us. I returned to the dining room but presently heard the family-room door open and Tremayne's voice calling.

"John, come back here, would you."

I went back. Doone was protesting about my presence, saying it was unnecessary and inadvisable.

Tremayne said stubbornly, "I want him to hear it. Will you repeat what you said?"

Doone shrugged. "I came to inform Mr. Vickers that some remains have been found which may prove to be those of a young woman who was once employed here."

"Angela Brickell," Tremayne said resignedly.

"Oh."

"What does 'Oh' mean, sir?" Doone inquired sharply.

"It means just oh," I said. "Poor girl. Everyone thought she'd just done a bunk."

"They have a photograph," Tremayne said. "They're trying to identify the man." He turned to Doone. "Show it to him." He nodded in my direction. "Don't take my word for it."

Unwillingly Doone handed me a photograph enclosed in a plastic holder.

"Do you know this man, sir?" he asked.

I glanced at Tremayne, who was not looking concerned.

"You may as well tell him," he said.

"Harry Goodhaven?"

Tremayne nodded. "That's Fiona's horse, Chickweed, the one they said was doped."

"How can you recognize a horse?" Doone asked.

Tremayne stared at him. "Horses have faces, like people. I'd know Chickweed anywhere. He's still here, out in the yard."

"Who is this man, this Harry Goodhaven?" Doone demanded.

"The husband of the owner of the horse."

"Why would Angela Brickell be carrying his photograph?"

"She wasn't," Tremayne said. "Well, I suppose she was, but it was the *horse's* photograph she was carrying. She looked after it."

Doone looked completely unconvinced.

"To a lad," I said, "the horses they look after are like children. They love them. They defend them. It makes sense that she carried Chickweed's picture."

Tremayne glanced at me with half-stifled surprise, but I'd been listening to the lads for a week.

"What John says," Tremayne nodded, "is absolutely true."

The attendant policeman, Constable Rich, was all the time taking notes, though not at high speed: not shorthand.

Doone said, "Sir, can you give me the address of this Harry Goodhaven?"

With slight irritation Tremayne answered, "This Harry

Goodhaven, as you call him, is Mr. Henry Goodhaven, who owns the Manor House, Shellerton."

Doone very nearly said "Oh" in his turn, and made a visible readjustment in his mind.

"I'm already running late," Tremayne said, making moves to leave.

"But, sir . . ."

"Stay as long as you like," Tremayne said, going. "Talk to John, talk to my secretary, talk to whoever you want."

"I don't think you understand, sir," Doone said with a touch of desperation. "Angela Brickell was *strangled*."

"What?" Tremayne stopped dead, stunned. "I thought you said . . ."

"I said we'd found some remains. Now that you've recognized the . . . er . . . horse, sir, we're pretty sure of her identity. Everything else fits: height, age, possible time of death. And, sir"—he hesitated briefly as if to summon courage—"only last week, sir, we had a Crown Court case about another young woman who was strangled . . . strangled here in this house."

There was silence.

Tremayne said finally, "There can't be any connection. The death that occurred in this house was an accident, whatever the jury thought."

Doone said doggedly, "Did Mr. Nolan Everard have any connections with Angela Brickell?"

"Yes, of course he did. He rides Chickweed, the horse in that photograph. He saw Angela Brickell quite often in the course of her work." He paused for thought. "Where did you say her . . . remains . . . were found?"

"I don't think I said, sir."

"Well, where?"

Doone said, "All in good time, sir," a shade uncomfortably, and it occurred to me that he was hoping someone would *know,* and anyone who knew would very likely have strangled her.

"Poor girl," Tremayne said. "But all the same, Chief Inspector, I do now have to go to the races. Stay as long as you like, ask whatever you want. John here will explain to my assistant and head lad. John, tell Mackie and Bob what's happened, will you? Phone the car if you need me. Right, I'm off."

He continued purposefully and at good speed on his way and one could see and hear the Volvo start up and depart. In some bemusement Doone watched him go: his first taste of the difficulty of deflecting Tremayne from a chosen course.

"Well, Chief Inspector," I said neutrally, "where do you want to begin?"

"Your name, sir?"

I gave it. He was a good deal more confident with me, I noticed: I didn't have a personality that overshadowed his own.

"And your . . . er . . . position here?"

"I'm writing a history of the stables."

He seemed vaguely surprised that anyone should be engaged on such an enterprise and said lamely, "Very interesting, I'm sure."

"Yes, indeed."

"And . . . er . . . did you know the deceased?"

"Angela Brickell? No, I didn't. She vanished last summer, I believe, and I've been here only a short time, roughly ten days."

"But you knew about her, sir," he said shrewdly.

"Let me show you how I knew," I said. "Come and look."

I led him into the dining room and showed him the piles of clippings, explaining they were the raw materials of my future book.

"This is my workroom," I said. "Somewhere in *that* pile of cuttings," I pointed, "is an account of Angela Brickell's disappearance. That's how I know about her, and that's all

I know. No one has mentioned her outside of this room since I've been here."

He looked through the past year's cuttings and found the pieces about the girl. He nodded a few times and laid them back carefully where he'd found them, and seemed reassured about me personally. I got the first hint of the garrulity to come.

"Well, sir," he said, relaxing, "you can start introducing me to all the people here and explain why I'm asking questions and, as I've found on other cases when only remains are found that people tend to think the worst and imagine all sorts of horrors so that it makes them feel sick and wastes a good deal of time altogether, I'll tell you, sir, and you can pass it on, that what was found was *bones,* sir, quite clean and no smell, nothing horrible, you can assure people of that."

"Thank you," I said, a shade numbly.

"Animals and insects had cleaned her, you see."

"Don't you think that fact alone will make people feel sick?"

"Then don't stress it, sir."

"No."

"We have her clothes and shoes and her handbag and lipstick back at the police station . . . they were scattered around her and I've had my men searching . . ." He stopped, not telling me then where the search had occurred; except that if she'd been scavenged it had to have been out of doors. Which for a stable girl, in a way, made sense.

"And, if you don't mind, sir, will you please just tell everyone she's been found, not that she was strangled."

"How do you know that she was strangled if there's nothing much left?"

"The hyoid bone, sir. In the throat. Fractured. Only a direct blow or manual pressure does that. Fingers, usually, from behind."

"Oh, I see. All right, I'll leave it to you. We'd better start with Mr. Vickers's secretary, Dee-Dee."

I steered him into the office and introduced him. Detective Constable Rich followed everywhere like a shadow, a non-speaking taker of notes. I explained to Dee-Dee that Angela Brickell had probably been found.

"Oh, good," she said spontaneously, and then, seeing it wasn't good at all, "Oh, dear."

Doone asked to use the telephone, Dee-Dee at once assenting. Doone called his people back at base.

"Mr. Vickers identified the horse as one that Angela Brickell tended in his stable, and the man as the owner of the horse, or rather the owner's husband. I'd say it's fairly sure we have Angela Brickell in the mortuary. Can you arrange to send round a woman police constable to her parents? They live out Wokingham way. The address is in my office. Do it pronto. We don't want anyone from Shellerton upsetting them first. Break it to them kindly, see? Ask if they could recognize any clothes of hers, or handbag. Ask Mollie to go to them, if she's on duty. She makes it more bearable for people. She mops up their grief. Get Mollie. Tell her to take another constable with her if she wants."

He listened for a moment or two and put down the receiver.

"The poor lass has been dead six months or more," he said to Dee-Dee. "All that's left is sweet clean bones."

Dee-Dee looked as if that thought were sick-making enough, but I could see that Doone's rough humanity would comfort in the end. He was like a stubby-fingered surgeon, I thought: delicate in his handiwork against the odds.

He asked Dee-Dee if she knew of any reason for Angela Brickell's disappearance. Had the girl been unhappy? Having rows with a boyfriend?

"I've no idea. We didn't find out until after she'd gone that she must have given chocolate to Chickweed. Stupid thing to do."

Doone looked lost. I explained about the theobromine. "That's in those clippings, too," I said.

"We found some chocolate bar wrappers with the lass," Doone said. "No chocolate. Is that what was meant in our notes by 'possibly doped a horse in her charge'?"

"Spot on," I said.

"Chocolate!" he said disgustedly. "Not worth dying for."

I said, enlightened, "Were you looking for a big conspiracy? A doping ring?"

"Have to consider everything."

Dee-Dee said positively, "Angela Brickell wouldn't have been in a doping ring. You don't know what you're talking about."

Doone didn't pursue it but said he'd like to talk to the rest of the stable staff, asking Dee-Dee meanwhile not to break the news to anyone else as he would prefer to do it himself. Also he didn't want anyone springing the tragedy prematurely onto the poor parents.

"Surely I can tell Fiona," she protested.

"Who's Fiona?" He frowned, perhaps trying to remember.

"Fiona Goodhaven, who owns Chickweed."

"Oh, yes. Well, not her either. *Especially* not her. I like to get people's first thoughts, first impressions, not hear what they think after they've spent hours discussing something with all their friends. First thoughts are clearer and more valuable, I've found."

He said it with more persuasion than command, with the result that Dee-Dee agreed to stay off the grapevine. She didn't ask how the girl had died. If she realized Doone's remarks best fitted a murder scenario, she didn't say so. Perhaps she simply shied away from having to know.

Doone asked to be taken out to the stables. On the way I asked him to remember, if he met Mackie, Tremayne's daughter-in-law and assistant trainer, that she was newly pregnant.

He gave me a sharp glance.

"You're considerate," I said mildly. "I thought you might want to modify the shocks."

He looked disconcerted but made no promise either way and, as it happened, by the time we reached the yard, Mackie had gone home and Bob Watson was alone there, beavering away with saw, hammer and nails, making a new saddle horse to hold the saddles in the tack room. We found him outside the tack-room door, not too pleased to be interrupted.

I introduced Bob to Doone, Doone to Bob. Doone told him that some human remains discovered by chance were thought to be those of Angela Brickell.

"No!" Bob said. "Straight up? Poor little bitch. What did she do, fall down a quarry?" He looked absentmindedly at a piece of wood he held, as if he'd temporarily forgotten its purpose.

"Why should you say that, sir?" Doone asked attentively.

"Manner of speaking," Bob said, shrugging. "I always thought she'd just scarpered. The guv'nor swore she'd given Chickweed chocolate, but I reckon she didn't. I mean, we all know you mustn't. Anyway, who found her? Where did she go?"

"She was found by chance," Doone said again. "Was she unhappy over a boyfriend?"

"Not that I know of. But there's twenty lads and girls here, and they come and go all the time. Truth to tell, I can't remember much about her, except she was sexy. Ask Mrs. Goodhaven, she was always kind to her. Ask the other girls here, some of them lived in a hostel with her. Why do you want to know about a boyfriend? She didn't take a high jump, did she? Is that what she did?"

Doone didn't say yes or no, and I understood what he'd meant by preferring to listen to unadulterated first thoughts, to the first pictures and conclusions that minds leaped to when questioned.

He talked to Bob for a while longer but as far as I could see learned nothing much.

"You want to see Mackie," Bob said in the end. "That's young Mrs. Vickers. The girls tell her things they'd never tell me."

Doone nodded and I led him and the ubiquitous Rich around the house to Mackie and Perkin's entrance, ringing the bell. It was Perkin himself who came to the door, appearing in khaki overalls, looking wholly an artisan and smelling, fascinatingly, of wood and linseed oil.

"Hello," he said, surprised to see me. "Mackie's in the shower."

Doone took it in his stride this time, introducing himself formally.

"I came to let Mrs. Vickers know that Angela Brickell's been found," he said.

"Who?" Perkin said blankly. "I didn't know anyone was lost. I don't know any Angela . . . Angela who did you say?"

Doone patiently explained she'd been lost for seven or more months. Angela Brickell.

"Good Lord. Really? Who is she?" A thought struck him. "I say, is she the stable girl who buggered off sometime last year? I remember a bit of a fuss."

"That's the one."

"Good then, my wife will be glad she's found. I'll give her the message."

He made as if to close the door but Doone said he would like to see Mrs. Vickers himself.

"Oh? All right. You'd better come in and wait. John? Come in?"

"Thanks," I said.

He led the way into a kitchen–dining room, where I hadn't been before and offered us rattan armchairs around a table made of a circular slab of glass resting on three gothic plaster pillars. The curtains and chair covers were bright turquoise overprinted with blowsy gray, black and white flowers, and all the kitchen fitments were faced with gray-white–streaked Formica; thoroughly modern.

Perkin watched my surprise with irony and said, "Mackie chose everything in a revolt against good taste."

"It's happy," I said. "Lighthearted."

The remark seemed somehow to disturb him, but Mackie herself arrived with damp hair at that point looking refreshed and pleased with life. Her reaction to Doone's first cautious words was the same as everyone else's. "Great. Where is she?"

The gradual realization of the true facts drained the contentment and the color from her face. She listened to his questions and answered them, and faced the implications squarely.

"You're telling us, aren't you," she said flatly, "that either she killed herself . . . or somebody killed her?"

"I didn't say that, madam."

"As good as." She sighed desolately. "All these questions about doping rings . . . and boyfriends. Oh, God." She closed her eyes briefly, then opened them to look at Doone and me.

"We've just had months and months of trouble and anxiety over Olympia and Nolan, we've had the TV people and reporters in droves, driving us mad with their questions, we're only just beginning to feel free of it all . . . and I can't bear it . . . I can't bear it . . . it's *starting all over again*."

10

I borrowed the Land-Rover and at Doone's request led him down to the village and into Harry and Fiona's drive. I was surprised that he still wanted me with him and said so, and he explained a little solemnly that he found people felt less *threatened* by a police officer if he turned up with someone they knew.

"Don't you want them to feel threatened?" I asked. "Many policemen seem to like it that way."

"I'm not many policemen." He seemed uninsulted. "I work in my own way, sir, and if sometimes it's not how my colleagues work then I get my results all the same and it's the results that count in the end. It may not be the best way to the highest promotion"—he smiled briefly—"but I do tend to solve things, I assure you."

"I don't doubt it, Chief Inspector," I said.

"I have three daughters," he said, sighing, "and I don't like cases like this one."

We were standing in the drive looking at the noble façade of a fine Georgian manor.

"Never make assumptions," he said absentmindedly, as if giving me advice. "You know the two most pathetic words a policeman can utter when his case falls apart around him?"

I shook my head.

" 'I assumed,' " he said.

"I'll remember."

He looked at me calmly in his unthreatening way and said it was time to trouble the Goodhavens.

As it happened, only Fiona was there, coming to the kitchen door in a dark-blue tailored suit with a white silk blouse, gold chains, high-heeled black shoes and an air of rush. She smiled apologetically when she saw me.

"John," she said. "What can I do for you? I'm going out to lunch. Can you make it quick?"

"Er . . ." I said, "this is Detective Chief Inspector Doone, Thames Valley Police. And Constable Rich."

"Policemen?" she asked, puzzled; and then in terrible flooding anxiety, "Nothing's happened to Harry?"

"No. No. Nothing. It's not about Harry. Well, not exactly. It's about Angela Brickell. They've found her."

"*Angela . . . ?* Oh, yes. Well, I'm glad. Where did she go?"

Doone was very adroit, I thought, at letting silence itself break the bad news.

"Oh, my dear," Fiona said after a few quiet revelationary seconds, "is she dead?"

"Yes, I'm afraid so, madam." Doone nodded. "I need to ask you a few questions."

"Oh, but . . ." She looked at her watch. "Can't it wait? It's not just a lunch, I'm the guest of honor."

We were still standing on the doorstep. Doone without arguing produced the photograph and asked Fiona to identify the man if she could.

"Of course. It's Harry, my husband. And that's my horse, Chickweed. Where did you get this?"

"From the young woman's handbag."

Fiona's face was full of kindness and regret. "She loved Chickweed," she said.

"Perhaps I could come back when your husband's at home?" Doone suggested.

Fiona was relieved. "Oh, yes, do that. After five tonight or tomorrow morning. He'll be here until about . . . um . . . eleven, I should think, tomorrow. 'Bye, John."

She hurried back into the house, leaving the door open, and presently, from beside our own cars, we saw her come out, lock the back door, hide the key under the stone ("Tut, tut, Doone said disapprovingly") and drive away in a neat BMW, her blond hair shining, cheerful hand waving good-bye.

"If you had to describe her in one word," Doone said to me, "what would it be?"

"Staunch," I said.

"That was quick."

"That's what she is. Steadfast, I'd say."

"Have you known her long?"

"Ten days, like the others."

"Mm." He pondered. "I won't have ten days, not living in their community, like you do. I might ask you again what people here are really like. People sometimes don't act natural when they're with policemen."

"Fiona did. Surely everyone did who you've met this morning?"

"Oh, yes. But there's some I haven't met. And there are loyalties . . . I read the transcript of part of that trial before I came here. Loyalty is strong here, wouldn't you agree? Staunch, steadfast loyalty, wouldn't you say?"

Doone might look gray, I thought, and his chatty, almost singsong Berkshire voice might be disarming, but there was a cunningly intelligent observer behind the waffle, and I did suddenly believe, as I hadn't entirely before, that usually he solved his cases.

He said he would like to speak to all the other stable girls before they heard the news from anyone else, and also the men, but the women first.

I took Doone and Rich to the house in the village which I knew the girls called their hostel, though I'd never been in it. It was a small modern house in a cul-de-sac, bought cheaply before it was built, Tremayne had told me, and appreciating nicely with the years. I explained to Doone that I didn't know all the girls' names: I saw them only at morning exercise and sometimes at evening stables.

"Fair enough," he said, "but they'll all know *you*. You can tell them I'm not an ogre."

I wasn't any longer so sure about that but I did what he asked. He sat paternally on a flower-patterned sofa in the sitting room, at home among the clutter of pot plants, satin cushions, fashion magazines and endless photographs of horses, and told them without drama that it looked possible Angela Brickell had died the day she hadn't returned for evening stables. They had found her clothes, her handbag and her bones, he said, and naturally they were having to look into it. He asked the by now familiar questions: did they think Angela had been deeply involved in doping horses, and did they know if she'd had rows with her boyfriend.

Only four of the six girls had been employed at the yard in Angela's time, they said. She definitely hadn't been doping horses; they found the idea funny. She wasn't bright enough, one of them said unflatteringly. She hadn't been their close friend. She was moody and secretive, they all agreed, but they didn't know of any one steady boyfriend. They thought Sam had probably had her, but no one should read much in that. Who was Sam? Sam Yaeger, the stable jockey, who rode more than the horses.

There were a few self-conscious giggles. Doone, father of

three daughters, interpreted the giggles correctly and looked disillusioned.

"Did Angela and Sam Yaeger quarrel?"

"You don't quarrel with Sam Yaeger," the brightest of them said boldly. "You go to bed with him. Or in the hay."

Gales of giggles.

They were all in their teens, I thought. Light-framed, hopeful, knowing.

The bold girl said, "But no one takes Sam seriously. It's just a bit of fun. He makes a joke of it. If you don't want to, you just say no. Most of us say no. He'd never try to force anyone."

The others looked shocked at the idea. "It's casual with him, like."

I wondered if Doone were thinking that maybe with Angela it hadn't been casual after all.

The bold girl, whose name was Tansy, asked when they'd found the poor little bitch.

"When?" Doone considered briefly. "Someone noticed her last Sunday morning. Mind you, he wasn't in a great hurry to do anything because he could see she'd been lying there peacefully a long time, but then he phoned us and the message reached me late Sunday afternoon while I was sleeping off my wife's Yorkshire pudding, great grub, that is, so Monday I went to see the lass and we started trying to find out who she was, because we have lists of missing people, runaways mostly, you see? Then yesterday we found her handbag, and it had this photo in it, so I came over this morning to check if she was the missing stable girl on our missing persons list. So I should think you could say we really found her this morning."

His voice had lulled them into accepting him on friendly terms and they willingly looked at the photograph he passed around.

"That's Chickweed," they said, nodding.

"You're sure you can tell one horse from another?"

"Of course you can," they said, "when you see them every day."

"And the man?"

"Mr. Goodhaven."

Doone thanked them and tucked the photo away again. Rich took slow notes, none of the girls paying him any attention.

Doone asked if by any chance Angela Brickell had owned a dog. The girls, mystified, said no. Why would he think so? They'd found a dog's collar near her, he explained, and a well-chewed ball. None of them had a dog, Tansy said.

Doone rose to go and told them if anything occurred to them, to send him a message.

"What sort of thing?" they asked.

"Well, now," he said kindly. "We know she's dead, but we want to know how and why. It's best to know. If you were found dead one day, you'd want people to know what happened, wouldn't you?"

Yes, they nodded, they would.

"Where did she go?" Tansy asked.

Doone as near as dammit patted her head, but not quite. I thought that that would have undone all his good fatherly work. Willing they might be, but feminists all, too smart to be patronized.

"We have to do more tests first, miss," he said obscurely. "But soon we hope to make a statement."

They all accepted that easily enough and we said our good-byes, traveling back through the village to a bungalow nearer Bob Watson's house, where the unmarried lads lived.

The living room in the lads' hostel, in sharp contrast to the girls', was plantless, without cushions and grubbily scattered with newspapers, empty beer cans, pornography, dirty plates and muddy boots. Only the televisions and video players in both places looked the same.

The lads all knew that Angela Brickell had been found dead as one of them had learned it from Bob Watson. None of them seemed to care about her personally (exactly like the girls) and had no information and few opinions about her.

"She rode all right," one of them said, shrugging.

"She was a bit of a hot pants," said another.

They identified Chickweed's picture immediately and one of them asked if he could have the photo when the police had finished with it.

"Why?" Doone asked.

"Because I look after the old bugger now, that's why. Wouldn't mind having a snap of him."

"Better take another one," Doone advised him. "By rights this belongs to the lass's parents."

"Well," he later demanded of me, after we'd left. "What do you think?"

"It's *your* job to think," I protested.

He half smiled. "There's a long way to go yet. If you think of anything, you tell me. I'll listen to everything anyone wants to say. I'm not proud. I don't mind the public telling me the answers. Make sure everyone knows that, will you?"

"Yes," I said.

The telephone in Shellerton House began ringing that afternoon in a clamor that lasted for days. However reticent Doone had been, the news had spread at once like a bush fire through the village that *another* young woman connected with Tremayne Vickers's house and stables had been found dead. Newspapers, quickly informed, brusquely demanded to be told where, when and why. Dee-Dee repeated and repeated that she didn't know until she was almost in tears. I took over from her after a while and dispensed enormous courtesy and goodwill but no facts, of which at that time anyway, I knew very few.

I worked on the book and answered the phone most of Friday and didn't see Doone at all, but on Saturday I learned that he had spent the day before scattering fear and consternation.

Tremayne had asked if I would prefer to go to Sandown with Fiona, Harry and Mackie, saying he thought I might find it more illuminating: he himself would be saddling five runners at Chepstow and dealing with two lots of demanding owners besides. "To be frank, you'd be under my feet. Go and carry things for Mackie."

With old-fashioned views he persisted in thinking pregnant women fragile, which Mackie herself tolerated with affection. I wondered if Tremayne understood how little Perkin would like my carrying things for Mackie and determined to be discreet.

"Fiona and Harry are taking Mackie," Tremayne said, almost as if the same thought had occurred to him. "I'll check that they'll take you too, though it's a certainty if they have room."

They had room. They collected Mackie and me at the appointed time and they were very disturbed indeed.

Harry was driving. Fiona twisted around in the front seat to speak to Mackie and me directly and with deep lines of worry told us that Doone had paid two visits to them the day before, the first apparently friendly and the second menacing in the extreme.

"He seemed all right in the morning," Fiona said. "Chatty and easygoing. Then he came back in the evening . . ." She shivered violently, although it was warm in the car, ". . . and he more or less accused Harry of strangling that bloody girl."

"What?" Mackie said. "That's ridiculous."

"Doone doesn't think so," Harry said gloomily. "He says she was definitely strangled. And did he show you that photo of me with Chickweed?"

Mackie and I both said yes.

"Well, it seems he got it enlarged. I mean, blown up really big. He said he wanted to see me alone, without Fiona, and he showed me the enlargement, which was just of me, not the horse. He asked me to confirm that I was wearing my own sunglasses in the photo. I said of course I was. Then he asked me if I was wearing my own belt, and I said of course. He asked me to look carefully at the buckle. I said I wouldn't be wearing anyone else's things. Then he asked me if the pen clipped onto the racecard I was holding in the photo was mine also . . . and I got a bit miffed and demanded to know what it was all about." He stopped for a moment, and then in depression went on. "You won't believe it . . . but they found my sunglasses and my belt and my gold pen lying with that girl, wherever she was, and Doone won't *tell* us where for some God-silly reason. I don't know how the hell those things got there. I told Doone I hadn't seen any of them for ages and he said he believed it. He thought they'd been with Angela Brickell all these months . . . that I'd dropped them when I was with her."

He stopped again, abruptly, and at that point added no more.

Fiona, in a strong mixture of indignation and alarm, said "Doone demanded to know precisely where Harry had been on the day that girl went missing and also he said he might want to take Harry's *fingerprints*."

"He thinks I killed her," Harry said. "It's obvious he does."

"It's ridiculous," Mackie repeated. "He doesn't know you."

"Where *were* you on that day?" I asked. "I mean you might have a perfect alibi."

"I might have," he said, "but I don't know where I was. Could you say for certain what you were doing on the Tuesday afternoon of the second week of June last year?"

"Not for sure," I said.

"If it had been the *third* week," Harry said, "we'd have been at Ascot races. Royal Ascot. Tarted up in top hats and things."

"We keep a big appointments diary," Fiona said fiercely. "I dug up last year's. There's nothing listed at all on that second Tuesday. Neither of us can remember what we were doing."

"No work?" I suggested. "No meetings?"

Harry and Fiona simultaneously said no. Fiona was on a couple of committees for good causes, but there'd been no meetings that day. Harry, whose personal fortune seemed to equal Fiona's in robust good health, had in the past negotiated the brilliant sale of an inherited tire-making company (so Tremayne had told me) and now passed his time lucratively as occasional consultant to other private firms looking for a golden corporate whale to swallow them. He couldn't remember any consultations for most of June.

"We went to see Nolan ride Chickweed at Uttoxeter near the end of May," Fiona said worriedly. "Angela was there looking after the horse. That was the day someone fed him theobromine and caffeine, and if she didn't give Chickweed chocolate herself then she must have let someone else do it. Sheer negligence, probably. Anyway, Chickweed won and Angela went back to Shellerton with him and we saw her a few days later and gave her an extra present, as we were so pleased with the way she looked after the horse. I mean, a horse's success is always partly due to whoever cares for it and grooms it. And I can't remember seeing the wretched girl again after that."

"Nor can I," Harry said.

They went over and over the same old ground all the way to Sandown and it was clear they had spoken of little else since Doone's devastating identification of Harry's belongings.

"Someone must have put those things there to incriminate Harry," Mackie said unhappily.

Fiona agreed with her, but it appeared that Doone didn't.

Harry said, "Doone believes it was an unpremeditated murder. I asked him why and he just said that most murders were unpremeditated. Useless. He said people who commit unpremeditated murder often drop things from extreme agitation and don't know they've dropped them. I said I couldn't even remember ever talking to the girl except in the company of my wife and he simply stared at me, not believing me. I'll tell you, pals, it was unnerving.''

"Awful,'' Mackie said vehemently. *"Wicked.''*

Harry, trying to sound balanced, was clearly horribly disconcerted and was driving without concentration, braking and accelerating jerkily. Fiona said they had thought of not going to Sandown as they weren't in a fun-day mood, but they had agreed not to let Doone's suspicions ruin everything. Doone's suspicions were nevertheless conspicuously wrecking their equilibrium and it was a subdued little group that stood in the parade ring watching Fiona's tough hunter, the famous Chickweed, walk around before the Wilfred Johnstone Hunter 'Chase.

No one, one hoped, had given him chocolate.

Fiona had told Nolan about Doone's accusations. Nolan told Harry that now he, Harry, knew what it was like to have a charge of murder hanging over him he would in retrospect have more sympathy for him, Nolan. Harry didn't like it. With only vestiges of friendliness he protested that he, Harry, had not been found with a dead girl at his feet.

"As good as, by the sound of things," Nolan said, rattled.

"Nolan!'' Fiona wasn't amused. "Everyone, stop talking about it. Nolan, put your mind on the race. Harry, not another word about that *bloody* girl. Everything will be sorted out. We'll just have to be patient.''

Harry gave her a fond but rueful glance and over her shoulder caught my eye. There was something more in his expression, I thought, and after a moment identified it as fear: maybe faint, but definitely present. Harry and fear hadn't, until then, gone together in my mind, particularly not since his controlled behavior in a frozen ditch.

Mackie, *in loco* Tremayne, saw Nolan into the saddle and the four of us walked towards the stands to see the race. With Mackie and Fiona in front, Harry fell into step beside me.

"I want to tell you something," he said, "but not Fiona."

"Fire away."

He looked quickly around him, checking no one could hear.

"Doone said . . . Christ . . . he said the girl had no clothes on when she died."

"God, Harry." I felt my mouth still open, and closed it consciously.

"I don't know what to do," he said.

"Absolutely nothing."

"Doone asked what I was doing there with my belt off." The shock still trembled in his voice.

"The innocent aren't found guilty," I protested.

He said miserably, "Oh, yes, they are. You know they are."

"But not on such flimsy evidence."

"I haven't been able to tell Fiona. I mean, we've always been fine together, but she might start *wondering* . . . I don't honestly know how I'd bear that."

We reached the stands and went up to watch, Harry falling silent in his torturing troubles amid the raucous calls of bookmakers and the enfolding hubbub of the gathering crowd. The runners cantered past on their way to the starting gate, Nolan looking professional as usual on the muscly chestnut that Fiona had ridden all autumn out hunting. Chickweed, Mackie had told me, was Fiona's special pet: her friend as much as her property. Chickweed, circling and lining up, running in the first hunter 'chase of the spring season, was going to win three or four times before June, Tremayne hoped.

We were joined at that point by pudgy unfit Lewis, who panted that he had only just arrived in time and asked if the Jockey Club had said anything about Nolan going on riding.

"Not a word," Fiona said. "Fingers crossed."

"If they were going to stop him," Lewis opined judiciously, taking deep breaths, "they'd surely have let him know by today, so perhaps the expletive sod's got away with it."

"Brotherly love," Fiona remarked ironically.

"He owes me," Lewis said darkly and with such growling intensity that all of us, I thought, recognized the nature of the debt, even if some hadn't wanted to believe it earlier.

"And will you collect?" Harry asked, his sarcasm showing.

"No, thanks to you," Lewis replied sharply.

"Perjury's not my best act."

Lewis smiled like a snake, all fangs.

"I," he said, "am the best bleep bleep actor of you all."

Fiona starkly faced the certainty that Lewis had not after all been too drunk to see straight when Olympia died. Mackie's clear face was pinched with dismay. Harry, who had known all along, would have shrugged off Lewis's admission philosophically were it not for his own ominous future.

"What would you have had me do?" Lewis demanded, seeing the general disapproval. "Say he called her every filthy name in the book and shook her by the neck until her eyes popped out?"

"Lewis!" Fiona exclaimed, not believing him. "Shut up."

Lewis gave me a mediumly hostile glance and wanted to know why I was always hanging around. No one answered him, me included.

Fiona said, "They're off" a split second before the official announcement and concentrated through her raceglasses.

"I asked you an expletive question," Lewis said to me brusquely.

"You know why," I replied, watching the race.

"Tremayne isn't here," he objected.

"He sent me to see Sandown."

Chickweed was easy to spot, I discovered, with the white blaze down his chestnut face that so clearly distinguished him in the photograph nodding away on the rails at every galloping step. The overall pace seemed slower to me than the other races I'd watched, the jumping more deliberate, but it wasn't, as Tremayne had warned me, an easy track even for the sport's top performers, and for hunters a searching test. "Watch them jump the seven fences down the far side," he'd said. "If a horse meets the first one right, the others come in his stride. Miss the first, get it wrong, legs in a tangle, you might as well forget the whole race. Nolan is an artist at meeting that first fence right."

I watched particularly. Chickweed flew the first fence and all the next six down the far side, gaining effortless lengths. "There's nothing like the hunting field for teaching a horse to jump," Tremayne had said. "The trouble is, hunters aren't necessarily fast. Chickweed is, though. So was Oxo, who won the Grand National years back."

Chickweed repeated the feat on the second circuit and then, a length in front of his nearest pursuer, swept around the long bend at the bottom end of the course and straightened himself for the third fence from home—the Pond fence, so called because the small hollow beside it had once been wet, though now held mostly reeds and bushes.

"Oh, come on," Fiona said explosively, the tension too much. "Chicky Chickweed . . . jump it."

Chicky Chickweed rose to it as if he'd heard her, his white blaze showing straight on to us before he veered right towards the second-last fence and the uphill pull to home.

"A lot of races are lost on the hill," Tremayne had told me. "It's where stamina counts, where you need the reserves. Any horse that has enough left to accelerate there is going to win. Same at Cheltenham. A race at either place can change dramatically after the last fence. Tired horses just fade away, even if they're in the lead."

Chickweed made short work of the second-last fence but didn't shake off his pursuer.

"I can't bear it," Fiona said.

Mackie put down her raceglasses to watch the finish, anxiety digging lines on her forehead.

It was only a race, I thought. What did it matter? I answered my own question astringently: I'd written a novel; what did it matter if it won or lost on its own terms. It mattered because I cared, because it was where I'd invested all thought, all effort. It mattered to Tremayne and Mackie the same way. Only a race . . . but also their skill laid on the line.

Chickweed's pursuer closed the gap coming to the last fence.

"Oh, no," Fiona groaned, lowering her own glasses. "Oh, Nolan, come on."

Chickweed made a spectacular leap, leaving unnecessary space between himself and the birch, wasting precious time in the air. His pursuer, jumping lower in a flatter trajectory, landed first and was fastest away.

"Damn," Harry said.

Fiona was silent, beginning to accept defeat.

Nolan had no such thoughts. Nolan, aggressive instincts in full flood, was crouching like a demon over Chickweed's withers delivering the message that losing was unacceptable. Nolan's whip rose and fell twice, his arm swinging hard. Chickweed, as if galvanized, reversed his decision to slow down now that he'd been passed and took up the struggle again. The jockey and horse in front, judging the battle won, eased up fractionally too soon. Chickweed caught them napping a stride from the winning post and put his head in front just where it mattered, the crowd cheering for him, the favorite, the fighter who never gave up.

It was Nolan, I saw, who had won that race. Nolan himself, not the horse. Nolan's ability, Nolan's character acting on Chickweed's. Through Nolan I began to understand how much more there was to riding races than fearlessness and being able to stay in the saddle. More than tactics, more than experience, more than ambition. Winning races, like survival, began in the mind.

Fiona, triumphant where all had looked lost, breathless and shiny-eyed, hurried ahead with Mackie to meet the returning warriors. Lewis, Harry and I pressed along in their wake.

"Nolan's a genius," Harry was saying.

"The other expletive jockey threw it away," Lewis had it.

Never assume, I thought, thinking of Doone. Never assume you've won until you hold the prize in your hand.

Doone *was* assuming things, I thought. Not taking his own advice. Or so it seemed.

We all went for a celebratory drink. though in Mackie's case it was ginger ale. Harry ordered the obligatory bubbles, his heart in his boots. Nolan was as high as Fiona, Lewis a grudging applauder. I, I supposed, an observer, still on the outside looking in. Six of us in a racecourse bar smiling in unison while the cobweb ghosts of two young women set traps for the flies.

We arrived back at Shellerton before Tremayne returned from Chepstow. Fiona dropped Mackie off at her side of the house and I walked round to Tremayne's, unlocking the door with the key he'd given me and switching on lights.

There was a message from Gareth on the family-room corkboard: GONE TO MOVIE. BACK FOR GRUB. Smiling, I kicked the hot logs together and blew some kindling sticks to life with the bellows to revive the fire and poured some wine and felt at home.

A knock on the back door drew me from comfort to see who it was, and I didn't at first recognize the young woman looking at me with a shy inquiring smile. She was pretty in a small way, brown-haired, self-effacing . . . Bob Watson's wife, Ingrid.

"Come in," I said warmly, relieved to have identified her. "But I'm the only one home."

"I thought maybe Mackie. Mrs. Vickers . . ."

"She's round in her own house."

"Oh. Well . . ." She came over the threshold tentatively and I encouraged her into the family room, where she stood nervously and wouldn't sit down.

"Bob doesn't know I'm here," she said anxiously.

"Never mind. Have a drink?"

"Oh, no. Better not."

She seemed to be screwing herself up to something, and out it all finally came in a rush.

"You were ever so kind to me that night. Bob reckons you saved me from frostbite at the least . . . and pneumonia, he said. Giving me your own clothes. I'll never forget it. Never."

"You looked so cold," I said. "Are you sure you won't sit down?"

"I was *hurting* with cold." She again ignored the chair suggestion. "I knew you'd come back just now . . . I saw Mrs. Goodhaven's car come up the road . . . I came to talk to you, really. I've got to tell someone, I think, and you're . . . well . . . easiest."

"Go on then. Talk. I'm listening."

She said in a small burst, unexpectedly, "Angela Brickell was a Roman Catholic, like I am."

"Was she?" The news meant very little.

Ingrid nodded. "It said on the local radio news tonight that Angela's body was found last Sunday by a gamekeeper on the Quillersedge Estate. There was quite a bit about her on the news, about how the police were proceeding with their enquiries and all that. And it said foul play was suspected. They're such stupid words, foul play. Why don't they just say someone probably did her in? Anyway, after she'd vanished last year Mrs. Vickers asked me to clear all

172

her things out of the hostel and send them to her parents, and I did."

She stopped, staring searchingly at my face for under-standing.

"What," I asked, feeling the way, "did you find in her belongings? Something that worries you . . . because she's dead?"

Ingrid's face showed relief at being invited to tell me.

"I threw it away," she said. "It was a do-it-yourself home kit for a pregnancy test. She'd used it. All I found was the empty box."

11

Tremayne came home and frightened Ingrid away like Miss Muffet and the spider.

"What did she want?" he asked, watching her scuttling exit. "She always seems scared of me. She's a real mouse."

"She came to tell me something she thinks should be known," I said reflectively. "I suppose she thought I could do the telling, in her place."

"Typical," Tremayne said. "What was it?"

"Angela Brickell was perhaps pregnant."

"What?" He stared at me blankly. *"Pregnant?"*

I explained about the used test. "You don't buy or use one of those tests unless you have good reason to."

He said thoughtfully, "No, I suppose not."

"So," I said, "there are about twenty lusty males connected with this stable and dozens more in Shellerton and throughout the racing industry, and even if she *were* pregnant, and from what Doone said about bones I don't see how they can tell yes or no, even if she were, it still might have nothing to do with her death."

"But it might."

"She was a Roman Catholic, Ingrid says."

"What's that got to do with it?"

"They're against abortion."

He stared into space.

I said, "Harry's in trouble. Have you heard?"

"No, what trouble?"

I told him about Doone's accusations, and also about Chickweed's way of winning and about Lewis's more or less explicit admission of perjury. Tremayne poured himself a gin and tonic of suitably gargantuan proportions and told me in his turn that he'd had a rotten day at Chepstow. "One of my runners broke down and another went crashing down arse over tip at the last fence with the race in his pocket. Sam dislocated his thumb, which swelled like a balloon, and although he's OK he won't realistically be fit until Tuesday, which means I have to scratch around for a replacement for Monday. And one lot of owners groused and groaned until I could have knocked their heads together and all I can do is be nice to them and sometimes it all drives me up the bloody wall, to tell you the truth."

He flopped his weight into an armchair, stretched out his legs and rested his gaze on his toecaps, thinking things over.

"Are you going to tell Doone about the pregnancy test?" he asked finally.

"I suppose so. It's on Ingrid's conscience. If I don't pass on what she's said, she'll find another mouthpiece."

He sighed. "It won't do Harry much good."

"Nor harm."

"It's a motive. Juries believe in motives."

I grunted. "Harry won't come to trial."

"Nolan did. And a good motive would have jailed him, you can't say it wouldn't."

"The pregnancy test is a nonstarter," I said. "Ingrid threw the empty box away, there's no proof it really existed, there's no saying if Angela used it or when, there's no certainty about the result, there's no knowing who she'd been sleeping with."

"You should have been a lawyer."

Mackie and Perkin came through for their usual drink and news exchange and even Chickweed's win couldn't disperse the general gloom.

"Angela pregnant?" Mackie shook her head, almost bewildered. "She didn't say anything about it."

"She might have done, given time," Tremayne said, "if the test was positive."

"Damned careless of her," Perkin said. "That bloody girl's nothing but trouble. It's all upsetting Mackie just when she should be feeling relaxed and happy, and I don't like it."

Mackie stretched out a hand and squeezed her husband's in gratitude, the underlying joy resurfacing, as persistent as pregnancy itself. Perhaps Angela Brickell too, I speculated, had been delighted to be needing her test. Who could tell?

Gareth gusted in full of plans for an expedition I'd forgotten about, a fact he unerringly read on my face.

"But you said you would teach us things, and we could light a fire." His voice rose high with disappointment.

"Um," I said. "Ask your father."

Tremayne listened to Gareth's request for a patch of land for a campfire and raised his eyebrows my way.

"Do you really want to bother with all this?"

"Actually, I suggested it, in a rash moment."

Gareth nodded vigorously. "Coconut's coming at ten."

Mackie said, "Fiona asked us to go down in the morning to toast Chickweed and cheer Harry up."

"But John *promised*," Gareth said anxiously.

Mackie smiled at him indulgently. "I'll make John's excuses."

* * *

176

Sunday morning crept in grayly on a near-freezing drizzle, enough to test the spirits of all would-be survivors. Tremayne, drinking coffee in the kitchen with the lights on at nine-thirty, suggested scrubbing the whole idea. His son would vehemently have none of it. They compromised on a promise from me to bring everyone home at the first sneeze, and Coconut arrived on his bicycle in brilliant yellow oil-skins with a grin to match.

It was easy to see how he'd got his name. He stood in the kitchen dripping and pulled off a sou'wester to reveal a wiry tuft of light-brown hair sticking straight up from the top of his head. (It would never lie down properly, Gareth later explained.)

Coconut was nearly fifteen. Below the topknot he had bright intelligent eyes, a big nose and a sloppy loose-lipped mouth, as if his face hadn't yet synthesized with his emerging character. Give him a year, I thought, maybe two, then the shell would firm to define the man.

"There's a bit of wasteland at the top of the apple orchard," Tremayne said. "You can have that."

"But, Dad . . ." Gareth began, raising objections.

"It sounds fine," I said firmly. "Survivors can't choose."

Tremayne looked at me and then at Gareth thoughtfully and nodded as if to confirm a private thought.

"But February's a bad month for food," I said, "and I suppose we'd better not steal a pheasant, so we'll cheat a bit and take some bacon with us. Bring gloves and a penknife each. We'll go in ten minutes."

The boys scurried to collect waterproofs for Gareth, and Tremayne asked what exactly I planned to do with them.

"Build a shelter," I said. "Light a fire, gather some lunch and cook it. That'll be enough, I should think. Everything takes forever when you start with nothing."

"Teach them they're lucky."

"Mm."

He came to the door to see off the intrepid expedition, all

of us unequipped except for the survival kit (with added bacon) that I wore around my waist and the penknives in their pockets. The cold drizzle fell relentlessly but no one seemed to mind. I waved briefly to Tremayne and went where Gareth led, which was through a gate in a wall, through a patch of long-deserted garden, through another gate and up a slow gradient through about fifty bare-branched apple trees, fetching up on a small bedraggled plateau roughly fenced with ruined dry-stone walling on one side and a few trees in the remains of a hawthorn hedge full of gaps around the rest. Beyond that untidy boundary lay neat prosperous open acres of winter plowing, the domain of the farmer next door.

Gareth looked at our terrain disgustedly and even Coconut was dismayed, but I thought Tremayne had chosen pretty well, on the whole. Whatever we did, we couldn't make things much worse.

"First of all," I said, "we build a shelter for the fire."

"Nothing will burn in this rain," Gareth said critically.

"Perhaps we'd better go back indoors, then."

They stared in faint shock.

"No," Gareth said.

"Right." I brought the basic survival tin out of my pocket and gave him the coil of flexible saw. "We passed at least four dead apple trees on the way up here. Slide a couple of sticks through the loops at the ends of this saw, and you and Coconut go and cut down one of those dead trees and bring it up here. Cut it as near the ground as you can manage."

It took them roughly three seconds to bounce off with renewed enthusiasm, and I wandered around the decrepit piece of what Tremayne had truly described as wasteland, seeing everywhere possibilities of a satisfactory camp. The whole place, for instance, was pale brown with the dead stalks of last year's unmown grass; an absolute gift.

By the time the boys returned, puffing, red faced and dragging the result of their exertions, I'd wrenched out a few rusty old metal fence posts, cut a lot of living hawthorn switches from the hedge and harvested a pile of the dead grass stalks from a patch near the last row of apple trees. We made a short trip down to the deserted garden to reap a patch of old stinging nettles for bindings, and about an hour after setting off were admiring a free-standing four-foot-square shelter made of a metal frame with a slightly sloping roof of closely latticed hawthorn switches thickly thatched on top with endless piled-on bundles of dried grass. While we watched, the drizzle trickled down the top layer of brownish stalks and dripped off to one side, leaving a small rain-free area underneath.

After that, by themselves, the boys made a simple square frame lashed with thickly crisscrossed hawthorn, which we could lean against any one side of the fire shelter to prevent the wind from blowing rain straight in. Gareth understood without telling and explained it to Coconut matter-of-factly.

"OK," I said. "Next, we find some flat dry stones from that broken-down wall to make a floor for the fire. Don't bring very wet stones, they can explode when they get hot. Then we go around looking for anything very small and dry that will burn. Dead leaves. Bits of fluff caught on fences. Anything inside that wrecked old greenhouse in the garden. When you find something, keep it dry in your pockets. When we've got enough tinder, we'll feather some kindling sticks. We also need enough dry wood, if you can find any. And bring any old cowpats you come across: they burn like peat."

After another hour's labor we had stacked under the fire shelter the remains of an old cucumber frame from the greenhouse and enough dry tinder to take kindly to a flame. Then, working with my hands under the shelter, I showed them how to strip the bark off a wet stick and make shallow lengthwise cuts in the dry deadwood underneath so that fine shavings curled outward and the stick looked feathered all over. They each made one with their knives: Gareth quick and neat, Coconut all thumbs.

Finally with a match, a piece of candle, the tinder of dead leaves and flower heads, the feathered kindling sticks, the cucumber frame and a good deal of luck (but no cowpats), a bright little fire burned healthily against the drizzly odds and Gareth and Coconut looked as if the sun had risen where they didn't expect it.

The smoke curled up and out over the edges of the thatched roofing. I remarked that if we'd had to live there for months we could hang spare meat and fish under the roof to smoke it. Applewood made sweet smoke. Oak would smoke some meats better.

"We couldn't live out here for months." Coconut couldn't imagine it.

"It wasn't always sunny in Sherwood Forest," I said.

We snapped all the smaller twigs off the felled apple tree and added them gradually to the blaze, then made the beginnings of a human-sized shelter by wedging the dead tree as a roof and rear wall between two live trees, bringing more hawthorn to weave through the branches, heaping onto the top and rear surface any boughs, dead plants and turves we could cut and thickly laying a floor below of grass stalks, the nearest thing to straw. Apart from a few drips, we were out of the rain.

Lunch, when we finally ate it after a long forage, consisted mainly of finds from the old garden: some tubers of wild parsley, comfrey and jerusalem artichoke, a handful of very small brussels sprouts (ugh, Gareth said) and a rather bitter green leaf salad of plantain, dock and dandelion (double ugh). Never eat poisonous buttercups, I said, be grateful for dandelions. Coconut flatly refused to contemplate worms, the only things plentiful. Both boys fell on the bacon, threaded and grilled on sharpened peeled sticks, and such was their hunger that they afterwards chewed for ages on strips of the inner sweet bark of a young birch tree that was struggling away in the hedge. Birch bark was good nourishing food, I said. Gareth said they would take my word for it.

We drank rather scummy rainwater found in an old watering can, and boiled in a Coke can Gareth collected from the Shellerton House trash. They declined my offer to make coffee from roast dandelion root. Next time they went camping they would take tea bags, they said.

We were sitting in the shelter, the fire burning red with embers on its stone base a few feet away, the drizzle almost a permanence, the odd foods eaten, the end of the experiment not far ahead.

"How about staying out here all night?" I asked.

They both looked horrified.

"You'd survive," I said, "with shelter and a fire."

"It would be miserable," Gareth said. "It's freezing cold."

"Yes."

There was a pause, then Gareth added, "Survival isn't really much fun, is it?"

"Often not," I agreed. "Just a matter of life or death."

"If we were outlaws in Sherwood Forest," he said, "the Sheriff's men would be hunting us."

"Nasty."

Coconut involuntarily looked around for enemies, shivering at the thought.

"We can't stay out all night. We have to go to school tomorrow," he said.

The relief on both their faces was comical, and I thought that perhaps for a second or two they'd had a vision of a much older, more brutal world where every tomorrow was a struggle, where hunger and cold were normal and danger ever present and cruel. A primitive world, far back from Robin Hood, back from the Druids who'd walked the ancient Berkshire Downs, back where laws hadn't been invented or rights thought of, back before organization, before tribes, before ritual, before duty. Back where the strong ate and the weak died, the bedrock and everlasting design of nature.

When a dark shade of iron seeped into the slate-gray light we pulled the fire to pieces and doused the hot ends in wet grass. Then we stacked the remaining pile of applewood neatly under the fire's roofing and started for home, carrying as little away as we'd brought.

Gareth looked back at the intertwined tree shelter and the dead fireplace and seemed for a moment wistful, but it was with leaps and whoops that he and Coconut ran down from there to re-embrace the familiar constraints of civilization.

"God," Gareth said, barging in through the back door, "lead me to a pizza. To two pizzas, maybe three."

Laughing, I peeled off my long-suffering ski suit and left them to it in the kitchen, heading myself for warmth in the family room; and there I found a whole bunch of depressed souls sprawling in armchairs contemplating a different sort of disastrous tomorrow where food was no problem but danger abounded.

Harry, Fiona, Nolan, Lewis, Perkin, Mackie and Tremayne, all silent, as if everything useful had been said already. Tight-knit, interlocked, they looked at me vaguely, at the stranger within their gates, the unexpected character in their play.

"Ah . . . John," Tremayne said, stirring, remembering, "are both boys still living?"

"More or less."

I poured myself some wine and sat on an unoccupied footstool, feeling the oppression of their collective thoughts and guessing that they all now knew everything I did, and perhaps more.

"If Harry didn't do it, who did?" It was Lewis's question, which got no specific reply, as if it had been asked over and over before.

"Doone will find out," I murmured.

Fiona said indignantly, "He's not trying. He's not looking beyond Harry. It's disgraceful."

Proof that Doone was still casting about, however, arrived noisily at that point in the shape of Sam Yaeger, who hooted his horn outside as a preliminary and swept into the house in a high state of indignation.

"Tremayne!" he said in the doorway, and then stopped abruptly at the sight of the gathered clan. "Oh. You're all here."

"You're supposed to be resting," Tremayne said repressively.

"To hell with bloody resting. There I was, quietly nursing my bruises according to orders, when this Policeman Plod turns up on my doorstep. Sunday afternoon! Doesn't the bugger ever sleep? And d'you know what little gem he tossed at me? Your sodding stable girls told him I'd had a bit of how's-your-father with Angela effing Brickell."

The brief silence which greeted this announcement wasn't exactly packed with disbelief.

"Well, did you?" Tremayne asked.

"That's not the point. The point is that it wasn't any Tuesday last June. So this Doone fellow asks me what I was doing that day, as if I could remember. Working on my boat, I expect. He asked if I logged the hours I worked on it. Is this man for real? I said I hadn't a sodding clue what I was doing, maybe it was a couple of willing maidens, and he has no sense of humor, it's in a permanent state of collapse, he said it wasn't a joking matter."

"He has three daughters," I said. "It worries him."

"I can't help his effing hangups," Sam said. "He said he had to check every possibility, so I told him he'd have a long job considering old Angie's opportunities, not to mention willingness." He paused. "She was even making goo-goo eyes at Bob Watson at one time."

"She wouldn't have got past Ingrid," Mackie said. "Ingrid looks meek and mild but you should see her angry. She

keeps Bob in her sight. She doesn't trust any girl in the yard.
I doubt if Angela got anywhere with Bob."

"You never know," Sam said darkly. "Can I have a
drink? Coke?"

"In the fridge in the kitchen," Perkin said, not stirring to
fetch it.

Sam nodded, went out and came back carrying a glass,
followed by Gareth and Coconut busily stoking their fur-
naces with pizza wedges.

Tremayne raised his eyebrows at the food.

"We're starving," explained his younger son. "We ate
roots, and birch bark and dandelion leaves, and no one in
their right mind would live in Sherwood Forest being chased
by the Sheriff."

Sam looked bewildered. "What *are* you on about?" he
demanded.

"Survival," Gareth said. He marched over to a table,
picked up *Return Safe from the Wilderness* and thrust it into
Sam's hands. "John wrote it," he said, "and five other books
like it. So we built a shelter and made a fire and cooked roots
and boiled water to drink . . ."

"What about Sherwood Forest?" Harry drawled, smiling
but looking strained notwithstanding.

Coconut explained, "We might be cold and hungry but
there weren't any enemies lurking behind the apple trees."

"Er . . ." Sam said.

Tremayne, amused, enlightened everyone about our day.

"Tell you what," Gareth said thoughtfully, "it makes you
realize how lucky you are to have a bed and a pizza to come
home to."

Tremayne looked at me from under lowered lids, his
mouth curving with contentment. "Teach them they're
lucky," he'd said.

"Next time," Coconut inquired, "why don't we make
some bows and arrows?"

"What for?" asked Perkin.

"To shoot the Sheriff's men, of course."

"You'd wind up hanged in Nottingham," Tremayne said. "Better stick to dandelion leaves." He looked at me. "Is there going to be a next time?"

Before I could answer, Gareth said, "Yes." He paused. "Well, it wasn't all a laugh a minute, but we did *do* something. I could do it again. I could live out in the cold and the rain . . . I feel good about it, that's all."

"Well done!" Fiona exclaimed sincerely. "Gareth, you're a great boy."

It embarrassed him, of course, but I agreed with her.

"How about it?" Tremayne asked me.

"Next Sunday," I said, "we could go out again, do something else."

"Do what?" Gareth demanded.

"Don't know yet."

The vague promise seemed enough for both boys, who drifted back to the kitchen for further supplies, and Sam, leafing through the book, remarked that some of my more ingenious traps looked as if they would kill actual people, not only big animals like deer.

"Eating venison in Sherwood Forest was a hanging matter too," Harry observed.

I said, agreeing with Sam, "Some traps aren't safe to set unless you know you're alone."

"If Gareth's confident after one day," Nolan said to me without much friendliness from the depths of an armchair, "what does that make you? Superman?"

"Humble," I said, with irony.

"How very goody-goody," he said sarcastically, with added obscenities. "I'd like to see you ride in a steeplechase."

"So would I," Tremayne said heartily, taking the sneering words at face value. "We might apply for a permit for you, John."

No one took him seriously. Nolan took offense. He didn't

like even a semihumorous suggestion that anyone else should muscle in on his territory.

Monday found Dee-Dee in tears over Angela Brickell's pregnancy test. Not tears of sympathy, it seemed, but of envy.

Monday also found Doone on our doorstep, wanting to check up on the dates when Chickweed had won and Harry had been there to watch.

"Mr. Goodhaven?" Tremayne echoed. "It's Mrs. Goodhaven's horse."

"Yes, sir, but it was Mr. Goodhaven's photo the dead lass was carrying."

"It was the *horse's* photo," Tremayne protested. "I told you before."

"Yes, sir," Doone agreed blandly. "Now, about those dates . . ."

In suppressed fury, Tremayne sorted the way through the form book and his memory, saying finally that there had been no occasion that he could think of when Harry had been at the races without Fiona.

"How about the fourth Saturday in April?" Doone asked slyly.

"The what?" Tremayne looked it up again. "What about it?"

"Your traveling head lad thinks Mrs. Goodhaven had flu that day. He remembers her saying later at Stratford, when the horse won but failed the dope test later, that she was glad to be there, having missed his last win at Uttoxeter."

Tremayne absorbed the information in silence.

"If Mr. Goodhaven went alone to Uttoxeter," Doone insinuated, "and Mrs. Goodhaven was at home tucked up in bed feeling ill . . ."

"You really don't know what you're talking about," Tremayne interrupted. "Angela Brickell was in charge of a *horse.* She couldn't just go off and leave it. And she came back here with it in the horse box. I'd have known if she hadn't, and I'd have sacked her for negligence."

"But I understood from your traveling head lad, sir," Doone said with singsong deadliness, "that they had to wait for Angela Brickell that day at Uttoxeter because when they were all ready to go home she couldn't be found. She *did* leave her horse unattended, sir. Your traveling head lad decided to wait another half hour for her, and she turned up just in time, and wouldn't say where she'd been."

Tremayne said blankly, "I don't remember any of this."

"No doubt they didn't trouble you, sir. After all, no harm had been done . . . had it?"

Doone left one of his silences hovering, in which it was quite easy to imagine the specific harm that could have been done by Harry.

"There's no privacy for anything odd on racecourses," Tremayne said, betraying the path his own thoughts had taken. "I don't believe a word of what you're hinting."

"Angela Brickell died about six weeks after that," Doone said, "by which time she'd used a pregnancy test."

"Stop it," Tremayne said. "This is supposition of the vilest kind, aimed at a good intelligent man who loves his wife."

"Good intelligent men who love their wives, sir, aren't immune to sudden passions."

"You've got it wrong," Tremayne said doggedly.

Doone rested a glance on him for a long time and then transferred it to me.

"What do you think, sir?" he asked.

"I don't think Mr. Goodhaven did anything."

"Based on your ten days' knowledge of him?"

"Twelve days now. Yes."

He ruminated, then asked me slowly, "Do you yourself have any feeling as to who killed the lassie? I ask about feeling, sir, because if it were solid knowledge you would have given it to me, wouldn't you?"

"Yes, I would. And no, I have no feeling, no intuition, unless it is that it was someone unconnected with this stable."

"She worked here," he said flatly. "Most murders are close to home." He gave me a long assessing look. "Your loyalties, sir," he said, "are being sucked into this group, and I'm sorry about that. You're the only man here who couldn't have any hand in the lassie's death, and I'll listen to you and be glad to, but only if you go on seeing straight, do you get me?"

"I get you," I said, surprised.

"Have you asked Mr. Goodhaven about the day he went racing without his wife?" Tremayne demanded.

Doone nodded. "He denies anything improper took place. But then, he would."

"I don't want to hear any more of this," Tremayne announced. "You're inventing a load of rubbish."

"Mr. Goodhaven's belongings were found with the lassie," Doone said without heat, "and she carried his photograph, and that's not rubbish."

In the silence after this somber reminder he took his quiet leave and Tremayne, very troubled, said he would go down to the Goodhavens' house to give them support.

Fiona however telephoned while he was on his way, and I answered the call because Dee-Dee had already gone home, feeling unwell.

"John!" she exclaimed. "Where's Tremayne?"

"On his way down to you."

"Oh. Good. I can't tell you how awful this is. Doone thinks . . . he says . . ."

"He's been here," I said. "He told us."

"He's like a bulldog." Her voice shook with distress. "Harry's strong, but this . . . this *barrage* is wearing him down."

"He's desperately afraid you'll doubt him," I said.

"What?" She sounded overthrown. "I don't, for a minute."

"Then tell him."

"Yes, I will." She paused briefly. "Who did it, John?"

"I don't know."

"But you'll see. You'll see what we're too close to see.
Tremayne says you understand things without being told,
more than most people do. Harry says it comes of all those
qualities his Aunt Erica wouldn't allow you, insight through
imagination and all that."

They'd been discussing me; odd feeling.

I said, "You might not want to know."

"Oh." It was a cry of admission, of revelation. "John
. . . save us all."

She put the phone down without waiting for a response to
her extraordinary plea, and I wondered seriously what they
expected of me, what they saw me to be: the stranger in their
midst who would solve all problems as in old-fashioned
westerns, or an eminently ordinary middling writer who was
there by accident and would listen to everyone but in the end
be ineffectual. Given a choice, I would without question
have opted for the latter.

By Tuesday the press had been drenched with leaks from
all quarters. Trial by public opinion was in full swing, the
libel laws studiously skirted by a profligate scattering of the
word "alleged" but the underlying meaning plain: Harry
Goodhaven had allegedly bedded a stable girl, got her pregnant and throttled her to save his marriage to a "wealthy
heiress," without whose money he would be penniless.

Wednesday's papers, from Harry's point of view, were
even worse, akin to the public pillory.

He phoned me soon after lunch.

"Did you see the bloody tabloids?"

"Yes," I said.

"If I come and pick you up, will you just come out driving with me?"

"Sure."

"Fine. Ten minutes."

Without many twinges of conscience I laid aside my notes on Tremayne's midcareer. With two weeks already gone of my four-week allocation I was feeling fairly well prepared to get going on the page, but as usual any good reason for postponing it was welcome.

Harry came in his BMW, twin of Fiona's, and I climbed in beside him, seeing more new lines of strain in his face and also rigidity in his neck muscles and fingers. His fair hair looked almost gray, the blue eyes altogether without humor, the social patina wearing thin.

"John, good of you," he said. "Life's bloody."

"I'll tell you one thing." I tried a shot at comfort. "Doone knows there's something wrong with his case, otherwise he would have arrested you already." I settled into the seat beside him, fastening the belt.

He glanced my way as he put the car into gear and started forward. "Do you think so? He keeps coming back. He's on our doorstep every day. Every day, a new pinprick, a new awkward bloody circumstance. He's building a cage round me, bar by bar."

"He's trying to break your nerve," I said, guessing. "Once he'd arrested and charged you, the papers would have to leave you alone. He's letting them have a field day, waiting for someone to remember something and waiting for you to crack and incriminate yourself. I shouldn't think he's tried to stop any of the leaks since the press found out where the girl was lying and he had to make an official statement. Maybe he's even organized a leak or two himself; I wouldn't put it past him."

Harry turned the nose of the car towards Reading to travel by the hilly route that would take us through the

Quillersedge Estate. I wondered why he'd gone that way but I didn't directly ask him.

"Yesterday," he said bitterly, "Doone asked me what Angela Brickell had been wearing. It's been in all the papers. He asked me if she'd undressed willingly. I could have strangled him . . . Oh, God, what am I saying?"

"Shall I drive?" I asked.

"What? Oh, yes—we nearly hit that post . . . I didn't see it. No, I'm all right. Really I am. Fiona says not to let him rattle me, she's being splendid, absolutely marvelous, but he *does* rattle me, I can't help it. He tosses out these lethal questions as if they were harmless afterthoughts . . . 'Did she undress willingly?' How can I answer? I wasn't there."

"That's the answer."

"He doesn't believe me."

"He isn't sure," I said. "Something's bothering him."

"I wish it would bother him into an early grave."

"His successor might be worse. Might prefer a conviction to the truth. Doone does at least seek the truth."

"You can't mean you like him!" The idea was an enormity.

"Be grateful for him. Be glad you're still free." I paused. "Why are we going this way?"

The question surprised him. "To get to where we're going, of course."

"So we're not just out for a drive?"

"Well, no."

"All around you," I said, "is the Quillersedge Estate."

"I suppose so," he said vaguely. Then: "Dear God, we go along this road all the time. I mean, everyone in Shellerton goes to Reading this way unless it's snowing."

A long stretch of the road was bordered on each side by mixed woodland, dripping now with yesterday's rain and looking bare-branched and bedraggled in the scrag end of winter. Part of the woodland was thinned and tamed and fenced neatly with posts and wire, policed with no-trespassing notices: part was wild and open to anyone caring to push through the tangle of trees, saplings and their assorted undergrowth. Five yards into that, I thought, and one would be invisible from the road. Only the strongly motivated, though, would try to go through it: it was no easy afternoon stroll.

"Anyway," Harry said, "the Quillersedge Estate goes on for miles. This is just the western end of it. The place where they found Angela was much nearer Bucklebury."

"How do you know?"

"Dammit, it was in the papers. Are *you* doubting me now?" He was angered and disconcerted by my question, then shook his head in resignation. "That was a Doone question. How do I know? Because the Reading papers printed a map, that's how. The gamekeeper put his X on the spot."

"I don't doubt you," I said. "If I doubted you I would doubt my own judgment too, and in your case I don't."

"I suppose that's a vote of confidence."

"Yes."

We drove a fair way along the roads and through villages unknown to me, going across country to heaven knew where. Harry, however, knew where, and down a mostly uninhabited lane turned through some broken gateposts into a rutted drive leading to a large sagging barn, an extensive dump of tangled metal and wood and a smaller barn to one side. Beyond this unprepossessing mess lay a wide expanse of muddy gray water sliding sluggishly by with dark wooded hills on the far side.

"Where are we?" I asked, as the car rolled to a stop, the only bright new thing in the general dilapidation.

"That's the Thames," Harry said. "Almost breaking its banks, by the look of things, after all that rain and melted snow. This is Sam's boatyard, where we are now."

"This?" I remembered what Sam had said about useful squalor: it had been an understatement.

"He keeps it this way on purpose," Harry confirmed. "We all came here for a huge barbecue party he gave to celebrate being champion jockey . . . eighteen months ago, I suppose. It looked different that night. One of the best parties we've been to . . ." His voice tailed off as if his thoughts had moved away from what his mouth was saying; and there was sweat on his forehead.

"What's making you nervous?" I asked.

"Nothing." It was clearly a lie. "Come with me," he said jerkily. "I want someone with me."

"All right. Where are we going?"

"Into the boathouse." He pointed to the smaller of the barns. "That big place on the left is Sam's workshop and dock where he works on his boats. The boathouse isn't used much, I don't think, though Sam made it into a grotto the night of the party. I'm going to meet someone there." He looked at his watch. "I'm a bit early. Don't suppose it will matter."

"Who are you going to meet?"

"Someone," he said, and got out of the car. "I don't know who. Look," he went on, as I followed him, "someone's going to tell me something which may clear me with Doone. I just . . . I wanted *support* . . . a witness, even. I suppose you think that's stupid."

"No."

"Come on, then."

"I'll come, but don't put too much hope on anyone keeping the appointment. People can be pretty spiteful, and you've had a rotten press."

"You think it's a hoax?" The idea bothered him, but he'd obviously considered it.

"How was the meeting arranged?"

"On the telephone," he said. "This morning. I didn't know the voice. Don't even know if it was a man or a woman. It was low. Sort of careful, I suppose, looking back."

"Why here," I asked, "of all places?"

He frowned. "I've no idea. But I can't afford not to listen, if it's something which will clear me. I can't, can I?"

"I guess not."

"I don't really like it either," he confessed. "That's why I wanted company."

"All right." I shrugged. "Let's wait and see."

With relief he smiled wanly and led the way across some rough ground of stones and gnarled old weeds, joining a path of sorts that ran from the big barn to the boathouse and following that to our destination.

Close to, the boathouse was if anything less attractive than from a distance, though there were carved broken eaves that had once been decorative in an Edwardian way and could have been again, given the will. The construction was mostly of weathered old brick, the long sidewalls going down to the water's edge, the whole built on and into the river's sloping bank.

True to Sam's philosophy, the ramshackle wooden door had no latch, let alone a padlock, and pushed inward, opening at a touch.

Windows in the walls gave plenty of light, but inside all one could see was a bare wooden floor stretching to double glass doors leading to a railed balcony overhanging the swollen river.

"Don't boathouses have water in them?" I inquired mildly.

"The water's underneath," Harry said. "This room was for entertaining. There's another door down by the edge of the river for going into the boat dock. That's where the grotto was. Sam had put colored lights all round and some actually in the water . . . it looked terrific. There was a bar up here in this room. Fiona and I went out onto the balcony with our drinks and looked at the skyful of stars. It was a warm night. Everything perfect." He sighed. "Perkin and Mackie were with us, smooching away in newlywed bliss. It all seems so long ago, when everyone was happy, everything simple. Nothing could go wrong . . . And Tremayne had a spectacular year and to crown it Top Spin Lob won the National . . . and since then not much has gone right."

"Did Sam invite Nolan to his party?"

Harry smiled briefly. "Sam felt good. He asked Dee-Dee, Bob Watson, the lads, everyone. Must have been a hundred and fifty people. Even Angela . . ." He stopped and looked at his watch. "It's just about time."

He turned and took a step towards the far-end balcony, the ancient floorboards creaking underfoot.

There was a white envelope lying on the floor about half-way to the balcony and, saying perhaps it was a message, he went towards it and bent to pick it up, and with a fearsome crack a whole section of the floor gave way under his weight and shot him, shouting, into the dock beneath.

12

It happened so fast and so drastically that I nearly slid after him, managing only instinctively to pivot on one foot and throw myself headlong back onto the boards still remaining solid behind the hole.

Harry, I thought ridiculously, was dead unlucky with cold dirty water. I wriggled until I could peer over the edge into the wet depths below and I couldn't see him at all.

Shit, I thought, peeling off my jacket. Come up, for God's sake, Harry, so I can pull you out.

No sign of him. Nothing. I yelled to him. No reply.

I kicked off my boots and swung down below, holding on to a bared crossbeam that creaked with threat, swinging from one hand while I tried to see Harry and not land on top of him.

All that was visible was brownish opaque muddy water. No time for anything except getting him out. I let go of the beam and dropped with bent legs so as to splash down softly and felt the breath rush out of my lungs from the iciness of the river. Letting the water buoy up my weight, I stretched my feet down to touch bottom and found the water came up to my ears; took a deep breath, put the rest of my head under and reached around for Harry, unable to see him, unable with open eyes to see anything at all.

He had to be there. Time was short. I stood up for a gasp of air, ducked down again, searching with fingers, with feet, with urgency turning to appalling alarm. I could feel things, pieces of metal, sharp spiky things, nothing living.

Another gasp of air. I looked for bubbles rising, hoping to find him that way, and saw not bubbles but a red stain in the water a short way off, a swirl of color against drab.

At least I'd found him. I dived towards the scarlet streaks and touched him at once, but there was no movement in him, and when I tried to pull him to the surface, I couldn't.

Shit . . . Shit . . . Stupid word kept repeating in my brain. I felt and slid my arms under Harry's and with my feet slipping on the muddy bottom yanked him upwards as fiercely as I could and found him still stuck and yanked again twice more with increasing desperation until finally whatever had been holding him released its grasp and he came shooting to the surface, only to begin falling sluggishly back again as a deadweight.

With my own nose barely above water I held him with his head just higher than mine, but he still wasn't breathing. I laced my arms around his back, under his own arms, letting his face fall on mine, and in that awkward position I blew my own breath into him, not in the accepted way with him lying flat with most things in control, but into his open nostrils, into his flaccid mouth, into either or both at once, as fast as I could, trying to pump his chest in unison, to do what his own intercostal muscles had stopped doing, pulling his rib cage open for air to flow in.

They tell you to go on with artificial respiration forever,

for long after you've given up hope. Go on and on, I'd been told. Don't give up. Don't ever give up.

He was heavy in spite of the buoyancy from the water. My feet went numb down on the mud. I blew my breath into him rhythmically, faster than normal breathing, squeezing him, telling him, ordering him in my mind to take charge of himself, come back, come back . . . Harry, come back . . .

I grieved for him, for Fiona, for all of them, but most for Harry. That humor, that humanity; they couldn't be lost. I gave him my breath until I was dizzy myself and I still wouldn't accept it was all useless, that I might as well stop.

I felt the jolt in his chest as I hugged it in rhythm against mine and for a long second couldn't believe it, but then he heaved again in my arms and coughed in my face and a mouthful of dirty water shot out in a spout and he began coughing in earnest and choking and gasping for air . . . gasping, gulping air down, wheezing in his throat, whooping like whooping cough, struggling to fill his functioning lungs.

He couldn't have been unconscious for long, looking back, but it seemed an eternity at the time. With coughing, he opened his eyes and began groaning, which was at least some sign of progress, and I started looking about to see how we were going to get out of what appeared to be uncomfortably like a prison.

Another door, Harry had said, down by the river's edge: and in fact, when I looked I could see it, a once-painted slab of wood set in brickwork, its bottom edge barely six inches above the water.

Across the whole end of the building, stretching from the ceiling down into the river, was a curtain of linked metal like thick oversized chicken wire, presumably originally installed to keep thieves away from any boat in the dock. Beyond it flowed the heavy main stream, with small eddies curling along and through the wire on the surface.

The dock itself, I well understood, was deeper than usual because of the height of the river. The door was still six inches above it, though . . . it didn't make sense to build a door high if the water was usually lower . . . not unless there was a step somewhere . . . a step or a walkway even, for the loading and unloading of boats . . .

Taking Harry gingerly with me, I moved to the left, towards the wall, and with great relief found that there was indeed a shelf there at about the height of my waist. I lifted Harry until he was sitting on the walkway and then, still gripping him tightly, wriggled up beside him so that we were both sitting there with our heads wholly above water, which may not sound a great advance but which was probably the difference between life and death.

Harry was semiconscious, confused and bleeding. The only good thing about the extreme cold of the water, I thought, was that whatever the damage, the blood loss was being minimized. Apart from that, the sooner we were out of there, the better.

The hole through which Harry had fallen was in the center of the ceiling. If I stood up on the walkway, I thought, I could probably stretch up and touch the ceiling, but wouldn't be able to reach the hole. Might try jumping . . . might pull more of the floor down. It didn't look promising. There seemed to be part of a beam missing in the area. Rotted through, no doubt.

Meanwhile I had to get Harry well propped so that he wouldn't fall forward and drown after all, and to do that I reckoned we needed to be in the corner. I tugged him gently along the walkway, which was made of planks, I discovered, with short mooring posts sticking up at intervals, needing me to lift his legs over one at a time. Still, we reached the end in a while, and I stood up and tugged him back until he was sitting wedged in the corner, supported by the rear and side walls.

He had stopped coughing, but still looked dazed. The blood streaking scarlet was from one of his legs, now stretched out straight before him but still not in view on account of the clouded water. I was debating whether to try to stop the bleeding first or to leave him in his uncertain state while I found a way out, trusting he wouldn't totally pass out, when I heard the main door creak open directly above our heads; the way Harry and I had come in.

My first natural impulse was to shout, to get help from whoever had come: and between intention and voice a whole stream of thoughts suddenly intruded and left me silent, open mouthed to call out but unsure of the wisdom.

Thoughts. Harry had come to this place to meet someone. He didn't know who. He'd been given a meeting place he knew of. He'd gone there trustingly. He'd walked into the boathouse and tried to pick up an envelope and the floor had given way beneath him and a piece of beam was missing, and if I hadn't been there with him he would certainly have drowned in the dock, impaled on something lurking beneath the surface.

Part of my later training had been at the hands of an ex-SAS instructor whose absolute priority for survival was evading the enemy; and with doubt but also awareness of danger I guessed at an enemy above our heads, not a savior. I waited for exclamations of horror from above, for someone to call Harry's name in alarm, for some natural innocent reaction to the floor's collapse.

Instead there was silence. Then the creak of a step or two, then the sound of the door being quietly closed.

Eerie.

All sounds from outside were muffled because of the dock being partly below ground level, set into the slope of the bank, but in a short while I heard the sound of a car door slamming and after that the noise of an engine starting up and being driven away.

Harry suddenly said, "Bloody hell." A couple of sweet words. Then he said, "What the hell's happening?" and then, "God, my leg hurts."

"We came through the boathouse floor." I pointed to the

hole. "The floorboards gave way. You landed on something that pierced your leg."

"I'm f–freezing."

"Yes, I know. Are you awake enough to sit here on your own for a bit?"

"John, for God's sake . . ."

"Not long," I said hastily. "I'll not leave you long."

As I stood on the walkway, the water level reached above my knees, and I waded along beside the wall in the direction of the lower door and the river. There were indeed steps by the door, three steps up and a flat landing along below the door itself. I went up the steps until the water barely covered my ankles and tried the doorlatch.

This time, no easy exit. The door was solid as rock.

On the wall beside the door there was a row of three electric switches. I pressed them all without any results from the electric-light bulbs along the ceiling. There was also a control box with cables leading to the top of the metal curtain: I opened the box and pressed the red button and the green button to be found inside there but again nothing changed in the boathouse.

The arrangement for raising the curtain was a matter of gear wheels designed to turn a rod to wind the metal mesh up onto it like a blind. The sides of the curtain were held in tracks to help it run smoothly. Without electricity however it wasn't going to oblige. On the other hand, because of its construction, the whole barrier had to be reasonably light in weight.

"Harry?" I called.

"God, John . . ." His voice sounded weak and strained.

"Sit there and don't worry. I'll come back."

"Where . . . are you going?" There was fear in his voice but also control.

"Out."

"Well . . . hurry."

"Yes."

I slipped back into the water and swam a couple of strokes to the curtain. Tried standing up, but the water was much deeper there. Hung on to the wire, feeling the tug of the eddies from the river.

With luck, with extreme luck, the curtain wouldn't go all the way down to the river's bed. It had no practical need to reach down further than the drought level of the river, which had to leave a gap of at least two or three feet. From the weight point of view, a gap was sensible.

Simple.

I took a breath and pulled myself hand over hand down the curtain, seeking to find the bottom of it with my feet: and there was indeed a gap between the bottom edge of the curtain and the mud, but only a matter of inches, and there was clutter down there, unidentifiable, pressing against the barrier, trying to get past it.

I came up for air.

"Harry?"

"Yes."

"There's a space under the metal curtain. I'm going out into the river and I'll be back for you very soon."

"All right." More control this time: less fear.

Deep breath. Dived, pulling myself down the wire. Came to the end of it, felt the mud below. The bottom edge of the curtain was a matter of free links, not a connecting bar. The links could be raised, but only singly, not altogether.

Go under it, I told myself. The temptation to return safely back up where I'd come from was enormous. Go *under* . . .

I swung down at the bottom, deciding to go headfirst, faceup, curling my back down into the soft riverbed, praying . . . *praying* that the links wouldn't catch on my clothes . . . in my knitted sweater . . . should have stripped . . . head under, metal lying on my face, push the links up with hands, full strength, take care, don't rush, don't snag clothes, get free of the jumble of things on the mud around me, hold on to the wire outside, don't let go, the current in the river was appreciable, tugging, keep straight, *hang on,* shoulders through, raise the links, back through, bottom through, legs . . . links . . . short of breath . . . lungs hurting . . . careful, careful . . . unknown things around my ankles, hampering . . . *had* to breathe soon . . . feet catching . . . feet . . . *through.*

The river immediately floated my free legs away as if it would have them, and I had to grab the wire fiercely to avoid going with the current. But I was through and not stuck in the dreadful clutch of metal links, not grasped by debris, not drowning without any chance of rescue.

I came up into the air, gasping deeply, panting, aching lungs swelling, feeling a rush of suppressed terror, clinging on to the curtain in a shaky state.

"Harry?" I called.

The dock looked dark beyond the curtain and I couldn't see him, but he could indeed see me.

"Oh, John . . ." His relief was beyond measure. "Thank God."

"Not long now," I said, and heard the strain in my own voice too.

I edged along the curtain in the upstream direction of the shut door and by hauling my way up the links at the side managed to scramble around the boathouse wall and up out of the water to roll at last onto the grassy bank. Bitterly cold, shivering violently from several causes, but *out.*

I stood up with knees that felt like buckling and tried to open the door into the dock; and it was as immovable from outside as from in. It had a mortise lock, a simple keyhole and no key.

Perhaps the best thing to do, I thought despairingly, was to find a telephone and get professional help: the fire brigade and an ambulance. If I couldn't find a telephone in Sam's big workshop I could drive Harry's car to the nearest house . . .

Big snag.

Harry's car had gone.

My mind started playing the shit tape monotonously.

Before I did anything, I thought, I needed to put on my boots. Went into the boathouse through the top door.

Another big snag.

No boots.

No ski-suit jacket either.

Harry's voice came from below, distant and wavery, "Is anyone there?"

"It's me—John," I shouted. "Just hold on."

No reply. He was weaker, perhaps. Better hurry.

There was now no doubt about murderous intention on someone's part and the certainty made me perversely angry, stimulating renewed strength and a good deal of bloody-mindedness. I ran along the stony path to Sam's large shed in my socks and hardly felt the discomfort, and found to my relief that I could get inside easily enough—no lock on the door.

The space inside looked as much like a junkyard as the space outside. The center, I saw briefly, was occupied by a large boat on blocks, its superstructure covered with light-weight gray plastic sheeting.

I spent a little precious time searching for a telephone, but couldn't find one. There was no office, no place partitioned off or locked. Probably Sam kept good tools somewhere, but he'd hidden them away.

All around lay old and rusting tools and equipment, but among the junk I found almost at once two perfect aids: a tire lever and a heavy mallet for driving in mooring pegs.

With those I returned at speed to the boathouse and at-tacked the lower door, first hammering the toe of the tire lever into a nonexistent crack between the wooden door-frame and the surrounding brickwork at a level just below the keyhole, then bashing the far end of that iron, to put heavy leverage against the doorframe, then wrenching out the lever and repeating the whole process above the lock, this time with fury.

The old wood of the doorframe gave up the struggle and splintered, freeing the tongue of the lock, and without much more trouble I pulled the door open towards me, swinging it wide. I left the tire lever and mallet on the grass and stepped down into the boathouse, the shocking chill of the water again a teeth-gritter.

At least, I thought grimly, it was a calm day. No windchill to speak of, to polish us off.

I waded along to Harry, who was sagging back against the corner, his head lolling only just above the surface.

"Come on," I said urgently. "Harry, wake up."

He looked at me apathetically through a mist of weakness and pain and one could see he'd been in that water a lot too long. Apathy, like cold, was a killer. I bent down and turned him until I had my hands under his arms, his back towards me, and I floated him along in the water to the steps and there strained to pull him up them and out onto the grass.

"My leg," he said, moaning.

"God, Harry, what do you weigh?" I asked, lugging.

"None of your bloody business," he mumbled.

I half laughed, relieved. If he could say that, for all his suffering, he wasn't in a dying frame of mind. It gave me enough impetus to finish the exit, though I dare say he, like me, felt only marginally warmer for being on land.

His leg seemed to have stopped bleeding, or very nearly, and he couldn't have severed an artery or he'd have bled to death by then, but all the same there had to be a pretty serious wound under the cloth of his trousers and the faster I could get him to a doctor the better.

As far as I remembered from our arrival, the boatyard lay down a lane with no houses nearby: I'd have a fair run in my socks to find help.

On the other hand, among the general clutter, only a few feet off, I could see the upturned keel of an old clinker-built rowboat. Small. Maybe six feet overall. A one-man job, big enough for two. If it weren't full of holes . . .

Leaving Harry briefly, I went to the dinghy and heaved it over right side up. Apart from needing varnish and loving care it looked seaworthy, but naturally there were no rowlocks and no oars.

Never mind. Any piece of pole would do. Plenty lying about. I picked up a likely length and laid it in the boat.

The dinghy had a short rope tied to its bow: a painter.

"Harry, can you hop?" I asked him.

"Don't know."

"Come on. Try. Let's get you in the boat."

"In the *boat*?"

"Yes. Someone's taken your car."

He looked bewildered, but the whole afternoon must have seemed so unbelievable to him that hopping into a boat would seem to be all of a piece. In any case, he made feeble efforts to help me get him to his left foot, and with my almost total support he made the few hops to reach the boat, though I could see it hurt him sorely. I helped him sit down on the one center thwart and arranged his legs as comfortably as possible, Harry cursing and wincing by turns.

"Hang on tight to the sides," I said. "Tight."

"Yes."

He didn't move, so I pulled his hands out and positioned them on the boat's edges.

"Grip," I said fiercely.

"Fine." His voice was vague, but his hands tightened.

I tugged and lugged the dinghy until it was sliding backwards down the bank, and then held on to the painter, digging my heels in, leaning back to prevent too fast and splashy a launch. At the last minute, when the stern hit the swollen water and the dinghy's progress flattened out, I jumped in myself and simply hoped against all reasonable hope that we wouldn't sink at once.

We didn't. The current took the dinghy immediately and

started it on its way downstream, and I edged past Harry into the stern space behind him and retrieved my piece of pole.

"What's that?" Harry asked weakly, trying to make sense of things.

"Rudder."

"Oh."

I made a crook of my left elbow on the back of the boat and laid the pole across it, the shorter end in my right hand, the longer end trailing behind in the water. The steering was rudimentary, but enough to keep us traveling bowfirst downstream.

Downstream was always the way to people . . . Bits of the guidebooks floated familiarly to the surface. *Some of your traps are horrific.*

Some of the traps described how to arrange for the prey to fall through seemingly firm ground into a pitful of spikes beneath.

Everyone had read the guides.

"John?" Harry said. "Where are we going?"

"Maidenhead, possibly. I'm not quite sure."

"I'm bloody cold."

There was some water in the boat now, sloshing about under our feet.

Shit.

Nowhere on the Thames was far from civilization, not even Sam's boatyard. The wide river narrowed abruptly with a notice on our left saying DANGER in huge letters, and a smaller notice saying LOCK with an arrow to the right.

I steered the dinghy powerfully to the right. DANGER led to a weir. A lock would do just fine. Locks had keepers.

At about then I took note that there weren't in fact any other boats moving on the river, and I remembered that often the locks closed for maintenance in winter and maybe the lockkeeper would have gone shopping . . .

Never mind. There were houses in sight on the right.

DICK FRANCIS

They proved to be summer cottages, all closed.

We floated on as if in a timeless limbo. The water in the bottom of the boat grew deeper. The current, away from the main stream, was much weaker. The lock cut seemed to last forever, narrowing though, with high dark trees on the left; finally, blessedly, on the right, there were moorings for boats wanting passage through the lock to the lower level of the river below. No boats there, of course. No helping hands. Never mind.

I took the dinghy as far as we could go, right up near to the lock gates. Tied the painter to a mooring post and stepped up out of the boat.

"Won't be long," I told Harry.

He nodded merely. It was all too much.

I climbed the steps up onto the lock and knocked on the door of the lockkeeper's house, and through great good fortune found him at home. A lean man; kind eyes.

"Fell in the river, did you?" he asked cheerfully, observing my soaked state. "Want to use the phone?"

13

I went with Harry in the ambulance to Maidenhead hospital, both of us swathed in blankets, Harry also in a foil-lined padded wrap used for hypothermia cases; and from then on it was a matter of phoning and reassuring Fiona and waiting to see the extent of Harry's injuries, which proved to be a pierced calf, entry and exit wounds both clean and clotted, with no dreadful damage in between.

While Fiona was still on her way, the medics stuffed Harry full of antibiotics and other palliatives and put stitches where they were needed, and by the time she'd wept briefly in my arms he was warm and responding nicely in a recovery room somewhere.

"But why," she asked, half cross, half mystified, "did he go to Sam's boatyard in the first place?" Like a mother scolding her lost child, I thought, after he's come back safe: just like Perkin with Mackie.

"He'll tell you about it," I said. "They say he's doing fine."

"You're damp!" She disengaged herself and held me at arm's length. "Did you fall through the floor too?"

"Sort of." The hospital's central heating had been doing a fine job of drying everything on me and I felt like one of those old-fashioned clotheshorses, steaming slightly in warm air. Still no shoes or boots; couldn't be helped.

Fiona looked at my feet dubiously.

"I was going to ask you to drive Harry's car home," she said, "but I suppose you can't."

I explained that Harry's car had already been driven away.

"Where is it, then?" she asked, bewildered. "Who took it?"

"Maybe Doone will find out."

"That man!" She shivered. "I hate him."

Before I could comment, a nurse came to fetch her to see Harry, and she went anxiously, calling over her shoulder for me to wait for her; and when she returned half an hour later she looked dazed.

"Harry's sleepy," she said. "He kept waking up and telling me silly things . . . How could you possibly get to this hospital in a *boat*?"

"I'll tell you on the way home. Would you like me to drive?"

"But . . ."

"It's quite easy with bare feet. I'll take off my socks."

She unlocked the car herself and handed me the keys without comment. We arranged ourselves in the seats, and as we headed for Shellerton in the early dark I told her calmly, incompletely and without terrors, the gist of what had befallen us in Sam's boatyard.

She listened with a frown, adding her own worry.

"Turn right here," she said once, automatically, and another time, "Sorry, we should have turned left there, we'll have to go back," and finally, "Go straight to Shellerton House. I'll drive home from there. I'm all right, really. It's just so upsetting. It made me shaky, seeing Harry dopey like that, pumped full of drugs."

"I know."

I pulled up outside Tremayne's house and while I put on my socks again she said she would come in for a while for company, "to cure the trembles."

Tremayne, Mackie and Perkin were all in the family room for the usual evening drinks. Tremayne made more than his usual fuss over Fiona, sensing some sort of turmoil, telling her comfortably that Mackie had just come back from Ascot races where he'd sent a runner for the three-mile chase which had proved a total waste of time.

The note I'd left for Tremayne, GONE OUT WITH HARRY, BACK FOR GRUB, was still pinned to the corkboard. He took my arrival with Fiona as not needing comment.

"I think someone tried to kill Harry," Fiona said starkly, cutting abruptly through Tremayne's continuing Ascot chat.

"What?"

There was an instant silence and general shock on all the faces, including Fiona's own.

"He went to Sam's boatyard and fell through some floorboards and was nearly drowned . . ." She told it to them much as I'd told her myself. "If John hadn't been with him to help . . ."

Tremayne said robustly, "My dearest girl, it must have been the most dreadful accident. Whoever would want to kill Harry?"

"No one," Perkin said, his voice an echo of Tremayne's. "I mean, what for?"

"Harry's a dear," Mackie said, nodding.

"You'd never think so to read the papers recently," Fiona pointed out, lines creasing her forehead. "People can be incredibly vicious. Even people in the village. I went into the shop this morning and everyone stopped talking and stared at me. People I've known for years. I told Harry and he was furious, but what can we do? And now this . . ."

"Did Harry say someone tried to kill him?" Perkin asked.

Fiona shook her head. "Harry was too dopey."

"Does John think so?"

Fiona glanced at me. "John didn't actually say so. It's what I think myself. What I'm afraid of. It scares me to think of it."

"Then don't, darling." Mackie put an arm around her and kissed her cheek. "It's a frightening thing to have happened, but Harry *is* all right."

"But someone stole his car," Fiona said, hollow-eyed.

"Perhaps he left the key in the ignition," Tremayne guessed, "and a passerby saw an opportunity."

Fiona agreed unwillingly. "Yes, he would have left his keys. He trusts people. I've told him over and over again that you simply *can't* these days."

They all spent time reassuring Fiona until the worst of the worry unwound from her body and I watched the movement of her silver-blond hair in the soft lights and made no attempt to throw doubts because it would have achieved nothing good.

With Doone, early the next afternoon, it was a different matter. He'd had my bald account of events over the telephone in the morning, his first knowledge of what had happened. Now he came into the dining room where I was working and sat down opposite me at the table.

"I hear you're a proper little hero," he said dryly.

"Oh, really? Who says so?"

"Mr. Goodhaven."

I stared back blandly with the same expression that he was trying on me. The morning's bulletin on Harry had been good, the prognosis excellent, his memory of events reportedly clarifying fast.

"Accident or attempted murder?" Doone asked, apparently seeking a considered answer.

I gave him one. "The latter, I'd say. Have you found his car?"

"Not yet." He frowned at me with a long look in which I read nothing. "Where would you search for it?" he asked.

After a pause I said, "At the top of a cliff."

He blinked.

"Don't you think so?" I said.

"Beachy Head? Dover?" he suggested. "A long drive to the sea."

"Maybe a metaphorical cliff," I said.

"Go on, then."

"Is it usual," I asked, "for policemen to ask for theories from the general public?"

"I told you before, I like to hear them. I don't always agree, but sometimes I do."

"Fair enough. Then what would you have thought if Harry Goodhaven had disappeared forever yesterday afternoon and you'd found his car later by a cliff, real or metaphorical?"

"Suicide," he said promptly. "An admission of guilt."

"End of investigation? Books closed?"

He stared at me somberly. "Perhaps. But unless we eventually found a body, there would also be the possibility of simple flight. We would alert Australia . . . look for him round the world. The books would remain open."

"But you wouldn't investigate anyone else, because you would definitely consider him guilty."

"The evidence points to it. His flight or suicide would confirm it."

"But something about that evidence bothers you."

I was beginning to learn his expressions, or lack of them. The very stillness of his muscles meant that I'd touched something he'd thought hidden.

"Why do you say so?" he asked eventually.

"Because you've made no arrest."

"That simple."

"Without your knowledge, I can only guess."

"Guess away," he invited.

"Then I'd say perhaps Harry's sunglasses and pen and belt were with Angela Brickell because she took them there herself."

"Go on," he said neutrally. It wasn't, I saw, a new idea to him.

"Didn't you say her handbag had been torn open, the contents gone except for the photo in a zipped pocket?"

"I did say so, yes."

"And you found chocolate wrappings lying about?"

"Yes."

"And traces of dogs?"

"Yes."

"And any dog worth his salt would bite open a handbag to get to the chocolate?"

"It's possible." He made a decision and a big admission. "There were toothmarks on the handbag."

"Suppose then," I said, "that she did in fact have a thing about Harry. He's a kind and attractive man. Suppose she did carry his photo with the horse, not Fiona's, who's the owner, after all. Suppose she'd managed to acquire personal things of Harry's, his sunglasses, a pen, even a belt, and wore them or carried them with her, as young people do. They'd only be evidence of her crush on Harry, not of his presence at her death."

"I considered all that, yes."

"Suppose someone couldn't understand why you didn't arrest Harry, particularly in view of all the hounding in the papers, and decided to remove any doubts you might be showing?"

He sat for a while without speaking, apparently debating how many of his thoughts to share. Not many more, it transpired.

"Whoever took Harry's car," I said, "removed my jacket and boots as well. I took them off before I went through the floor into the dock."

"Why didn't you tell me that?" He seemed put out, severe.

"I'm telling you now." I paused. "I would think that whoever took those things is very worried indeed now to find that I was with Harry and that he is alive. I'd say there wasn't supposed to be any reason to think Harry had gone to Sam's boatyard. No one would ever have looked for him there. I'd say it was an attempt to confirm Harry's guilt that went disastrously wrong, leaving you with bristling new doubts and a whole lot more to investigate."

He said formally, "I would like you to be present at the boatyard tomorrow morning."

"What do you think of the place?" I asked.

"I've taken statements from Mr. and Mrs. Goodhaven and others," he said stiffly. "I haven't been to the boatyard yet. It has however, been cordoned off. Mr. Yaeger is meeting me there tomorrow at nine A.M. I would have preferred this afternoon but it seems he is riding in three races at Wincanton."

I nodded. Tremayne had gone there, also Nolan. Another clash of the Titans.

"You know," Doone said slowly, "I had indeed started to question others besides Mr. Goodhaven."

I nodded. "Sam Yaeger for one. He told us. Everyone knew you'd begun casting wider."

"The lass had been indiscriminate," he said regretfully.

Tremayne lent me his Volvo to go to the boatyard in the morning, reminding me before I set off that it was the day of the awards dinner at which he was to be honored.

I'd seen the invitation pinned up prominently by Dee-Dee in the office: most of the racing world, it seemed, would be there to applaud. For Tremayne, though he made a few self-deprecating jokes about it, the event gave proof of the substance of his life, much like the biography.

Sam and Doone were already in the boatyard by the time I'd found my way there, neither of them radiating joy, Sam's multicolored jacket only emphasizing the personality clash with gray plainclothes. They'd been waiting for me, it seemed, in a mutual absence of civility.

"Right, sir," Doone said, as I stood up out of the car, "we've done nothing here so far. Moved nothing. Please take us through your actions of Wednesday afternoon."

Sam said crossly, "Asking for bloody trouble, coming here."

"As it turned out," Doone said placidly. "Go on, Mr. Kendall."

"Harry said he was due to meet someone in the boathouse, so we went over there." I walked where we'd gone, the others following. "We opened this main door. It wasn't locked."

"Never is," Sam said.

I pushed open the door and we looked at the hole in the floor.

"We walked in," I said. "Just talking."

"What about?" Doone asked.

"About a great party Sam gave here once. Harry was saying there had been a bar here in the boathouse and a grotto below. He began to walk down to the windows and saw an envelope on the floor and when he bent to pick it up the floor creaked and gave way."

Sam looked blank.

"Is that likely?" Doone asked him. "How long ago was the floor solid enough to hold a party on it?"

"A year last July," Sam said flatly.

"Quick bit of rot," Doone commented in his singsong voice.

Sam made no answer, in itself remarkable.

"Anyway," I said, "I took off my boots and jacket and left

them up here and I dropped into the water, because Harry hadn't come up for air, like I told you."

"Yes," Doone said.

"You can see better from the lower door," I remarked, turning to go down the path. "This door down here leads into the dock."

Sam disgustedly fingered the splintered doorframe.

"Did you do this?" he demanded. "It wasn't locked."

"It was," I said. "With no key in sight."

"The key was in the keyhole on the inside."

"Absolutely not," I said.

Sam pulled the door open and we looked into the scene that was all too familiar to my eyes: an expanse of muddy water, the hole in the ceiling overhead and the curtain of iron mesh across the exit to the river; a dock big enough for a moderate-sized cabin cruiser or three or four smaller boats.

The water smelled dankly of mud and winter, which I hadn't seemed to notice when I'd been in it.

"There's a sort of walkway along this right-hand wall," I told Doone. "You can't see it now because of the flood-water."

Sam nodded. "A mooring dock, with bollards."

"If you care to walk along there," I suggested, deadpan, "I'll show you an interesting fact about that hole."

They both stared at the water with reluctance stamped all over their faces, then Sam's cleared as he thought of a more palatable solution.

"We'll go and look in a boat."

"How about the curtain?"

"Roll it up, of course."

"Now, wait," Doone said. "The boat can wait. Mr. Kendall, you came through the hole, found Mr. Goodhaven and brought him to the surface. You sat him on the dock, then dived out under the curtain and climbed onto the bank. Is that right?"

"Yes, except that while I was pulling Harry along to that far corner to give him better support, someone opened the main door above our heads, like I told you, and then went away without saying anything, and I heard a car drive off, which might have been Harry's."

"Did you hear any car *arriving*?" Doone asked.

"No."

"Why didn't you call out for help?"

"Harry had been enticed here . . . It all felt like a trap. People who set traps come back to see what they've caught."

Doone gave me another of his assessments.

Sam said, frowning, "You can't have dived out under the curtain, it goes right down to the riverbed."

"I sort of slithered under it."

"You took a bloody risk."

"So do you," I said equably, "most days of the week. And I didn't have much choice. If I hadn't found a way out we'd both eventually have died of cold or drowning, or both. Certainly by now. Most likely Wednesday night."

After a short thoughtful silence Doone said, "You're out on the bank. What next?"

"I saw the car had gone. I went to collect my boots and jacket, but they'd gone too. I called to Harry to reassure him, then I went over to that big shed to find a telephone, but I couldn't."

Sam shook his head. "There isn't one. When I'm here I use the portable phone from my car."

"I couldn't find any decent tools, either."

Sam smiled. "I hide them."

"So I used a rusty tire lever and a mallet, and I'm sorry about your woodwork."

Sam shrugged.

"Then what?" Doone asked.

"Then I got Harry out here and put him in a dinghy and we . . . er . . . floated down to the lock."

"My dinghy!" Sam exclaimed, looking at the imitation scrapyard. "It's gone!"

"I'm sure it's safe down at the lock," I said. "I told the lockkeeper it was yours. He said he'd look after it."

"It'll sink," Sam said. "It leaks."

"It's out on the bank."

"You'll never make a writer," he said.

"Why not?"

"Too bloody sensible."

He read my amusement and gave me a twisted grin.

I said, "What happens to the rubbish lying in the dock when you roll up the curtain?"

"Bloody sodding hell!"

"What are you talking about?" Doone asked us.

"The bed of this dock is mud, and it slopes downwards towards the river," I said. "When the curtain's rolled up, there's nothing to stop things drifting out by gravity into the river and being moved downstream by the current. Bodies often float to the surface, but you of all people must know that those who drown in the Thames can disappear altogether and are probably taken by undercurrents down through London and out to sea." Sometimes from my high Chiswick window I'd thought about horrors down below the surface, out of sight. Like hidden motives, running deadly, running deep.

"Everyone in the Thames Valley knows they disappear." Doone nodded. "We lose a few holidaymakers every year. Very upsetting."

"Harry's leg was impaled on something," I said mildly. "He was stuck underwater. He'd have been dead in a very few minutes. Next time Sam rolled the curtain up, Harry would have drifted quietly out of here, I should think, and no one would ever have known he'd been here. If his body were found anywhere downstream, well then, it could be suicide. If it wasn't found, then he'd escaped justice." I paused, and asked Sam directly, "How soon would you have rolled up the curtain?"

He answered at once. "Whenever I'd found the hole in the floor. I'd have gone to take a look from beneath. Like we're going to now. But I hardly ever come over here. Only in summer." He gave Doone a sly look. "In the summer I bring a mattress."

"And Angela Brickell?" Doone asked.

Sam, silenced, stood with his mouth open. A bull's-eye, I thought, for the detective chief inspector.

I asked Sam, "What's under the water in the dock?"

"Huh?"

"What did Harry get stuck on?"

He brought his mind back from Angela Brickell and said vaguely, "Haven't a clue."

"If you raise the curtain," I said, "we may never know."

"Ah." Doone stared judiciously at Sam, all three of us still clustered around the open door. "It's a matter for grappling irons, then. Can we get a light inside there?"

"The main switch for here is over in the shed," Sam said as if automatically, his mind's attention elsewhere. "There's nothing in the dock except maybe a couple of beer cans and a radio some clumsy bimbo dropped when she was teetering out of a punt in high heels. I ask you . . ."

"Harry wasn't impaled on a radio," I said.

Sam turned away abruptly and walked along the path to his workshop. Doone made as if to go after him, then stopped indecisively and came back.

"This could have been an accident, sir," he said uneasily.

I nodded. "A good trap never looks like one."

"Are you quoting someone?"

"Yes. Me. I've written a good deal about traps. How to set them. How to catch game. The books are lying about all over the place in Shellerton. Everyone's dipped into them. Follow the instructions and kill your man."

"You're not joking by any chance, are you, sir?"

I said regretfully, "No, I'm not."

"I'll have to see those books."

"Yes."

Sam came back frowning and, stretching inside without stepping into the water, pressed the three switches that had been unresponsive two days earlier. The lights in the ceiling came on without fuss and illuminated the ancient brick walls and the weathered old gray beams which crossed from side to side, holding up the planks of the floor above: holding up the planks, except where the hole was.

Doone looked in briefly and made some remark about returning with assistance. Sam looked longer and said to me challengingly, "Well?"

"There's a bit of beam missing," I said, "isn't there?"

He nodded unwillingly. "Looks like it. But I didn't know about it. How could I?"

Doone, in his quiet way a pouncer, said meaningfully, "You yourself, sir, have all the knowledge and the tools for tampering with your boathouse."

"I didn't." Sam's response was belligerence, not fear. "Everyone knows this place. Everyone's been here. Everyone could cut out a beam that small, it's child's play."

"Who, precisely?" Doone asked. "Besides you?"

"Well . . . anybody. Perkin! He could. Nolan . . . I mean, most people can use a saw, can't they? Can't you?"

Doone's expression assented but he said merely, "I'll take another look upstairs now, if you please, sir."

We went in gingerly, but as far as one could tell the floor was solid except for the one strip over the missing bit of beam. The floorboards themselves were gray with age, and dusty, but not worm-eaten, not rotten.

Sam said, "The floorboards aren't nailed down much. Just here and there. They fit tightly most of the time because of the damp, but when we have a hot dry summer they shrink and you can lift them up easily. You can check the beams for rot."

"Why are they like that?" Doone asked.

"Ask the people who built it," Sam said, shrugging. "It was like this when I bought it. The last time I took the floorboards up was for the party, installing colored spotlights and strobes in the ceiling underneath."

"Who knew you took the floorboards up?" Doone asked.

Sam looked at him as if he were retarded. "How do I know?" he demanded. "Everyone who asked how I'd done the lighting, I told them."

I went down on my knees and edged towards the hole.

"Don't do that," Doone exclaimed.

"Just having a look."

The way the floorboards had been laid, I saw, had meant that the doctored beam had been a main load-bearer. Several of the planks, including those that had given way under Harry's weight, had without that beam's support simply been hanging out in space, resting like a seesaw over the previous beam but otherwise supported only by the tight fit of each plank against the next. The floorboards hadn't snapped, as I'd originally thought: they'd gone down into the dock with Harry.

I tested a few planks carefully with the weight of my hand, then retreated and stood up on safer ground.

"Well?" Doone said.

"It's still lethal just each side of the hole."

"Right." He turned to Sam. "I'll have to know, sir, when this tampering could have been carried out."

Sam looked as if he'd had too much of the whole thing. With exasperation he said, "Since when? Since Christmas?"

Doone said stolidly, "Since ten days ago."

Sam briefly gave it some thought. "A week last Wednesday I dropped off a load of wood here on my way to Windsor races. Thursday I raced at Towcester. Friday I spent some time here, half a day. Saturday I raced at Chepstow and had a fall and couldn't ride again until Tuesday. So Sunday I spent nursing myself until you came knocking on my door, and Monday I spent here, pottering about. Tuesday I was back racing at Warwick. Wednesday I went to Ascot, yesterday Wincanton, today Newbury . . ." He paused. "I've never been here at nights."

"What races did you ride in on Wednesday afternoon?" Doone asked. "At Ascot."

"What races?"

"Yes."

"The two-mile hurdle, novice hurdle, novice chase."

I gathered from Doone's face that it wasn't the type of answer he'd expected, but he pulled out a notebook and wrote down the reply as given, checking that he'd got it right.

Sam, upon whom understanding had dawned, said, "I wasn't here driving Harry's bloody car away, if that's what you're thinking."

"I'll need to ascertain a good many people's whereabouts on Wednesday afternoon," Doone said placidly in a flourish of jargon. "But as for now, sir, we can proceed with our investigations without taking any more of the time of either of you two gentlemen, for the present."

"Class dismissed?" Sam said with irony.

Doone, unruffled, said we would be hearing from him later.

Sam came with me to where I'd parked Tremayne's car on stone-strewn grass. The natural jauntiness remained in his step but there was less confidence in his thoughts, it seemed.

"I like Harry," he said, as we reached the Volvo.

"So do I."

"Do you think I set that trap?"

"You certainly could have."

"Sure," he said. "Dead easy. But I didn't."

He looked up into my face, partly anxious, partly still full of his usual machismo.

"Unless you killed Angela Brickell," I said, "you wouldn't have tried to kill Harry. Wouldn't make sense."

"I didn't do the silly little bimbo any harm." He shook his head as if to free her from his memory. "She was too intense for me, if you want to know. I like a bit of a giggle, not remorse and tears afterwards. Old Angie took everything seriously, always going on about mortal sin, and I got bloody damned tired of it, and of her, tell the truth. She wanted me to marry her!" His voice was full of the enormity of such a thought. "I told her I'd got my sights set on a high-born heiress and she damned near scratched my eyes out. A bit of a hellcat, she could be, old Angie. And hungry for it! I mean, she'd whip her clothes off before you'd finished the question."

I listened with fascination to this insider viewpoint, and the moody Miss Brickell suddenly became a real person, not a pathetic collection of dry bones, but a mixed-up pulsating young woman full of strong urges and stronger guilts who'd piled on too much pressure, loaded her need of penitence and her heavy desires and perhaps finally her pregnancy onto someone who couldn't bear it all, and who'd seen a violent way to escape her.

Someone, I thought with illumination, who knew how easily Olympia had died from hands around the neck.

Angela Brickell had to have invited her own death. Doone, I supposed, had known that all along.

"What are you thinking?" Sam asked, uncertainly for him.

"What did she look like?" I said.

"Angie?"

"Mm."

"Not bad," he said. "Brown hair. Thin figure, small tits, round bottom. She agonized about having breast implants. I told her to forget the implants, what would her babies think? That turned on the taps, I'll tell you. She bawled for ages. She wasn't much fun, old Angie, but bloody good on a mattress."

What an epitaph, I thought. Chisel it in stone.

Sam looked out over the flooding river and breathed in the damp smell of the morning as if testing wine for bouquet, and I thought that he lived through his senses to a much greater degree than I did and was intensely alive in his direct approach to sex and his disregard of danger.

He said cheerfully, as if shaking off murder as a passing inconvenience, "Are you going to this do of Tremayne's tonight?"

"Yes. Are you?"

He grinned. "Are you kidding? I'd be shot if I wasn't there to cheer. And anyway"—he shrugged as if to disclaim sentiment—"the old bugger deserves it. He's not all bad, you know."

"I'll see you there, then," I said, agreeing with him.

"If I don't break my neck." It was flippantly said, but an insurance against fate, like crossed fingers. "I'd better tell this sodding policeman where the main electric switch is. I've got it rigged so no one can find it but me, as I don't want people being able to walk in here after dark and turn the lights on. Inviting vandalism, that is. When the force have finished here, they can turn the electric off."

He bounced off towards Doone, who was writing in his notebook, and they were walking together to the big boatshed as I drove away.

Even after having done the week's shopping en route, I was back at Shellerton House as promised in good time for Tremayne to drive his Volvo to Newbury races. He had sent three runners off in the horse box and was taking Mackie to assist, leaving me to my slowly growing first chapter in the dining room.

When they'd gone Dee-Dee came in, as she often did now, to drink coffee over the sorted clippings.

I said, "I hope Tremayne won't mind my taking all these with me when I go home."

"Home . . ." Dee-Dee smiled. "He doesn't want you to go

home, didn't you know? He wants you to write the whole book here. Any day now he'll probably make you an offer you can't refuse."

"I came for a month. That's what he said."

"He didn't know you then." She took a few mouthfuls of coffee. "He wants you for Gareth, I think."

That made sense, I thought; and I wasn't sure which I would choose, to go or to stay, if Dee-Dee was right.

When she'd returned to the office I tried to get on with the writing but couldn't concentrate. The trap in Sam's boathouse kept intruding and so did Angela Brickell; the cold threat of khaki water that could rush into aching lungs to bring oblivion and the earthy girl who'd been claimed back by the earth, eaten clean by earth creatures, become earth-digested dust.

Under the day-to-day surface of ordinary life in Shellerton the fish of murder swam like a shark, silent, unknown, growing new teeth. I hoped Doone would net him soon, but I hadn't much faith.

Fiona telephoned during the afternoon to say that she'd brought Harry home and he wanted to see me, so with a sigh but little reluctance I abandoned the empty page and walked down to the village.

Fiona hugged me like a long-lost brother and said Harry still couldn't be quite clear in his mind as he was saying now that he remembered drowning. However could one remember drowning?

"Quite hard to forget, I should think."

"But he didn't drown!"

"He came close."

She led me into the pink and green chintzy sitting-room where Harry, pale with blue shadows below the eyes, sat in an armchair with his bandaged leg elevated on a large upholstered footstool.

"Hello," he said, raising a phantom smile. "Do you know a cure for nightmares?"

"I have them awake," I said.

"Dear God." He swallowed. "What's true, and what isn't?"

"What you remember is true."

"Drowning?"

"Mm."

"So I'm not mad."

"No. Lucky."

"I told you," he said to Fiona. "I tried not to breathe, but in the end I just did. I didn't mean to. Couldn't help it."

"No one can," I said.

"Sit down," Fiona said to me, kissing Harry's head. "What's lucky is that Harry had the sense to take you with him. And what's more, everyone's apologizing all over the place except for one vile journalist who says it's possible a misguided vigilante thought getting rid of Harry the only path to real justice, and I want Harry to sue him, it's truly vicious."

"I can't be bothered," Harry said in his easygoing way. "Doone was quite nice to me! That's enough."

"How's the leg?" I asked.

"Lousy. Weighs a couple of tons. Still, no gangrene as yet."

He meant it as a joke but Fiona looked alarmed.

"Darling," he said placatingly, "I'm bloated with antibiotics, punctured with tetanus jabs and immunized against cholera, yellow spotted mountain fever and athlete's foot. I have it on good authority that I'm likely to live. How about a stiff whisky?"

"No. It'll curdle the drugs."

"For John, then."

I shook my head.

"Take Cinderella to the ball," he said.

"What?"

"Fiona to Tremayne's party. You're going, aren't you?"

I nodded.

"I'm not leaving you," Fiona protested.

"Of course you are, love. It wouldn't be the same for Tremayne if you weren't there. He dotes on you. John can take you. And"—his eyes brightened mischievously with reawakening energy—"I know who'd love to use my ticket."

"Who?" his wife demanded.

"Erica. My sainted aunt."

14

The Lifetime Award to Tremayne was the work of a taken-over revitalized hotel chain aiming to crash the racing scene with sponsorship in a big way. They, Castle Houses, had put up the prize for a steeplechase and had also taken over a prestigious handicap hurdle race already in the program for Saturday.

The cash on offer for the hurdle race had stretched the racing world's eyes wide and excited owners into twisting their trainers' arms so that the entries had been phenomenal (Dee-Dee said). The field would be the maximum allowed on the course for safety, and several lightweights had had to be balloted out.

As a preliminary to their blockbuster, Castle Houses had arranged the award dinner and subsidized the tickets so that more or less everyone could afford them. The dinner was being held on the racecourse, in the grandstand with its almost limitless capacity; and the whole affair, Mackie had told me, was frankly only a giant advertisement, but everyone might as well enjoy it.

Before we went we met in the family room, Tremayne pretending nonchalance and looking unexpectedly sophisticated in his dinner jacket: gray hair smooth in wings, strong features composed, bulky body slimmed by ample expert tailoring. Perkin's jacket by contrast looked a shade too small for him and in hugging his incipient curves diminished the difference between the sizes of father and son.

Gareth's appearance surprised everyone, especially Tremayne: he made a bravado entrance to cover shyness in a dinner jacket no one knew he had, and he looked neat, personable and much older than fifteen.

"Where did you get that?" his father asked, marveling.

"Picked it off a raspberry bush." He smiled widely. "Well, actually, Sam said I was the same height as him now and he happened to have two. So he's lent it to me. OK?"

"It's great," Mackie said warmly, herself shapely in a shimmering black dress edged with velvet. "And John's jacket, I see, survived the plunge into the ditch."

The ditch seemed a long time ago: two weeks and three days back to the lonely silent abandoned struggle in the attic, to the life that seemed now to be the dream, with Shellerton the reality. Shellerton the brightly lit stage, Chiswick the darkened amphitheater where one sat watching from the balcony.

"Don't get plastered tonight, John," Tremayne said. "I've a job for you in the morning."

"Do you know how to avoid a hangover forever?" Gareth asked me.

"How?" I said.

"Stay drunk."

"Thanks a lot," I said, laughing.

Tremayne, happy with life, said, "You feel confident riding Drifter now, don't you?"

"More or less," I agreed.

"Tomorrow you can ride Fringe. I own a half-share in him. He's that five-year-old in the corner box. You can school him over hurdles."

I must have looked as astonished as I felt. I glanced at Mackie, saw her smiling, and knew she and Tremayne must have discussed it.

"Second lot," Tremayne said. "Ride Drifter first lot as usual."

"If you think so," I said a shade weakly.

"If you stay here a bit longer," Tremayne said, "and if you ride schooling satisfactorily, I don't see why you shouldn't eventually have a mount in an amateur race, if you put your mind to it."

"*Cool,*" Gareth said fervently.

"I shouldn't think he wants to," Perkin remarked as I hadn't answered in a rush. "You can't make him."

An offer I couldn't refuse, Dee-Dee had said; and I'd thought only of money. Instead he was holding out like a carrot a heart-stopping headlong plunge into a new dimension of existence.

"Say you will," Gareth begged.

Here goes impulse again, I thought. To hell with the helium balloon, it could wait a bit longer.

"I will." I looked at Tremayne. "Thank you."

He nodded, beaming and satisfied, saying, "We'll apply for your permit next week."

We all loaded into the Volvo and went down to Shellerton Manor where everyone trooped in to see Harry. Tired but cheerful, he held court from his chair and accepted Mackie's heartfelt kiss with appreciative good humor.

"I'm so glad you're alive," she said, with a suspicion of tears, and he stroked her arm and said lightly that he was too, on the whole.

"What did it feel like?" Perkin said curiously, glancing at the bandaged leg.

"It happened too fast to feel much," Harry said, smiling lopsidedly. "If John hadn't been there I'd have died without knowing it, I dare say."

"Don't!" Fiona exclaimed. "I can't bear even to think of it. Tremayne, off you go or you'll be late. John and I will pick up Erica and see you soon." She swept them out, following them, fearing perhaps that they would add to Harry's fatigue, and he and I looked at each other across the suddenly empty room in a shared fundamental awareness.

"Do you know who did it?" he asked, weariness and perhaps despair returning, stress visible.

I shook my head.

"Couldn't be someone I know." He meant that he didn't want it to be. "They meant to *kill* me, dammit."

"Dreary thought."

"I don't want to guess. I try not to. It's pretty awful to know someone hates me enough . . ." He swallowed. "That hurts more than my leg."

"Yes." I hesitated. "It was maybe not hate. More like a move in a chess game. And it went wrong, don't forget. The strong presumption of guilt has changed to a stronger presumption of innocence. Entirely and diametrically the wrong result. That can't be bad."

"I'll hang on to that."

I nodded. "Better than a funeral."

"Anything is." He dredged up a smile. "I've got a neighbor coming in to be with me tonight while you're all out. I feel a bit of a coward."

"Rubbish. Bodyguards make good sense."

"Do you want a permanent job?"

Fiona returned, pulling on a fluffy white wrap over her red silk dress, saying she really didn't want to go to the dinner and being persuaded again by her husband. He would be fine, he said, his friend would be there in a moment and good-bye, have a good time, give Tremayne the evening of his life.

Fiona drove her own car, the twin of Harry's (still lost) and settled Erica Upton in the front beside her when we collected her on a westerly detour. The five-star novelist gave me an unfathomable glimmer when I closed the car door for her and remarked that she'd had a long chat with Harry that afternoon on the telephone.

"He told me to lay off you, as you'd saved his life," she announced baldly. "A proper spoilsport."

I said in amusement, "I don't suppose you'll obey him."

I heard the beginning of a chuckle from the front seat, quickly stifled. The battle lines, it seemed, had already been drawn. Hostilities however were in abeyance during arrival at the racecourse, disrobing, hair tidying and first drinks. Half the racing world seemed to have embraced the occasion, for which after the last race that afternoon there had been much speedy unrolling of glittering black and silver ceiling-to-floor curtaining, transforming the workaday interior of the grandstand into something ephemerally magnificent.

"Theatrical," Erica said disapprovingly of the décor, and so it was, but none the worse for that. It lifted the spirits, caused conversation, got the party going. Background music made a change from bookies' cries. Fiona looked at the seating plan and said to meet at table six. People came and surrounded her and Erica, and I drifted away from them and around, seeing a few people I knew by sight and hundreds I didn't. Like being at a gravediggers' convention, I thought, when one had marked out one's first plot.

My thoughts ran too much on death.

Bob Watson was there, dapper in a dark-gray suit, with Ingrid shyly pretty in pale blue.

"Couldn't let down the guv'nor," Bob said cheerfully. "Anyway, he gave us the tickets."

"Jolly good," I said inanely.

"You're riding Fringe tomorrow," he said, halfway be-

tween announcement and question. "Schooling. The guv'-
nor just told me."

"Yes."

"Fringe will look after you," he said inscrutably, looking
around. "Done this place up like an Egyptian brothel,
haven't they?"

"I don't really know."

"Oh, very funny."

Ingrid giggled. Bob quelled her with a look, but I noticed
slightly later and indeed all evening that she stuck very
closely to his side, which could have been interpreted as her
own insecurity if I hadn't remembered Mackie saying that
meek little Ingrid never gave Bob much chance to stray with
the likes of Angela Brickell and God help him if he did.

Sam Yaeger, ever an exhibitionist, had come in a white
dinner jacket, having lent Gareth his black. He also had a
frilled white shirt, a black shoestring tie and a definite air of
strain under the confident exterior. Doone, it appeared, had
more or less accused him straight out of sabotaging his own
boathouse.

"He says I had the tools, the knowledge, the opportunity
and the location, and he looked up those races I rode at
Ascot and worked out that I could have had time between
the first two and the last to drive to Maidenhead and remove
Harry's car. I asked why should I bother to do that when
presumably if I had set the trap I would expect Harry's car
still to be there *after* the races, and he just wrote down my
answer as if I'd made a confession."

"He's persistent."

"He listens to you," Sam said. "We've all noticed. Can't
you tell him I didn't bloody do it?"

"I could try."

"And he whistled up his cohorts after you'd gone," Sam
complained, "and they came with wet-suits and grappling
irons and a heavy magnet and dredged up a lot of muck
from the dock. An old broken bicycle frame, some rusted

railings, an old disintegrating metal gate . . . it had all been lying here and there on the property. They clammed up after a bit and wouldn't show me everything, but he thinks I put it all in the water hoping Harry would get tangled in it."

"Which he did."

"So I'm asking you how come *you* didn't get spiked when you went down there after him?"

"I learned how to jump into shallow water very young. So I didn't go down far. Put my feet down cautiously after I was floating."

He stared. "How do you do that?"

"Jump shallow? The second your feet touch the water you raise your knees and crumple into a ball. The water itself acts as a brake. You must have done it yourself sometime or other. And I had the air in my clothes to hold me up, don't forget."

"Doone asked me if I'd left your jacket and boots in Harry's car. Tricky bastard. I know now how Harry's been feeling. You get that flatfoot looking to tie you in knots and it's like being squeezed by coils and coils of a sodding boa constrictor. Everything you say, he takes it in the wrong way. And he looks so damned harmless. He got me so riled I lost a race this afternoon I should have won. Don't say I said that. I don't bloody know why we all tell you things. You don't belong here."

"Perhaps that's why."

"Yeah, perhaps."

He seemed to have let out sufficient steam and resentment for the moment and turned to flirt obligingly with a middle-aged woman who touched his arm in pleased anticipation. Owners, Tremayne had said, either loved or hated Sam's manner: the women loved, the men put up with it in exchange for winners.

Nolan, glowering routinely at Sam from a few feet away, switched his ill-humor to me.

"I don't want you treading on my effing toes," he said forcefully. "Why don't you clear off out of Shellerton?"

"I will in a while."

"I told Tremayne there'll be trouble if he gives you any of my rides."

"Ah."

"He has the effing gall to say I suggested it myself and he knows bloody well I was taking the piss." He glared at me. "I don't understand what Fiona sees in you. I told her you're just a bag of shit with a pretty face who needs his arse kicked. You keep away from her horses, understand?"

I understood that he like everyone else was suffering from the atmospheric blight cast by Angela Brickell, he perhaps most because the strain of his own trial and conviction was so recent. There was no way I was ever going to ride as well as he did and he surely knew it. Fiona would never jock him off, in racing's descriptive phrase.

He stomped away, his place almost immediately taken by his brother, who gave me a malicious imitation of a smile and said, "Nolan doesn't expletive like you, dear heart."

"You don't say."

Lewis was sober, so far. Also unaccompanied, like Nolan, though Harry had mentioned at one time that Lewis was married: his reclusive wife preferred to stay at home to avoid the fuss and fracas of Lewis drunk.

"Nolan likes to be the center of attention and you've usurped his pinnacle," Lewis said.

"Rubbish."

"Fiona and Mackie look to you, now, not to him. And as for Tremayne, as for Gareth . . ." He gave me a sly leer. "Don't put your neck within my brother's reach."

"Lewis!" His lack of fraternal feeling shocked me more than his suggestion. "You stuck *your* neck out for him, anyway."

"Sometimes I hate him," he said with undoubted truth, and wheeled away as if he had said enough.

Glasses in hand, the chattering groups mixed and mingled, broke and re-formed, greeted each other with glad cries as if they hadn't seen each other for years, not just that afternoon. Tremayne, large smile a permanence, received genuinely warm congratulations with believable modesty and Gareth, appearing eel-like at my elbow, said with gratification, "He deserves it, doesn't he?"

"He does."

"It makes you think a bit."

"What about?"

"I mean, he's just Dad." He struggled to get it right. "Everyone's two people, aren't they?"

I said with interest, "That's profound."

"Get away." He felt awkward at the compliment. "I'm glad for him, anyway."

He snaked off again and within minutes the throng began moving towards dinner, dividing into ten to a table, lowering bottoms onto inadequate chairs, fingering menus, peering at the print through candlelight, scanning their allotted neighbors. At table number six I found myself placed between Mackie and Erica Upton, who were already seated.

Erica was inevitable, I supposed, though I suspected Fiona had switched a few place cards before I reached there: a certain bland innocence gave her away.

"I did ask to sit next to you," Erica remarked, as if reading my thoughts as I sat down, "once I knew you'd be here."

"Er . . . why?"

"Do you have so little self-confidence?"

"It depends who I'm with."

"And by yourself?"

"In a desert, plenty. With pencil and paper, little."

"Quite right."

"And you?" I asked.

"I don't answer that sort of question."

I listened to the starch in her voice, observed it in the

straightness of her backbone, recognized the ramrod will that made no concessions to hardship.

"I could take you across a desert," I said.

She gave me a long piercing inspection. "I hope that's not an accolade."

"An assessment," I said.

"You've found your courage since I met you last."

She had a way of leaving one without an answer. She turned away, satisfied, to talk to Nolan on her other side, and I, abandoned, found Mackie on my right smiling with enjoyment.

"She's met her match," she said.

I shook my head regretfully. "If I could write like her . . . or ride like Sam or Nolan . . . if I could do *anything* that well, I'd be happy."

Her smile sweetened. "Try cooking."

"Dammit . . ."

She laughed. "I hear the power of your bananas flambées made Gareth oversleep."

Perkin, on her other side, murmured something to get her attention and for a while I watched Tremayne make the best of our table having been graced by the sponsor's wife, a gushing froth of a lady in unbecoming lemon. He would clearly have preferred to be talking to Fiona on his other side, but the award was having to be paid for with politeness. He glanced across the table, saw me smiling, interpreted my thought and gave me a slow ironic blink.

He soldiered manfully through the salmon soufflé and the beef Wellington while Lewis on the lady's other side put away a tumblerful of vodka poured from a half-bottle in his pocket. Fiona watched him with a frown: Lewis's drinking, even to my eyes, was increasingly without shame. Almost as if, having proclaimed himself paralytic in court, he was setting about proving it over and over again.

Glumly fidgeting between Lewis and Perkin, Gareth ate everything fast and looked bored. Perkin with brotherly bossiness told him to stop kicking the table leg and Gareth uncharacteristically sulked. Mackie made a placatory remark and Perkin snapped at her too.

She turned her head my way and with a frown asked, "What's wrong with everyone?"

"Tension."

"Because of Harry?" She nodded to herself. "We all pretend, but no one can help *wondering* . . . This time it's much worse. Last time at least we knew how Olympia died. Angela Brickell's on everyone's nerves. Nothing feels safe anymore."

"You're safe," I said. "You and Perkin. Think about the baby."

Her face cleared as if automatically: the thought of the baby could diminish to trivia the grimmest forebodings.

Perkin on her other side was saying contritely, "Sorry, darling, sorry," and she turned to him with ever-ready forgiveness, the adult of the pair. I wondered fleetingly if Perkin, as a father, would be jealous of his child.

Dinner wound to a close: speeches began. Cultured gents, identified for me by Mackie as being the Himalayan peaks of the Jockey Club, paid compliments to Tremayne from an adjacent table and bowed low to the sponsor. He, the lemon lady's husband, eulogized Tremayne, who winced only slightly over Top Spin Lob being slurred to Topsy Blob, and a minion in the livery of Castle Houses brought forth a tray bearing the award itself, a silver bowl rimmed by a circle of small galloping horses, an award actually worthy of the occasion.

Tremayne was pink with gratification. He accepted the bowl. Everyone cheered. Photos flashed. Tremayne made a brief speech of all-around thanks: thanks to the sponsors, to his friends, his staff, his jockeys, to racing itself. He sat down, overcome. Everyone cheered him again and clapped loudly. I began to wonder how many of them would buy

Tremayne's book. I wondered whether after that night Tremayne would need the book written.

"Wasn't that great?" Mackie exclaimed, glowing.

"Yes, indeed."

The background music became dance music. People moved about, flocking around Tremayne, patting his back. Perkin took Mackie to shuffle on the square of dance floor adjoining the table. Nolan took Fiona, Lewis got drunker, Gareth vanished, the sponsor retrieved his lady: Erica and I sat alone.

"Do you dance?" I asked.

"No." She looked out at the still-alive party. "The Duchess of Richmond's Ball," she said.

"Do you expect Waterloo tomorrow?"

"Sometime soon. Who is Napoleon?"

"The enemy?"

"Of course."

"I don't know," I said.

"Use your brains. What about insight through imagination?"

"I thought you didn't believe in it."

"For this purpose, I do. Someone tried to kill Harry. That's extremely disturbing. What's disturbing about it?"

It seemed she expected an answer, so I gave it. "It was premeditated. Angela Brickell's death may or may not have been, but the attack on Harry was vastly thought out."

She seemed minutely to relax.

"My God!" I said, stunned.

"What? What have you thought of?" She was alert again, and intent.

"I'll have to talk to Doone."

"Do you know who did it?" she demanded.

"No, but I know what he knew." I frowned. "Everyone knows it."

"What? Do explain."

I looked at her vaguely, thinking.

"I don't believe it's very important," I said in the end.

"Then what is it?" she insisted.

"Wood floats."

She looked bemused. "Well, of course it does."

"The floorboards that went down to the water with Harry, they stayed under. They didn't float."

"Why not?"

"Have to find out," I said. "Doone can find out."

"What does it matter?"

"Well," I said, "no one could be absolutely certain that Harry would be spiked and drown immediately. So suppose he's alive and swimming about. He's been in that place before, at Sam's party, and he knows there's a mooring dock along one wall. He knows there's a door and he has daylight and can see the river through the metal curtain. So how does he get out?"

She shook her head. "Tell me."

"The door opens outward. If you're inside, and you're standing in only six inches of water, not six feet, and you've got three or four floorboards floating about, you use one of them as a ram to break the lock or batter the door down. You're big and strong like Harry and also wet, cold, desperate and angry. How long does it take you to break out?"

"I suppose not long."

"When Napoleon came to the boathouse," I said, "there wasn't any sound of Harry battering his way out. In fact"—I frowned—"there's no saying how long the enemy had been there, waiting. He might have been hiding . . . heard Harry's car arrive."

Erica said, "When your book's published, send me a copy."

I looked at her openmouthed.

"Then I can tell you the difference between invention and insight."

"You know how to pierce," I said, wincing.

She began to say something else but never completed it.

Instead our heads turned in unison towards the dancers, among whom battle seemed already to have started. There was a crash and a scream and bizarrely against the unrelentingly cheerful music two figures could be seen fighting.

Sam . . . and Nolan.

Sam had blood on his white jacket and down the white ruffles. Nolan's shirt was ripped open, showing a lot of hairy chest. They were both reeling about exchanging swinging blows not ten feet from table six and I stood up automatically, more in defense than interference.

Perkin tried to pull them apart and got smartly knocked down by Nolan, quick and tough with his fists as with his riding. I stepped without thinking onto the polished square and tried words instead.

"You stupid fools," I said: not the most inventive sentence ever.

Nolan took his attention off Sam for a split second, lashed out expertly at my face and whirled back to his prime target in time to parry Sam's wildly lunging arm and kick him purposefully between the legs. Sam's head came forward. Nolan's fist began a descent onto the back of Sam's vulnerable neck.

With instinct more than thought I barged into Nolan bodily, pushing him off line. He turned a face of mean-eyed fury in my direction and easily transferred his hatred.

I was vaguely aware that the dance floor had cleared like morning mist and also acutely conscious that Nolan knew volumes more about bare-knuckle fisticuffs than I did.

Racing people were extraordinary, I thought. Far from piling into Nolan in a preventive heap, they formed an instant ring around us and, as the band came to a straggling sharp-flat unscheduled halt, Lewis's drunken aristocratic voice could be heard drawling, "Five to four the field."

Everyone laughed. Everyone except Nolan. I doubted if he'd heard. He was high on the flooding wave from the bursting dam of his dark nature, all the anxiety, guilt, hate and repressions sweeping out in a reckless torrent, no longer containable.

In a straight fight I wasn't going to beat him. All I would be was a punchbag for his escaping fury, the entity he saw as a new unbearable threat to his dominance in Tremayne's stable; the interloper, usurper, legitimate target.

I turned my back on him and took a step or two away. All I knew about fighting was ruse and trickery. I could see from the onlooking faces that he was coming for me, and at what speed, and when I felt the air behind me move and heard the brush of his clothes I went down fast on one knee and whirled and punched upward hard into the bottom of his advancing rib cage and then shifted my weight into his body and upward so as to lift him wholesale off the floor, and before he'd got that sorted out I had one of his wrists in my hand and he ended up on his feet with me behind him, his arm in a nice painful lock and my mouth by his ear.

"You stupid shit," I said intensely. "The Jockey Club are here. Don't you care about your permit?"

For answer he kicked back and caught me on a shin.

"Then I'll ride all your horses," I said unwisely.

I gave him a hard releasing shove in the general direction of Sam, Perkin and an openmouthed Gareth and at last watched a dozen restraining hands clutch and keep him from destroying himself entirely, but he struggled against them and turned his vindictive face my way and shouted in still exploding rage, *"I'll kill you."*

I stood unmoving and listened to those words, and thought of Harry.

15

I apologized to Tremayne.

"Nolan started it," Mackie said.

She peered anxiously at the reddening bruise on Perkin's cheek, a twin to one on mine.

Perkin sat in angry confusion at table six while the racing crowd, entertaining skirmish over, drifted away and got the band restarted.

Nolan was nowhere in sight. Sam took off his stained jacket, wiped his bloody nose, sucked his knuckles and began making jokes as a form of released tension.

"I bumped into him, that's all I did," he proclaimed with tragicomic gestures. "Well, say I then took Fiona off him and maybe I told him to go find himself another filly and the next thing was he got a pincer hold on my ear and was bopping me one on the nose and there I was bleeding fit to fill the Frenchy furrows so naturally I gave him one back."

He collected an appreciative audience which definitely didn't include Tremayne. The shambles at the end of his splendid evening was aggravating him sorely and he propelled Fiona into a seat at the table with some of the disgruntled force he'd shown in Ronnie Curzon's office.

Fiona said anxiously, "But, Tremayne, Sam meant it as a joke."

"He should have had more sense." Tremayne's voice was rough. Gareth, next to Perkin, looked at his father with apprehension, knowing the portents.

"Nolan's been through a lot," Fiona said excusingly.

"Nolan's a violent man," Tremayne stated with fierce irritation. "You don't go poking a stick at a rattlesnake if you don't want to get bitten."

"Tremayne!" She was alarmed at his brusqueness, which he immediately softened.

"My dear girl, I know he's your cousin. I know he's been through a lot, I know you're fond of him, but he and Sam shouldn't be in the same room together just now." He looked from her to me. "Are you all right?"

"Yes."

"John was splendid!" Mackie exclaimed, and Perkin scowled.

Erica grinned at me like a witch, saying, "You're much too physical for the literati."

"Let's go home," Tremayne said abruptly. He stood, kissed Fiona, picked up the box containing his silver bowl and waited for obedience from his sons, his daughter-in-law and his prospective biographer. We stood. We followed him meekly. He made a stately, somewhat forbidding exit, his displeasure plainly visible to all around, his mien daring unkind souls to snigger.

No one did. Tremayne was held in genuine respect and I saw more sympathy than smirks: yet he in many respects was the stoker of the ill-feeling between his warring jockeys, and putting me among them wasn't a recipe for a cease-fire.

"Perhaps I'd better not ride schooling in the morning," I suggested, as we reached the gate to the car park.

"Are you scared?" he demanded, stopping dead.

I stopped beside him as the other three went on ahead.

"Nolan and Sam don't like it, that's all," I said.

"You bloody well ride. I'll get you that permit. I'll tame Nolan by threats. Understand?"

I nodded.

He stared at me intently. "Is that why Nolan said he would kill you? Besides your making a public fool of him?"

"I think so."

"Do you want to ride in a race or two, or don't you?"

"I do."

"School Fringe tomorrow, then. And as for now, you'd better go back with Fiona. Make sure she gets home safe. Harry won't want Nolan pestering her and he's quite capable of it."

"Right."

He nodded strongly and went on towards his Volvo, and I returned to find Fiona arguing with Nolan in the entrance hall. She and Erica beside her saw me with relief, Nolan with fresh fury.

"I was afraid you'd gone," Fiona said.

"Thank Tremayne."

Nolan said angrily, "Why is this bag of slime always hanging about?"

He made no move, though, to attack me.

"Harry asked him to see me home," Fiona said placatingly. "Get some rest, Nolan, or you won't be fit for Groundsel tomorrow."

He heard, as I did, the faint threat in the cousinly concern, and at least it gave him an excuse for a face-saving exit. Fiona watched his retreating back with a regret neither Erica nor I shared.

* * *

I rode Drifter with the first lot in the morning and crashed off onto the wood chippings halfway up the gallop.

Tremayne showed a modicum of anxiety but no sympathy, and the anxiety was for the horse. He sent a lad after it to try to catch it and with disgust watched me limp towards him rubbing a bruised thigh.

"Concentrate," he said. "What the hell do you think you were doing?"

"He swerved."

"You weren't keeping him straight. Don't make excuses, you weren't concentrating."

The lad caught Drifter and brought him to join us.

"Get up," Tremayne said to me testily.

I wriggled back into the saddle. I supposed he was right about not concentrating: a touch of the morning afters.

They'd all gone to bed the night before when I'd returned from a last noggin with Harry. I'd walked up from the village under a brilliantly starry sky, breathing cold shafts of early-morning air, thinking of murder. Sleep had come slowly with anxiety dreams. I felt unsettled, not refreshed.

I rode Drifter back with the rest of the string and went into breakfast half expecting to be told I wouldn't be allowed to ride Fringe. Tremayne's own mood appeared to be a deepening depression over the evening's finale, and I was sorry because he deserved to look back with enjoyment.

He was reading a newspaper when I went in, and scowling heavily.

"How did they get hold of this so damned fast?"

"What?"

"This." He pushed the opened paper violently across the table and I read that a brace of brawling jockeys had climaxed the prestigious award dinner with a bloody punch-up. Ex-champion Yaeger and amateur champion Nolan Everard (recently convicted of manslaughter) had been restrained by friends. Tremayne Vickers had said "no comment." The sponsor was furious. The Jockey Club were "looking into it." End of story.

"It's rubbish," Tremayne snorted. "I never said 'no comment.' No one asked me for any comment. The sponsor had left by the time it happened, so how can he be furious? So had the Jockey Club members. They went after the speeches. I talked to some of them as they were leaving. They congratulated me. Huh!"

"The fuss will die down," I assured him.

"Makes me look a bloody fool."

"Make a joke of it," I suggested.

He stared. "I don't feel like joking."

"No one does."

"It's this business about Harry, isn't it? Upsets everyone. Bloody Angela Brickell."

I made the toast.

He said, "Are you fit enough to ride Fringe?"

"If you'll let me."

He studied me, some of his ill-feeling fading. "Concentrate, then."

"Yes."

"Look," he said a touch awkwardly, "I don't mean to take my bad temper out on you. If you hadn't been here we'd all be in a far worse pickle. Best thing I ever did, getting you to come."

In surprise I searched for words to thank him but was forestalled by the telephone ringing. Tremayne picked up the receiver and grunted "Hullo?", not all his vexation yet dissipated.

His face changed miraculously to a smile. "Hello, Ronnie. Calling to find out how the book's going? Your boy's been working on it. What? Yes, he's here. Hold on." He passed me the receiver, saying unnecessarily, "It's Ronnie Curzon."

"Hello, Ronnie," I said.

"How's it going?"

"I'm riding a good deal."

"Keep your mind on the pages. I've got news for you."

"Good or bad?"

"My colleague in America phoned yesterday evening about your book."

"Oh." I felt apprehensive. "What did he say?"

"He says he likes *Long Way Home* very much indeed. He will gladly take it on, and he is certain he can place it with a good publisher."

"Ronnie!" I swallowed, unable to get my breath. "Are you sure?"

"Of course I'm sure. I always told you it was all right. Your English publisher is very enthusiastic. She told my American colleague the book is fine and he agrees. What more do you want?"

"Oh . . ."

"Come down from the ceiling. A first novel by an unknown British writer isn't going to be given a huge advance." He mentioned a sum which would pay my rent until I'd finished the helium balloon and leave some over for sandwiches. "If the book takes off like they hope it will, you'll get royalties." He paused. "Are you still there?"

"Sort of."

He laughed. "It's all beginning. I have faith in you."

Ridiculously, I felt like crying. Blinked a few times instead and told him in a croaky voice that I'd met Erica Upton twice and had sat next to her at dinner.

"She'll destroy you!" he said, horrified.

"I don't think so. She wants a copy of the book when it's published."

"She'll tear it apart. She likes making mincemeat of new writers." He sounded despairing. "She does hatchet jobs, not reviews."

"I'll have to risk it."

"Let me talk to Tremayne."

"OK, and Ronnie . . . thanks."

"Yes, yes . . ."

I handed back the receiver and heard Ronnie being agitated on the other end.

"Hold on," Tremayne said, "she likes him."

I distinctly heard Ronnie's disbelieving *"What?"*

"Also she's very fond of her nephew, Harry, and on Wednesday John saved Harry's life. I grant you she may write him a critical review, but she won't demolish him." Tremayne listened a bit and talked a bit and then gave me the receiver again.

"All right," Ronnie said more calmly, "any chance you get, save her life too."

I laughed, and with a sigh he disconnected.

"What happened?" Tremayne asked. "What did he tell you?"

"I'm going to be published in America. Well . . . probably."

"Congratulations." He beamed, pleased for me, his glooms lifting. "But that won't change things, will it? I mean here, between us. You will still write my book, won't you?"

I saw his anxiety begin to surface and promptly allayed it.

"I will write it. I'll do the very best I can and just hope it does you justice. And will you excuse me if I run and jump and do handsprings? I'm bursting . . . Ronnie said it's all beginning. I don't know that I can bear it." I looked at him. "Did you feel like this when Top Spin Lob won the National?"

"I was high for days. Kept smiling. Topsy Blob, I ask you!" He stood up. "Back to business. You'll come up with me in the Land-Rover. Fringe's lad can ride him up, then change with you."

"Right."

Ronnie's news, I found, had given me a good deal more confidence on Fringe than I had had on Drifter, illogical though it might be.

It's all beginning . . .

Concentrate.

Fringe was younger, whippier and less predictable than Drifter: rock music in place of classical. I gathered the reins and lengthened the stirrup leathers a couple of holes while Fringe made prancing movements, getting used to his new and heavier rider.

"Take him down below the three flights of hurdles," Tremayne said, "then bring him up over them at a useful pace. You're not actually racing. Just a good half-speed gallop. Bob Watson will be with you for company. Fringe jumps well enough but he likes guidance. He'll waver if you don't tell him when to take off. Don't forget, it's you that's schooling the horse, not the other way round. All ready?"

I nodded.

"Off you go, then."

He seemed unconcerned at letting me loose on his half-share investment and I tried telling myself that ahead lay merely a quick pop over three undemanding obstacles, not the first searching test of my chances of racing. I'd ridden over many jumps before, but never on a racehorse, never fast, never caring so much about the outcome. Almost without being aware of it I'd progressed from the hesitancy of my first few days there to a strong positive desire to go down to the starting gate: any starting gate, anywhere. I had to admit that I envied Sam and Nolan.

Bob was circling on his own horse, waiting for me. Both his horse and Fringe, aware they would be jumping, were stimulated and keen.

"Guv'nor says you're to set off on the side nearest him," Bob said briefly. "He wants to see what you're doing."

I nodded, slightly dry-mouthed. Bob expertly trotted his mount into position, gave me a raised-eye query about readiness and kicked forward into an accelerating gallop. Fringe took up his position alongside with familiarity and eagerness, an athlete doing what he'd been bred for, and enjoyed.

First hurdle ahead. Judge the distance . . . give Fringe the message to shorten his stride . . . I gave it to him too successfully, he put in a quick one, got too near to the hurdle, hopped over it nearly at a standstill, lost lengths on Bob.

Damn, I thought. *Damn.*

Second hurdle, managed it a bit better, gave him the signal three strides from the jump, felt him lift off at the right time, felt his assurance flow back and his faith in me revive, even if provisionally.

Third hurdle, I left him too much to his own devices as the distance was awkward. I couldn't make up my own mind whether to get him to lengthen or shorten and in consequence I didn't make his mind up to do either and we floundered over it untidily, his hooves rapping the wooden frames, my weight too far forward . . . a mess.

We pulled up at the end of the schooling stretch and trotted back to where Tremayne stood with his binoculars. I didn't look at Bob; didn't want to see his disapproval, all too wretchedly aware that I hadn't done very well.

Tremayne with pursed lips offered no direct opinion. Instead he said, "Second pop, Bob. Off you go," and I gathered we were to go back to the beginning and start again.

I seemed to have more time to get things together the second time and Fringe stayed beside Bob fairly smoothly to the end. I felt exalted and released and newly alive in myself, but also I'd watched Sam Yaeger in a schooling session one morning and knew the difference.

Tremayne said nothing until we were driving back to the stable and then all he did was ask me if I were happy with what I'd done. Happy beyond expression in one way, I thought, but not in another. I knew for certain I wanted to race. Knew I had elementary skill.

"I'll learn," I said grimly, and he didn't answer.

When we reached the house however he rummaged about in the office for a while complaining that he could never find anything on Dee-Dee's days off and eventually brought a paper into the dining room, plonked it on the table and instructed me to sign.

It was, I saw, an application for a permit to race as an amateur jockey. I signed it without speaking, incredibly delighted, grinning like a maniac.

Tremayne grunted and bore the document away, coming back presently to say I should stop working and go with him to Newbury races, if I didn't mind. Also Mackie would be coming with us and we'd be picking up Fiona.

"And frankly," he said, coming to the essence of the matter, "those two don't want to go without you, and Harry wants you to be there and . . . well . . . so do I."

"All right," I said.

"Good."

He departed again and, after a moment's thought, I went into the office to put through a call to Doone's police station. He was off duty, I was told. I could leave my name and a message.

I left my name.

"Ask him," I said, "why the floorboards in the boathouse didn't float."

"Er . . . would you repeat that, sir?"

I repeated it and got it read back with skepticism.

"That's right," I confirmed, amused. "Don't forget it."

We went to the races and watched Nolan ride Fiona's horse Groundsel and get beaten by a length into second place, and we watched Sam ride two of Tremayne's runners unprofitably and then win for another trainer.

"There's always another day," Tremayne said philosophically.

Fiona told us on the way to the races that the police had phoned Harry to say they'd found his car in the station car park at Reading.

"They said it looks OK but they've towed it off somewhere to search for clues. I never knew people really said 'search for clues,' but that's what they said."

Tremayne nodded. "They talk like their notebooks."

From Reading station one could set off around the world.

Metaphorical cliff, I thought. A guilty disappearance had been the intended scenario, not a presumption of suicide. Unless of course the car had been moved again after Harry had made his unscheduled reappearance.

The racecourse was naturally buzzing with accounts of the row at Tremayne's dinner, most of the stories inflamed and inaccurate because of the embroidery by the press. Tremayne bore the jokes with reasonable fortitude, cheered by the absence of inquiry or even remarks from the Jockey Club, not even strictures about "bringing racing into disrepute," which I'd learned was the yardstick for in-house punishment.

By osmosis of information, both Sam and Nolan knew details of Fringe's schooling. Sam said, "You'll be taking my sodding job next," without meaning it in the least, and Nolan, bitter-eyed and cursing, saw Tremayne's warning glare and subsided with festering rancor.

"How on earth do they know?" I asked, mystified.

"Sam phoned Bob to find out," Tremayne said succinctly. "Bob told him you did all right. Sam couldn't wait to tell Nolan. I heard him doing it. Bloody pair of fools."

All afternoon Fiona kept me close by her side, looking around for me any time I fell a step behind. She tried unsuccessfully to hide what she described as "preposterous fear," and I understood that her fear had no focus and no logic, but was becoming a state of mind. Tremayne, sensing it also, fussed over her even more than usual and Fiona herself made visible efforts to act normally and as she said "be sensible."

Whenever Mackie wasn't actively helping Tremayne she stayed close also to Fiona, and although I tried I couldn't dislodge the underlying anxiety in their eyes. Silver-blond and redhead, they clung to each other occasionally as long-time friends, and spoke to Nolan, cousin of one, ex-fiancé of the other, with an odd mixture of dread, exasperation and compassion.

Nolan was disconcerted by having lost on Groundsel though I couldn't see that he'd done anything wrong. Tremayne didn't blame him, still less did Fiona, but the nonsuccess intensified if possible his ill-will towards me. I was truly disconcerted myself to have acquired so violent an enemy without meaning to and could see no resolution short of full retreat; and the trouble was that since that morning's schooling, any inclination to retreat had totally vanished.

I looked back constantly to the morning with huge inward joy; to Ronnie's phone call, to the revelation over hurdles. Doors opening all over the place. All beginning.

The afternoon ending, we took Fiona home and went on to Shellerton House, where Perkin came through for drinks, Tremayne went out to see the horses and Gareth returned from a football match. An evening like most others in that house, but to me the first of a changed life.

The next day, Sunday, Gareth held me to my promise to take him and Coconut out on another survival trip.

The weather was much better; sunny but cold still with a trace of a breeze, a good day for walking. I suggested seven miles out, seven miles back; Gareth with horror suggested two. We compromised on borrowing the Land-Rover for positioning, followed by walking as far as their enthusiasm took them.

"Where are you going?" Tremayne asked.

"Along the road over the hills towards Reading," I said. "There's some great woodland there, unfenced, no signs saying keep out."

Tremayne nodded. "I know where you mean. It's all part of the Quillersedge Estate. They only try to keep people out just before Christmas, to stop them stealing the fir trees."

"We'd better not light a fire there," I said, "so we'll take our food and water with us."

Gareth looked relieved. "No fried worms."

"No, but it will be survival food. Things you could pick or catch."

"OK," he said with his father's brand of practical acceptance. "How about chocolate instead of dandelion leaves?"

I agreed to the chocolate. The day had to be bearable. We set off at ten, collected Coconut and bowled along to the woods.

There were parking places all along that road, not planned official tarmacked areas but small inlets of beaten earth formed by the waiting cars of many walkers. I pulled into one of them, put on the handbrake and when the boys were out, locked the doors.

Gareth wore of course his psychedelic jacket. Coconut's yellow oilskins had been superseded by an equally blinding anorak and I, in the regrettable absence of my ski-suit jacket, looked camouflaged against the trees in stone-washed jeans and a roomy olive-drab Barbour borrowed from Tremayne.

"Right," I said, smiling, as they slid the straps of bright-blue nylon knapsacks over their shoulders, "we'll take a walk into the Berkshire wilderness. Everyone fit?"

They said they were, so we stepped straight into the tangled maze of alder, hazel, birch, oak, pine, fir and laurel and picked our steps over dried grass, scratchy brambles and the leafless knee-high branching shoots of the wood's next generation. None of this had been cleared or replanted; it was scrub woodland as nature had made it, the real thing as far as the boys were concerned.

I encouraged them to lead but kept them going towards the sun by suggesting detours around obstructing patches, and I identified the trees for them, trying to make it interesting.

"We're not eating the bark again, are we?" Coconut said, saying ugh to a birch tree.

"Not today. Here is a hazel. There might still be some nuts lying round it."

They found two. Squirrels had been there first.

We went about a mile before they tired of the effort involved, and I didn't mean to go much further in any case because according to the map I had in my pocket we were by then in about the center of the western spur of the Quillersedge woods. We'd come gently up and down hill, but not much further on the ground fell away abruptly, according to the map's contour lines, with too hard a climb on the return.

Gareth stopped in one of the occasional small clearings and mentioned food hopefully.

"Sure," I said. "We can make some reasonable seats with dead twigs to keep our bottoms off the damp ground, if you like. No need today for a shelter."

They made flat piles of twigs, finished them off with evergreen, then emptied their rucksacks and spread the blue nylon on top. We all sat fairly comfortably and ate the things I'd bought for the occasion.

"Smoked trout!" Gareth exclaimed. "That's an advance on roots."

"You could catch trout and smoke them if you had to," I said. "The easiest way to catch them is with a three-pronged spear, but don't tell that to fishermen."

"How do you smoke them?"

"Make a fire with lots of hot embers. Cover the embers thickly with green fresh leaves: they'll burn slowly with billows of smoke. Make a latticed frame to go over the fire and put the trout on it or otherwise hang them over the smoke, and if possible cover it all with branches or more leaves to keep the smoke inside. The best leaves for smoking are things like oak or beech. The smell of the smoke will go into the fish to some extent, so don't use anything you don't like the smell of. Don't use holly or yew, they're poisonous. You can smoke practically anything. Strips of meat. Bits of chicken."

"Smoked salmon!" Coconut said. "Why not?"

"First catch your salmon," said Gareth dryly.

He had brought a camera and he took photos of everything possible: the seats, the food, ourselves.

"I want to remember these days when I'm old like Dad," Gareth said. "Dad wishes he'd had a camera when he went round the world with his father."

"Does he?" I asked.

He nodded. "He told me when he gave me this one."

We ate the trout with unleavened bread and healthy appetites and afterwards filled up with mixed dried fruit and pre-roasted chestnuts and almonds. The boys declared it a feast compared with the week before and polished off their chocolate as a bonus.

Gareth said casually, "Was it in a place like this that someone killed Angela Brickell?"

"Well . . . I should think so. But five miles or so from here," I said.

"And it was summer," he commented. "Warm. Leaves on the trees."

"Mm." Imaginative of him, I thought.

"She wanted to kiss me," he said with a squirm.

Both Coconut and I looked at him in astonishment.

"I'm not as ugly as all that," he said, offended.

"You're not ugly," I assured him positively, "but you're young."

"She said I was growing up." He looked embarrassed, as did Coconut.

"When did she say that?" I asked mildly.

"In the Easter holidays, last year. She was always out there in the yard. Always looking at me. I told Dad about it, but he didn't listen. It was Grand National time and he couldn't think of anything but Top Spin Lob." He swallowed. "Then she went away and I was really glad. I didn't like going out into the yard when she was there." He looked at me anxiously. "I suppose it's wrong to be glad someone's dead."

"Is glad what you feel?"

He thought about it.

"Relieved," he said finally. "I was afraid of her." He looked ashamed. "I used to think about her, though. Couldn't help it."

"It won't be the last time someone makes a pass at you," I said prosaically. "Next time, don't feel guilty."

Easier said than done, I supposed. Shame and guilt tormented the innocent more than the wicked.

Gareth seemed liberated by having put his feelings into words and he and Coconut jumped up and ran around, throwing mock punches at each other, swinging on tree branches, getting rid of bashfulness with shouts and action and shows of strength. I supposed I'd been like that too, but I couldn't remember.

"Right," I said, as they subsided onto the seats and panted while I packed away our food wrappings (which would have started a dinky fire). "Which way to the Land-Rover?"

"That way," said Gareth immediately, pointing east.

"That way," Coconut said, pointing west.

"Which way is north?" I asked.

They both got it instinctively wrong, but then worked it out roughly by the sun, and I showed them how to use a watch as a compass, which Gareth half remembered, having learned before.

"Something to do with pointing the hands at the sun," he guessed.

I nodded. "Point the hour hand at the sun, then halfway between the hand and twelve o'clock is the north-south line."

"Not in Australia," Gareth said.

"We're not in Australia," Coconut objected. He looked at his watch and around him. "That way is north," he said, pointing. "But which way is the Land-Rover?"

"If you go north you'll come to the road," I said.

"What do you mean 'you'?" Gareth demanded. "You're coming too. You've got to guide us."

"I thought," I said, "that it would be more fun for you to find your own way back. And," I went on as he tried to interrupt, "so as you don't get lost if the sun goes in, you can paint the trees as you go with luminous paint. Then you can always come back to me."

"Cool," he said, entranced.

"What?" Coconut wanted to know.

Gareth told him about finding one's way back to places by blazing the trail.

"I'll follow you," I said, "but you won't see me. If you go really badly wrong, I'll tell you. Otherwise, survival's up to you."

"Ace," Gareth said happily.

I unzipped the pouch around my waist and gave him the small jar of paint and the sawn-off paintbrush.

"Don't forget to paint so you can see the splash from both directions, coming and going, and don't get out of sight of your last splash."

"OK."

"Wait for me when you hit the road."

"Yes."

"And take the whistle." I held it out to him from the pouch. "It's just a backup in case you get stuck. If you're in trouble, blow it, and I'll come at once."

"It's only a mile," he protested, slightly hurt, not taking it.

"What do I say to your father if I mislay you?"

He grinned in sympathy, giving way, and put the best of all insurances in his pocket.

"Let's go back the way we came," Coconut said to Gareth.

"Easy!" Gareth agreed.

I watched them decide on the wrong place and paint the first mark carefully around a sapling's trunk. They might just possibly have been able to find the morning's path if they'd been starting again from the road, but tracking backwards was incredibly difficult. All the identifiable marks of our passage, like broken twigs and flattened grass, pointed forward into the wood, not out of it.

They consulted their watches and moved north through the trees, looking back and painting as they went. They waved once and I waved back, and for some time I could see their bright jackets in the dappled shade of the afternoon sun. Then, when they had gone, I began slowly to follow their splashes.

I could go much faster than they could. When I saw them again I dropped down on one knee, knowing that even though they were constantly looking back they wouldn't see me at that low level, in my nature-colored clothes.

Besides the map, I'd brought along my faithful compass, and by its reckoning checked the boys' direction all the time. They wandered off to the northeast a bit but not badly enough to get really lost, and after a while made a correction to drift back to north.

The pale-cream splashes were easy to spot, never far apart. Gareth had intelligently chosen smooth-barked saplings all the way, and all the marks were at the same height, at about waist level, where painting came to him most naturally, it seemed.

I kept the boys in sight intermittently all the way. They were talking to each other loudly as if to keep lurking wood-spirits at bay, and I did vividly remember that teenage spooky feeling of being alone in wild woodland and at the mercy of supernatural eyes. Even in sunshine one could be nervous. At night a couple of times at fifteen I'd been terrified.

On that day, as I slowly followed the trail, I simply felt at home and at peace. There were birds singing, though not yet many, and apart from the boys' voices the quiet was as old and deep as the land. The woods still waited the stirring of spring, lying chilly and patient with sleeping buds and butterflies in cocoons. The smells of autumn, of compost and rot, still faintly lingered into the winter thaw, only the pines and firs remaining fragrant if one brushed them. Pine resin, collected by tapping, dried to lumps that made brilliant firelighters.

It was a slow-going mile, but towards the end one could hear occasional cars along the road ahead and Gareth and Coconut with whoops crashed through the last few yards, again, as the week before, relieved to be back in the space age.

I speeded up and stepped out behind them, much to Gareth's surprise.

"We thought you were miles back," he exclaimed.

"You laid an excellent trail."

"The paint's nearly finished." He held it up to show me and the jar slipped out of his hand, rolling the remains of its contents onto the earth. "Hey, sorry," he said. "But there wasn't much left."

"Doesn't matter." I picked up the jar, which was slippery on the outside from dripped paint and, screwing its lid on, dropped it with the brush into a plastic bag before stowing it again in my pouch.

"Can we get some more?" Coconut asked.

"Sure. No problem. Ready to go home?"

The boys, both pumped up by their achievement, ran and jumped all along the road to the Land-Rover that we found around the next bend, and rode back in euphoric good spirits.

"Terrific," Gareth told Tremayne, bursting into the family room after we'd dropped Coconut and returned to Shellerton. "Fantastic."

Whether they wanted to or not, Tremayne, Mackie and Perkin received a minute-by-minute account of the whole day with the sole exception of the discussion about Angela

Brickell. Tremayne listened with veiled approval, Mackie with active interest, Perkin with boredom.

"It's real wilderness," Gareth said. "You can't hear *anything*. And I took lashings of photos—" He stopped, suddenly frowning. "Hold on a minute."

He sped out of the room and came back with his blue knapsack, searching the contents worriedly.

"My camera's not here!"

"The one I gave you for Christmas?" Tremayne asked, not overpleased.

"Perhaps Coconut's got it," Perkin suggested languidly.

"Thanks." Gareth leaped to the telephone in hopes that were all too soon dashed. "He says he didn't see it after lunchtime." He looked horrified. "We'll have to go back at once."

"No, you certainly won't," Tremayne said positively. "It sounds a long way and it'll be getting dark soon."

"But it's *luminous* paint," Gareth begged. "That's the whole point, you can see it in the dark."

"No," said his father.

Gareth turned to me. "Can't we go back?"

I shook my head. "Your father's right. We could get lost in those woods at night, paint or no paint. You've only got to miss one mark and you'd be out there till morning."

"*You* wouldn't get lost."

"I might," I said. "We're not going."

"Did you drop it on the path back?" Mackie asked sympathetically.

"No . . ." He thought about it. "I must have left it where we had lunch. I hung it on a branch to keep it from getting damp. I just forgot it."

He was upset enough for me to say, "I'll get it tomorrow afternoon."

"Will you?" Disaster swung back to hope. "Oh, *great*."

Tremayne said doubtfully, "Will you find one little camera hanging in all those square miles of nothing?"

"Of course he will," Gareth told him confidently. "I told you, we left a *trail*. And oh!" He thought of something. "Isn't it lucky I dropped all the paint, because now you can see where the trail starts, because we didn't paint any trees once we could see the road."

"Do explain," Mackie said.

Gareth explained.

"Will you really find the trail?" Mackie asked me, shaking her head.

"As long as someone hasn't parked on the patch of paint and taken it all away on their tires."

"Oh, no," Gareth said, anguished.

"Don't worry," I told him. "I'll find your camera if it's still in the clearing."

"It is. I'm sure. I remember hanging it up."

"All right then," Tremayne said. "Let's talk about something else."

"Grub?" Gareth asked hopefully. "Pizza?"

16

On Monday morning, first lot, I was back on Drifter.

"He's entered in a race at Worcester the day after tomorrow," Tremayne said as we walked out to the yard at seven in the half-dawn. "Today's his last training gallop before that, so don't fall off again. The vet's been here already this morning to test his blood."

Tremayne's vet took small blood samples of all the stable's runners prior to their last training gallop before they raced, the resulting detailed analysis being able to reveal a whole host of things from a raised lymphocyte count to excreted enzymes due to muscle damage. If there were too many contraindications in the blood, the vet would advise Tremayne that the horse was unlikely to run well or win. Tremayne said the process saved the owners from wasting money on fruitless horse-box expenses and jockey fees and also saved himself a lot of inexplicable and worrying disappointments.

"Are you going to Worcester yourself?" I asked.

"Probably. Might send Mackie. Why?"

"Er . . . I wondered if I could go to see Drifter race."

He turned his head to stare at me as if he couldn't at once comprehend my interest, but then, understanding, said of course I could go if I wanted to.

"Thanks."

"You can gallop Fringe this morning, second lot."

"Thanks again."

"And thanks to you for giving Gareth such a good day yesterday."

"I enjoyed it."

We reached the yard and stood watching the last preparations as usual.

"That's a good camera," Tremayne said regretfully. "Stupid boy."

"I'll get it back."

"Along his precious trail?" He was doubtful.

"Maybe. But I had a map and a compass with me yesterday. I know pretty well where we went."

He smiled, shaking his head. "You're the most competent person . . . Like Fiona says, you put calamities right."

"It's not always possible."

"Give Drifter a good gallop."

We went up to the Downs and at least I stayed in the saddle, and felt indeed a new sense of being at home there, of being at ease. The strange and difficult was becoming second nature in the way that it had when I'd learned to fly. Racehorses, helicopters; both needed hands responsive to the messages reaching them, and both would usually go where you wanted if you sent the right messages back.

Drifter flowed up the gallop in a smooth fast rhythm and Tremayne said he would have a good chance at Worcester if his blood was right.

When I'd left the horse in the yard and gone in for breakfast I found both Mackie and Sam Yaeger sitting at the table with Tremayne, all of them discussing that day's racing at Nottingham. The horse that Tremayne had been going to run had gone lame, and another of Sam's rides had been withdrawn because its owner's wife had died.

"I've only got a no-hoper left," Sam complained. "It's not bloody worthwhile going. Reckon I'll catch flu and work on the boat." He telephoned forthwith, made hoarse-voiced excuses and received undeserved sympathy. He grinned at me, putting down the receiver. "Where's the toast, then?"

"Coming."

"I hear you played cowboys and Indians all over Berkshire with Gareth and Coconut yesterday."

"News travels," I said resignedly.

"I told him," Mackie said, smiling. "Any objections?"

I shook my head and asked her how she was feeling. She'd stopped riding out with the first lot because of nausea on waking, and Tremayne, far from minding, continually urged her to rest more.

"I feel sick," she said to my inquiry. "Thank goodness."

"Lie down, my dear girl," Tremayne said.

"You all fuss too much."

Sam said to me, "Doone spent all Saturday afternoon at the boatyard."

"I thought he was off duty."

"He got a message from you, it seems."

"Mm. I did send one."

"What message?" Tremayne asked.

"I don't know," Sam answered. "Doone phoned me yesterday to say he'd been to the boatyard and taken away some objects for which he would give me a receipt."

"What objects?" asked Tremayne.

"He wouldn't say." Sam looked at me. "Do you know what they were? You steered him to them, it seems. He sounded quite excited."

"What was the message?" Mackie asked me.

"Um . . ." I said. "I asked him why the floorboards didn't float."

Tremayne and Mackie appeared mystified but Sam immediately understood and looked thunderstruck.

"Bloody hell—how did you think of it?"

"Don't know," I said. "It just came."

"Do explain," Mackie begged.

I told her what I'd told Erica at Tremayne's dinner, and said it might not lead to anything helpful.

"But it certainly might," Mackie said.

Sam said to me thoughtfully, "If you hadn't stopped me, I'd have rolled up the curtain so as to go into the dock in a boat, and all that stuff under the water would have slithered away into the river and no one would have been any the wiser."

"Fiona's sure John will find out, before Doone does, who set that trap for Harry," Mackie said.

I shook my head. "I don't know who it was. Wish I did."

"Matter of time," Tremayne said confidently. He looked at his watch. "Talking of time, second lot." He stood up. "Sam, I want a trial of that new horse Roydale against Fringe. You ride Roydale, John's on Fringe."

"OK," Sam said easily.

"John." Tremayne turned to me. "Don't try to beat Sam as if it were a race. This is a fact-finder. I want to see which has most natural speed. Go as fast as you can but if you feel Fringe falter, don't press him, just ease back."

"Right."

"Mackie, talk to Dee-Dee or something. I'm not taking you up there to vomit in the Land-Rover."

"Oh, Tremayne, as if I would."

"Not risking it," he said gruffly. "Don't want you bouncing about on those ruts."

"I'm not an invalid," she protested, but she might as well have argued with a rock. He determinedly left her behind and drove Sam and me up to the gallops.

On the way, Sam said to me dryly, "Nolan usually rides any trials. He'll be furious."

"Thanks a lot."

Tremayne said repressively, "I've told Nolan he won't be riding work here again until he cools off."

Sam raised his eyebrows comically. "Do you want John shot? Nolan's a whiz with a gun."

"Don't talk nonsense," Tremayne said a shade uneasily, and bumped the Land-Rover across the ruts of the track and onto the smooth upland grass before drawing to a halt. "Keep your mind on Roydale. He belongs to a new owner. I want your best judgment. His form's not brilliant, but nor is the trainer he's come from. I want to know where we're at."

"Sure," Sam said.

"Stay upsides Fringe as long as you can."

Sam nodded. We took Roydale and Fringe from the lads and when Tremayne had driven off and positioned himself on his hillock we started together up the all-weather gallop, going the fastest I'd been ever. Fringe, flat-out at racing pace, had a wildness about him I couldn't really control and I guessed it was that quality which won him races. Whenever Roydale put his nose in front, Fringe found a bit extra, but it seemed there wasn't much between them, and with the end of the wood chippings in sight the contest was still undecided. I saw Sam sit up and ease the pressure, and copied him immediately, none too soon for my taxed muscles and speed-starved lungs. I finished literally breathless but Sam pulled up nonchalantly and trotted back to Tremayne for a report in full voice.

"He's a green bugger," he announced. "He has a mouth like elephant skin. He shies at his own shadow and he's as stubborn as a pig. Apart from that, he's fast, as you saw."

Tremayne listened impassively. "Courage?"

"Can't tell till he's on a racecourse."

"I'll enter him for Saturday. We may as well find out.

Perhaps you'd better give him a pop over hurdles tomorrow."

"OK."

We handed the horses back to their respective lads and went down the hill again with Tremayne and found Doone waiting for us, sitting in his car.

"That man gives me the bloody creeps," Sam said as we disembarked.

The grayly persistent detective chief inspector emerged like a turtle from his shell when he saw us arrive, and he'd come alone for once: no silent note-taker in his shadow.

"Which of us do you want?" Tremayne inquired bullishly.

"Well, sir." The singsong voice took all overt menace away, yet there was still a suggestion that collars might be felt at any minute. "All of you, sir, if you don't mind."

Just the same if we did mind, he meant.

"You'd better come in, then," Tremayne offered, shrugging.

Doone followed us into the kitchen, removed a gray tweed overcoat and sat by the table in his much-lived-in gray suit. He felt comfortable in kitchens, I thought. Tremayne vaguely suggested coffee, and I made a mug of instant for us each.

Mackie came through from having breakfasted with Perkin, saying she wanted to know how the trial had gone. She wasn't surprised to see Doone, only resigned. I made her some coffee and she sat and watched while Doone picked a piece of paper out of his breast pocket and handed it to Sam.

"A receipt, sir," he said, "for three lengths of floorboard retrieved from the dock in your boathouse."

Sam unfolded the paper and looked at it dumbly.

"Why didn't they float?" Tremayne asked bluntly.

"Ah. So everyone knows about that?" Doone seemed disappointed.

Tremayne nodded. "John just told us."

Doone gave me a sorrowful stare, but I hadn't given a thought to his wanting secrecy.

"They didn't float, sir, because they were weighted."

"With what?" Sam asked.

"With pieces of paving stone. There are similar pieces of paving stone scattered on a portion of your boatyard property."

"*Paving* stone?" Sam sounded bemused, then said doubtfully, "Do you mean broken slabs of pink and gray marble?"

"Is that what it is, sir, marble?" Doone didn't know much about marble, it appeared.

"It might be."

Doone pondered, made up his mind, went out to his car and returned carrying a five-foot plank which he laid across the kitchen table. The old gray wood, though still dampish, looked as adequate for its purpose as its fellows still forming the boathouse floor and didn't seem to have been weakened in any way. Slightly towards one end, on the surface that was now uppermost on the table, rested a long, unevenly shaped darkish slab of what I might have thought was rough-faced granite.

"Yes," Sam said, glancing at it. "That's marble." He stretched out his hand and tried to pick it up, and the plank came up an inch with it. Sam let it drop, frowning.

"It's stuck on," Doone said, nodding. "From the looks of the other pieces lying about, the surface that's stuck to the wood is smooth and polished."

"Yes," Sam said.

"Superglue, we think," Doone said, "would make a strong enough bond."

"A lot of plastic adhesives would," Sam said, nodding.

"And how do you happen to have chunks of marble lying about?" Doone asked, though not forbiddingly.

"It came with a job lot of stuff I bought from a demolition firm," Sam explained without stress. "They had some paneling I wanted for a boat I did up, and some antique bathroom fittings. I had to take a lot of oddments as well, like the marble. It came from a mansion they were pulling down. They sell off things, you know. Fireplaces, doors, anything."

Doone asked conversationally, "Did you stick the marble onto the floorboards, sir?"

"No, I bloody well did *not*," Sam said explosively.

"Onto the underside of the floorboards," I said. "There were no slabs of marble in sight when Harry and I went into the upstairs room of the boathouse. I expect, if there are some other blocks still in place, that you can see them from underneath, in the dock."

Doone with slight reluctance admitted that there seemed to be marble stuck to the underside of one more floorboard on each side of the hole.

The plank on the table was about eight inches across. Harry had taken three of them down with him; five altogether had been doctored. The trap with its missing section of beam had been three and a half feet across, and Harry, taking the envelope bait, had gone through its center.

"Have you finished snooping round my place now?" Sam demanded, and Doone shook his head.

"I want to work on my boat," Sam objected.

"Go ahead, sir. Never mind my men, if they're there."

"Right." Sam stood up with bouncing energy, quite unlike a patient suddenly stricken with flu. " 'Bye, Tremayne. 'Bye Mackie. See you, John."

He went out to his car, carrying his jazzy jacket, and tooted as he drove away. The kitchen seemed a lot less alive without him.

"I'd like to talk to Mr. Kendall alone," Doone said placidly.

Tremayne's eyebrows rose but he made no objection. He suggested I take Doone into the dining room while he told Mackie about Roydale's gallop, and Doone followed me docilely, bringing the plank.

The formality of the dining-room furnishings seemed at first to change his mood from ease to starch, but it appeared to me after a short while that he was troubled rather by indecision as to which side I was now on, them or us.

He seemed to settle finally for us, us being the police, or at least the fact-seekers and, clearing his throat, he told me that his men with grappling irons and magnets had missed finding the floorboards the first time, probably because the floorboards weren't magnetic. Did I, he wanted to know, think the trap-setter had taken magnetism into account?

I frowned. "Stretching it a bit," I said. "I should think he looked around for something heavy that would take glue, and with all that junk lying around there was bound to be something. The marble happened to be perfect. But the whole thing was so thoroughly thought out, you really can't tell."

"Do you know who did it?" he asked forthrightly.

"No," I said truthfully.

"You must have opinions." He shifted on his chair, looking around him. "I'd like to hear them."

"They're negative more than positive."

"Often just as valuable."

"I'd assume the trap-setter had been a guest at Sam Yaeger's boatyard party," I said, "only you warned me never to assume."

"Assume it," he said, almost smiling and in some inner way contented.

"And," I went on, "I'd assume it was the person who killed Angela Brickell, who wanted to fix the blame forever on Harry by making him disappear, only . . ."

"Assume it," he said.

"Anyone could have killed Angela Brickell, but only a hundred and fifty or so people went to Sam's party, and half of those were women."

"Don't you think a woman could have set that trap?" he asked neutrally.

273

"Sure, a woman could have thought it out and done the carpentering. But what woman could have lured Angela Brickell and persuaded her to take all her clothes off in the middle of a wood?"

He sucked his teeth.

"All right," he said, "I agree, a man killed her." He paused. "Motive?"

"I'd guess . . . to keep a secret. I mean, suppose she was pregnant. Suppose she went out into the woods with . . . *him*, and they were going to make love . . . or they'd done it . . . and she said, 'I'm pregnant, you're the father, what are you going to do about it?' She was full of jumbled religious guilts, but it was she who was the seducer . . ." I paused. "I'd think perhaps she was killed because she wanted too much . . . and because she wouldn't have an abortion."

He made a sound very like a purr in his throat.

"All right," he said again. "Method: strangulation. Guaranteed to work, as everyone around here knew, after the death of that other girl, Olympia."

"Yes."

"Opportunity?" he said.

"No one can remember what they were doing the day Angela Brickell disappeared."

"Except the murderer," he observed. "What about opportunity on the day Mr. Goodhaven fell through the floor?"

"Someone was there to drive his car away . . . no fingerprints, I suppose?"

"Gloves," he said succinctly. "Too few of Mr. Goodhaven's prints are still there. No palm print on the gear lever, for instance. I don't know if we'd have worried about that if we'd thought he'd done a bunk. It was a cold day, after all. He might have worn gloves himself."

"You might have guessed at collusion," I suggested.

"Did you ever consider police work?"

"Not good at that sort of discipline."

"You don't like taking orders, sir?"

"I prefer giving them to myself."

He smiled without criticism. "You'd be no good in uniform."

"None at all."

He was entitled, I supposed, to his small exploratory excursion around my character; and if he himself, I thought, had been wholly fulfilled by uniform, he would still be in it.

Perkin in his overalls appeared in the open doorway, hovering.

"Is Mackie over here?" he said. "I can't find her."

"In the kitchen with Tremayne," I said.

"Thanks." He swept a gaze over Doone and the plank and said with irony, "Sorting it out, then?"

Doone said a shade heavily, "Mr. Kendall's always helpful," and Perkin made a face and went off to join Mackie.

"About Harry's car," I said to Doone. "There must have been just a small problem of logistics. I mean, perhaps our man parked his own car in Reading station car park, then took a train to Maidenhead station and a bus from there to near the river, and went on foot from there to the boatyard . . . wouldn't that make sense?"

"It would, but so far we haven't found anyone who noticed anything useful."

"Car park ticket?"

"There wasn't one in the car. We don't know when the car arrived in the car park. It could have been parked somewhere else on Wednesday and repositioned when our man discovered Mr. Goodhaven was still alive."

"Mm. It would mean that our man had a lot of time available for maneuvering."

"Racing people do have flexible hours," he observed, "and they mostly have free afternoons."

"I don't suppose there's a hope that my jacket and boots were still in the car?" I asked.

"No sign of them. Sorry. They'll be in a dump somewhere, shouldn't wonder." He was looking around the room again, and this time revealed his purpose. "About those guide-books of yours. I'd like to see them."

They were in the family room. I went to fetch them and returned with only three I'd found, *Jungle*, *Safari* and *Ice*. The others, I explained, could be anywhere, as everyone had been reading them.

He opened *Jungle* and quickly flipped through the opening chapters, which were straightforward advice for well-equipped jungle holidays: "Never put a bare foot on the earth. Shower in slippers. Sleep with your shoes inside your mosquito netting. Never drink untreated water . . . never brush your teeth with it . . . don't wash fruit or vegetables in it, avoid suspect ice cubes."

"Never get exhausted!" Doone said aloud. "What sort of advice is that?"

"Exhausted people can't be bothered to stick to lifesaving routines. If you don't drive yourself too hard you're more likely to survive. For instance, if you've a long way to go, it's better to get there slowly than not at all."

"That's weak advice," he said, shaking his head.

I didn't argue, but many died from exhaustion every year through not understanding the strengths of weakness. It was better to stop every day's travel early so as to have good energy for raising a tent, digging an igloo, building a platform up a tree. Dropping down exhausted without shelter could bring new meaning to the expression "dead tired."

" 'Food,' " Doone read out. " 'Fishing, hunting, trapping.' " He flicked the pages. "In the jungle, hang fishhooks to catch birds. Don't forget bait. You always need bait." He looked up. "That envelope was bait, wasn't it?"

I nodded. "Good bait."

"We haven't found it. That water's like liquid mud. You can't see an inch through it, my men say."

"They're right."

He stared for a second. "Oh, yes. I'd forgotten you'd been in it." He went back to the book. " 'It's possible to bring down game with a spear or a bow and arrow, but these take considerable practice and involve hours spent lying in wait. Let a trap do the waiting . . . ' " He read on. " 'The classic trap for large animals is a pit with sharpened staves pointing upwards. Cover the pit with natural-looking vegetation and earth, and suspend the bait over the top.' " He looked up. "Very graphic illustrations and instructions."

"Afraid so."

Eyes down again to the book, he went on. "All sharpened staves for use in traps (and also spears and arrows) can be hardened to increase their powers of penetration by being charred lightly in hot embers, a process which tightens and toughens the wood fibers." Doone stopped reading and remarked, "You don't say anything about sharpening old bicycle frames and railings."

"There aren't many bicycle frames in the jungle. Er . . . were they sharpened?"

He sighed. "Not artificially." He read on. "If digging or scraping out a pit is impracticable because of hard or water-logged ground, try netting. Arrange a net to entangle game when it springs the trap. To make a strong net you can use tough plant fibers . . ." He silently read several pages, occasionally shaking his head, not, I gathered, in disagreement with the text, but in sorrow at its availability.

"How to skin a snake," he read. "Dear God."

"Roast rattlesnake tastes like chicken," I said.

"You've eaten it?"

I nodded. "Not at all bad."

"First aid. How to stop heavy bleeding. Pressure points . . .To close gaping wounds, use needle and thread. To help blood clot, apply cobwebs to the wound. *Cobwebs!* I don't believe it."

"They're organic," I said, "and as sterile as most bandages."

"Not for me, thanks." He put down *Jungle* and flipped

277

through *Safari* and *Ice*. Many of the same suggestions for traps appeared in all the books, modified only by terrain.

"Don't eat polar bear liver," Doone read in amazement, "it stores enough vitamin A to kill humans." He smiled briefly. "That would make a dandy new method for murder."

First catch your polar bear . . .

"Well, sir," Doone said, laying the books aside, "we can trace the path of ideas about the trap, but who do you think put them into practice?"

I shook my head.

"If I throw names at you," he said, "give your reasons for or against."

"All right," I said cautiously.

"Mr. Vickers."

"Tremayne?" I must have sounded astonished. "All against."

"Why, exactly?"

"Well, he's not like that."

"As I told you before, I don't know these people the way you do. So give me reasons."

I said, thinking, "Tremayne Vickers is forceful, a bit old-fashioned, straightforward, often kind. Angela Brickell would not have been to his taste. If, and to my mind it's a colossal if, *if* she managed to seduce him and then told him he was the father-to-be, and if he believed it, it would have been more his style to pack her off home to her parents and provide for her. He doesn't shirk responsibility. Also I can't imagine him taking any woman out into deep woods for sex. Impossible. As for trying to kill Harry . . ." Words failed me.

"All right," Doone said. He brought out a notebook and methodically wrote *Kendall's assessments* at the top of the page. Underneath he wrote *Tremayne Vickers,* followed by a cross, and under Tremayne, *Nolan Everard.*

"Nolan Everard," he said.

Not so easy. "Nolan is brave. He's dynamic and determined . . . and violent."

"And he threatened to kill you," Doone said flatly.

"Who told you that?"

"Half the racing world heard him."

Sighing, I explained about my riding.

"And when he attacked you, you picked him up like a baby in front of all those people," Doone said. "A man might not forgive that."

"We're talking about Angela Brickell and Harry," I pointed out mildly.

"Talk about Nolan Everard then. *For,* first."

"*For* . . . Well, he killed Olympia, not really meaning to, but definitely by putting her life at risk. He couldn't afford another scandal while waiting for trial. If Angela Brickell had seduced him—or the other way round—and she threatened a messy paternity suit . . . I don't know. That's again a big if, but not as impossible as Tremayne. Nolan and Sam Yaeger often bed the same girl, more or less to spite each other, it seems. Nolan regularly rides the horse Chickweed, that Angela Brickell had care of, and there would have been opportunities for sex at race meetings, like in a horse box, if he wanted to take the risk. He could sue me for slander over this."

"He won't hear of it," Doone said positively. "This conversation is just between you and me. I'll deny I ever discussed the case with you if anyone asks."

"Fair enough." I thought a bit. "As for the trap for Harry, Nolan would be mentally and physically capable."

"But? I hear your but."

I nodded. "*Against.* He's Fiona's cousin, and they're close. He depends on Fiona's horses to clinch his amateur-champion status. He couldn't be sure she would have the heart to go on running racehorses if she were forced to believe Harry a murderer . . . if she thought he had left her without warning, without a note, if she were worried sick by not knowing where he'd gone, and was also haunted by the thought of Harry with Angela Brickell."

"Would Everard have stopped to consider all that?" he mused doubtfully.

"The trap was well thought out."

Doone wrote a question mark after Nolan's name.

"Doesn't *anyone* have a solid alibi for Wednesday afternoon?" I asked. "That's the one definite time our man has to explain away."

"And don't think we don't know it." Doone nodded. "Not many of the men connected with this place can account for every hour of that afternoon, though the women can. We've been very busy this morning, making enquiries. Mrs. Goodhaven went to a committee meeting, then home in time to be there when you telephoned. Mrs. Perkin Vickers was at Ascot races, vouched for by saddling a horse in the three-mile chase. Mr. Vickers's secretary, Dee-Dee, made several telephone calls from the office here and Mrs. Ingrid Watson went shopping in Oxford with her mother and can produce receipts."

"Ingrid?"

"She can't vouch for what her husband did."

He wrote *Bob Watson* under Nolan.

"*For* him being our man," I said dubiously, "is, I suppose Ingrid herself. She wouldn't put up with shenanigans with Angela Brickell. But whether Bob would kill to stay married to Ingrid . . ." I shook my head. "I don't know. He's a good head lad, Tremayne trusts him, but I wouldn't stake my life on his loyalty. Also he's an extremely competent carpenter, as you saw yourself. He was serving drinks at the party when Olympia died. He went to the boatyard party as a guest."

"Against?"

I hesitated. "Killing Angela Brickell might have been a moment's panic. Setting the trap for Harry took cunning and nerve. I don't know Bob Watson well enough for a real opinion. I don't know him like the others."

Doone nodded and put a question mark after his name also.

Gareth Vickers, he wrote.

I smiled. "It can't be him."

"Why not?" Doone asked.

"Angela Brickell's sexuality frightened him. He would never have gone into the woods with her. Apart from that, he hasn't a driving license, and he was at school on Wednesday afternoon."

"Actually," Doone said calmly, "he is known to be able to drive his father's jeep on the Downs expertly, and my men have discovered he was out of school last Wednesday afternoon on a field trip to Windsor Safari Park. That's not miles from the boatyard. The teacher in charge is flustered over the number of boys who sneaked off to buy food."

I considered Gareth as a murderer. I said, "You asked me for my knowledge of these people. Gareth couldn't possibly be our man."

"Why are you so sure?"

"I just am."

He wrote a cross against Gareth's name, and then as an afterthought, a question mark also.

I shook my head. Under Gareth's name he wrote *Perkin Vickers.*

"What about *him*?" he asked.

"Perkin . . ." I sighed. "He lives in another world, half the time. He works hard. *For,* I suppose, is that he makes furniture, he's good with wood. I don't know that it's *for* or *against* that he dotes on his wife. He's very possessive of her. He's a bit childlike in some ways. She loves him and looks after him. *Against* . . . he doesn't have much to do with the horses. Seldom goes racing. He didn't remember who Angela Brickell was, the first morning you were here."

Doone pursed his lips judiciously, then nodded and wrote a cross against Perkin, and then again a question mark.

"Keeping your options open?" I asked dryly.

"You never know what we don't know," he said.

"Deep."

"It might be reasonable to assume that Mr. Goodhaven didn't set the trap himself, to persuade me of his innocence," he said, writing *Henry Goodhaven* on the list.

"A hundred percent," I agreed.

"However, he took you along as a witness." He paused. "Suppose he planned it and it all went wrong? Suppose he needed you there to assert he'd walked into a trap?"

"Impossible."

He put a question mark against Harry, all the same.

"Who drove his car away?" I said, a shade aggressively.

"A casual thief."

"I don't believe it."

"You like him," Doone said. "You're unreliable."

"That page is headed '*Kendall's* assessments,' " I protested. "My assessment of Harry merits a firm cross."

He looked at what he'd written, shrugged and changed the question mark to a negative. Then he made a question mark way to the right on the same line. "My assessments," he said.

I smiled a little ruefully and said reflectively, "Have you worked out when the trap was set? Raising the floorboards, finding the marble and sticking it on, cutting out the bit of beam—and I bet that went floating down the river—remembering to lock the lower door . . . It would all have taken a fair time."

"When would *you* say it was done, then?" he asked, giving nothing away.

"Any time Tuesday, or Wednesday morning, I suppose."

"Why, exactly?"

"Anti-Harry fever was publicly at its height on Monday, Tuesday and Wednesday, but by the Sunday before, at least, you'd begun to spread your investigation outward . . . which must horribly have alarmed our man. Sam Yaeger spent Monday at the boatyard because he'd been medically stood down from racing as a result of a fall, but by Tuesday he was racing again, and on Wednesday he rode at Ascot, so the boathouse was vulnerable all day Tuesday and again Wednesday morning."

Doone looked at me from under his eyelids.

"You're forgetting something," he said, and added *Sam Yaeger* to his list.

17

"Put a cross," I said.

Doone shook his head. "You admire him. You could be blinded."

I thought it over. "I do in many ways admire him, I admit. I admire his riding, his professionalism. He's courageous. He's a realist." I paused. "I'll agree that on the *For* side you could put the things you listed the other day, that he has all the skills to set the trap and the perfect place to do it."

Doone nodded. "Go on."

"You'd begun actively investigating him," I said.

"Yes, I had."

"He'd rolled around a bit with Angela Brickell," I said, "and that's where we come to the biggest *Against*."

"You're not saying he couldn't have had the irritation, the nerve, the strength to strangle her?"

"No, I'm not, though I don't think he did it. What I'm

284

saying is that he wouldn't have taken her out into the woods. He told you himself he moves a mattress into the boathouse on such occasions. If he'd strangled her on impulse it would have been *there,* and he could have slid her weighted body into the river, no one the wiser."

Doone listened with his head on one side. "But what if he'd deliberately planned it? What if he'd suggested the woods as being far away from his own territory?"

"I wouldn't think he'd need to cover his sins with strangulation," I said. "Everyone knows he seduces anything that moves. He would pass off an Angela Brickell sort of scandal with a laugh."

Doone disapproved, saying "Unsavory," and maybe thinking of his assailable daughters.

"We haven't got very far," I said, looking at his list. All my own assessments were a cross except the question mark against Nolan. Not awfully helpful, I thought.

Doone clicked his pen a few times, then at the bottom wrote *Lewis Everard.*

"That's a longshot," I said.

"Give me some *Fors* and *Againsts.*"

I pondered. "*Against* first. I don't think he's bold enough to have set that trap, but then"—I hesitated—"there's no doubt he's both clever and cunning. I wouldn't have thought he would have gone into the woods with Angela Brickell. Can't exactly say why, but I'd think he'd be too fastidious, especially when he's sober."

"For?" Doone prompted, when I stopped.

"He gets drunk . . . I don't know if he'd tumble Angela Brickell in that state or not."

"But he knew her."

"Even if not in the biblical sense," I agreed.

"Sir!" he said with mock reproach.

"He would have seen her at the races," I said, smiling. And *For* . . . he is a good liar. According to him, he's the best actor of the lot."

"A question mark, then?" Doone's pen hovered.

I slowly shook my head. "A cross."

"The trouble with you," Doone said with disillusion, looking at the column of negatives, "is that you haven't met enough murderers."

"None," I agreed. "You can't exactly count Nolan Everard."

"And you wouldn't know a murderer if you tripped over one."

"Your list is too short," I said.

"It seems so." He put away the notebook and stood up. "Well, Mr. Kendall, thank you for your time. I don't discount your impressions. You've helped clarify my thoughts. Now we'll have to step up our enquiries. We'll get there in the end."

The singsong accent came to a stop and he shook my hand and let himself out, a gray man in gray clothes following his own informal idiosyncratic path towards the truth.

I sat for a while thinking of what I'd said and of what he'd told me, and I still couldn't believe that any of the people I'd come to know so well was really a murderer. No one was a villain, not even Nolan. There had to be someone else, someone we hadn't begun to consider.

I worked on and off on Tremayne's book for the rest of the morning but found it hard to concentrate.

Dee-Dee drifted in and out, offering coffee and company, and Tremayne put his head in to say he was going to Oxford to see his tailor, and to ask if I wanted an opportunity to shop.

I thanked him and declined. I would probably have liked to replace my boots and ski jacket, but I still hadn't much personal money. It was easy at Shellerton House to get by without any. Tremayne would doubtless have lent me some of the quarter-advance due at the end of the month, but my lack was my own choice, and as long as I could survive as I was, I wouldn't ask. It was all part of the game.

Mackie came through from her side to keep company with Dee-Dee, saying Perkin had gone to Newbury to collect some supplies, and presently the two women went off to lunch together, leaving me alone in the great sprawling house.

I tried again and harder to work and felt restless and uneasy. Stupid, I thought. Being alone never bothered me: in fact, I liked it. That day, I found the size of the silent house oppressive.

I went upstairs, showered and changed out of riding clothes into the more comfortable jeans and shirt I'd worn the day before and pulled on sneakers and the red sweater for warmth. After that I went down to the kitchen and made a cheese sandwich for lunch and wished I'd gone with Tremayne if only for the ride. It was all part of the usual pattern of finding something to do—*anything*—rather than sit down and face the empty page, except that that day the uneasiness was extra.

I wandered in a desultory fashion into the family room, which looked dead without the fire blazing and began to wonder what I could make for dinner. Gareth's BACK FOR GRUB message was still pinned to the corkboard, and it was with a distinct sense of release that I remembered I'd said that I would go back for his camera.

The unease vanished. I found a piece of paper and left my own message: I'VE BORROWED THE LAND-ROVER TO FETCH GARETH'S CAMERA. BACK FOR COOKING THE GRUB! I pinned it to the corkboard with a red drawing pin and a light heart, and went upstairs again to change back into jodhpur boots to deal with the terrain and to pick up the map and the compass in case I couldn't find the trail. Then I skipped downstairs and went out to the wheels, locking the back door behind me.

It was a good day, sunny like the day before but with

more wind. With a feeling of having been unexpectedly let out of school, I drove over the hills on the road to Reading and coasted along the unfenced part of the Quillersedge Estate until I thought I'd come more or less to where Gareth had dropped the paint: parked off the road there and searched more closely for the place on foot.

No one had driven the paint away on their tires. The splash was dusty but still visible and, without much trouble, I found the beginning of the trail about twenty feet straight ahead in the wood and followed it as easily through the tangled trees and undergrowth as on the day before.

Gareth a murderer . . . I smiled to myself at the absurdity of it. As well suspect Coconut.

The pale paint splashes, the next one ahead visible all the time, weren't all that marked the trail: it showed signs in broken twigs and scuffed ground of our passage the day before. By the time I came back with the camera it would be almost a beaten track.

Wind rattled and swayed the trees and filled my ears with the old songs of the land, and the sun shone through the moving boughs in shimmering ever-changing patterns. I wound my slow way through the maze of unpruned growth and felt at one with things there and inexpressibly happy.

The trail strayed around and eventually reached the small clearing. Our improvised seats were frayed by the wind but still identified the place with certainty, and almost at once I spotted Gareth's camera, prominently hanging, as he'd said, from a branch.

I walked across to collect it and something hit me very hard indeed in the back.

Moments of disaster are disorientating. I didn't know what had happened. The world had changed. I was falling. I was lying facedown on the ground. There was something wrong with my breathing.

I had heard nothing but the wind, seen nothing but the

moving trees but, I thought incredulously, *someone had shot me.*

From total instinct as much as from injury I lay as dead. There was a zipping noise beside my ear as something sped past it. I shut my eyes. There was another jolting thud in my back.

So this was death, I thought numbly; and I didn't even know who was killing me, and I didn't know why.

Breathing was terrible. My chest was on fire. A wave of clammy perspiration broke out on my skin.

I lay unmoving.

My face was on dead leaves and dried grass and pieces of twig. I could smell the musty earth. Earth-digested, come to dust.

Someone, I thought dimly, was waiting to see if I moved: and if I moved there would be a third thud and my heart would stop. If I didn't move someone would come and feel for a pulse and, finding one, finish me off. Either way, everything that had been beginning was now ending, ebbing away without hope.

I lay still. Not a twitch.

I couldn't hear anything but the wind in the trees. Could hear no one moving. Hadn't heard even the shots.

Breathing was dreadful. A shaft of pain. Minimum air could go in, trickle out. Too little. In a while . . . I would go to sleep.

A long time seemed to pass, and I was still alive.

I had a vision of someone standing not far behind me with a gun, waiting for me to move. He was shadowy and had no face, and his patience was forever.

Clammy nausea came again, enveloping and ominous. My skin sweated. I felt cold.

I didn't exactly try to imagine what was happening in my body.

Lying still was anyway easier than moving. I would slide unmoving into eternity. The man with a gun could wait forever, but I would be gone. I would cheat him that way.

That's delirium, I thought.

Nothing happened in the clearing. I lay still. Time drifted.

After countless ages I seemed to come back to a real realization that I was continuing to breathe, even if with difficulty, and didn't seem in immediate danger of stopping. However ghastly I might feel, however feeble, I wasn't drowning in blood. Wasn't coughing it up. Coughing was a bleak thought, the way my chest hurt.

My certainty of the waiting gun began to fade. He wouldn't be there after all this time. He wouldn't stand forever doing nothing. He hadn't felt my pulse. He must have thought it unnecessary.

He believed I was dead.

He had gone. I was alone.

It took me a while to believe those three things utterly and another while to risk acting on the belief.

If I didn't move I would die where I lay.

With dread but in the end inevitability, I moved my left arm.

Christ, I thought, that *hurt.*

Hurt it might, but nothing else happened.

I moved my right arm. Just as bad. Even worse.

No more thuds in the back, though. No quick steps, no pounce, no final curtain.

Perhaps I really was alone. I let the thought lie there for comfort. Wouldn't contemplate a cat-and-mouse cruelty.

I put both palms flat on the decaying undergrowth and tried to heave myself up onto my knees.

Practically fainted. Not only could I not do it, but the effort was so excruciating that I opened my mouth to scream and couldn't breathe enough for that either. My weight settled back on the earth and I felt nothing but staggering agony and couldn't think connectedly until it abated.

Something was odd, I thought finally. It wasn't only that

I couldn't lift myself off the ground but that I was stuck to it in some way.

Cautiously, sweating, with fiery stabs in every inch, I wormed my right hand between my body and the earth, and came to what seemed like a rod between the two.

I must have fallen onto a sharp stick, I thought. Perhaps I hadn't been shot. But yes, I had. Hit in the back. Couldn't mistake it.

Slowly, trying to ration the pain into manageable portions, I slid my hand out again, and then after a while, hardly believing it, I bent my arm and felt around my back and came to the rod there also, and faced the grim certainty that someone had shot me not with a bullet but an *arrow*.

I lay for a while simply wrestling with the enormity of it.

I had an arrow right through my body from back to front, somewhere in the region of my lower ribs. Through my right lung, which was why I was breathing oddly. Not, miraculously, through any major blood vessels, or I would by now have bled internally to death. About level with my heart, but to one side.

Bad enough. Awful. But I was still alive.

Survival begins in the mind.

I'd written that, and knew it to be true. But to survive an arrow a mile from a road with a killer around to make sure I didn't make it . . . where in one's mind did one search for will to survive that? Where, when just getting to one's knees loomed as an unavoidable torture and to lie and wait to be rescued appeared to be merely common sense.

I thought about rescue. A long long way off. No one would start looking for me for hours; not until after dark. The sun on my back was warm, but the February nights were still near zero and I was wearing only a sweater. Theoretically the luminous trail should lead rescuers to the clearing even at night . . . but any sensible murderer would have obliterated the road end of it after he'd found his own way out.

I couldn't realistically be rescued before tomorrow. I thought I might die while I waited: might die in the night. People died of injuries sometimes because their bodies went into shock. General trauma, not just the wound, could kill.

One thought, one decision at a time.

Better die trying.

All right. Next decision.

Which way to go.

The trail seemed obvious enough, but my intended killer had come and gone that way—must have done—and if he should return for any reason I wouldn't want to meet him.

I had a compass in my pocket.

The distant road lay almost due north of the clearing and the straightest line to the road lay well to the left of the paint trail.

I waited for energy, but it didn't materialize.

Next decision: get up anyway.

The tip of the arrow couldn't be far into the earth, I thought. I'd fallen with it already through me. It could be only an inch or so in. No more than a centimeter, maybe.

I shut my mind to the consequences, positioned my hands, and pushed.

The arrow tip came free and I lay on my side in frightful suffering weakness, looking down at a sharp black point sticking out from scarlet wool.

Black. The length of a finger. Hard and sharp. I touched the needle tip of it and wished I hadn't.

Only one arrow. Only one all the way through, at least.

Not much blood, surprisingly. Or perhaps I couldn't tell, blood being the same color as the jersey, but there was no great wet patch.

A mile to the road seemed an impossible distance. Moving an inch was taxing. Still, inches added up. Better get started.

First catch your compass . . .

With an inward smile and a mental sigh I retrieved the compass carefully from my pocket and took a bearing on north. North, it seemed, was where my feet were.

I rolled with effort to my knees and felt desperately, appallingly, overwhelmingly ill. The flicker of humor died fast. The waves of protest were so strong that I almost gave up there and then. Outraged tissues, invaded lungs, an overall warning.

I stayed on my knees, sitting back on my heels, head bowed, breathing as little as possible, staring at the protruding arrow, thinking the survival program was too much.

There was a pale slim rod sticking into the ground beside me. I looked at it vaguely and then with more attention, remembering the thing that had sung past my ear.

An arrow that had missed me.

It was about as long as an arm. A peeled fine-grained stick, dead straight. A notch in its visible end, for slotting onto a bowstring. No feather to make a flight.

The guidebooks all gave instructions for making arrows.

"Char the tips in hot embers to shrink and toughen the fibres for better penetration . . ."

The charred black tip had penetrated all right.

"Cut two slots in the other end, one shallow one for the bowstring, one deep one to push a shaped feather into, to make a flight so that the arrow will travel straighter to the target."

Illustrations thoughtfully provided.

If the three arrows had all had flights . . . if there'd been no wind . . .

I closed my eyes weakly. Even without flights, the aim had been deadly enough.

Gingerly, sweating, I curled my left hand behind my back and felt for the third arrow, and found it sticking out of my jersey though fairly loose in my hand. With trepidation I took a stronger hold of it and it came away altogether but with a sharp dagger of soreness, like digging out a splinter.

The black tip of that arrow was scarlet with blood, but I reckoned it hadn't gone in further than a rib or my spine. I only had the first one to worry about.

Only the one.

Quite enough.

It would have been madness to pull it out, even if I could have faced doing it. In duels of old it hadn't always been the sword going *into* the lungs that had killed so much as the drawing of it out. The puncture let air rush in and out, spoiling nature's enclosed vacuum system. With holes to the outer air, the lungs collapsed and couldn't breathe. With the arrow still in place, the holes were virtually blocked. With the arrow in place, bleeding was held at bay. I might die with it in. I'd die quicker with it out.

The first rule of surviving a disaster, I had written, was to accept that it had happened and make the best of what was left. Self-pity, regrets, hopelessness and surrender would never get one home. Survival began, continued and was accomplished in the mind.

All right, I told myself, follow your own rules.

Accept the fact of the arrow. Accept your changed state. Accept that it hurts, that every movement will hurt for the foreseeable future. Take that for granted. Go on from there.

Still on my knees, I edged around to face north.

The clearing was all mine: No man with a gun. No archer with a bow.

The day in some respects remained incredibly the same. The sun still threw its dappled mantle and the trees still creaked and resonantly vibrated in the oldest of symphonies. Many before me, I thought, had been shot by arrows in ancient woodland and faced their mortality in places that had looked like this.

But I, if I stirred myself, could reach surgeons and antibiotics and hooray for the National Health Service. I slowly shifted on my knees across the clearing, aiming to the left of the painted trail.

It wasn't so bad . . .

It was awful.

For God's sake, I told myself, ignore it. Get used to it. Think about north.

It wasn't possible to go all the way to the road on one's knees: the undergrowth was too thick, the saplings in places too close together. I would have to stand up.

So, OK, hauling on branches, I stood up.

Even my legs felt odd. I clung hard to a sapling with my eyes closed, waiting for things to get better, telling myself that if I fell down again it would be much much *much* worse.

North.

I opened my eyes eventually and took the compass out of my jeans pocket, where I'd stowed it to have hands free for standing up. Holding on still with one hand, I took a visual line ahead from the north needle to mark into memory the furthest small tree I could see, then put the compass away again and with infinite slowness clawed a way forward by inches and after a while reached the target and held on to it for dear life.

I had traveled perhaps ten yards. I felt exhausted.

"Never get exhausted," I had written. Dear God.

I rested out of necessity, out of weakness.

In a while I consulted the compass, memorized another young tree and made my way there. When I looked back I could no longer see the clearing.

I was committed, I thought. I wiped sweat off my forehead with my fingers and stood quietly, holding on, trying to let the oxygen level in my blood climb back to a functioning state.

A functioning mode, Gareth might have said.

Gareth . . .

Sherwood Forest, I thought, eight hundred years ago. Whose face should I pin on the Sheriff of Nottingham . . .

I went another ten yards, and another, careful always not

to trip, holding on to branches as on to railings. My breath began wheezing from the exertion. Pain had finally become a constant. Ignore it. Weakness was more of a problem, and lack of breath.

Stopping again for things to calm down, I began to do a few unwelcome sums. I had traveled perhaps fifty yards. It seemed a marathon to me, but realistically it was roughly one thirty-fifth of a mile, which left thirty-four thirty-fifths still to go. I hadn't timed the fifty yards but it had been no sprint. According to my watch it was already after four o'clock, a rotten piece of information borne out by the angle of the sun. Darkness lay ahead.

I would have to go as fast as I could while I could still see the way, and then rest for longer, and then probably crawl. Sensible plan, but not enough strength to go fast.

Fifty more yards in five sections. One more thirty-fifth of the way. Marvelous. It had taken me fifteen minutes.

More sums. At a speed of fifty yards in fifteen minutes it would take me another eight hours to reach the road. It would then be half-past midnight, and that didn't take into account long rests or crawling.

Despair was easy. Survival wasn't.

To hell with despair, I thought. Get on and walk.

The shaft of the arrow protruding from my back occasionally knocked against something, bringing me to a gasping halt. I didn't know how long it was, couldn't feel as far as the end, and I couldn't always judge how much space I needed to keep it clear.

I'd come out on the simple camera-fetching errand without the complete zipped pouch of gadgets, but I did have with me the belt holding my knife and the multipurpose survival tool, and on the back of that tool there was a mirror. After the next fifty yards I drew it out and took a look at the bad news.

The shaft, straight, pale and rigid, stuck out about eighteen inches. There was a notch in the end for the bowstring, but no flight.

I didn't look at my face in the mirror. Didn't want to confirm how I felt. I returned the small tool to the pouch and went another fifty yards, taking care.

North. Ten yards visible at a time. Go ten yards. Five times ten yards. Short rest.

The sun sank lower on my left and the blue shadows of dusk began gathering on the pines and firs and creeping in among the sapling branches and the alders. In the wind the shadows threw barred stripes and moved like prowling tigers.

Fifty yards, rest. Fifty yards, rest. Fifty yards, rest.

Think of nothing else.

There would be moonlight later, I thought. Full moon was three days back. If the sky remained clear, I could go on by moonlight.

Dusk deepened until I could no longer see ten yards ahead, and after I'd knocked the shaft of the arrow against an unseen hazard twice within a minute I stopped and sank slowly down to my knees, resting my forehead and the front of my left shoulder against a young birch trunk, drained as I'd never been before.

Perhaps I would write a book about this one day, I thought.

Perhaps I would call it . . . Longshot.

A long shot with an arrow.

Perhaps not so long, though. No doubt from only a few yards out of the clearing, to get a straight view. A short shot, perhaps.

He'd been waiting there for me, I concluded. If he'd been following me he would have had to be close because I had gone straight to the camera, and I would have heard him, even in the wind. He'd been there first, waiting, and I'd walked up to the carefully prominent bait and presented him with a perfect target, a broad back in a scarlet sweater, an absolute cinch.

Traps.

I'd walked into one, as Harry had.

I leaned against the tree, sagging into it. I did feel comprehensively dreadful.

If I'd been the archer, I thought, I would have been waiting in position, crouched and camouflaged, endlessly patient, arrow notched on bow. Along comes the target, happily unaware, going to the camera, putting himself in position. Stand up, aim . . . a whamming direct hit, first time lucky.

Shoot twice more at the fallen body. Pity to waste the arrows. Another nice hit.

Target obviously dead. Wait a bit to make sure. Maybe go near for a closer look. All well. Then retreat along the trail. Mission accomplished.

Who was the Sheriff of Nottingham . . .

I tried to find a more comfortable position but there wasn't one, really. To save my knees a bit I slid down onto my left hip, leaning my head and my left side against the tree. It was better than walking, better than fighting the tangle of woodland, but whether it was better than lying in the clearing, I couldn't decide. Yet he, the archer, might have gone back there to check again after all and if he had he would know I was alive, but he would never find me where I was now, deep in impenetrable shadow along a path he couldn't follow in the dark.

It was ironic, I thought, that for the expedition for Gareth and Coconut I'd deliberately chosen to aim for a spot on the map that looked as remote from any road as possible. I should have had more sense.

The darkness intensified down in the wood though I could see stars between the boughs. I listened to the wind. Grew cold. Felt extremely alone.

I let go of things a bit. Simply existed. Let thoughts drift.

I felt formless, part of time and space, an essence, a piece of cosmos. The awareness of the world's antiquity which was often with me seemed to intensify, to be a solace. Everything was one. Every being was integral, but alone. One could dissolve and still exist . . . I hovered on the edge of consciousness, semiasleep, making nonsense.

I relaxed too far. My weight shifted against the tree, slipping downwards, and the shaft of the arrow hit the ground. The explosive pain of it brought me hellishly back to full savage consciousness and to a revived desire not to become part of the eternal mystery just yet. I struggled back into equilibrium and tried to ride the pulverizing waves of misery and found to my desperate dismay that the finger of arrow in front was almost an inch longer.

I'd pushed the arrow further through. I'd done hell knew what extra damage in my lung. I didn't know how to bear what my body felt.

I went on breathing. Went on living. That's all one could say.

The worst of it got better.

I sat for what seemed a long time in the cold darkness, breathing shallowly, not moving at all, just waiting, and eventually there was a lightening of the shadows and a luminosity in the wood, and the moon rose clear and bright in the east. To eyes long in the dark, it was like daylight.

Time to go. I pulled out the compass, held it horizontally close to my eyes, let the needle settle onto north, looked that way and mapped the first few feet in my mind.

Putting thought into action was an inevitable trial. Everything was sore, every muscle seemed wired directly to the arrow. Violent twinges shot up my nerves like steel lightning.

So what, I told myself. Stop bellyaching. Ignore what it feels like, concentrate on the journey.

Concentrate on the Sheriff . . .

I pulled myself to my feet again, rocked a bit, sweated,

clung on to things, groaned a couple of times, gave myself lectures. Put one foot in front of the other, the only way home.

Knocking the arrow seemed after all not to have been the ultimate disaster. Moving seemed to require the same amount of breath as before, which was to say more than could be easily provided.

I couldn't always see so far ahead by moonlight and needed to consult the compass more often. It slowed things up to keep putting it in and out of my jeans pocket so after a while I tucked it up the sleeve of my jersey. That improvement upset the old fifty-yard rhythm but it didn't much matter. I looked at my watch instead and stopped every fifteen minutes for a rest.

The moon rose high in the sky and shone unfalteringly into the woods, a silver goddess that I felt like worshiping. I became numb again to discomfort to a useful degree and plodded on methodically, taking continual bearings, breathing carefully, aiming performance just below capability so as to last out to the end.

The archer had to have a face.

If I could think straight, if every scrap of attention didn't have to be focused on not falling, I could probably get nearer to knowing. Things had changed since the arrow. A whole lot of new factors had to be considered. I tripped over a root, half lost my balance, shoved the new factors into oblivion.

Slowly, slowly, I went north. Then one time when I put my hand in my sleeve to bring out the compass, it wasn't there.

I'd dropped it.

I couldn't go on without it. Had to go back. Doubted if I could find it in the undergrowth. I felt swamped with liquefying despair, weak enough for tears.

Get a bloody grip on things, I told myself. Don't be stupid. Work it out.

I was facing north. If I turned precisely one hundred and eighty degrees I would be facing where I'd come from.

Elementary.

Think.

I stood and thought and made the panic recede until I could work out what to do, then I took my knife out of its sheath on my belt and carved an arrow in the bark of the tree I was facing. An arrow pointing skyward. I had arrows on the brain as well as through the lungs, I thought.

The tree arrow pointed north.

The compass had to be somewhere in sight of that arrow. I would have to crawl to have any hope of finding it.

I went down on my knees carefully and as carefully turned to face the other way, south. The tangle of brown foot-long dried grass and dead leaves and the leafless shoots of new growth filled every space between saplings and established trees. Even in daylight with every faculty at full steam it wouldn't have been an easy search, and as things were it was abysmal.

I crawled a foot or two, casting about, trying to part the undergrowth, hoping desperate hopes. I looked back to the arrow on the tree, then crawled another foot. Nothing. Crawled another and another. Nothing. Crawled until I could see the arrow only because it was pale against the bark, and knew I was already further away than when I'd taken the last bearing.

I turned around and began to crawl back, still sweeping one hand at a time through the jumbled growth. Nothing. Nothing. Hope became a very thin commodity. Weakness was winning.

The compass had to be *somewhere.*

If I couldn't find it, I would have to wait for morning and steer north by my watch and the sun. If the sun shone. If I lasted that long. The cold of the night was deepening and I was weaker than I'd been when I set out.

I crawled in a fruitless search all the way back to the tree and then turned and crawled away again on a slightly different line, looking, looking, hope draining away yard by yard in progressive debility, resolution ebbing with failure.

One time when I turned to check on the arrow on the tree, I couldn't see it. I no longer knew which was north.

I stopped and slumped dazedly back on my heels, facing utter defeat.

Everything hurt unremittingly and I could no longer pretend I could ignore it. I was wounded to death and dying on my knees, scrabbling in dead grass, my time running out with the moonlight, the shadows closing in.

I felt that I couldn't endure any more. I had no will left. I had always believed that survival lay in the mind but now I knew there were things one couldn't survive. One couldn't survive unless one could believe one could, and belief had leaked out of me, gone with sweat and pain and weakness into the wind.

18

Time . . . unmeasured time . . . slid away.

I moved in the end from discomfort, from stiffness: made a couple of circling shuffles on my knees, an unthought-out search for a nest to lie in, to die in, maybe.

I looked up and saw again the arrow cut into the tree. It hadn't been and wasn't far away, just out of sight behind a group of saplings.

Apathetically, I thought it of little use. The arrow pointed in the right direction, but ten feet past it, without the compass, which way was north?

The arrow on the tree pointed upwards.

I looked slowly in that direction, as if instructed. Looked upwards to the sky: and there, up there, glimpsed now and then between the moving boughs, was the constellation of the Great Bear . . . and the polestar.

* * *

No doubt from then on my route wasn't as straight or as accurate as earlier, but at least I was moving. It wasn't possible after all to curl up and surrender, not with an alternative. Clinging on to things, breathing little, inching a slow way forwards, I achieved again a sort of numbness to my basic state, and in looking upwards to the stars at every pause felt lighter and more disembodied than before.

Lightheaded, I dare say.

I looked at my watch and found it was after eleven o'clock, which meant nothing really. I couldn't reach the road by half-past midnight. I didn't know how long I'd wasted looking for the compass or for how long I'd knelt in capitulation. I didn't know at what rate I was now traveling and no longer bothered to work it out. All that I was really clear about was that this time I would go on as long as my lungs and muscles would function. Survival or nothing. It was settled.

The face of the archer . . .

In splinters of thought, unconnectedly, I began to look back over the past three weeks.

I thought of how I must seem to them, the people I'd grown to know.

The writer, a stranger, set down in their midst. A person with odd knowledge, odd skills, physically fit. Someone Tremayne trusted and wanted around. Someone who'd been in the right place a couple of times. Someone who threatened.

I thought of Angela Brickell's death and of the attacks on Harry and me and it seemed that all three had had one purpose, which was to keep things as they were. They were designed not to achieve but to prevent.

One foot in front of the other . . .

Faint little star, half hidden, revealed now and then by the wind; flickering pinpoint in a whirling galaxy, the prayer of navigators . . . see me home.

Angela Brickell had probably been killed to close her mouth. Harry was to have died to cement his guilt. I wasn't to be allowed to do what Fiona and Tremayne had both foretold, that I would find the truth for Doone.

They all expected too much of me.

Because of that expectation, I was half dead.

All guesses, I thought. All inferences. No actual objects that could prove guilt. No statements or admissions to go on, but only probability, only likelihood.

The archer had to be someone who knew I was going to go back for Gareth's camera. It had to be someone who knew how to find the trail. It had to be someone who could follow instructions to make an effective bow and sharp arrows, who had time to lie in wait, who wanted me gone, who had a universe to lose.

The way information zoomed around Shellerton, anyone theoretically could have heard of the lost camera and the way to find it. On the other hand the boys' expedition had occurred only yesterday . . . dear God, only *yesterday* . . . and if . . . *when* . . . I got back, I could find out for certain who had told who.

One step and another. There was fluid in my lungs, rattling and wheezing at every breath. People lived a long time with fluid . . . asthma . . . emphysema . . . years. Fluid took up air space . . . you never saw anyone with emphysema run upstairs.

Angela Brickell had been small and light; a pushover.

Harry and I were tall and strong, not easy to attack at close quarters. Half the racing world had seen me pick up Nolan and knew I could defend myself. So, sharp spikes for Harry and arrows for John, and it was only luck in both cases that had saved us. I'd been there for Harry and the arrow had bypassed my heart.

Luck.

The clear sky was luck.

I didn't want to see the face of the archer.

The sudden admission was a revelation in itself. Even with

305

his handiwork through me, I thought of the sadness inevitably awaiting the others; yet I would have to pursue him, for someone who had three times seen murder as a solution to problems couldn't be trusted never to try it again. Murder was habit-forming, so I'd been told.

Endless night. The moon moved in silver stateliness across the sky behind me. Left foot. Right foot. Hold on to branches. Breathe by fractions.

Midnight.

If ever this ended, I thought, I wouldn't go walking in woodland for a very long time. I would go back to my attic and not be too hard on my characters if they came to pieces on their knees.

I thought of Fringe and the Downs and wondered if I would ever ride in a race, and I thought of Ronnie Curzon and publishers and American rights and of Erica Upton's reviews and it all seemed as distant as Ursa Major but not one whit as essential to my continued existence.

Grapevine around Shellerton. A mass of common knowledge. Yet this time . . . this time . . .

I stopped.

The archer had a face.

Doone would have to juggle with alibis and charts, proving opportunity, searching for footprints. Doone would have to deal with a cunning mind in the best actor of them all.

Perhaps I was wrong. Doone could find out.

I tortoised onwards. A mile was sixty-three thousand three hundred and sixty inches. A mile was roughly one point six kilometers or one hundred and sixty thousand centimeters.

Who cared.

I might have traveled at almost eight thousand inches an hour if it hadn't been for the stops. Six hundred and sixty feet. Two hundred and twenty yards.

A furlong! Brilliant. One furlong an hour. A record for British racing.

Twinkle twinkle little star . . .

No one but a bloody fool would try to walk a mile with an arrow through his chest. Meet J. Kendall, bloody fool.

Lightheaded.

One o'clock.

The moon, I thought briefly, had come down from the sky and was dancing about in the wood not far ahead. Rubbish, it couldn't be. It certainly was. I could see it shining.

Lights. I came to sensible awareness; to incredulous understanding. The lights were traveling along the road.

The road was real, was there, was not some lost myth in a witch-cursed forest. I had actually got there. I would have shouted with joy if I could have spared the oxygen.

I reached the last tree and leaned feebly against it, wondering what to do next. The road had for so long been the only goal that I'd given no thought to anything beyond. It was dark now: no cars.

What to do? Crawl out onto the road and risk getting run over? Hitchhike? Give some poor passing motorist a nightmare?

I felt dreadfully spent. With the trunk's support I slid down to kneeling, leaning head and left shoulder against the bark. By my reckoning, if I'd steered anything like a true course, the Land-Rover was way along the road to the right, but it was pointless and impossible to reach it.

Car lights came around a bend from that direction and seemed not to be traveling too fast. I tried waving an arm to attract attention but only a weak flap of a hand was achieved.

Have to do better.

The car braked suddenly with screeching wheels, then backed rapidly until it was level with me. It was the Land-Rover itself. How could it be?

Doors opened. People spilled out. People I knew.

Mackie.

Mackie running, calling, "John, John," and reaching me and stopping dead and saying, "Oh, my *God*."

Perkin behind her, looking down, his mouth shocked open in speechlessness. Gareth saying, "What's the matter," urgently, and then seeing and coming down scared and wide-eyed on his knees beside me.

"We've been looking for you for *ages*," he said. "You've got an arrow . . ." His voice died.

I knew.

"Run and fetch Tremayne," Mackie told him, and he sprang instantly to his feet and sprinted away along the road to the right, his feet impelled as if by demons.

"Surely we must take that arrow out," Perkin said, and put his hand on the shaft and gave it a tug. He hardly moved it in my chest but it felt like liquid fire.

I yelled . . . it came out as a croak only but it was a yell in my mind . . . "Don't."

I tried to move away from him but that made it worse. I shot out a hand and gripped Mackie's trouser leg and pulled with strength I didn't know I still had left. Strength of desperation.

Mackie's face came down to mine, frightened and caring.

"Don't . . . move . . . the arrow," I said with terrible urgency. "Don't let him."

"Oh, God." She stood up. "Don't touch it, Perkin. It's hurting him dreadfully."

"It would hurt less out," he said obstinately. The vibrations from his hand traveled through me, inducing terror as well.

"No. No." Mackie pulled at his arm in a panic. "You must leave it. You'll kill him. Darling, you *must* leave it alone."

Without her Perkin would have had his way, but he finally took his dangerous hand off the shaft. I wondered if he

308

believed that it would kill me. Wondered if he had any idea what force he would have needed to pull the arrow out, like a wooden skewer out of meat. Wondered if he could imagine the semiasleep furies he'd already reawakened. The furies had claws and merciless teeth. I tried to breathe even less. I could feel the sweat running down my face.

Mackie leaned down again. "Tremayne will get help." Her voice was shaky with stress, with the barbarity of things.

I didn't answer: no breath.

A car pulled up behind the Land-Rover and disgorged Gareth and then Tremayne, who moved like a tank across the earthy shoulder and rocked to a halt a yard away.

"Jesus Christ," he said blankly. "I didn't believe Gareth." He took charge of things then as a natural duty but also, it seemed, with an effort. "Right, I'll call an ambulance on the car phone. Keep still," he said to me unnecessarily. "We'll soon have you out of here."

I didn't answer him either. He sped away back to the car and we could hear his urgent voice, though not the words. He returned shortly, telling me to hang on, it wouldn't be for long; and the shock had made him breathless too, I noticed.

"We've looked for you for hours," he said, anxious, I thought, to prove I hadn't been forgotten. "We telephoned the police and the hospitals and they had no news of a car crash or anything, so then we came out here . . ."

"Because of your message," Mackie said, "on the corkboard."

Oh, yes.

Gareth's camera was swinging from Perkin's hand. Mackie saw me watching it and said, "We found the trail, you know."

Gareth chimed in, "The paint by the road had gone but we looked and looked in the woods. I remembered where we'd been." He was earnest. "I remembered pretty well where it started. And Perkin found it."

"He went all the way along it with a torch," Mackie said,

stroking her husband's arm, "clever thing—and he came back after absolutely ages with Gareth's camera and said you weren't there. We didn't know what to do next."

"I wouldn't let them go home," Gareth said. A mixture of stubbornness and pride in his voice. Thank God for him, I thought.

"What happened exactly?" Tremayne asked me bluntly. "How did you get like this?"

"Tell you . . . later." It came out not much above a whisper, lost in the sound of their movements around me.

"Don't bother him," Mackie said. "He can hardly speak."

They waited beside me making worried encouragements until the ambulance arrived from the direction of Reading. Tremayne and Mackie went to meet the men in uniform, to tell them, I supposed, what to expect. Gareth took a step or two after them and I called him in an explosive croak, "Gareth," and he stopped and turned immediately and came back, bending down.

"Yes? What? What can I do?"

"Stay with me," I said.

It surprised him but he said, "Oh, OK," and stayed a pace away, looking troubled.

Perkin said irritably, "Oh, go on, Gareth."

I said, "No," hoarsely. "Stay."

After a pause Perkin put his back towards Gareth and his face down near mine and asked with perfect calmness, "Do you know who shot you?" It sounded like a natural question in the circumstances, but it wasn't.

I didn't reply. I looked for the first time straight into his moonlit eyes, and I saw Perkin the son, the husband, the one who worked with wood. I looked deep, but I couldn't see his soul. Saw the man who thought he'd killed me . . . saw the archer.

"Do you really know?" he asked again.

He showed no feeling, yet my knowledge held the difference between his safety and destruction.

After a long moment, in which he read the answer for
himself, I said, "Yes."

Something within him seemed to collapse, but he didn't
outwardly fall to pieces or rant or rave or even again try to
pull out the arrow or finish me in any other way. He didn't
explain or show remorse or produce justification. He
straightened and looked across to where the men from the
ambulance were advancing with his father and his wife.
Looked at his brother, a pace away, listening.

He said to me, "I love Mackie very much."

He'd said everything, really.

I spent the night thankfully unaware of the marathon
needlework going on in my chest and drifted back late in the
morning to a mass of tubes and machines and techniques I'd
never heard of. It seemed I was going to live: the doctors
were cheerful, not cautious.

"Constitution like a horse," one said. "We'll have you
back on your feet in no time."

A nurse told me a policeman wanted to see me, but visitors had been barred until tomorrow.

By tomorrow, which was Wednesday, I was breathing
shallowly but without mechanical help, sitting propped up
sideways and drinking soup; talking, attached to drainage
tubes and feeling sore. Doing just fine, they said.

The first person who came to see me wasn't Doone after
all but Tremayne. He came in the afternoon and he looked
white, fatigued and many years older.

He didn't ask about my health. He went over to the window of the post-operation side ward I was occupying alone
and stood looking out for a while, then he turned and said,
"Something awful happened yesterday."

He was trembling, I saw.

"What?" I asked apprehensively.

"Perkin . . ." His throat closed. His distress was overwhelming.

"Sit down," I said.

He fumbled his way into the chair provided for visitors and put a hand over his lips so that I shouldn't see how close he was to tears.

"Perkin," he said after a while. "After all these years you'd think he'd be careful."

"What happened?" I asked, when he stopped.

"He was carving part of a cabinet by hand . . . and he cut his leg open with the knife. He bled . . . he tried to reach the door . . . there was blood all over the floor . . . pints of it. He's had cuts sometimes before but this was an artery . . . Mackie found him."

"Oh, no," I said in protest.

"She's in a terrible state and she won't let them give her sedatives because of the baby."

Despite his efforts, tears filled his eyes. He waited for his face to steady, then took out a handkerchief and fiercely blew his nose.

"Fiona's with her," he said. "She's been marvelous." He swallowed. "I didn't want to burden you with this but you'd soon have wondered why Mackie didn't come."

"That's the least of things."

"I have to go back now, but I wanted to tell you myself."

"Yes. Thank you."

"There's so much to see to." His voice wavered again. "I wish you were there. The horses need to go out. I need your help."

I wanted very much to give it but he could see I couldn't.

"In a few days," I said, and he nodded.

"There has to be an inquest," he said wretchedly.

He stayed for a while, sitting exhaustedly as if loath to take up his burdens again, postponing the moment when he would have to go back to supporting everyone else. Eventually he sighed deeply, pushed himself to his feet and with a wan smile departed.

Admirable man, Tremayne.

Doone arrived very soon after Tremayne had gone and came straight to the point.

"Who shot you?"

"Some kid playing Robin Hood," I said.

"Be serious."

"Seriously, I didn't see."

He sat in the visitor's chair and looked at me broodingly.

"I saw Mr. Tremayne Vickers in the car park," he said. "I suppose he told you their bad news?"

"Yes. Dreadful for them."

"You wouldn't think, would you," he added, "that this could be another murder?"

He saw my surprise. "I hadn't thought of it," I said.

"It looks like an accident," he said with a certain delicacy, "but he was experienced with that knife, was young Mr. Vickers, and after Angela Brickell, after Mr. Goodhaven, after your little bit of trouble . . ." He left the thought hanging and I did nothing to bring it to earth. He sighed after a while and asked how I was feeling.

"Fine."

"Hm." He bent down and picked up a paper bag that he'd laid on the floor. "Thought you might like to see this." He drew out a sturdy transparent plastic inner bag and held it up to the light to show me the contents.

An arrow, cut into two pieces.

One half was clean and pale, and the other stained and dark, with a long black section sharpened at the tip.

"We've had our lab take a look at this," he said in his singsong way, "but they say there are no distinctive tool marks. It could have been sharpened by any straight blade in the kingdom."

"Oh," I said.

"But charring the point, now, that's in your books."

"And in other books besides mine."

He nodded. "Yesterday morning, at Shellerton House, Mr. Tremayne Vickers and young Mr. and Mrs. Perkin Vickers all told me they'd spent three or four hours looking for you on Monday night. Young Gareth didn't want them to give up, they said, but Mr. Vickers senior told him you'd be all right even if you had got lost. You knew how to look after yourself, he said. They were just about to go home when they found you."

"Lucky me."

He nodded. "An inch either way and you'd be history, so I hear. I told them all not to worry, I would go on working with you as soon as you were conscious and we would see our way together to a solution of the whole case."

"Did you?" He took away what breath I still had.

"Mr. Tremayne Vickers said he was delighted." He paused. "Did you follow that trail of paint towards the clearing they talk about?"

"Mm."

"And was it along the trail that someone shot at you?"

"Mm."

"We'll be taking a look at it ourselves, I shouldn't wonder."

I made no comment and he looked disappointed.

"You should be wanting your assailant brought to justice." Textbook words again. "You don't seem to care."

"I'm tired," I said.

"You wouldn't be interested then in the glue."

"What glue?" I asked. "Oh, yes, glue."

"For sticking marble to floorboards," he said. "We had it analyzed. Regular impact adhesive. On sale everywhere. Untraceable."

"And the alibis?"

"We're working on them, but everyone moved about so

much except poor young Mr. Vickers, who was in his work-room all the time."

He seemed to be waiting for me to react, rather as if he'd floated a fly in front of a fish.

I smiled at him a little and displayed no interest. His mustache seemed to droop further from the lack of good results. He rose to go and told me to take care. Good advice, though a bit too late. He would proceed, he said, with his inquiries.

I wished him luck.

"You're too quiet," he said.

When he'd gone I lay and thought for a long time about poor young Mr. Vickers, and of what I should have told Doone, and hadn't.

Perkin, I thought, was one of the very few people who'd known about the camera and the trail. I'd listened to Gareth tell him in detail on Sunday evening.

Mackie had told Sam Yaeger on Monday morning.

Theoretically she could also have told Fiona on the telephone, who could have told Nolan or Lewis, but it wasn't the sort of item one would naturally bother to pass on.

On Monday morning Doone had turned up at Shellerton House with the plank. Perkin knew it was I who had remembered that the floorboards should have floated, and on Monday he'd seen the plank on the dining-room table and heard Doone and me talking in close private consultation. Everything Fiona and Tremayne believed of me must have looked inevitable at that moment. John Kendall would lead Doone to the quarry, who was himself. Any quarry was entitled to take evasive action: to pre-empt discovery by striking first.

By lunchtime Perkin had driven off, going to Newbury for supplies, he'd said. Going to the Quillersedge woods, more like.

Tremayne had gone to Oxford to his tailor. Mackie was out to lunch with Dee-Dee. Gareth was at school. I'd abandoned the empty house and walked joyfully into the woods and only by chance did I know what had hit me.

I imagined Perkin threading along that trail at night, following the paint quite easily as he'd been that way already in daylight, and being secretly pleased with himself because if he had inadvertently left any traces of his passage the first time they could be explained away naturally by the second. That satisfaction would smartly have evaporated when he reached the clearing and found me gone. A nasty shock, one might say. He might have been intending to go back to his family and appear utterly horrified while breaking the news of my death. Instead, he'd looked shocked and utterly horrified at seeing me still alive. Openmouthed. Speechless. Too bad.

If I'd tried to walk out along the trail, I would have met Perkin face-to-face.

I shivered in the warm hospital room. Some things were better unimagined.

For Perkin, making arrows would have been like filing his nails, and he'd had a stove right in his workroom for the charring. He must have constructed a pretty good strong bow too (according to my detailed instructions), which would by now no doubt be broken in unidentifiable pieces in distant undergrowth. Perhaps he'd risked time to practice with a few shots before I got there. Couldn't tell unless I went back to look for spent arrows, which I wasn't going to do.

Random thoughts edged slowly into my mind for the rest of the day.

For instance, Perkin thought in wood, like a language. Any trap he made would be wooden.

Nolan had knocked Perkin down at Tremayne's dinner. I'd picked Nolan up and made a fool of him. Perkin wouldn't have risked any way to kill me that meant creeping up on me, not after what he'd seen.

Perkin had had to get over the shock of finding my familiar ski jacket and boots in the boathouse and then the far worse shock of the cataclysmic reversal of his scheme when Harry and I both lived.

The best actor of them all, he had contained those shocks within himself with no screaming crises of nerves. Many a convicted murderer had displayed that sort of control. Maybe it was something to do with a divorce from reality. There were books on the subject. One day I might read them.

Perkin had resented Mackie's friendly feelings towards me. Not strongly enough to kill me for that, but certainly strongly enough to make killing me satisfying in that respect also.

Never assume . . .

Perkin had always been presumed to be busy in his workshop, and yet there were hours and days when he might not have been, when Mackie was out of the house seeing to the horses. On the Wednesday of Harry's trap, Mackie had been saddling Tremayne's runner in the three-mile chase at Ascot.

Perkin had made none of the classic mistakes. Hadn't scattered monogrammed handkerchiefs about or faked alibis or carelessly dropped dated train tickets or shown knowledge he shouldn't have had. Perkin had listened more than he'd talked, and he'd been cunning and careful.

I thought of Angela Brickell and of all the afternoons Perkin had spent alone in the house. She had tried to seduce even Gareth. Not hard to imagine she'd set her sights also on Perkin. Intelligent men in love with their wives weren't immune to blatantly offered temptations. Sudden arousal. Quick, casual gratification. End of episode.

Except not the end of the episode if there were a failure of a birth control measure and the result was conception. Not the end if the woman asked for money or threatened disclosure. Not the end if she could and would destroy the man's marriage.

Say Angela Brickell had definitely been pregnant. Say she

was sure who the father was; and working in a racing stable with thoroughbreds she would know that proving paternity was increasingly an exact science. The father wouldn't be able to deny it. Say she enticed him into the woods and became demanding in every way and heavily emotional, piling on pressure.

Perkin had not long before seen Olympia lying dead at Nolan's feet. He'd heard over and over again how fast she'd died. Say that picture, that certainty, had flashed into his mind. The quick way out of all his troubles lay in his own two strong hands.

I imagined what Perkin might have been feeling. Might have been facing.

Mackie at that time had been unable to conceive and was troubled and unhappy because of it. Angela Brickell however was devastatingly carrying Perkin's child. Perkin loved Mackie and all too probably couldn't face her knowing what he'd done. Couldn't bear to hurt her so abominably. Was perhaps ashamed. Didn't want his father to find out.

Irresistible solution: a fast death for Angela too. Easy.

Perhaps he, not she, had chosen the woods. Perhaps he'd planned it, perhaps it hadn't been a lightning urge but the first of his traps.

Impossible to know now if either scenario were right. Possible, likely, probable; no more than one of those.

I wondered if he had gone home feeling anything but relief.

Long before Doone came knocking on the door, Perkin could have decided, in case the girl's body were ever found, to say he didn't remember her. No one had thought it odd that he didn't; he was seldom seen with the horses.

His one catastrophic mistake had been to try to settle the mystery forever by making Harry disappear.

By his actions shall you know him . . .

By his arrows.

I thought that Doone might not think of looking in Perkin's workroom for a match to the arrow's wood. Perkin hadn't had much time to hunt elsewhere for anything suitable. He would have used a common wood, not exotic, but all the same, there would be more of it to be found, perhaps even in the cabinet he was making of bleached oak.

He hadn't had any handy feathers, so no flights.

Perkin would have known that a wood match could be made. He knew more about wood than anyone else.

Doone, with his promise of instant detection once I woke up, must have been the end of hope.

He did love Mackie. His universe was lost. One way out remained.

I thought of Tremayne and his pride in Perkin's work. Thought of Gareth's vulnerable age. Thought of Mackie, her face alive with the wondrous joy of discovering she was pregnant. Thought of that child growing up, loved and safe.

Nothing could be gained by trying to prove what Perkin had done. Much would be smashed. They all would suffer. The families always suffered most.

No child would become a secure and balanced adult with a known murderer for a father. Without knowledge, Mackie's grief would heal normally in time. Tremayne and Gareth wouldn't be crippled by undeserved shame. All of them would live more happily if they and the world remained in ignorance, and to try to achieve that I would give them the one gift I could.

Silence.

At the short uncomplicated inquest on Perkin a week later the coroner found unhesitatingly for "Accident" and expressed sympathy with the family. Tremayne came to collect me from the hospital afterwards and told me on the way to Shellerton that Mackie had got through the court ordeal bravely.

"The baby?" I asked.

"The baby's fine. It's what's giving Mackie strength. She says Perkin is with her, will always be with her that way."

"Mm."

Tremayne glanced briefly across at me and back to the road.

"Has Doone found out yet who put that arrow through you?" he asked.

"I don't think so," I said.

"You don't know, yourself?"

"No."

He drove for a while in silence.

"I just wondered . . ." he said uncertainly.

After a while I said, "Doone came to see me twice. I told him I didn't know who shot me. I told him I had no ideas of any sort anymore."

I certainly hadn't told him where to look for arrow wood.

Doone had been disgustedly disillusioned with me: I had closed ranks with *them,* he said. Goodhavens, Everards, Vickerses and Kendall. "Yes," I'd agreed, "I'm sorry." Doone said there was no way of proving who had killed Angela Brickell. "Let her lie," I'd said, nodding. After a silence he'd risen grayly to his feet to leave and told me to look after myself. Wryly I'd said, "I will." He'd gone slowly, regretfully, seeing regret in my face also, an unexpected mutual liking slipping inevitably into memory.

"You don't think," Tremayne said painfully. "I mean, it had to be someone who knew you would fetch Gareth's camera who shot you."

"I told Doone it was a kid playing Robin Hood."

"I'm . . . afraid . . ."

"Block it out," I said. "Some kid did it."

"John . . ."

He knew, I thought. He was no fool. He could have worked things out the same way I had, and he'd have had a hellish time believing it all of his own son.

"About my book," he said, hesitating. "I don't know that I want to go on with it."

"I'm going to write it," I said positively. "It's going to be an affirmation of your life and your worth, just as was intended. It's all the more important now, for you especially, but for Gareth, for Mackie and your new grandchild as well. For you and for them, it's essential I do it."

"You do know," he said.

"It was a kid."

He drove without speaking the rest of the way.

Fiona and Harry were with Mackie and Gareth in the family room. Perkin's absence was to me almost a shock, so accustomed had I become to his being there. Mackie looked pale but in charge of things, greeting me with a sisterly kiss.

"Hi," Gareth said, very cool.

"Hi yourself."

"I've got the day off from school."

"Great."

Harry said, "How are you feeling?" and Fiona put her arms carefully around me and let her scent drift in my senses.

Harry said his Aunt Erica sent good wishes, his eyes ironic.

I asked Harry how his leg was. All on the surface and polite.

Mackie brought cups of tea for everyone; a very English balm in troubles. I remembered the way Harry had laced the coffee after the ditch, and would have preferred that, on the whole.

It was a month yesterday, I thought, that I came here.

A month in the country . . .

Harry said, "Has anyone found out who shot at you?"

He was asking a simple unloaded question, not like Tremayne. I gave him a simple answer, the one that eventually became officially accepted.

"Doone is considering it was a child playing out a fantasy," I said. "Robin Hood, cowboys and Indians. That sort of thing. No hope of ever really knowing."

"Awful," Mackie said, remembering.

I looked at her with affection and Tremayne patted my shoulder and told them I would be staying on as arranged to write his book.

They all seemed pleased, as if I belonged; but I knew I would leave them again before summer, would walk out of the brightly lit play, and go back to the shadows and solitude of fiction. It was a compulsion I'd starved for, and even if I never went hungry again I would feel that compulsion forever. I couldn't understand it or analyze it, but it was there.

After a while I left the family room and wandered through the great central hall and on into the far side of the house, into Perkin's workroom.

It smelled aromatically and only of wood. Tools lay neatly as always. The glue pot was cold on the stove. Everything had been cleaned and tidied and there were no stains on the polished floor to show where his life had pumped out.

I felt no hatred for him. I thought instead of the extinction of his soaring talent. Thought of consequences and seduction. What's done is done, Tremayne would say, but one couldn't wipe out an enveloping feeling of pathetic waste.

A copy of *Return Safe from the Wilderness* lay on a workbench, and I picked it up idly and looked through it.

Traps. Bows and arrows. All the familiar ideas.

I flipped the pages resignedly and they fell open as if from use at the diagram in the first-aid section showing the pressure points for stopping arterial bleeding. I stared blankly at the carefully drawn and accurate illustration of exactly where the main arteries could be found nearest the surface in the arms and wrists . . . and in the legs.

Dear God, I thought numbly. I taught him that too.

*Catch up with
Dick Francis's
other national bestsellers....*

BANKER

Young investment banker Tim Ekaterin has decided to join the exciting world of horse racing. When the multimillion-dollar loan he arranges to finance the purchase of Sandcastle, a champion, is threatened by an apparent defect in the horse, Tim searches desperately for an answer. Violence and murder do not deter him. He must find the key to the murders. And to Sandcastle.

BLOOD SPORT

When English agent Gene Hawkins agreed to search for millionaire Dave Teller's prized missing stallion, he didn' know his retainer would include the attention of his boss's beautiful teenage daughter—or Teller's seldom sober wife. He also didn't know that his search would lead eventually to murder.

BOLT

In Kit Fielding's breakneck world of steeplechase racing, the ultimate catastrophe strikes: someone is shooting the horses with a weapon fiendishly called a "humane killer." Kit must stop the murdering madness, and everyone in his upper-crust circle becomes a suspect.

BREAK IN

Kit Fielding, proud heir to tradition and sporting hero to legions of fans, is drawn into a crusade to save the marriage of his twin sister, Holly, from ruinous scandal. His intercession proves more costly than he'd imagined, thrusting him into a deadly contest with a ruthless media czar, a black-hearted robber baron, and a violent adversary far too close to home for comfort.

THE DANGER

Kidnapping is Andrew Douglas's business: they take them, he finds them. But it isn't so simple when Alessia Cenci, golden-girl jockey, disappears, followed by the young child of a derby winner and the senior steward of the Jockey Club. Andrew's caseload is suddenly, violently overflowing.

DEAD CERT

As he rode through the thick English fog, jockey Alan York was looking at an all-too-familiar sight: the back of champion rider Bill Davidson astride the great racehorse Admiral. But this was one race York was destined to win. Before Admiral jumped the last fence, Bill Davidson would be dead. Alan knew racing was a dangerous sport, but he also knew this had been no accident.

THE EDGE
The Great Transcontinental Mystery Race, a rail junket that offers the passengers a chance to race thoroughbreds and a mystery to solve. For Tor Kelsey, undercover agent for the British Jockey Club, this imaginary mayhem is about to become a nightmare of real murder.

ENQUIRY
Jockey Kelly Hughes and trainer Dexter Cranfield had been barred from racing, a devastating event for them both. The charge at the secret Enquiry? Throwing a race for personal profit. It was a vicious frame-up, but Hughes refuses to take the phony verdict lying down—even though his personal Enquiry might have him lying down permanently.

FLYING FINISH
According to just about everybody, Henry Grey has a bad disposition. But Henry knew a new job was all he needed. So he took a new job, air transport of racehorses, which would let him see the world, maybe change his luck. His luck changed all right—when he found there was something more than horseflesh in the cargo hold.

FOR KICKS

Daniel Roke couldn't leave his Australian stud farm to go help look into an English horse-doping scandal. So he said. But soon he was in England taking over investigative duties vacated by a racing journalist who had died in an "auto accident." Then Daniel learned that men who would give drugs to horses would do much worse to human beings.

FORFEIT

James Tyrone, a racing reporter, knew that fellow writer Bert Checkov was a drunk. But when Bert suddenly died in an "accidental" fall from a window, Tyrone suspected that Bert's death might be related to some columns he'd written touting can't-lose horses—who mysteriously failed to show up on race day. Tyrone vowed to prove that Checkov was murdered, despite the terrifying risk involved.

HOT MONEY

With five ex-wives and nine children, it's no great surprise that wealthy gold trader Malcolm Pembroke should preside over a motley clan in constant conflict with one another. When Malcolm's least likable ex-wife dies violently, he calls on his son, Ian, the family jockey, to protect him from their nearest, if not always dearest, relatives. Ian must delve for the final, critical clue in the darkly buried Pembroke past, simmering with the greed, hate, and vengefulness that could motivate blood to strike against blood.

NERVE

Rob Finn was a bit of a misfit: a struggling jockey in a family of musicians, a man in love with a beautiful woman who wouldn't have him, a rider who—just as it looked like he'd break into racing's big time—lost his nerve. Or did he? The horses felt too sluggish beneath him; he knew there had to be a reason. When he found it, he could barely believe it. And when it found him, he could barely breathe.

ODDS AGAINST

Ex-jockey Sid Halley had a wrecked hand, a mean case of depression, and a need for a new career. He joined a detective agency, took a bullet in his side, and was sent out on a case of his own. Then he met Zanna Martin, a woman who could make life worth living again. But it was an even-money bet that he'd be killed before she had the chance.

PROOF

Wine merchant Tony Beach finds himself caught in the terrifying midst of a mystery that begins with sham scotch and counterfeit claret and escalates to hijacking and murder. Tony must draw on every reserve of hidden courage to crack a sophisticated scam and to save many lives—especially his own.

REFLEX

Jockey Philip Nore is no ordinary hero. When he begins to suspect that a track photographer's fatal accident was really murder, he sets out to discover the truth and to trap the killer. Slowly, he unravels some nasty secrets of corruption, blackmail, and murder—and unwittingly sets himself up as the killer's next target.

SLAY RIDE

British investigator David Cleveland came to Norway in search of Robert Sherman, a champion jockey, who had disappeared right before the Norwegian national—a race he was certain to win. Cleveland was sure that Sherman's disappearance was tied to a gruesome string of deaths that he soon found was meant to include his own.

TRIAL RUN

How can you say no to a Prince? You can't. But the Prince's brother-in-law had his heart set on riding in the Olympics, and it seemed some jealous Russian had her heart set on killing him if he did. So Randall Drew left his well-bred horses and high-born girlfriend and went to Moscow. He did not expect the sabotage and murder he found there, nor the unspeakable terror that followed.

TWICE SHY

Young physicist Jonathan Derry is given some musical tapes by a friend. But the tapes are really an elaborate computerized horse-betting system that can make the owner a rich man—or a dead one.

WHIP HAND

Sid Halley had one good hand and another made of metal. No longer able to jockey, he became a private investigator, quite a good one, though his new life could never erase the haunting memories of his past glories. When the wife of one of England's top trainers came to beg for his help in preventing some foul play at the track, Sid Halley began to know what being haunted really was.

DICK FRANCIS